ACCIDENTAL TOURBOOK

ACCIDENTAL HONEYMOON

MIRANDA MACLEOD

Apple Blossom Press
Boston, MA

Accidental Honeymoon

Copyright © 2020 Miranda MacLeod

All rights reserved. No part of this publication may be reproduced, distributed, or transmitted in any form or by any means, including photocopying, recording, or other electronic or mechanical methods, without the prior written permission of the publisher or author, except in the case of brief quotations embodied in critical reviews and certain other noncommercial uses permitted by copyright law.

Find out more: www.mirandamacleod.com
Contact the author: miranda@mirandamacleod.com

Cover Design by: Victoria Cooper
Edited by Kelly Hashway

ISBN: 9798560116187

This is a work of fiction. Any resemblance of characters to actual persons, living or dead, is purely coincidental.

Apple Blossom Press
PO Box 547
Bolton MA 01740

ALSO BY MIRANDA MACLEOD

Stand Alone Novels

Telling Lies Online

Holly & Ivy (cowritten with T.B. Markinson)

Heart of Ice (cowritten with T.B. Markinson)

Love's Encore Trilogy:

A Road Through Mountains

Your Name in Lights

Fifty Percent Illusion

Americans Abroad Series:

Waltzing on the Danube

Holme for the Holidays

Stockholm Syndrome

Letters to Cupid

London Holiday

Check mirandamacleod.com for more about these titles, and for other books coming soon!

ABOUT THE AUTHOR

Originally from southern California, Miranda now lives in New England and writes heartfelt romances and romantic comedies featuring witty and charmingly flawed women that you'll want to marry. Or just grab a coffee with, if that's more your thing. She spent way too many years in graduate school, worked in professional theater and film, and held temp jobs in just about every office building in downtown Boston.

To find out about her upcoming releases and take advantage of exclusive sales, be sure to sign up for her newsletter at her website: mirandamacleod.com.

CHAPTER ONE

"Who the hell are you?"

Monica gripped the front doorknob, her knuckles turning white as she surveyed the dark-haired woman who was blocking her departure. Though usually a sucker for short, choppy curls and freckle-spattered cheeks, this was one of those rare times when Monica was impervious to an attractive woman's charms. It had taken her weeks to book today's meeting at The Walters Art Museum, and with a wedding contract in the six figures on the line, she couldn't afford to be a minute late, no matter how pretty the obstacle standing in her path might be. Besides, it was much too early on a Monday morning to feel anything but grumpy.

"You're Monica?" The woman spoke with an easy confidence that made it seem like she'd never experienced a moment of self-doubt in her life. Deep blue eyes peered at Monica from beneath partially closed lids, and it felt like the stranger could see right through her and knew she was all bark and no bite. How annoying.

"Do you always answer a question with a question?" Monica snapped. She eyed the woman's baggy denim jeans and rumpled plaid shirt that topped a white V-neck tank top that had shifted downward to give Monica much more of an eyeful than had probably been intended. Talk about being put at an immediate disadvantage. It would be all she could do to keep her eyes politely above neck level while giving the interloper the third degree. "I still have no idea who you are."

"I'm Ray." She hoisted her left arm to reveal a sizable toolbox, shaking it effortlessly so the contents rattled. "I'm the handy ma'am."

"I'm sorry, the what?"

"Handy. Ma'am," she repeated, punctuating each word with a lift of the eyebrows that sent sparks to the tips of Monica's toes.

Monica stepped to the left and closed the door ever so slightly in an effort to prevent the possibility of Ray pushing her way in. She seemed like exactly the type of woman who would do that, the domineering kind who didn't easily take no for an answer. In other words, pretty much *her* type exactly, though Monica would be loath to admit it. Not in real life, of course. She had a professional image to maintain, and that meant being seen with the right kind of woman, someone as put together and polished as she was. Secretly, though? Yeah, a soft butch with a tool belt showing up on her doorstep was a scenario that could've been lifted straight from any number of her late-night fantasies.

But what were the odds of it playing out in real life?

"Wait a minute." Monica's eyes widened as an explanation for the situation sharpened into focus. "Did my girl squad send you?"

"Did who do what?" For the first time, the cocky stranger seemed thrown off her game.

"That's it, isn't it?" Monica grinned triumphantly at Ray. "How many times have my twin cousins Trish and Maddie jokingly threatened to send me a stripper to help loosen me up? But I never thought they'd go through with it."

Ray took a step back, her jaw tightening as her eyes flashed with what could only be anger. "I don't know who you think you are—"

"Is this part of the act?" Monica tapped her fingertips together. "I've always had a weakness for combative women, which, if you ask my therapist, is part of the reason I keep ending up alone."

A hint of surprise flickered across Ray's face at the mention of women, but it was far from the first time that had happened to Monica. With her long blonde hair and penchant for pencil skirts and dangly earrings, the word *lesbian* didn't even make the top ten of assumptions people made when meeting her. To the woman's credit, Ray made a quicker recovery than most.

"Listen. I don't want to hear about your private life. I have a job to do." Ray reached into her back pocket and pulled out a business card.

Monica scanned the details. The card looked legit, featuring a list of common household repair tasks that, despite her initial assumption, were probably not code for anything sexual. So, this was not a stripper sent by her mischievous younger cousins to entertain her. How disappointing.

"Rachel Walsh. Tell me; do you call yourself Ray so people will think you're a dude? If that's the case, you might want to adjust your shirt. That cleavage is a dead giveaway."

Ray gave a nonchalant shrug that resulted in her plaid shirt slipping a few inches down one arm, exposing a very shapely shoulder. "Nobody said you had to look."

Damn. Monica swallowed, feeling like a rock was caught in her throat. Had that shoulder move been intended to seduce her? Probably not, but even so, Monica thought she knew how a mouse felt when being toyed with by a cruel cat. A few more swipes and she'd be a goner. Time to strike back. "It's a weird name for a woman, if you ask me."

"I didn't, but as it happens, I was nicknamed Ray after my grandfather, who also gave me my stubborn streak. You see this?" Ray tapped the dimple in her chin. "Grandpa Ray had one just like it. If it turns red, you've done pissed me off beyond belief."

Monica squirmed. "It's approaching the color of a fire engine right now."

"Exactly," Ray said, gnashing her teeth together so her jaw became square as a lantern.

"There's no exactly about it," Monica retorted, suddenly recalling *she* was the one who'd been wronged. "You can't show up and barge into my house with a toolbox unannounced. I'm on my way to a very important business meeting."

"Your house?" Ray scoffed. "It's my understanding you're just a renter."

"Yes." A chill crept into Monica's tone as she bristled at that word *just*. That she was renting the house was a technicality she did not enjoy being reminded of, like she was some kind of second-class citizen. "My lease clearly states I should receive twenty-four-hours' notice for any work on the property."

"Have you checked your messages?"

"I never listen to voice mail." Monica tossed her head slightly to remove some stray strands of hair from her face. "Anything important comes by text."

Ray sucked in a deep breath. "Do you think that could be the source of your problem?"

Monica stiffened, her neck growing hot. "Who do you think you are, telling me I have a problem?"

Another bored shrug, accompanied by an additional

inch of bare shoulder in what was quickly becoming an accidental strip-tease. "You're the one who introduced yourself by announcing you're in therapy."

"Everyone's in therapy." Monica made a show of rolling her eyes. "I don't have time for this today. I already explained I'm running late for my meeting."

Ray glanced down at Monica's feet. "I take it shoes are one of your other trouble spots."

Monica's eyes darted to the floor, at which point she realized she was wearing only a single shoe. She'd been in the middle of searching for the other one when the doorbell had interrupted her. She started to speak, burning with the desire to explain she was a victim of circumstance, but could only open and close her mouth like a goldfish.

"Right, let's sort this out before we both die of old age, shall we?" Ray pulled out her phone and held it to her ear. "It's Ray. It's like you said. She hadn't gotten the message about you putting the house on the market, and she won't let me in to start the work."

An angry chirping came from the phone, which, even at a distance, Monica recognized as belonging to her ex-girlfriend. Not bothering to ask permission, Monica snatched the phone from Ray's hand and turned her back so the handy girl, or whatever it was she called herself, couldn't gawk at the look of wide-eyed terror that surely had taken over her face at the phrase "putting the house on the market."

"What the hell, Brianna? You're selling my house?"

"Your house?" Her ex's mocking laugh made Monica wince. "I think you mean my house—"

"We had an agreement—"

"For you to *rent* it from me for a little while until you got back on your feet."

"The only reason I'm not on my feet is because you knocked me on my ass by leaving me for Judith."

"Which is why I'm only charging you the cost of the mortgage and taxes instead of the full market rate." Brianna sighed dramatically, and Monica could clearly picture the look of self-pity that was almost certainly etched on her ex's face. "I didn't think you'd be so cruel as to punish me like this, Monica. How long do you plan to take advantage of me?"

"Take advantage? You're the one who suggested the deal, I assume because it made you feel less guilty when I found out you were cheating on me. On my birthday. I didn't even get to enjoy my cake. You know how I feel about cake." At the sound of shuffling behind her, Monica flipped around to see Ray was standing inside the house. Oops. She'd kind of forgotten the woman was there and wished too late she'd kept that humiliating cake detail to herself. "It's only been a couple months. Do you know how hard it is to find a decent rental?"

"I do, actually. I'm a real estate investor, remember?"

"Then you should understand," Monica pleaded,

even though she knew understanding anyone else's position wasn't one of Brianna's strong points.

"Yeah, I understand the market is way hotter right now than I thought it would be for that crappy townhouse. It's not my fault everyone wants to move to the suburbs to get away from crowded cities and set up home offices."

"I happen to like this crappy townhouse." Monica let out a low-throated growl as Ray chuckled. As if she needed some day laborer judging her on her lack of snappy comebacks.

"I'm sorry, Monica. You know I'll always love you, but I have to make the best financial decision for me and Judith. She has her eye on a three-unit penthouse in the Inner Harbor. It's a total steal right now, but even so, I'll need to sell one of my other properties to make the down payment, and yours will yield the highest return."

"This is so like you. Money always comes first."

"Yep. Everything is my fault. Poor little Moany can't be blamed for anything."

"Don't call me that! You know I hate that nickname."

"Moany Monica, Moany Monica," Brianna chanted like a three-year-old.

Monica covered the earpiece so Ray couldn't hear the dreadful nickname. After several seconds, she tried pleading with her ex. "You can't sell my house. I'll have no place to go."

"You keep calling it your house, but my name is on the mortgage. If you ask me, I've been a saint letting you stay there—"

"I pay enough in rent to cover all your out-of-pocket expenses on the place."

"Oh, please. I could easily get three hundred and seventy-five dollars more a month on the open market."

"There you go again with exact dollar figures."

"It's called the real-estate business. It's how I afforded the house in the first place, instead of flitting around from party to party, drinking champagne all night with celebrities."

"That's what I do for a living!" Monica squeezed her eyes shut. How many times had they argued about this since Monica had launched her own event planning business? Brianna had been so supportive at first, but she should've anticipated her ex would get jealous the minute her clientele started including B-list celebrities.

"You barely worked for a year, and I was the one who had to carry your dead weight."

"It was the worst economy in decades. The entire world was basically shut down!"

Admittedly, it had been terrible timing to venture out on her own mere months before the whole planet ground to a halt, but it's not like she could've seen that coming. Besides, hadn't she dipped into her savings to make sure she never missed contributing her portion to the bills? That was half the reason she couldn't afford to buy the house, not that Brianna cared to remember that. Her ex was the type who could only recall the details that were convenient for her.

Monica tried to settle her breathing, noticing again Ray watching her intently. Having this humiliating conversation in front of the hottest woman she'd seen in ages just added insult to injury. "Come on, Brianna. I'm sure we can come to an agreement."

"Sure. You can buy the house from me. I'll give you a great deal."

Monica could picture Brianna's phony professional smile, and she wished they were having this conversation in person so Monica could strangle her backstabbing ex. "You know I can't do that. Not for another year, according to the spreadsheet you put together for me. You said you'd give me that long."

"No, I said you would be able to buy *something* in a year. I didn't promise you could stay in my house for that long. That's your problem. You only hear the words that suit you. Not reality."

Talk about the pot calling the kettle black. Monica felt the world around her go red. "I'm not moving!"

"Either buy me out," Brianna shouted, "or I'll have you kicked out."

"I have a lease!" Monica choked on the words, knowing it wouldn't matter. She was done with stubborn women. Hell, she was done with women, period. They were nothing but trouble.

"I know." Brianna's voice was as cold as her heart. "I wrote it and included an escape clause saying I could sell it if the market heated up. Well, guess what? It's fucking on fire. So either fork over twenty percent or start packing."

The phone went dead.

"I hate you!" Monica screamed into the phone before tossing it down onto the couch, stomping her foot as she did so for good measure.

"Hey! That's my phone!" Ray rushed over to inspect the damage. Maybe it was Monica's imagination, but she seemed disappointed there wasn't any. She'd probably wanted to sue. Typical woman: heartless to the core. Monica was done with all of them for good, no matter how hot they were. Or in Ray's case, ridiculously hot. Her plaid shirt was now tied around her waist, exposing the muscles of her upper arms, which rippled in a way nobody's muscles had a right to do.

Damn it.

"How long will you be here?" Monica growled, turning her head away so as not to stare at those biceps a moment longer. Unfortunately, she could still see them, even with her eyes closed. How did arms even begin to look like that?

"A day," Ray replied. "Two tops. Depends how many rooms end up needing paint."

"Are you doing the master bedroom?"

"It's not on the initial order."

"Well, I hate the color," Monica huffed, as if the hue were somehow Ray's fault. She turned around and looked the woman in the eyes. Such a deep, sparkling blue. A moment later her gaze veered dangerously downward, and it took all her self-control to focus on Ray's chin, that stubborn appendage with its color-coded dimple. Seriously, all females should come with a similar warning system. "Can you add that room to your list?"

"That'll take a couple of extra days, but yeah, sure...no problem." Ray's eyes twinkled like she'd heard the ca-ching of a cash register ringing up a sale. Monica didn't care. This was all on Brianna's dime. "What color were you thinking?"

"A light blue." Monica looked at her Fitbit. "Look, I really am running late now, and if I lose this contract, I'm screwed. This is the biggest thing I've had a shot at in ages."

"I can come up with a color if you'd like."

Monica eyed the ragged hem of the woman's cut-off shorts. "Do you know anything about interior design?"

"I have a first edition Wharton and Codman on my nightstand. I read a chapter every night before bed."

Monica had no idea what that was, but it sounded legit, and she'd rather die than admit a handyman—

excuse me, *ma'am*—might know more about something than she did, so she responded with a curt nod.

"I guess I can trust you to pick out the paint color, then. Maybe like the stripes in your shirt? It really brings out—" She was about to say Ray's eyes but stopped short. "The room. It brings out the room."

Ray grabbed the sleeve dangling from her waist. "I got it. Anything else?"

"Maybe you could suggest a whole color palette for the house while you're at it. Knowing my ex, she's playing it safe with a boring beige."

"Brandy cream, actually."

"What color is that?"

"Boring beige." Ray sucked in her cheeks like she was trying to stifle a laugh. Good. The enemy of your enemy is your friend, or something like that. It meant she was on Monica's side, at least for the moment, which was worth taking advantage of.

"I always wanted a ceiling fan in the office. Brianna never got around to it. And new switch plate covers, and the overhead fixtures in the bathroom. Good ones, not the cheap kind." It'd serve her skinflint of an ex right, sticking her with these extra fees. "Add those to your design plan. I'll text you if I can think of anything else."

"You're the boss." Ray jotted down something in a small notebook.

"How many days of work are we up to now?" If she could add more items to the handy ma'am's to-do list, how much time would that buy her to figure out a way to beat Brianna at this game? "More importantly, how many days can I have you?"

Ray shrugged, a motion that made the muscles in her shoulders tighten in a way that defied nature. "My calendar's pretty light all week."

"Cool. I'll see what else I can think of."

"You've got my card, which has my number on it." Ray smirked. "Unlike some people, I check my voice mail daily."

Monica's eyes narrowed. "Very funny."

Brianna may have fired the first shot in the house war, but Monica would win in the long run. Even if it killed her.

Not giving the matter too much more thought, she rushed into her office and grabbed her missing heel, slipping it over her polished toes before racing out the door. She'd have just enough time to make it to The Walters as long as traffic wasn't too heavy.

Sliding on her shades, Monica climbed behind the steering wheel of her beloved Benz. The lease was about to expire, and there was no way Brianna would sign for another one, but Monica might as well enjoy it while she had it, right? She fired up the engine, and it purred like a kitten.

Shit.

She'd forgotten to tell that handy lady person about Mr. Fluffles, the Persian in need of a serious attitude adjustment that Brianna had stuck her with when she'd skipped out on her. Oh, well. Ray would figure it out. Or, maybe the cat would escape through the open front door. As if Monica could be so lucky. Considering how much fancy cat food that beast ate every day, she should've deducted the cost from her rent. Her ex had some real nerve to accuse her of laziness when that puff of white fur did nothing but sit on a silk cushion all day and sharpen its claws. Of course, in the end, Brianna had dumped them both.

Monica put the car in gear and sped toward the highway, praying she'd make it to her meeting on time. If she was late and lost the chance to plan this wedding, it would be Brianna's fault. Hers and that hot handy woman's with her distracting eyes and muscular arms. How dare she wear a tank top when she had arms like that?

This was just one more reason on a growing list of why Monica would never fall for another woman, not ever again. They were nothing but trouble, the whole lot of them. And at thirty-two years old, Monica had already had enough trouble to last herself a lifetime.

CHAPTER TWO

The sound of a car engine roared through an open window, and even without seeing it, Ray could tell it was expensive. Probably flashy, too, in that entirely unnecessary way that was only about showing off to other people how rich you were, or how rich you wanted them to *think* you were.

Kinda like this place, Ray thought as she studied her surroundings. The exterior of the two-story townhouse sported deep red brick and a balcony supported by white pillars like it was some sort of plantation. Meanwhile, its sides and back were covered in just about the lowest quality vinyl siding available on the market. So typical of modern construction. That meant that while the foyer floor was marble and lit by a shiny crystal chandelier hanging from a cathedral ceiling, Ray would bet ten bucks the rest of the house had been outfitted with beige wall-to-wall carpet and cheap hollow core doors.

That's the problem with the world nowadays, she could almost hear Grandpa Ray's voice saying in her mind as he launched into one of his favorite diatribes. New things weren't built to last, and people would rather tear down something than put the work into making it shine again. Ray shared her grandfather's old-world values, which had caused trouble with more than a few of the women she'd dated who wanted nothing but the latest trends, no matter how disposable.

If only she could break herself of the habit of falling hard for a pretty face who had nothing in common with her. Women like Monica, for example, with that silky hair and the oh-so-feminine wiles that could turn Ray on as easily as flipping a switch. Even if she *was* hot—or hotter than hot, if Ray were completely honest about it—that was beside the point.

Make no mistake, Ray could get her into bed with less effort than it would take to prime the walls. That much had been obvious. Ray almost felt bad for Monica, given how much effort she'd put into trying not to be too obvious about all the staring she'd been doing. The truth was Ray was used to having that effect on women.

Attracting recent divorcees who were experiencing the sudden onset of bi-curiosity seemed to be a particular specialty of hers. They would hire her for a job and flirt with her nonstop while explaining how overrated men were. Ray had no desire to be someone's experiment, but she'd become adept at letting them down gently, a necessity when her livelihood depended on getting as many five-star reviews as she could. In fact, she'd pegged Monica for this type of woman the minute the door had opened to reveal all that golden hair, and those shapely legs beneath her form-fitting skirt. Ray had been shocked to discover Brianna was her ex.

Of course, considering that, plus the fact Monica wasn't the one who had hired her, it technically wouldn't have been against her rules if Ray had decided to sleep with her. But with an entitled princess like Monica, the bedroom was all there was. She could never understand the passion for hard work that made Ray tick, the thrill that came with taking something that had been written off as old and broken and restoring it to a new life with her own two hands. That woman's disdain for anything blue collar had been all too obvious. Ray had plenty of experience with that type of woman, too. More than enough to want a repeat.

Move along, Ray, she cautioned herself. *She's not worth the trouble.*

As if to remind herself how little she and Monica had in common, Ray pulled out her phone and scrolled to the first decorating blog post in her inbox. Due to the nature of her business, she'd gotten signed up on more of those mailing lists than she could count, with article titles like "15 Must Have Trends to Wow Your Friends," and content that served as a house-in-a-box starter kit for aspiring basic white girls everywhere. Which, if you looked that phrase up in the urban dictionary, they might as well put a photo of Monica in place of a definition. Ray didn't need to assess the rest of the house to know what she would find.

Oh, yeah. With a crooked smile, she studied the photos of her chosen newsletter. *This one.*

Open shelving in the kitchen, a navy blue accent wall, floral removable wallpaper, a curved sofa. The list went on, and she could picture it now, in all its cookie-cutter glory. Grabbing her toolbox, Ray bet herself a beer after work she'd find at least ten of these elements in Monica's house. All fifteen and she'd treat herself to a six-pack for the weekend. Something cheap and domestic, the kind of beer a woman like Monica would rather die than drink.

Ray scored four points in the living room alone, because holy rattan, Batman. Her trusty blogger had hinted that wicker would be making a comeback, but with two end tables, a coffee table, and an accent chair made out of the stuff, Ray might as well have been standing on her great aunt Bessie Mae's veranda sipping a mint julep. Plus, she earned a bonus point for one of the items being painted white, offering what the article promised was an unexpected twist on a classic. Because, yeah, no one had ever thought to paint wicker white before. She made a note to suggest a shade of blush for the walls, which had been declared the Color of the Year by at least three different sources, thereby almost guaranteeing anyone who had already gone all-in on the wicker bandwagon would consider the addition of pink to the room a homerun.

She scored an additional two points in the kitchen for the aforementioned open shelving and navy accent wall, which Ray had to admit was almost too easy. The shelves had literally been mounted *on* the dark blue wall. At the rate she was going, she'd end up earning a twelve pack and spending most of her holiday Monday with an end-of-summer hangover.

After entering two other rooms, and earning one point from each thanks to animal print hand towels in the guest bath that offered a *touch of whimsy*, plus a fake olive tree in the dining room that added a pop of *sophisticated sage green*, Ray found her way to the master bedroom. Bracing herself for a high-contrast color scheme and a canopy bed made from acrylic and metal, which her blogger promised added a much-needed modern upgrade to a traditional classic—a phrase that honestly made a part of Ray's soul wither and die—she turned the doorknob and was nearly bowled over by a streak of white that disappeared around the corner of the hallway with an angry shake of a very fluffy tail.

"Here, kitty kitty," Ray called out, taking a best guess at the type of animal that had raced past her. She peered down the hallway expectantly, but nothing appeared. Ray shrugged. Wherever the cat had gone, it seemed in no hurry to return. She'd make an effort not to let it outside, of course, but if Monica preferred to keep her pet confined to the bedroom all day, she really should've told Ray the rules before heading out.

Turning her attention back to the bedroom, Ray was momentarily thrown off to realize the space looked nothing like she'd anticipated. It was actually, well…good. Or at least, not too far off the mark. With a muted color palette and real wood furnishings, it exuded a touch of class instead of the gaudy New Jersey casino feel she'd dreaded. Though the awful wall color gave Ray the final point she needed to win herself a beer, Monica couldn't technically be blamed for it since she'd already requested a change. What was more, the shade of blue the woman had selected was exactly what Ray would've suggested. Weird.

She wouldn't be earning a six-pack, but all in all, the bedroom made Ray surprisingly happy by putting a tick in the good taste column. Maybe she'd judged Monica too harshly. Her eyes landed on a desktop covered with clippings of dresses from bridal magazines, any one of which probably cost more than Ray made in a month.

Maybe her first impression had been on the money, after all. Money being the operative word. Not only did Monica appear to be completely obsessed with getting married, but her expensive taste was a one-way ticket to the poor house. No wonder the woman's ex had run off.

With a roll of her eyes at Monica's collection of matrimonial monstrosities, Ray set to work taping all of the woodwork and draping plastic sheets over the furniture and baseboards to protect the carpet. Who still had carpet in their bedroom? If this was her place, she'd rip it up and put in a spectacular hardwood floor. Real wood, too, for sure. She'd been hired to install no less than three of those laminate floating floors that summer, in *fashion colors* because apparently good old brown wood wasn't good enough for people these days.

After a quick trip to the local hardware store, Ray returned and poured a beautiful robin's egg blue paint into her tray. She dipped the pad of the edger into it ever so lightly so as not to overload it and cause drips. Ray wasn't as fast as some of the people who specialized in nothing but painting, but she was meticulous and prided herself on producing a perfectly finished room. She'd yet to have a client complain.

"Meow."

She flipped around, her eyes scanning all the plastic, until she spotted the white Persian, who had returned to the bedroom in her absence.

"Of course. Princess Monica had to have a cat as high maintenance as she was. Tell me, do you get your food in a crystal goblet like in the commercials?"

The cat hissed in response.

Ray took a step back. "Hey now. I don't want to get into it with you after already dealing with your human today. You stay over there, and I'll stay on this side. Got it?"

The cat flopped onto the plastic, lifting a leg to clean its butt.

"Unbelievable. Well, they say pets act like their owners. I bet your mommy would expect an audience for everything she does, too. Although, staring at her ass would be much more appealing than—nope. You know what? I'm not letting my imagination go there, kitty. That's a sure way to ruin my day."

Ray started edging one of the walls. Resolving to banish Monica from her thoughts while she worked, she turned to conversing with the cat for amusement. "This house wouldn't be half bad, really. I mean, it's newer construction, so it's not my cup of tea, but I've seen a lot worse. The real problem is that, with the exception of the bedroom, it's decorated all wrong."

The cat blinked then yawned. It wasn't a stellar response, but compared to the outright hostility from earlier, Ray thought they might be on the verge of establishing a rapport.

"People are in too much of a rush to finish a room and move on, only to redo it a few years later because it isn't quite right. Did you know, I didn't have a proper bed frame for over two years? Nope, just a mattress on the floor, until I was in a consignment shop and spied a particular carved mahogany headboard from across the room. It spoke to me. That's how you know if you have the right piece. There has to be a connection."

Ray applied more paint to the pad while the cat followed her every move with rapt attention. She'd been living on her own since Grandpa Ray died, so it was a nice change to have an engaged audience for her ramblings.

"You might not know this, being a cat and all, but the problem with human connections is we tend to base them on the wrong things, like shiny hair and a nice ass."

The cat, who had lifted one gleaming white paw to her tongue, paused and gave Ray the stink eye.

"Nothing against you, babe. I'm sure the boy cats in the neighborhood go crazy for all that nice fur of yours. Probably some of the girl cats, too. But when it comes to people, first impressions are not a good basis for a relationship. Maybe not second impressions, either. I mean, I walked in here, and for a split second, I thought I might have something in common with that princess mommy of yours. Then I caught sight of her serial killer wedding collage, and it brought me back to my senses."

The cat was still watching her intently, but now Ray got the impression it was less out of interest and more that she was keeping an eye on Ray as if suspicious she would steal something.

"Yep," Ray huffed, "you're the spitting image of

your mom. A judgmental diva. I'll have you know this whole handy ma'am thing is just a side gig. I'm a lot more than just the hired help, okay?"

The cat did not look convinced. Ray crossed her arms and glared.

"I may not have gone the traditional college route, but I spent two years earning a certificate in restoration carpentry in one of the best programs there is. When a historical mansion needs repair, who do you think they call? That's right, me. My boss at Grant's Restorations promised me he's reeling in something huge in September. He won't say what, but I'm thinking it's a federal contract, maybe even the White House." She sighed. "I only wish my grandfather had lived to see me finally make my mark. He's missing it by less than a year. That really kills me. Imagine what he would've thought of his granddaughter doing a major renovation on the Lincoln Bedroom."

She looked over to see the cat's response, but her conversation buddy had vanished. A ripping sound behind her caused Ray to wheel around. "Hey! What are you doing?"

The Persian was on its hind legs, scratching its claws through the plastic that covered the mattress.

"Don't do that! Bad kitty!" Ray lunged at the cat, causing it to dash to the other side of the room. "That's it. Your socializing privileges have been revoked. I'm kicking you out."

Again, Ray tried to capture the cat, but it dodged

her, and in the process of escaping Ray's grasp, the cat splashed into the paint tray.

What had up to that point been a pristine white cat was now masquerading as a robin's egg blue tabby. What a shame those didn't exist in nature, as Monica was sure to notice the difference.

"Now look what you've done!"

The Persian rubbed against the freshly painted wall, texturing it with a layer of fur.

"No! Don't do that. You'll ruin everything!"

As if finally realizing the extent of its predicament, the cat held still long enough for Ray to scoop it into her arms.

"This is why I'm a dog person." Ray held the cat close to her, smudging her white tank with liberal streaks of blue paint. That was the least of her problems. She eyed the cat's matted mess of fur in dismay. "I know cats hate water, but you're getting a shower."

As if understanding her words, the cat let out a desperate hiss.

"I don't want to hear a single complaint out of you." She gave the pitiful bundle in her arms an imploring look. "If we work together, this won't be too painful; I promise. Do we have a deal?"

The cat didn't move a muscle, clearly an indication that whatever fun it had derived from using itself as a feline paint brush had dissipated, and it wanted a thorough cleaning, maybe even badly enough to cooperate.

Ray carried the cat into the bathroom, whistling

under her breath at the gleaming fixtures and spotless white towels. How did Monica keep it so clean? Everything was perfectly folded, as if it never got used. Did she have some other bathroom and kept this one prepped for impromptu photo shoots? As Ray pondered this, the cat started to fuss.

"Oh, no. We had a deal. You're getting clean no matter if you like it or not."

She kicked on the shower, warming it up just enough so as not to shock or scald the feline. "Okay, here goes nothing."

As soon as the water penetrated its fur, the cat let out a howl that made Ray's blood turn cold. It was accompanied by a potentially lethal assault of teeth and claws.

"Ow!" Ray yelped, tightening her grip. "I'm not enjoying this either, but you got us into this mess."

The cat struggled, clawed, and howled, but Ray didn't let go until every last speck of blue had been washed away. The minute she loosened her grip, the cat ran out of the room and down the hall. Ray quickly blocked off the bedroom to avoid a repeat performance.

Ray plucked her tank from where it was plastered to her chest. Her jeans were equally soaked through and through. *Damn it,* she thought, *I can't keep working like this.* The AC was blasting against a humid end-of-summer day. Working in wet clothing would freeze her to the core, and besides being uncomfortable, in her line of work, steady hands were a must. Reluctantly, she stripped down and reached for one of the pristinely folded towels. No way. She'd ruin it for sure. Instead, she opted to don the luxurious terry cloth robe that hung from a hook on the back of the door. She topped off the ensemble with a spa-like hair towel for her dripping hair before going off in search of the laundry room to dry her soaking clothes.

Just as she was crossing the foyer, the doorbell rang.

Ray's first instinct was to ignore it. With a sense of relief, she found the laundry area and put her clothes in the dryer.

The bell rang again.

Followed by pounding.

Geez, talk about persistent. Had Monica pissed off a mob boss or something? There was no way Ray could continue to ignore it, and the person on the other side of the door seemed to have no intention of going away.

Ray stormed to the door and opened it with force, grasping the collar of her borrowed robe to preserve whatever dignity she could.

"You're not Monica." The older gentleman who stood on the threshold looked confused for a moment. Then it flitted away, and he stuck out a hand and cheerily added, "It's nice to meet you!" He shook Ray's hand up and down like an old fashion water pump.

"Er, likewise," Ray said, trying to free her fingers from the man's grasp.

"Is Moany here?"

"I don't think she likes that nickname," Ray said, recalling the snippets of the phone conversation she'd overheard between Monica and her ex.

"My daughter lacks a sense of humor sometimes."

Ray couldn't exactly argue, but on the other hand, she kinda had to side with Monica on this one. Who in the world would want to be called Moany? It was a terrible name. "Oh, you're Monica's dad?"

"Sure am. Do you know if she got my voice-mail message?"

Ray snorted. "I doubt it. Voice mail isn't really her thing."

"You've got her all figured out already, I see," he said with a laugh. "That's why I dropped by to let her know her mom and I were going to take her up on that dinner she offered. We were thinking Friday night. Is she around?"

"No, she's at a work meeting, but I can give her the message when she gets home."

"Excellent." He took Ray's hand again. "Gosh, I'm so embarrassed, my dear, but I'm terrible with names, and I've plum forgotten yours."

"Ray," she replied, almost certain she hadn't mentioned her name before.

"My memory's not what it was." The sheepish look of doubt that clouded his face reminded Ray so much of her grandfather in the early days of his struggles with his memory that it nearly broke her heart. She grabbed up the business card she'd given Monica, which the woman had discarded on the hall table. "Here, take my card. It'll help you remember.

"Thanks!" Monica's dad beamed with obvious relief. "And don't forget to tell Monica about Friday."

"No worries," Ray replied, tapping her head. "I've got it locked up here, safe and sound."

"See you on Friday!" the man called over his shoulder as he descended the front stairs.

Not a chance, she thought. No matter how many extra projects Monica managed to throw at her, the work would be done by Friday afternoon at the latest. Between bossy Monica and her hellion cat, Ray was pretty sure she'd never been happier at the prospect of wrapping up a job. But the door was nearly shut by the time Monica's dad called out, so Ray allowed it to click in place without responding. She was the hired help, after all. He had no reason to remember who she was, even if it was sweet of him to try.

CHAPTER THREE

Early Thursday evening, Monica followed Ray through her townhouse, which had been transformed from ceiling to floor in every room. She surveyed the master bedroom with a particularly satisfied sigh. The color was perfect, and the workmanship —or should that be work*woman*ship?—was superb, as it had been on every project Ray had shown her. But of all the rooms in the house, this was the one where the biggest difference could be felt, like the ghost of Brianna had finally been chased out, and Monica could breathe again.

"This looks incredible." Monica flashed Ray an appreciative grin, or at least that had been her intention. She hadn't expected to come face-to-face with an eyeful of exposed cleavage and flexed biceps as the woman bent to retrieve her tools. Whatever expression had ended up plastered to her face, Monica was fairly certain it was frozen there for good and could probably get her arrested in at least six states.

"I'm glad you like it." Ray tucked her toolbox under her arm, a ghost of a smirk letting Monica know she was well aware she was being ogled, though whether she was enjoying it remained a mystery. "I'm all packed up and should be out of your hair in a few minutes, as soon as I get your signature on the paperwork. Should I email you the final invoice?"

Monica waved her hand dismissively, unconcerned with financial details. "Don't bother cc'ing me. Just send it to Bri."

Ray's face clouded, apparently no longer interested in cloaking her emotions. "I've already sent her one for her portion of the job. I was talking about the bill for all the extras."

Monica frowned. "What extras?"

"Uh, all the stuff you added the first day. Specialty paint colors, the ceiling fan." Ray ticked off the items on her fingers as she went. "Cleaning the grout in the kitchen. The new switch plates. It's all listed on the invoice."

"Oh, that." Monica let out a relieved laugh. "No, go ahead and send those to Bri, as well."

"But, you're the one who requested the work," Ray argued, cocking her head to one side in a way that Monica would've found adorable if it weren't for the fact the woman was actively contradicting her.

"Sure, but my ex was very clear the other day that

ACCIDENTAL HONEYMOON

this is her house. So," Monica said with a smirk, "her house, her bills, right?"

Ray's head swiveled slowly from side to side in a clear sign of disagreement. "That's not how money works."

"Of course, it is." Monica shrugged, ready for the handy woman to leave so she could unwind with a glass of wine. She'd just found out the wedding contract at The Walters Art Museum was coming down to her or a rival event planner, and they'd be battling it out tomorrow afternoon. She needed her beauty rest for the final presentation. "Send her the bill. She's good for it; trust me. She and the new bitch she's with are both loaded."

"She's already seen the bill." The dimple in Ray's chin that Monica had been warned about was turning a bright pink. "She said you were on your own for the upgrades."

"Well, I…" Monica spluttered, her own temper flaring. "Does she think I don't know how the real estate game works?"

"Game?" Ray gave Monica a dubious look. "Sounds more like you're running a con, skipping out on a bill and trying to get someone else to pay."

"I'm not conning anyone out of anything." Monica ran her fingers through her long hair, stopping to pick at a tangled spot. It was a soothing action, something to help bring down her simmering blood pressure. Too bad Ray's hair wasn't long enough to get knotted, because judging by the crimson glow of that chin dimple, she needed to learn some techniques for taking things down a notch or two herself, before she boiled over. "Look, here's how it works. Bri pays for the extra work I ordered, which makes me feel better, because who doesn't enjoy sticking it to an ex, right? Then she adds twice that amount to the price of the house when she goes to sell it to me, and we spend several weeks haggling about it. It all works out in the end."

At this point, Ray's eyes had become so squinted Monica wasn't convinced she could see out of them. "You mean, in the end, you're paying for the repairs and maybe more?"

"I guess so." Monica didn't like the sound of *maybe more*. It wasn't like the economic downturn had left her with money to burn, and she hadn't considered the possibility she might end up on the losing end of the bargain. She was good at negotiations, and Brianna had rarely come out the winner when they were together. Even so, it was a possibility she had to consider. She tossed her head defiantly. "Who cares? The exasperation it will cause Bri while we argue over it should be well worth any premium."

"Why not save everyone a headache and pay me now?"

"Where's the satisfaction in that?" Monica replied with an airy laugh. She turned to go, desperate to get to the kitchen and uncork that nice chardonnay she had chilling in the fridge. The handy ma'am's presence in the house had left her all hot and bothered, in more ways than one. Had there ever been such an exasperating woman?

Ray stood with her hands on her hips, blocking Monica's exit from the bedroom, looking anything but amused. "If you don't pay me, I'll sue."

"Sue?" Monica put her own hands on her hips, mimicking Ray's stance. "I spent a semester as a pre-law major."

"A whole semester? Any longer and you'd be Supreme Court material."

"It was long enough to know you're out of luck, because I didn't sign a contract."

Ha. Gotcha.

Ray sucked in a breath as if to argue, then let it out like a slowly deflating balloon as Monica's words seemed to sink in. "Look. I'm sure we can come to an agreement. I won't charge you overtime."

"You won't charge me a dime—" She stopped when a flash of light shone through the bedroom window and hit her in the eyes. "That's weird."

"What, you mean a grown woman thinking she doesn't have to pay people for their work?" Ray quipped. "You're right, that's the weirdest thing I've heard in a long time."

"No, those headlights." Monica approached the window and did her best to peer through the opening in the blinds without moving them and making it obvious she was spying. "A car's pulled in and parked in my driveway, but I'm not expecting anyone."

An odd, almost sheepish expression crossed Ray's face. "Um, it's Thursday, right?"

"Yeah, why?"

"Nothing, just that your dad stopped by the other day and told me to tell you he and your mom were taking you up on your dinner offer, only"—Ray cleared her throat, looking nervous—"I kind of forgot to mention it."

Monica's stomach clenched, and the anger that had subsided earlier roared to a boil. "They're coming tonight, and you're only telling me now?"

"No, not tonight," Ray said, waving her hands as if trying to literally smooth the situation out like it was a wrinkled tablecloth. "He said Friday, which is tomorrow, so there's no problem."

A woman swung her legs out of the car, and the minute Monica recognized the shoes, she groaned. "There's a problem all right. Only one person I know wears silver loafers like those. My mother."

"Your mother?" Ray's eyes widened.

"This is your fault." Monica pointed her finger accusingly at the hapless handy ma'am, whose usual cocky demeanor was evaporating by the second. "You must've gotten the date wrong."

"Check your messages," Ray urged. "I'm positive your father said Friday."

"Then why are they outside my house tonight?"

Monica demanded, even while doing what Ray had asked and pulling out her phone. Sure enough, there was a voice mail alert. Locking eyes with Ray, she put it on speaker and hit play.

Hello, pumpkin. It's Dad. Your mother and I are looking forward to catching up with you over dinner. We can hardly wait to get to know your girlfriend better. She seems like a really lovely girl. We'll see you Friday!

"There." Ray smacked her palm against her thigh. "See? He clearly said Friday."

Monica had heard him say it, too, but she had turned her attention to a different part of the call. "What did he mean by my girlfriend seemed like a lovely girl?"

"I don't know. In my opinion, Brianna seems almost as high strung as—" Ray stopped in mid-sentence, as if suddenly remembering she and Monica were in the middle of a money dispute and deciding to err on the side of professionalism by not insulting her directly. "Never mind. We still have a bill to settle."

"Oh, no." Monica took another look out the window. Her parents were both standing in her driveway but had not yet started toward the front door. Her father appeared to be on the phone. "Not until we get to the bottom of why my dad said Brianna seemed lovely."

"Are you seriously upset because your parents like your girlfriend? Talk about a first world problem."

"Ex-girlfriend, but that's not the issue." Monica

sucked in her cheeks, knowing Ray was to blame, even if she wasn't sure how. "My parents were already at their second home in Florida when Bri and I started dating, and with the economy tanking and everything, they decided to stay for the long term and have only just gotten back to Baltimore. Which means they've never even met Bri and certainly have no way of knowing if she's lovely."

"They probably just assumed. Why wouldn't she be?" But as she said it, Ray's face bore an uncanny resemblance to a kindergartener who'd been caught sneaking cookies during nap time.

"Something's going on here." As she was trying to puzzle it out, Monica's attention was diverted to the bed where Mr. Fluffles had flopped down on her comforter, rolling to expose his belly for rubs. A belly that appeared to have been dyed the exact same shade as her bedroom walls.

Monica squinted. "What's wrong with the cat?"

"What cat?" Ray feigned innocence.

"What are you not telling me?"

Ray swallowed hard as she stared at the cat she'd pretended not to see. "I am so sorry, but when I was painting this room the other day, there was a little mishap with your cat and a paint tray. To be fair, you didn't tell me you had a cat."

"Exactly what was the nature of this mishap?" Monica drilled, refusing to fall for the trap of debating whose fault the cat's existence was.

"It was no big deal, I swear. Little Princess Powderpuff over there wandered through the paint, and I washed her off."

"Him."

"That cat's a he?" Ray's expression said that was one of the most ridiculous things she'd ever heard.

Monica stiffened, suddenly protective of Brianna's cast-off devil cat. "Yes. His name is Mr. Fluffles."

"His name is…oh, my God."

Ray dissolved into a fit of laughter that made the skin at the base of Monica's neck prickle, even as it sent a shot of heat through her groin. Monica's brain wanted to throttle Ray for acting like a jerk about the cat. Her body, on the other hand, had significantly different ideas of what to do with the woman. Monica was pretty sure all these mixed messages might be putting her in imminent danger of having her head explode.

"This isn't funny," Monica insisted. "We still haven't figured out why my dad thinks Bri is lovely. Did she come by when he was here and you're hiding it from me?"

"Of course not." Ray looked genuinely offended. "However, if she had stopped by to see the progress, it would've been within her rights as the homeowner. But, I don't hide things. I would've told you."

"Sure, like you told me my parents were coming for dinner." Out in the driveway, her father slipped the phone back into his pocket and took her mom's arm to lead her toward the house. Monica let out a growl of frustration. Time was running out. "When my dad came by the other day, what happened? Tell me every detail."

Ray placed the tip of her finger against the dimple on her chin, her brow furrowing in thought. "I had just finished giving Mr. Fluffles a shower—"

"And you lived to tell about it?"

"Barely." Ray glared at the cat, who was grooming his baby blue belly without a care in the world. "That beast soaked me from head to toe. I had to throw my clothes in the dryer. In fact, I'd just done that when your dad arrived."

Monica gaped. "You answered the door naked?"

"Are you insane?" Ray gave her a look like she was pretty sure Monica was a few cards shy of a full deck. "I threw on one of the bathrobes from upstairs. There's no way I'd go traipsing through a client's house in my birthday suit."

As the answer clicked in Monica's head, the doorbell rang.

"Come on." Monica fixed Ray with a steely stare. "Let's go greet my parents."

Ray took a step back. "Under no circumstances do I meet parents. Ever."

"But that's the problem. You already have." There was a hint of triumph in Monica's tone. "When he saw you in my house, wearing nothing but a bathrobe in the middle of the afternoon, my dad obviously thought

ACCIDENTAL HONEYMOON

you were Bri. So come along, dearest, and let's say hello."

Ray dug in her heels, gluing herself to her spot even as Monica grabbed her elbow. "Why would I do that?"

"Because all my life, I've disappointed my family. My older cousins all went to Ivy League schools and got jobs as doctors and lawyers, while the twins, troublemakers that they are, still manage to be practically perfect in every way."

Shit. She had absolutely not planned to say any of that. It was true but none of Ray's business. Why had it all come tumbling out? Monica blinked rapidly. No way would she let a tough woman like Ray see her on the brink of tears over what amounted to self-pity. She waited for Ray to make fun of her but was surprised to find the woman watching her quietly, like she was waiting to hear the rest.

Wait. Could telling her the truth actually work? With no better plan, Monica decided it was worth a try.

"I was the flighty one. The artist. Now, if they were actually coming here tomorrow like they said they would be, I'd be able to share the news with them that I've been chosen for a huge contract at The Walters Art Museum, propelling my small business to the big leagues."

"Really? That's great." Though Monica braced

herself for the addition of a snarky comeback, Ray seemed oddly sincere. "Congratulations."

"Thanks. But it hasn't happened yet. Not until after tomorrow's final presentation. Right now, the only thing I have to tell them is Brianna broke up with me and is trying to kick me out of my house. I'd really rather not. Which is where you come in." The doorbell rang again. Monica tightened her grip on Ray's arm. "Please, come downstairs with me and pretend to be my girlfriend, just for a few minutes."

"What's in it for me?" Ray asked, though Monica was encouraged that she had stopped resisting and started walking with her.

"I'll pay that invoice of yours, no questions asked," Monica offered, knowing it was the only way. Any leverage she might have held by the fact she hadn't signed a contract was negated by the enormity of the favor she was asking. "Even the overtime."

"You admit my time has value?" Ray slowed her pace as the bell rang for a third time, followed by a loud knock.

"Yes, of course, it does," Monica snapped, impatient to make it to the door.

"But you didn't think it was worth paying me for my work."

"I wanted to make Bri pay." Monica's cheeks burned as she realized how spoiled she sounded. "That was unfair of me, and I apologize. You have every right to be compensated for your time."

"Thank you."

Darn her. Was the exasperating woman going to make Monica come right out and grovel for her help? "Do we have a deal?"

"I assume that means you'll be paying me for my time tonight."

Monica stopped in her tracks and stared. This was much more outrageous than groveling. "You think I should pay you to shake hands with my parents and then be on your way. Now who's off her rocker?"

Ray shrugged. "If that's really all it is, I'll write it off as a free fifteen-minute design consultation. But I think we both know when it comes to parents, the chances of them wrangling me into a full dinner is not insignificant."

"Pumpkin?" Monica's dad called through the closed door. She had to answer it before they got worried and called the police or something.

"Fine." Monica seethed as she grasped the doorknob. "Whatever you want, poopsie."

"Quick, what's your last name?"

"Why, so you can write out a contract in blood?"

"No, so I know what to call your mom and dad. Mister and missus…" Ray waved her hand, inviting a response.

"Panagiotopoulos."

"Are you fucking kidding me?" Ray's lips moved as if she were trying to silently pronounce the last name while Monica suppressed a giggle. "Even your last name is high maintenance."

"We're Greek." Plastering an everything is hunky-dory smile on her face, Monica wrenched the door open. "Hi, Mom. Hi, Dad. Silly me. I could've sworn we agreed on tomorrow night for dinner."

"I'm sure it was my fault," Ray said jovially, wrapping an arm around Monica's shoulder and giving her a squeeze. She reached the other hand toward Monica's dad. "It's great to see you again Mr. Panty-oh—"

"Rachel, dear. Call me George." He shook Ray's hand then nodded toward Monica's mother. "And this is Helen."

"George. Helen." Ray looked from one to the other, repeating their names in that way that's always suggested by business coaches to help remember names. "I really do apologize, but I honestly thought dinner was tomorrow night. I'm afraid I already have plans this evening."

Monica's mom's hand shot out, grasping Ray by the forearm. "Oh, no. You can't leave now."

Ray flashed Monica an *I told you so* look.

Damn. Why did Ray have to be right all the time?

"Mom, I'm sure we can try to include Ray some other time. Since I didn't cook anything, why don't we head into the city and grab a bite at Cypriana? You always love that place."

"I'm afraid there's no time," her mother replied,

and the grim look on her face sparked worry in Monica's belly.

"We didn't come over for dinner, Moany. It's your *yiayia*."

Monica's eyes grew wide. "Oh no."

"We have to get to the hospital in New York tonight," her mother said. "Dad's booked four tickets on a flight leaving in a few hours. You'll barely have time to pack."

Monica blinked. "Why four?"

"Well, for Rachel, of course," her mom replied. She held out the tickets, and Monica saw one was preprinted with Ray's full name, Rachel Walsh.

Feeling lightheaded, Monica reached for Ray's arm to steady herself. "Can you excuse us for a minute?"

"Of course, pumpkin," her dad said.

"Not too long, though, dear," her mom added. "We'll need to call for a taxi to the airport very soon."

Monica nodded, then dragged a befuddled-looking Ray down the hall and into the kitchen. "What are we going to do?"

"What's a *yiayia*?" Ray's voice was tinged with an unusual amount of what could only be described as panic. "Is it something to do with your *you know what*?"

Monica snorted as Ray pointed in the general direction of her crotch. "Oh my...no. Geez. *Yiayia* is the Greek word for grandmother."

"Thank God." Most of the color returned to Ray's face as she let out a long breath. "Now that I think about it, I was confusing that with *hoohaa*. But wait, what's going on with your grandmother?"

"Uh-uh. Are you expecting me to forget that you confused my dad's mother with your lady parts?" Monica snickered as Ray's face flushed scarlet, but the gravity of the situation cut her teasing short. "She's ninety-six years old and in poor health."

Ray's brow creased in concern. "Your mom said she's in the hospital?"

Monica swallowed a lump in her throat. "For my parents to book the trip without asking, it has to be serious. I'm afraid she's dying."

"I'm really sorry." Ray fidgeted with her fingers, clearly at a loss for what to say. "If there's anything I can do—"

"There is, actually." The thought had entered her brain like a bolt of lightning. Monica gulped quickly and plowed ahead so she could get it out before she lost the nerve. "You can come with me to New York."

"No way."

"I thought you'd say that," Monica persisted, "but hear me out."

Ray cocked her head to one side. "Come on, Monica. It's one thing to play pretend girlfriend for an hour or two over dinner, but this? This is over-the-top nuts. Your whole clan's going to be there."

"Clans are Scottish, not Greek."

Ray balled her fists, looking like she wished she could wring Monica's neck. It had the odd effect of making Monica feel a little better. "Then whatever the Greek word is for a whole bunch of nosy relatives I don't want to meet. I can't fool your entire extended family."

"You would be fulfilling my grandmother's dying wish."

Ray grimaced. "Tell me you did *not* just play that card. That's low."

"It's not low," Monica pleaded. "It's true. My grandmother has always been a thoroughly modern woman in so many ways. Like, when I came out to my family, she accepted me immediately and made it clear that anyone who did otherwise would face her wrath. But in other ways, she's very traditional. Like wanting to see me settle down."

"Tell her you have. Here." Ray reached for her phone and pulled Monica toward her, holding it out as far as she could with one arm. "We can take a selfie, and you can show it to her as proof."

"After my parents have promised her a real flesh and blood girlfriend is coming to see her?" Monica yanked her thumb in the direction of the foyer, where her parents were waiting. "You know they've already told her you'll be there, right? No way they didn't lead with that news."

"Brianna's the one who should be doing this." But as Ray chewed her bottom lip, it was clear her resolve was softening.

Maybe a little bit of eyelash batting would do the

trick. But, no. Somehow Monica sensed that wouldn't work on a no-nonsense woman like Ray. Instead, Monica pressed her hands together and spoke from the heart. Hey, against all odds, it had worked on her before.

"Do you know what it's like to have a grandparent you completely adore?"

Ray shrugged, looking away.

"What about that grandfather of yours?" Monica pressed. "The one with the chin?"

"Yes." Ray closed her eyes and sighed. "Grandpa Ray. He died early this year."

"Then you know." Monica weighed how personal she should get. Ray was basically a stranger, and they'd done nothing but butt heads since they met. On the other hand, Monica needed this woman's help for what was admittedly a harebrained scheme, and the only way to get it would be to convince her how important it truly was. "I told you how I've always been the failure in my family. My *yiayia* might be the only one who never looked at me that way, no matter how big a mistake I made. She believed in me, even when it took me six years to graduate from college because I kept changing my major. When I wanted to start my own business, she told me I could do it when no one else thought I could."

"She sounds really special." Ray's voice was soft, thick with unspoken loss that made Monica want to reach out and give her a hug. Monica refrained. If she actually did it, Ray would be out the door for good, running as fast as she could away from the crazy lady.

"You have to understand why I can't disappoint her by showing up all alone. Not this time."

"I get it. I do. But—"

"I'll pay you." She was already on the hook for an unintended handyman bill, and raiding her savings for even more would set her home buying dream back by months. But whatever it cost, her grandmother was worth it to her. Besides, she'd be doing fine financially once the wedding at The Walters was finalized. With one last, desperate bid, Monica went all in and sweetened the deal. "I'll pay you double time. If we leave tonight and take the earliest flight back in the morning, we'll be gone twelve hours at the most. Please, Ray."

Ray sucked in a deep breath, nodding slightly as understanding filled her eyes. "I'm going to regret this."

"No, you won't." With a squeal, Monica pulled Ray into a hug, no longer caring whether the woman would think she was insane. "I'll be the best fake girlfriend you've ever had; I promise."

CHAPTER FOUR

As the flight attendants made their last checks of the overhead bins before takeoff, Ray snapped the buckle and tightened the belt across her lap before stretching her legs in front of her as far as they would go in the cramped middle seat.

This is insane. And it wasn't just the fact that she'd offered her prime aisle seat to Monica within seconds of boarding, even though she'd sworn to herself during the entire cab ride to the airport that she wouldn't. No mentally sound person would volunteer for a middle seat unless under extreme duress, but Ray chalked it up to the good old-fashioned manners Grandpa Ray had instilled in her from an early age. Elbows don't belong on tables, take your ball cap off indoors, and always give up your seat for a lady. Even a really annoying lady, whose eyes got beguilingly crinkly in the corners when she smiled, and…

And that's quite enough of that, she chastised herself.

No, the truly crazy part was being on the flight at all. Had she honestly agreed to fly to New York to be someone's fake girlfriend? It was the type of thing that only happened in movies, like the madcap comedies she and her grandfather used to watch late at night on the classic movie channel when he'd had trouble sleeping. If she'd learned anything from them, it was things never went according to plan. This whole situation was destined to blow up in her face. So why had she said yes?

Because I'm a big ol' softy.

There. She'd finally said it. Not out loud so Monica could hear, because who knew what a pampered princess like her would do with that knowledge, but she'd admitted it to herself. It wasn't that she found Monica attractive. She did, of course, but it was something else. She cared. As much as she liked to act tough, and generally shunned anything outwardly feminine when it came to her appearance, deep down, Ray was as sentimental as they came. She loved small animals and had a soft spot for pretty flowers. God help her, she even liked the color pink. But apparently, recent events had shown her there was nothing like a dying grandparent to light up every one of her emotional buttons and spur her to act in colossally stupid ways.

As soon as they were in the air, Ray turned to

Monica. "Okay, give it to me straight. What am I getting myself into with this family of yours?"

Pulling off the headphones she'd donned when they sat down, Monica shrugged. "You've met my parents."

Ray craned her neck for a quick glimpse of George and Helen who, due to the last-minute nature of their trip, had been seated several rows away. She noted that, like her, Monica's father was seated in the middle while his wife rested her head on a pillow she'd propped against the window. Another high maintenance female. In her mind, she pumped her fist in a salute to her put-upon compatriot. *Solidarity, George.*

"So, that's it?" Ray asked hopefully. "No other relatives?"

"Are you kidding? Tons."

Naturally. Ray shuddered. "Lay it on me."

"Let's see." Monica tilted her head from side to side, appearing to run through a mental list. "*Yiayia* had three sisters, but they've all died, so that leaves their kids: Don, Sophia, Philip, Annie, Jennifer, and Lawrence. Then there are the cousins. Nina, Maddie, Trish, David, Seth, Erik, Josh, Pam, Debbie, Terry, Mark, Jessica, Sophia, Matt, Bryce, and Clark. All of them have kids, of course, except Maddie and Trish, who are still in college."

"Uh-huh." Ray was already overwhelmed by the number of branches on this family tree. "And I assume the kids all have names, too?"

"Probably, but the only one of the extended cousins I can ever remember off the top of my head is Agamemnon."

"You have a cousin named Agamemnon? Agamemnon Panty-topless?"

Monica's eyes narrowed to slits as Ray grinned at her own cleverness. "That's Panagiotopoulos, thank you very much. But, no. His last name is Jones. I think his mom felt bad for marrying someone with such an Anglo last name, so she made up for it by giving her son the most Greek first name she could think of. If you ask me, it's absolutely terrible."

"I didn't want to be rude," Ray said, "but...yeah. Will they all be at the hospital?"

"I'm sure they will be at some point. *Yiayia*'s the matriarch of the family."

"Vying to see who gets her millions?" Ray joked, then immediately regretted how callous she must have sounded. "I'm sorry. I didn't mean it like that. My dark sense of humor gets me into trouble sometimes, especially when I'm nervous. Which I definitely am. I had no idea I was going to be meeting half of Greece on this trip."

"No worries." Monica waved her hand dismissively. "The truth is, my grandmother was left with a modest nest egg when my grandfather died—some insurance money, a few pieces of property—but none of us will see any of it when she's gone. She made it clear a long time back that whatever's left after paying her bills would be going to charity."

"Less fighting that way?" Ray guessed.

"You'd think so, but no. I'm sure they're fighting over who gets what this very minute. For the past five years, relatives have been putting color-coded stickers under items all over *Yiayia*'s house, so everyone would know they'd called dibs. Last Thanksgiving when we were all there for dinner, Annie's purple sticker had been peeled off a particular vase and replaced with one of Jennifer's green stickers, and they nearly knocked the turkey off the table duking it out."

"You've got to be joking."

"Nope. Saw it with my own eyes."

"Have you tagged anything?"

"Me?" Monica put a hand on her chest and fixed Ray with an innocent look. "No way."

"Too much dignity to get caught up in the fleeting quest for material goods?" Ray said it with as straight a face as she could manage, but from the light punch she received on her upper arm, she had a feeling Monica wasn't buying it.

"Are you kidding? The old lady's got some prime merchandise. That vase alone could've been sold for a pretty penny. I just didn't trust my skills wielding a carving knife across a crowded table to put a bid in for it."

"Now I know you're joking." At least, Ray sure hoped so.

To Ray's relief, Monica laughed. "Honestly? I know where I stand with all of them. I've always been the black sheep in the family. Why invite trouble, you know?"

"Don't take this the wrong way, but I'm glad I'm only your fake girlfriend," Ray confided. "I'm not sure I could handle more than a few hours of a family like that."

"From the way you reacted to having to meet my parents tonight, I kind of got the impression you felt that way about any girlfriend's family."

"I feel that way about anyone's family, period." Ray's face grew warm. "Family stuff is fine if you're in a serious relationship, but I'm not the type for that kind of thing."

"You don't spend time with your own family?"

"Don't have much to speak of. No clue who my dad was. Mom was unreliable at best, coming and going when it suited her. Growing up, it was mostly me and my grandpa, and now that he's gone, I'm a lone wolf."

"What, you don't have a little missus back at home? A couple of wolf cubs?" Monica's nose crinkled as she bit down on her lip. "I guess I should've asked that before recruiting you for this charade."

"If there had been, I wouldn't be here," Ray assured her. "Not my style, even for pretend."

"Good to know."

"Frankly, though, settling down has never appealed to me. The thought of even going to a wedding makes me break out in hives." Ray pressed her hand to her lips, the look on Monica's face reminding her that the woman's bedroom had been filled with photos of wedding ideas.

"I feel a bit differently about them."

Yikes. Ray had really stepped in it this time. Monica had probably expected to be introducing Brianna to her family on a night like this, sporting some massive diamond engagement ring on her finger. Talk about rubbing salt in her wound. "Look, I'm sorry to bring up a sore subject. I didn't mean anything by it."

"What subject?"

"I saw those magazine clippings in your bedroom," Ray confessed, surprised at the sudden stab of sympathy she felt for the woman. "I guess you and your ex must've been planning a pretty spectacular wedding when she walked out. That's gotta hurt."

To her surprise, Monica burst out laughing. "You thought those were for my wedding?"

Ray's brow crinkled. "Weren't they?"

"Maybe if my dad was the King of Persia."

Ray scratched her head. How crazy did a broad have to be to snip pictures out of magazines of weddings she couldn't afford? "So, weddings are like a hobby or something?"

"I beg your pardon?" Monica's back had stiffened, and her face had the expression of someone who'd received a rude comment about their mother. "Is that what Bri told you?"

"Huh?" Ray blinked, unsure how else to respond since she had no idea what she'd done. She had to have done something, though, because her companion was getting downright huffy.

"That's so typical of Bri." Monica folded her arms tightly across her chest. "Never mind that we discussed it for months before I took the plunge."

"You discussed what, your engagement?" Ray guessed, feeling like she was stumbling around in a pitch-black room full of alligators.

"No, my business." Monica studied her through narrowed eyes. "I'm a party planner."

"That's a job?" Even as she said it, Ray knew she'd made a mistake, and she would probably be made to pay for it in some unknown but no doubt painful way in the future.

"You're as bad as my ex."

Monica's eyes teared up. She sniffled. Oh, shit. The payback was even worse than Ray had feared. Monica was about to cry. In front of a plane full of people, who would all start staring at Ray and thinking she was to blame. She kinda was.

"Please, don't do that. I'm sorry." Ray put a hand on Monica's chin, nudging her face upward so she could look in the woman's eyes, which were a striking blue that shone even brighter through the unshed tears. "I honestly didn't know that was something people got paid to do, at least not as full-time employment. Explain to me how it works, like I'm an idiot."

"You *are* an idiot." But a ghost of a smile teased Monica's lips, and the crying crisis appeared to be averted. "As for how it works, people pay me to plan their events. I mostly do weddings but also corporate events, birthday parties—"

"Look, we both agree I'm not bright," Ray interrupted, "but how dumb must someone be to not be able to manage a birthday party on their own? It's balloons and a cake."

Monica leaned forward conspiratorially. "I did a fiftieth birthday party for a congressman last year that had a budget of 70k. There was a live rock band."

Ray's jaw dropped. "Seriously? Wow. I guess if you're working with congressmen, you must be raking it in."

Monica made a face. "Unfortunately, that was with the company I used to work for, before I struck out on my own. It's been a little slower since then."

Thinking back on the terrible economy of the past year, Ray grimaced. "That's rotten luck."

Monica shrugged. "To hear Bri tell it, you'd think a global downturn was all part of my plan to not have to go to work. Things are looking up, though. I'm competing tomorrow for a senator's daughter's wedding. Their budget is well over a hundred thousand dollars."

"That's big money."

Monica nodded. "That's why I have to get back to Baltimore on the first flight tomorrow, so I have enough time to get ready to do the pitch."

"A hundred grand for a wedding, though." Ray shuddered.

"The thought of lifelong commitment making you feel a little green around the gills there, Ms. Walsh?"

"It isn't commitment itself I have a problem with," Ray explained. "I mean, I might not be a huge believer in everlasting love, but I don't like the idea of spending my life alone, either. If the right woman came along someday, it's not like I would break up with her on principle or something."

"Spoken like a true romantic," Monica ribbed. "What is it you don't like, then?"

"All the trappings of weddings. I hate how otherwise intelligent women develop an overnight obsession with dresses and shoes the minute they have a ring on their finger."

Monica's eyes lit up. "Right? The worst part is how everyone expects, by virtue of being female, that you must love weddings and be dying to go to them and to have one of your own."

Ray laughed. "Tell me about it. Since hitting the big three-oh a few years back, I've been to over a dozen weddings. Pretty much every person I know has tied the knot. Sometimes I wish we could go back to gay people not getting married because geez. I'm so over it."

"At least I bet you've never had the dubious honor of being a bridesmaid."

Ray arched an eyebrow. "What makes you say that? I've done it twice. I even had to go as far as wearing a dress for one of them."

"You wore a dress?" Monica's mouth gaped. "I think I would pay to see that."

"So you could laugh?"

"Nah, I bet you'd look hot in a dress." Monica pinched her lips together as soon as she'd said it, immediately looking mortified. Despite herself, Ray's heart skipped a beat.

"I'll have you know I can rock a dress if I have to, but not this one. It was a hideous peach thing. I almost died when I pulled it out of the box."

"Why'd you do it?"

"Because it was my best friend from high school, and I'd always said I'd do anything for her."

Monica gave her a knowing look. "And you were in love with her, I'll bet."

Ray looked sheepishly at the other woman. "No comment. The thing is, when I told her I'd do anything, I was thinking of something more reasonable, like giving her a kidney."

"Clearly, you should've been more specific." Monica nibbled on her lip for a few moments, like she was debating saying something. "Can I tell you a secret?"

Ray leaned forward slightly. "Please do."

"Sometimes I hate weddings, too."

"What?" It came out screechier than she'd intended, and Ray clapped a hand over her mouth, stifling a sudden onset of giggles. "But that's your job."

"I know, and I'm good at it, too. Do you know, when business started to dry up, I launched a wedding podcast and blog, and I already have almost a million followers? That makes me a macro-influencer."

"Is there a special salute I should be giving?" Ray deadpanned, loving the expression Monica got when she was being teased, the one that promised it was only a matter of time until the tables were turned. Why that expression worked for her was a mystery, but man, it sure did. "Do I need to kiss your ring?"

"Smart-ass."

"You're not the first to notice." Ray looked at her thoughtfully. "Seriously, though, why do you do what you do if you hate it?"

"Because I love the idea of two people coming together with the people they love and making a promise. Simple. Beautiful. But too often, the people who hire me don't care about that, or their parents don't, and it turns into a big, ugly nightmare. That's the part I don't like."

"Keeping up with the Joneses," Ray said. "Or the Agamemnons. Did I get that name right?"

"You did!" Monica clapped playfully. "Want to take a stab at mine now?"

"Not a chance." Ray did not have a death wish.

"Also," Monica lowered her voice to barely more than a whisper. "Sometimes I'm afraid I'm a wedding Grim Reaper."

"A what?"

"I've planned five weddings since I started my own business, and four of them have ended in disaster."

Ray spent a moment rechecking her math. "That seems like a lot, percentage wise."

"It's off the charts."

"When you say disaster…" Ray prompted.

"Let's see. One of them, the groom disappeared two thirds of the way through the reception. They found him in bed the next morning—"

"With a bridesmaid?" Ray guessed.

"No, with a tire track across his chest."

"Oh my God. But if he was dead, how did he get back to his bed?"

"He wasn't dead, just passed out drunk with no idea what happened or how his shirt had gotten a tire track on it. God help his wife. Then, there've been two divorces."

"Times have been stressful lately," Ray pointed out, wanting for some reason to try to cheer her up. "A lot of couples didn't make it."

"One marriage lasted eight weeks. The other was less than a month. The bride spent longer choosing her cake flavor."

"Ouch. To be fair, cake is a serious matter that should not be taken lightly."

"There's another thing we agree on," Monica said. "I bet when you met me, you doubted we'd have this much in common."

Ray stroked her chin with an amused smirk. "I take it by the way you said it that you were under a similar suspicion."

Monica's cheeks turned pink. "Perhaps."

"So, will you stick with it, do you think?"

"The wedding business? I have to for now. It pays the bills. Maybe someday, though, I'll have a chance to plan the types of events I'd actually want for myself."

"That would be nice," Ray said and meant it. Everyone should have something in life that made them feel complete, and since it was unlikely a relationship would ever fit the bill, the next best thing was work.

They landed at LaGuardia a short time later and breezed through the airport to the taxi stand, being encumbered by nothing more than a single overnight bag, which Monica had packed but Ray carried. Apparently, it included a toothbrush and other essentials of some kind for both Monica and Ray, though she hadn't bothered to ask for the details. They wouldn't be in New York longer than the morning, as Monica had made it clear she had to get back to Baltimore on the earliest flight because of her work. What could they possibly need in that short a time? Judging by the weight of the bag, Ray suspected they had different definitions of what was essential.

Shocking.

Sure, they'd had a pleasant conversation on the plane, during which they'd established they both disliked weddings and thought very highly of cake. It hardly made them soul mates. As far as Ray could see, she and Monica were as different as night and day. So why had Ray spent the whole flight feeling like she had butterflies in her belly?

Because I'm an idiot.

It was only as the cab driver pulled up to the hospital entrance that Ray truly began to regret her impulsive decision. If there was one thing in the world she hated more than weddings, it was hospitals. She stared at the foreboding entrance, gripping the *oh shit* handle above the window, her heart beating wildly.

"I'm not sure I can go in there." Ray swallowed, her throat like sandpaper. "All last year, my grandfather was sick. In and out of the hospital. I…"

Ray had expected a tantrum, but instead, Monica placed a hand on Ray's back. "It's okay. Take your time. What can I do to help?"

"I need a minute. I know we have a deal—" Ray swiped her eyes. "What's wrong with me? I can't stop them."

"It's going to be okay."

Monica wrapped her arms around Ray's quivering body. It was the second time that day, and while definitely not the hugging type, Ray melted into the embrace with complete gratitude and more than a little embarrassment. She was supposed to be the strong one, the one offering Monica a comforting shoulder to cry on. It wasn't her grandfather behind the door, but Monica's grandmother. Instead, as she inhaled the citrus scent of Monica's shampoo and absorbed the heat that radiated from her body, she felt a sense of peace wash over her like she'd never experienced before. Some part deep inside her wanted to stay that way forever, while the rest of her—the rational part—knew she needed to escape immediately.

Time to rally.

She screwed up her courage, pulling away from the warmth of Monica's arms and facing the hospital doors. Straightening her back, she took Monica's hand and held it as they joined George and Helen at the revolving doors.

Ray stared straight ahead as they followed Monica's parents down endless corridors, until they reached the room where Monica's grandmother was.

"The doctors say only two visitors at a time," George told them, "so why don't you two go first while Helen and I find some coffee? Unless, that is, you'd rather get a drink first."

Yeah, a whiskey, straight up, Ray thought but bit her tongue before she could say it. Monica wouldn't appreciate it if they thought their daughter was dating a lush. "No, that's fine. You go get something. I'm sure you'd like to settle your nerves."

When they'd left, Ray entered the hospital room just ahead of Monica, as if to protect her from the terrible sight that surely awaited them of a withered woman on the bed, hooked up to scary machines with beeping and flashing lights.

Instead, she saw a spitfire of a woman—tiny and wrinkled, yes, but with hair dyed fire engine red and topped with a bright green turban—sitting up in bed, grinning.

"Moany!"

The old woman opened her arms for Monica to hug her, and Monica obliged immediately, not seeming to be bothered in the slightest by the use of her despised nickname. Even so, it surprised Ray that she would call her granddaughter that, given how highly Monica had spoken of her. It was only when she repeated it that Ray realized what she'd heard was not the mean-spirited moniker but the name *Monica* spoken with a hint of a Greek accent.: Moany-ca.

This made Ray like her a lot better, but one fact remained; if that woman was on her deathbed, Ray would eat her left shoe.

Had she been conned by the entire family?

CHAPTER FIVE

Monica clasped her grandmother tightly, alarmed that she could feel every bone in the woman's narrow shoulders almost as if she were hugging one of those skeletons in a science lab.

"*Yiayia*, you're too thin," she scolded, pulling back enough to look her grandmother in the eyes. "Haven't they been feeding you in here?"

"Nothing worth mentioning," her grandmother responded with a scowl. "You know they're trying to make me stay on a low-cholesterol, low-sodium diet?"

"Well, they're trying to keep you healthy," Monica told her, even if it was the last thing her grandmother would want to hear.

"That's what the doctor said—and by the way, I think I have shoes older than he is—so I says to him, I says Doctor, I'm ninety-six years old. Something's going to kill me. It might as well taste good."

She couldn't help laughing, but Monica felt a pang of sympathy for whoever was in charge of her grandmother's care. Knowing how *Yiayia* felt about a good meal, Monica suspected the woman may have smuggled a leg of lamb in her purse. Low cholesterol diet? Good luck with that.

In the middle of her laughter, the older woman began to cough, gulping in anguished breaths that turned her face as unnaturally red as her hair.

"Are you okay?" Panic spread through Monica's body like wildfire. "Do I need to call a nurse?"

The woman shook her head with steely determination. "I'm fine. Just dandy."

She was far from fine, but Monica knew a few things for certain, her grandmother was tough and a fighter. They'd all raced here in a panic, but Monica wouldn't put it past the woman to live another decade. She'd probably gotten lonely and wanted the family to visit.

"Who's this?" *Yiayia*'s eyes sparkled as she looked past Monica, zeroing in on Ray like she'd spied the biggest present under the tree on Christmas morning.

"Oh, right. I almost forgot. This is my… This is Ray." Monica reached for Ray's hand, hoping her grandmother hadn't noticed her stumble over the introduction. She was willing to mislead about the nature of their relationship in any number of ways, but when it came down to it, she'd found it impossible to outright lie to her grandmother.

"Ray." The old woman nodded thoughtfully. "That's a curious name."

"It's Rachel," Ray said, inching a little closer to the bed. "My grandfather was named Ray, and we had a lot in common, so the name stuck."

"It's a good name," *Yiayia* proclaimed in the tone she used that said "that should settle it for everybody." "It's the name of my favorite actor. Have you ever heard of Ray Mi—"

"*Yiayia*." Monica cleared her throat in gentle warning, dreading what she knew was about to come. When her grandmother started down the road of classic movies, she was impossible to stop. They'd be here for days. "I'm sure Ray doesn't want to get into a long conversation about old Hollywood."

But Ray's expression was animated with unusual excitement. Monica was probably going to get charged extra for this Academy Award worthy performance, but it might be worth it. The woman's interest in her grandmother's ramblings was absolutely convincing. "Were you about to say Ray Milland?"

"Yes!" *Yiayia* clapped her hands together with such force she jostled the hospital bed. "You know who that is?"

"You bet I do!" As Ray came as close to dancing a jig as Monica had ever seen outside a tourism video for Ireland, it occurred to her that maybe Ray wasn't acting. She actually seemed to be bonding with the old woman.

"What's your favorite Milland movie?" *Yiayia* demanded. Monica held her breath as Ray considered. Her grandmother had strong opinions on almost everything, and this would be no exception. She prayed Ray wasn't bluffing.

"Well," Ray began after several seconds spent rubbing the dimple in her chin, "most will tell you *The Lost Weekend* is his best movie, and I won't argue he was brilliant in it. *Dial M for Murder* is another knockout performance, but I have to admit, I have a soft spot for one of his lesser known films. *The Well Groomed—*"

"*Bride!*" The older woman was so ecstatic she nearly shot up out of the bed. "Oh, how I loved that film. 1946. I remember like it was yesterday. We were living in California because my husband, Niko, had just gotten out of the Navy and got a job at a winery up in Napa Valley. He loved it there. It reminded him of the old country. We went to see movies every week, and for our anniversary that year, he took me to Hollywood, where I actually saw Olivia de Havilland *in person* when we were standing in line to get a hot dog at Pink's."

"Are you serious?" Ray seemed to have forgotten she was still holding Monica's hand. She was squeezing it so hard it felt like Monica's fingers had lost circulation. "I can't imagine seeing her for real. You know, *The Well Groomed Bride* was her first role after her contract dispute with Warner Bros."

"Men always think they can control a woman. She showed them!"

"She sure did," Ray said with an admiring chuckle. Between the young woman and the old, it was hard to tell who was the bigger fan. "Even if it did cost her two years of work."

"A marriage should only have one quarterback!" Monica's grandmother bellowed.

Monica jumped in alarm, certain her grandmother must be manifesting signs of a stroke. "Should I call a nurse?"

Ray laughed. "No, that's one of the lines from the movie. See, Olivia de Havilland was marrying a football player, and she was fighting with Ray Milland over the last bottle of champagne in the city—not a normal bottle but one of those big ones."

"A magnum, they're called," *Yiayia* interjected. "Niko sometimes brought them home for a special occasion."

"That's right, a magnum. Well, it's a complicated story, but you wouldn't believe the shenanigans over a champagne bottle. Predictably, it all led to true love in the end."

"Yeah, I bet," said Monica, who had lost the thread of the conversation.

"I'm sorry, Moany-ca," *Yiayia* said. "I've gotten so caught up reminiscing over movies with your lovely girlfriend that I haven't been paying any attention to you. What have you been up to?"

"Uh, let's see." With the spotlight turned on her, Monica's brain went blank. Considering what a chatterbox Ray had turned out to be, there had to be something she could talk about with her own grandmother. What did the woman like? "Well, a few days ago, I was at a wedding venue that's to die for. Er, I mean..." Under the circumstances, Monica immediately regretted her word choice and looked desperately to Ray for backup.

"Monica's right." Placing her hands on the back of one of the chairs provided for visitors, Ray motioned for Monica to sit, then settled into the other chair. "The Walters Art Museum is an absolutely stunning place for weddings."

"What wonderful manners you have, Ray. Reminds me of my dear husband." Monica's grandmother beamed. "So, you like this museum, too, then?"

"Oh, yes," Ray said amiably. "It's one of the nicest venues in the area. Expensive, though. Way out of my league for sure."

Yiayia's face grew thoughtful. "What is it you do for a living, Ray?"

"She's a handy ma'am," Monica interjected, not relishing the loss of attention so soon. This was her grandmother, after all. It wasn't fair her fake girlfriend got all the limelight. "That's like a handyman but a woman."

"Oh, how clever," *Yiayia* clucked approvingly. "Handy ma'am. I love it."

"That's only a side job. I'm actually a professionally trained restoration carpenter." Ray, however, looked at Monica with a less than pleased expression.

"Okay." Monica failed to see the difference. She still worked with tools, right?

"It means," Ray explained with a tone that suggested she was running thin on patience, "I specialize in the fine craftsmanship needed to bring old, historic houses back to their original splendor."

Nope. Monica still didn't get it. Her grandmother, however, looked impressed enough for the both of them.

"Two jobs? I admire your work ethic. It sounds like a wonderful career. Can you restore people, too?" *Yiayia* joked, pointing to her wrinkled cheeks. "I could also use a return to my original splendor. Believe it or not, I used to be almost as pretty as your Moany-ca."

"Oh, I believe it, Mrs. Panty...er, Pan-yee..."

"Call me *Yiayia*," she said, placing her gnarled hand on Ray's arm. "You're part of the family now."

Family? Jealousy bubbled up in Monica's chest. Her grandmother had been talking to Ray all night and barely said two words to her. It wasn't fair! Ray was the hired help, after all. Monica was about to set the record straight, consequences be damned, when her dad poked his head into the room.

"Okay, you two. It's my turn to visit," he said. "You have to share."

The older woman's smile dulled, but she recovered

quickly and turned first to Monica and then to Ray. "That's okay. I'm so glad you came to see me. I have a good feeling about you two, and something tells me you're going to have good fortune come your way very soon."

They exited the room holding hands, but as soon as they were safely down the hallway, Monica pulled hers away. She looked expectantly at Ray. "I could use some coffee."

There was a flicker of an emotion in Ray's eyes that Monica couldn't quite place. Hurt, perhaps? It didn't matter. Monica was drained from the visit with her grandmother and lacked both the energy and the desire to contemplate whatever hidden meaning might be lurking in the woman's facial expressions. The more she thought about how much Ray had monopolized her grandmother's attention, the more annoyed she became.

Monica's gaze swept the hallway, landing on a sign for the cafeteria. "Looks like we can get some over there."

They filled their cups in silence, and when they reached the register, Monica stepped in front of Ray, pulling out her wallet. "I guess I should pay, since you're still on the clock."

Ray frowned but didn't argue. When they found a small table that was empty, Ray went to pull out the chair, but Monica waved her away. "I've got it."

Ray shrugged and sat in the opposite chair. "Your grandmother's a real hoot."

Monica nodded sullenly. "She was more animated tonight with you than I've seen her in several years."

"Well," Ray responded good-naturedly, "we Ray Milland fans have to stick together. It's really a shame we have to leave for the airport in a few hours. I'd love to be able to talk with her some more."

Monica gritted her teeth, her nostrils flaring slightly. Just what she needed, for Ray to monopolize her grandmother for another day. "At least it looks like it was a false alarm. *Yiayia* will probably outlive us all."

Ray's expression grew thoughtful. "I'm not so sure. This happened with Grandpa Ray. He had a burst of energy toward the end, and I was convinced he was recovering, but then he took a sudden turn and went downhill quickly. His nurse told me it was common, especially once the patient has had a chance to see all their family one last time."

"What are you saying, that because I came to visit, I've killed my grandmother?"

"Of course not. I'm just suggesting you need to be prepared that you might not have much time left with her. Have you considered extending your visit?"

"I wish I could, but I have to get back for my meeting in the morning, or I'll lose the contract."

"Surely, under the circumstances, you could get them to reschedule for Monday."

"Maybe." Honestly, Monica doubted it. The bride-to-be was a senator's daughter. "I guess I could call the museum as soon as it opens and see if I can reschedule. If not, I'd still have time to catch the next shuttle flight if I went straight from the airport to my meeting.

"I'm really proud of you, Monica." Ray's voice was gravelly with emotion. "I'll admit when we first met, I may not have had the best opinion of you, but putting your grandmother first like this is the right choice. You won't regret it."

How dare that woman? If she'd been a teakettle, Monica would've been on the verge of whistling. Had this handy ma'am—and what a dumb, gimmicky name, seriously—just lectured her on the importance of family? Of all the nerve! As if Monica needed a nobody like Ray to be proud of her to provide some sort of validation.

She checked her watch with an exaggerated motion. "Looks like it's time for me to call you a cab."

Ray's face clouded. "A cab? You mean you don't need me to stay here with you?"

As if.

"No, you might as well catch the early flight. Your services won't be required any longer. Make sure you send me a full invoice for today, including overtime." Monica looked away so as not to have to face the devastating pain in Ray's eyes.

Was she proud of her behavior? Of course not. But Ray was already halfway to the door, and there was nothing to be done about it now.

WHAT WAS THAT POUNDING?

Monica sat up in bed, pulling the satin sleep mask from her eyes and squinting at the alarm clock on her nightstand. It was only seven o'clock, much too early for construction. Yet, the racket continued. She swung her legs out from under the covers, every part of her body aching after spending two nights sleeping on the chair in her grandmother's hospital room, and then on the sofa for five additional nights at her grandmother's apartment as her family squabbled around her after the old woman had passed away.

It had been a terrible week. As Ray had predicted, *Yiayia* had made a sudden turn for the worse just hours after they'd discussed the possibility, almost like them talking about it had put the idea into her grandmother's head. And while Monica's meeting with the museum had been rescheduled, when Monica was still unable to return in time for it due to the funeral, that must-win had gone to her competitor instead. Now that she'd finally made it back home, all she wanted was decent sleep, and lots of it. Apparently, even something so simple was too much to ask for.

She shuffled to the window. A man stood on her driveway, whacking a piece of wood with a mallet, driving it deep into the square of green that passed for her front lawn. That explained the pounding she'd heard. But why was he doing it? The answer became clear when he stepped away, and Monica caught sight of the bright red for sale sign that hung from the newly installed post.

Fuck.

Her grandmother hadn't even been in the ground for twenty-four hours, and Brianna thought that was a good time to put the house on the market? There had to be something illegal in that level of callousness. At least the guy was getting into his truck and driving off. There was a stack of posts and signs in the truck bed, and Monica wondered if the next poor sap knew he was coming.

With quiet restored, Monica returned to bed.

The phone rang.

"Yep?" was as good a greeting as she could manage.

"Monica Panagiotopoulos?"

"Uh-huh." The caller had pronounced her last name correctly and without hesitation, meaning there was a good chance she actually knew him, but she couldn't place the voice. "Who is this?"

"It's Larry Donahue, from Donahue and Taite. I handled your grandmother's affairs for many years, and first I'd like to say how sorry I am for your loss."

"Oh, thanks." Right. Donahue and Taite, the attorneys. "Funny, I was thinking about calling a lawyer. Do you know if it's illegal to pound a for sale sign into someone's yard at seven on a Friday morning?"

"Well, uh…" The man hesitated. "It's not my area

ACCIDENTAL HONEYMOON

of expertise, but I could have an associate look into noise ordinances in your municipality."

Wow. Larry did not have a sense of humor.

"That's okay. What was it you were calling about? If it's the death certificate, you should probably call the funeral home directly."

"No, this has to do with something else. You see, the day before she died, your grandmother gave a sealed envelope to one of the nurses to put in the mail for her, addressed to our offices, along with a cover letter. We need to know the contents of the envelope before we can begin processing her estate."

"Have you considered opening it?" Seriously, was this guy actually a lawyer, or was she being pranked?

"There's an issue," he said, the overly precise tone of voice suggesting his patience was being strained by her attempt at levity. "The accompanying letter instructed us in no uncertain terms that the envelope could only be opened in the presence of the addressees."

Now Monica was catching on. Her grandmother had written her a letter and didn't want anyone to open it but her. "Wait, I was there the whole time she was in the hospital, right up until she died. Why didn't she give me the letter then?"

"Presumably there is something inside she didn't want you to see until she'd passed," Larry replied.

Monica's stomach clenched. That couldn't be good news. No way. When was the last time anyone had something good to say that they'd rather be dead than have you hear? Had she done something to offend *Yiayia* on her death bed, and she'd died with one of her legendary grudges? With Monica's luck, the old lady was planning to haunt her for all eternity.

Monica sighed. "I wish I'd known about this last night. I only just returned from New York City. I could've taken care of it then."

"Actually, I'm calling from the Boston offices. Your grandmother retained our services when she and your grandfather still resided in Massachusetts."

"That had to have been over forty years ago," Monica said. "I wasn't even born."

"Forty-eight years, actually," Larry said. "She was one of my father's clients. I inherited her when he retired."

"Oh." What more was there to say? "I want to make sure I'm getting this straight. I need to come to Boston so you can open an envelope and give my grandmother's estate away to a couple of animal shelters and the local public radio station? Let me drop everything and get right on that."

"Please, Ms. Panagiotopoulos, you really do need to take this seriously. We're only trying to do our jobs."

Monica felt a twinge of guilt. It wasn't this guy's fault she'd woken up with a stiff neck to the sound of her ex-girlfriend's inevitable betrayal. Besides, now that she'd lost out on the big wedding contract she'd been counting on, it's not like she had a busy calendar weighing her down. "Okay, I can head to Boston early next week. Can you text me the address and any other pertinent details? I don't really do voice mail."

"Of course," Larry assured her, the tension easing from his voice. "One other thing. You'll need to bring Ms. Walsh with you."

Monica clearly was suffering from her lack of morning coffee, because she'd become completely lost. "I'm sorry, who is that, the nurse?"

"The envelope says Rachel Walsh."

Her memory clicked, if not her comprehension. "The handy ma'am?"

"Enough horsing around, young lady." Judging by the very loud sigh he didn't even attempt to muffle, Larry was impatient again. He'd reverted to treating her like a naughty child. It was very unfair, because for once, she really wasn't trying to be funny.

"But, why?"

"Because the envelope is addressed to you both, ergo you both must be present for it to be opened."

"I'm still not following. Why did she want Ray to be there?"

"I assume because, as we've learned from your grandmother's cover letter, the two of you are engaged to be married. Please accept my congratulations."

Too stunned to respond, Monica ended the call without a word. Engaged? Her grandmother had believed she and Ray were getting married and had written them a letter on her death bed, the contents of which only Ray's presence with her in Boston could shed light on?

Monica stared at the bedroom walls, the ones that were painted the same blue as the handy ma'am's shirt. The same handy ma'am she'd treated like absolute crap in a fit of childish jealousy, who would definitely never want to speak with her again.

What the hell was she supposed to do now?

CHAPTER SIX

The sun was bright on Monday morning as Ray headed into the office of Grant's Restorations for the much-anticipated September staff meeting, during which it was assumed Mr. Grant would finally reveal the identity of that amazing mystery contract he'd been teasing all summer. Ray could hardly wait. This was the moment she'd been waiting to ask for more responsibility, to finally be promoted to lead project manager. She had more experience than her colleague Tom Jenkins, and a better eye for detail, too. After three years on the job, she hoped her boss had finally learned to look past the fact she was a woman in what he considered a man's job and really appreciated what she had to offer.

Ray pulled at the open front of her plaid flannel, fastening a few buttons in the middle to keep it in place. Though it would be warm later in the day, enough of a chill lingered in the air from overnight that there was no denying the approach of fall. In Ray's opinion, it was the best time of the year. The hassle of jackets and gloves was still many weeks away, but the joys of the season were already popping up all around in the form of Halloween decorations in shop windows and signs for pumpkin spice everything.

"Morning, Barb," Ray greeted the barista at the coffee place across the street from the office. "So, tell me, which one's better, the pumpkin spice latte, the pumpkin flavored coffee, or the new signature chai?"

"Ray, I've barely seen you all summer," Barb chided playfully. "I thought you'd found another coffee joint."

"No way," Ray assured her. "I've been on hiatus a while. Summer at Grant's was slow so I was working my handy ma'am gig. But I'm back in the office today, so which option's going to get me through the staff meeting without falling asleep?"

"Pumpkin spice lattes are definitely the best," Barb said with a wink, "but even more so because if you order one today, it comes with a free apple cider donut."

"A free donut? This is my lucky day." Ray rubbed the top of her head. "Maybe I should buy a lottery ticket."

"If I were you, I think I would." Barb slid the cup into a cardboard sleeve and handed it over. "It can't hurt, and man, can you imagine what it would be like to suddenly find out you're a millionaire?"

"That would be something," Ray replied with a chuckle, though she was too smart to really bother buying a ticket. A dollar not wasted was as good as a dollar won, Grandpa Ray used to say. It would be amazing, though, to suddenly stumble into a fortune. "Tell me, Barb. If you won the big prize, would you let it change you, or would you stick around here and keep working?"

"Stay in this dump?" Barb looked at Ray like she'd sprung an extra head. "Honey, I'd be in the Caribbean so fast the coffee wouldn't even be finished brewing. I've got a boat all picked out, gonna call her *Barbarella*. Don't tell me you'd keep showing up to work every day, with that boss of yours who doesn't fully appreciate you."

Poor Barb may have gotten an earful several months back when Tom had been made lead on a project instead of Ray. She checked her watch, and since she still had plenty of time to make it to the meeting, Ray decided to indulge in a few minutes of fantasy.

"I suppose I wouldn't," she decided after mulling it over a bit, "but I would still want to work."

"Start your own business where you could be the boss?" Barb suggested.

Ray shook her head. "That's the problem. In my

line of work, the owner of the property is the real boss. It's their money we're spending, and if they decide to go with mass-produced resin moldings instead of real carved wood because it's cheaper, or to remove damaged ceiling medallions instead of repairing them because they're in a hurry, ultimately I don't get a say in it."

"Sounds frustrating," Barb said, sliding a plump apple cider donut into a small paper bag.

"It really is," Ray said, taking the donut. "I guess if I was suddenly so rich I didn't have to worry about the cost, I'd get myself an old, run-down place that I knew no one in their right mind would be willing to spend the time or money fixing up, and I'd do every part of it exactly the way it was meant to be done."

"That sounds really nice, and I'd wish you luck with it," Barb told her as she turned to go, "only I'm afraid I've already got the winning ticket in my purse. *Barbarella*, here I come!"

Most of the team had already assembled in the meeting room when Ray arrived, though the boss was nowhere in sight. There were eight men seated around the large rectangular table, with Ray the only woman, with the exception of the receptionist, who sat perched on the edge of her swivel chair like a nervous bird.

Ray couldn't blame her. Though great guys when you got to know them as well as Ray had, they were bruisers with arms the size of tree trunks, and they were more than a little rambunctious. It had taken Ray the better part of six months not to tremble inside when telling them what to do on a jobsite, but she'd mastered it eventually and more than earned her spot at the head of this motley crew. Now to see if Mr. Grant, the boss, thought so, too.

Mr. Grant entered a few minutes past nine, and the first thing Ray noticed was he looked positively green. His forehead was shiny with sweat, his collar disheveled, and he seemed on the verge of throwing up. Maybe he'd had some bad seafood for dinner. He stood shakily at the front of the room, grasping the back of a chair as if he needed it to stay upright. Whatever job he was about to announce, it had to be a real humdinger not to postpone the meeting until he was feeling better.

"When my father started this business," Mr. Grant began, "I know he never thought a day like today would come."

Off to a good start. Ray looked around the room at all the other anticipation-filled faces and wished she'd started an office pool on what the big job would be. She might not buy lottery tickets, but there was nothing more satisfying than a bet between friends.

Mr. Grant drew a shaky breath. "As you know, this past year has been a rough one. We've had furloughs, faced jobsite restrictions that ate away at profits, and the overall economy has taken a real beating. Through it all, I've held out hope because I knew I had a contract in the works that would easily see us through the next two years. I got the call this morning."

Ray crossed her fingers. *Come on, Lincoln Bedroom.*

"The contract has been put on hold until at least next spring." At this, Mr. Grant's face crumpled, and he pressed a meaty hand to his face to cover his eyes.

Had she heard that right? Ray's own hand began to shake so badly she had to set her latte cup on the table. She turned to Tom, who was seated beside her, and whispered, "What does this mean?"

Tom didn't say a word but lifted one hand and made a slicing motion across his throat by way of reply.

At the front of the room, the boss did his best to pull himself together. "I'm really sorry, all of you. You're like family to me. But this is too big a storm for Grant's Restoration to weather. As of today, we're closing up shop. I'll give each one of you a glowing recommendation. I know you'll land on your feet."

With that, Mr. Grant fled the room. Ray thought she could hear him bawling in the hallway, or possibly barfing. Not that she'd blame him if he was. She was starting to feel queasy herself. She looked helplessly at the others on her team, each appearing more stunned than the last. After several moments of awkward silence, Tom stood and pushed in his chair.

"I guess that's it. Nice knowin' ya'll." He left the room.

Two others followed.

Ray opened her mouth. "But…"

It was no use. The room was emptying out. Ray rose from her seat and made her way to the meeting room door. She paused in the hallway, looking toward her desk, but she didn't have anything personal there, so she continued to the front door.

Three years on the job, countless hours, and it had come to this. Unemployed. What the hell was she going to do now?

What she needed to do was scrape her pride off the pavement, walk back to her car, and start calling around for more handy ma'am gigs. What she wanted to do was drive to the nearest liquor store, grab a six-pack, and crawl into bed. However, the good place near her house didn't open until noon, and besides, there was something about actually giving in to the temptation to buy alcohol in the morning and drink it alone in her pajamas that screamed, "Red flag!"

She did know one thing she didn't want to do, though: talk to Monica Panty-topless. Which was a real problem, because as soon as she emerged from the building, she spotted the woman in the parking lot, striding toward her with the sternest look Ray had ever seen. If she was here to apologize for her deplorable behavior in New York, this was not the right way to start out, all angry as a hornet.

"What's the matter with you?" Ray grumbled, anger making her chin burn. "Somebody die?"

"Yeah." Monica sniffed, but in a way that made Ray think she was more on the verge of lashing out than crying. "My grandmother."

"Oh, no. Monica... I'm sorry." *Stupid, stupid Ray,* she scolded herself. Sometimes she had such a hard time telling the difference between when a person was sad or mad. She stumbled around for a way to explain. "I really didn't mean to be callous. I tend to say the one heartless thing I know I shouldn't say, because my brain is telling me not to say it, so naturally it bubbles out. And, at the worst possible time."

To her surprise, Monica let out a breath that could almost be mistaken for a soft chuckle. "Yeah, I'm starting to pick up on that trait."

Ray's memory flashed back to the old woman she'd met with the fiery red hair and bright green turban. It brought a smile to her face. "Your grandmother was a lovely woman, and I'm lucky to have met her, even if my time with her was so short."

"Apparently, she felt the same." Monica paused, like she was thinking over what to say next. "The thing is, she took a real shine to you, which is why I'm here."

"I think I understand." Ray straightened her shoulders and did her best to slick back her short, unruly waves. She wasn't the type to hold a grudge, after all, and the fact Monica looked particularly amazing standing there with the morning sun turning her hair to gold had absolutely nothing to do with it, either.

Nothing at all. "I would be honored to revise my role as your fake girlfriend for *Yiayia*'s funeral, free of charge. Tell me when."

"Well, I do need you to come with me somewhere, but it's not to the funeral," Monica said. "Do you have time to grab a coffee so I can explain?"

Ray looked down at her hands and realized they were empty. "Sure. I seem to have left my coffee inside. There's a great place across the street."

Ray led the way. Once she'd procured two pumpkin spice lattes and two apple cider donuts—still free, thank goodness, since she was fresh out of a job—Ray sat with Monica at a small table in the back of the shop.

Monica took a long sip of her drink, as if for courage. Ray could see her vulnerability in the way she clutched the cup, her knuckles white, but it was also clear she was fighting with admirable courage to stay in control. The woman was stubborn all right, and Ray had to admire her a little for it.

Setting her cup down, Monica looked Ray in the eyes, confident and in control. "I need you to fly to Boston with me."

"Boston?" Ray blinked several times, wondering if all of this was a dream because nothing seemed natural. "Why Boston? Is that where the funeral's going to be? I guess I can go, but I'm not sure I can swing the airfare at the moment."

"Never mind that," Monica said. "I'll cover the

expenses—it's the least I can do for the inconvenience to you—but I should say once again, it's not for the funeral. It's a little more complicated. We need to visit my grandmother's attorney."

"I'm not following." Ray frowned. What was wrong with this woman? There had to be something, because she was definitely not normal. Gorgeous, but then again, weren't the pretty ones always a little off-kilter? They were in Ray's experience. "Don't take this the wrong way, but you must have someone in your life who's better equipped to be a shoulder to cry on during this difficult time than a fake girlfriend. Don't you have any friends?"

"A few, sure. But you know how it is in your thirties. Everybody's settled down, living their own lives, saying they want to get together and never finding the time. Anyway, even if someone else *could* go with me, it's not company I'm looking for. I'm sorry to have to ask; I really am." Monica rested her head on one hand with a weary look that tugged on Ray's heartstrings. Her earlier confidence had evaporated, and it seemed like she hadn't had a good night's sleep in a while. "My grandmother sent something to her lawyer's office right before she died, but the lawyer can't open it unless you're present in the office with me."

"Do you think she changed her will?" Ray shot a look toward the front of the shop where Barb was wiping the counter with a rag. Hadn't they been joking about coming into a fortune? But no. There had to be another explanation. That kind of thing only happened in dreams.

"Don't get too excited," Monica warned her, but all Ray could think was she hadn't said no. "I doubt it'll be much."

"But you think she left me something?"

"*Us* something," Monica corrected. "She was under the impression we were getting married."

"You told her we were engaged?" Ray stared in disbelief. "How could you have lied to that sweet old lady like that?"

"I did nothing of the sort," Monica retorted. "I don't know what you said to her—"

"What *I* said to her?" Ray poked at her chin dimple, certain it was glowing red. "You were there the whole time I was talking to her, and never once did I say anything about getting married. I wouldn't marry you if you were the last woman on earth."

"Likewise," Monica spat, crossing her arms and glaring at Ray with an intensity that could've set kindling on fire. "But here's the thing. We're still going to have to pretend we're engaged long enough to find out what she left us."

"I don't know. I don't think I'd feel right about taking any money under false pretenses. You and I, we're nothing but a lie. Profiting from that seems like we're on the express train to"—Ray pointed to the ground and whispered—"the Bad Place."

"It's not like it would be much," Monica argued.

"I've given this some thought, and my guess is when we were talking about my visit to The Walters Art Museum, she thought I went there because we were planning a wedding. Then you said you liked it, but it was out of your price range, and she jumped to conclusions."

Ray pursed her lips. "Fine. Maybe I did contribute to the misunderstanding, but I would like to point out that you did, too."

"Agreed. Whatever." Monica uncrossed her arms and took a long sip of her latte. "What I think may have happened is she changed her will so we'd have enough money for a wedding, or what she thinks is enough for a wedding. She got married at city hall during the war in a dress she borrowed from her sister. The whole thing probably cost a buck-fifty."

"How much are you thinking, ballpark?"

"Probably ten, maybe twenty thousand, tops. It's not a fortune, but it's nothing to sneeze at."

Ray bit her lip. "I don't know, Monica. It still feels wrong."

"I didn't want to bring this up before, but I know you lost your job today."

Ray twisted in her seat. "How?"

"I overheard some of the guys talking in the parking lot right before you came out. And you know I'd rather die than tell you this, but Bri put the house up for sale while I was in New York. This morning I came out, and the sign had been switched to sold. She didn't even bother to tell me in person. She sent a text."

"At least it wasn't a voice mail, or you still wouldn't know." For once, her joke landed as intended, and a flicker of a smile showed on Monica's lips. On impulse, Ray reached for Monica's hand and gave it a quick squeeze. "That's rotten of her."

"It is, and so is me losing out on the biggest wedding of my career and you having your company close with no warning."

"Oh no. You mean you didn't get hired for that after all?"

"I don't want to talk about it." Monica lifted her chin defiantly. "While I admire your principles, you can't eat them or use them to pay the rent. I don't think the money will be much, but it might save both of us from disaster for a month or two."

Ray sat back and studied her companion. The little lady had a point. "If I say yes?"

"I pay for the trip to Boston, and we split the proceeds sixty/forty."

"Sixty percent of twenty is twelve. I guess I could do it for twelve grand."

"Your take would be eight. *I* get the sixty." Monica jabbed her thumb into her chest. "She was my grandmother."

Ray smirked at how hot under the collar her

teasing had made Monica and decided to push her a little further to see what would happen. "Fact is, princess, you can't get a dime without me. And you know it, or you wouldn't be here."

Monica glared. "What happened to having principles?"

Ray shrugged. "You talked me right out of them. Good job! Have you considered becoming a life coach?"

"There's no way I'm giving you sixty percent of my grandmother's money," Monica said through clenched teeth.

"I'll settle for half."

Monica let out a little growl. "Fine. We'll plan to leave first thing in the morning. Don't bother to pack, I think we can get it all taken care of in one day. I'll text you the flight info as soon as I have it."

Ray stuck out her hand, arching an eyebrow as Monica stared at it and refused to shake. "Come on, now. This is no way to start our honeymoon, darling."

Monica made a face. "The sooner we get this trip over with, the sooner we never have to see each other again, poopsie."

Ray continued to hold her hand out until Monica had no choice but to shake it to end the awkward standoff. Ray burst out laughing, pointing to her chin. "I told you. Stubbornness runs deep in these genes. But as for never seeing each other? I'll drink to that."

Ray lifted her cup to her lips and drank down the

spicy, pumpkin-y goodness in one long gulp. Monica was a handful, the type of woman who brought trouble with her wherever she went. That made her a temptation, one Ray had learned the hard way was best avoided. Never see her again? Oh, yes. She would drink to that for sure.

CHAPTER SEVEN

The law offices of Donahue and Taite were housed in an old brownstone whose front windows overlooked Boston Common. The building had no lobby to speak of, just an ornate but small foyer that opened to a winding staircase of marble and gold. An old-fashioned cage elevator ran up the center of the staircase, and Monica regarded it dubiously.

"Do you think this thing is safe?" She tapped a freshly manicured finger on the wrought iron gate that served as a door, wanting nothing to do with the thing. She'd dressed in a pantsuit for the occasion, blow drying her hair until it shone so as to put her most professional foot forward. Her companion? Not so much. As Ray slid the cage open and poked her head inside, all Monica could think was that anyone seeing the woman now would assume she was there to perform maintenance on the thing.

"Inspection certificate's up-to-date," Ray announced, "and the call buttons appear to have been modernized. I think we'll live, unless you'd rather walk up."

A sign listing the building's occupants hung beside the elevator. Monica searched it and made a face when she found the law office. "Sixth floor? I'll take a risk in this contraption, because I know for sure the stairs would kill me."

Aside from some bumping and creaking, the ride to the top floor was surprisingly smooth. They exited the elevator into a short hallway, at the far end of which was a door fitted with a window that had *Donahue and Taite, Attorneys at Law* painted on it in gold block letters. It reminded Monica of the type of office in which you'd expect to find a 1930s private investigator. Appropriate, considering they were here to solve a mystery.

The interior of the office was very much that of a modern law firm, with a massive bookcase of leather-bound law tomes on one wall and a receptionist who looked up from a sleek glass and chrome desk as they entered.

"Can I help you?" she asked.

"Monica Panagiotopoulos, here to see Larry Donahue."

"Of course," the receptionist said as she consulted an appointment book on her desk. She shifted her gaze to Ray. "And you are?"

"This is my f-fiancée." Monica stumbled over the word as if speaking a foreign language, and her cheeks began to burn.

"Okay, then."

The woman behind the desk lifted an eyebrow quizzically, and Monica could almost hear her thinking she'd never seen a less compatible couple in her life. With Monica's tailored suit and Ray's tattered work clothes, there was no way anyone would ever think they were a match. It was humiliating. When the receptionist departed to announce their arrival, Monica turned to Ray with her jaw clenched.

"I thought I told you to dress appropriately for this meeting."

"I did." Ray plucked at her polo shirt defensively. "This shirt has a collar. That means it's business casual."

"It has a logo embroidered on it, which makes it a work uniform." Monica pointed to Ray's thigh. "And those jeans, aside from being *jeans*, and at least two sizes too big for you, have a spot of paint on them."

Ray looked down. "That isn't paint. I dripped mustard on them, and the stain remover stuff I used took some of the color out. Not much, though. And there's not even one hole in these. I checked. Twice."

Monica let out a strangled groan. "Clearly, we have very different taste."

"Yeah, well," Ray grumbled, "it must be limiting

finding clothes that can accommodate that stick you always have up your—"

"Ladies, thank you for coming in." A gray-haired man greeted them, interrupting before Ray could finish what was certain to have been a less than flattering observation. "Please, follow me back to my office. Now that both of you are here, we can find out what's in that mystery envelope."

Once Monica and Ray were seated in the two chairs reserved for clients, Larry Donahue settled into the leather chair behind his desk and pulled out an antique gold letter opener, which he used to open a cream-colored envelope that sat on his desk. Monica's breath hitched as she recognized her grandmother's handwriting across the front. It was as bold as ever and only slightly shaky with age. A lump formed in her throat as it hit her she would never see that writing again on a birthday or Christmas card.

"Okay." Larry pulled a single sheet of paper from inside and scanned the contents, his eyes widening slightly as they moved down the page. "Well, this is a bit of a change."

"What?" Monica edged forward in her seat, her heart pounding. "What did she change?"

"You're familiar with the terms of your grandmother's most recent will?" he asked.

"Yes," Monica replied. "She had decided to give most of her estate to charity."

"Under the new terms that she outlines here, the

charities do still receive the bulk of her liquid assets, but there are two notable amendments. I'll let you read it for yourself."

He handed the letter to Monica, who started reading silently until Ray cleared her throat loudly.

"Wanna read that so the whole class can hear?"

Monica shot her a dirty look then began to read out loud from the top.

"'To my dearest granddaughter and her lovely wife-to-be. Beginning a new life together is a grand adventure, one that can be full of hardships as well as happiness. It brings me such joy to know you have found one another, and while I am certain you can weather any difficulties life throws your way with love and good humor, I hope you will let me help in this small way while I'm still able.'"

Tears streamed down Monica's face, blurring the page and making the rest impossible to read. She handed it to Ray, who continued where Monica had left off.

"'I am instructing my attorney to bequeath to you both the savings bonds Niko's parents gave us when we married,'" Ray paused from her reading to comment, "I used to get those for Christmas when I was a kid. When I graduated from high school, I used them to buy an old junker of a car."

"Not much of an inheritance." Monica gave a noncommittal shrug. Then, realizing her words may have come across as callous, which had not been her intent, she added, "It's lovely that she thought of us at all, of course. Can I take another look?"

"I wasn't finished," Ray said, handing her the letter anyway.

Monica scanned it quickly, her face settling into a thoughtful frown. "I'm confused. It says something about a property, but she didn't own her apartment in New York. It was rent-controlled, but unfortunately that's not something you can inherit."

"No," Larry said, shuffling through a pile of folders beside him. "This would be an older property, a parcel she and your grandfather bought when they lived in Massachusetts."

"She's left us a house?" Monica's face brightened. That would certainly be worth more than savings bonds.

Larry tilted his hand as if to say *so-so*. "There's an old house on the property, but it's not so much residential as agricultural."

"A farm?" Ray asked.

"No," Larry replied. "A vineyard."

"A vineyard." Monica's head spun as she contemplated the news. "I didn't even know there were vineyards in Massachusetts."

"Quite a few. There's a whole coastal wine trail and wineries all throughout New England. Yours is out in the center of the state, not too far from the New Hampshire line."

Hers. Considering what Bri had put her through

with the townhouse, Monica should've been thrilled to have her own property at last, but all she could wonder was what she was going to do with a vineyard. "I can't even keep houseplants alive. Even the ones everyone swears up and down are unkillable."

Larry chuckled. "There's a caretaker, an older gentleman named Christos. Your grandmother made some provisions for him in her will as well. He's tended the property for years. The output's minimal. He's more of a hobbyist and getting up there in years, but there's no reason it couldn't produce more down the line, enough to cover the costs."

"Larry," Ray spoke up, "are you saying her vineyard loses money?"

"Now, technically, it isn't hers," Larry corrected. "It belongs to both of you. Or, it will after you're married. Your grandmother was clear about that in the instructions that accompanied this letter."

"We have to be married?" Monica's throat constricted. Her eyes darted to Ray, who was busy picking something out of her teeth with her fingernail. There was no one on the planet Monica felt less inclined to marry. "What happens if we aren't?"

"If you haven't married within a year, we revert to the previous version of your grandmother's will. The property would be put in a trust to be sold after the caretaker's death, with his designated heirs being given the first chance to buy it, after which all proceeds would go to charity."

Monica caught Ray's eye, trying to gauge what she was thinking, but it was hard to tell. Hopefully, they were on the same page, which was to say "no way." As much as Monica adored her grandmother, a vineyard that was losing money and a handful of savings bonds wasn't exactly an earth-shattering inheritance. Certainly not worth getting married to someone as ill-suited to her as Ray was. The best thing all around would be to walk away.

"I'm sorry, Larry," Monica said, pinching the bridge of her nose, "but could you give us a minute alone?"

"Of course," he said, rising from his desk and heading to the door. "Take all the time you need."

When they were by themselves, Monica was overtaken with the urge to laugh. "Wow, I guess I got our hopes up for nothing with all of this."

"That's okay." Ray gave a good-natured shrug. "It was fun to dream for a little while, like thinking for a minute you might have a winning lottery ticket."

"A couple acres of grapes and some savings bonds." Monica shook her head.

Ray laughed softly. "It was really sweet of your *Yiayia* to think of us at all. It's almost sad to let it go. It obviously meant something to her."

"Yeah, but it sounds like we're in agreement," Monica said with a sigh. It was hard not to feel a little deflated. Between her lack of work and no place to live, a few thousand dollars really would've been nice right now. "We'd better let Larry know it's not happening."

When the lawyer came back into the room, Monica was about to break the news to him that she and Ray were going to pass, but as she opened her mouth, Ray spoke up first.

"Hey, Larry, I'm curious. Ballpark figure, how much is this little inheritance worth?"

"Let me see." He hummed softly as he shuffled through papers, jotting down notes on a tablet of yellow legal paper. "I'd have to have an associate look into the exact market value of a fifty-two-acre parcel of land, but I do know the current value of the savings bonds is right around 84k."

"K, like thousand?" Ray's eyes grew wide. "Eighty-four thousand dollars?"

"And did you say fifty-two acres?" Monica gulped. She'd learned enough about real estate to know you could fit a lot of houses on that much land. Plus, hadn't Bri told her how buyers were fleeing the cities for more space in the country? They were sitting on a potential gold mine. If only…

Larry sat back in his chair. "You ladies had something you wanted to tell me?"

Monica looked at Ray. They nodded and answered in unison.

"We're getting married."

"Come on," Monica urged, reaching for Ray's hand. Her motivation wasn't a sudden rush of sentimental feelings toward her newly betrothed. Far from it. Her patience was worn to the breaking point by Ray's lollygagging, and Monica had every intent of dragging her the rest of the way up the hill. "According to my phone, City Hall's over that way."

"When you said we were getting married"—Ray huffed, pausing in the middle of the sidewalk to draw a few labored breaths—"I didn't realize you meant right now."

"I don't see any benefit to waiting," Monica admonished. "You heard what Larry said. All he needs from us is a marriage certificate, and the inheritance is ours."

"Well, technically, he said the property would be ours." Ray started walking again, too slowly for Monica's taste, but any forward movement was good if it got her up the hill. "We can have the money from the savings bonds right now, to pay for the wedding, your grandma said."

"We're not spending a dime more than we have to on the wedding," Monica snapped.

Ray rolled her eyes. "Of course, we're not. I'm just saying we don't have to be too hasty, either. The 84k is ours no matter what."

"The land is probably worth millions."

"Sure, but earlier today, we both would've been happy with a few thousand."

Monica grabbed Ray's arm, fixing her with a steely stare. "You better not be getting cold feet."

"No, I'm..." Ray tossed her hands in the air. "You know what? You're right. We'd better go through with this immediately, before either one of us comes to our senses and runs for the hills."

"Now you're talking!" Monica said, though she was starting to wish Ray would stop talking and give her ears a rest.

"The funniest part," Ray said, showing no signs of being quiet, "is I've never wanted to get married, and now I'm racing to the altar to tie the knot with someone I would never consider under any normal circumstance. Is that the definition of irony?"

"I think it's the definition of asshole," Monica muttered at a near whisper.

"How do you figure?" Apparently, Ray had excellent hearing.

Monica stopped walking and turned to Ray with her hands on her hips. She'd about had it with this raggedy woman implying *she* was somehow on the losing end of this bargain, when Monica was the one being forced to share her inheritance with a total stranger who dressed like a hobo.

"I have nice hair, good teeth, a decent figure." Monica pointed to each general region on her body as she ticked off her assets. "What is it, exactly, you find so very wrong with me?"

Ray stopped and gave Monica a once-over. "It's not your looks, babe. It's your personality."

"I beg your pardon?" Monica tossed her head back, her aforementioned nice hair flying backward. "Name one thing wrong with my personality."

"Just one?" Ray laughed. "Where do I start? Judgmental. Temperamental. High maintenance—"

"I'm not high maintenance!" Monica's nostrils flared like a dragon about to breathe fire.

"Really? Out of my whole list, *that's* the hill you want to die on. Besides this actual hill, that is. The entire city of Boston is at sea level. Was there really not a single flat path between the lawyer's office and city hall?"

"How is it I—the high maintenance one—am handling this gradual slope better than the woman who spends her life going up and down a ladder for a living?"

"They're very different muscle groups." Ray let out an exasperated groan. "Can we get to the court house and get this over with? The sooner we marry, the sooner we settle things with the lawyer, and the sooner we can file for divorce."

"I'm not the one who's been dillydallying up this hill. If I have to spend one extra minute with you, I may do something drastic." Monica mimed taking Ray by the throat and giving her a good shake.

"Please. The only reason I won't murder you," Ray

jabbed a finger at Monica, "is because the spouse is always the prime suspect."

Fortunately, as a double homicide seemed inevitable, their destination came into view. In contrast to the elegant brick buildings of Beacon Hill, Boston city hall was a grimy concrete structure that sat in the middle of a windswept plaza that seemed devoid of life.

Monica eyed the monstrosity with utter distaste. "It looks like an upside-down cake."

"The style was called Brutalist architecture," Ray explained. "It's ugly as sin, and such a shame, considering the beautiful Second Empire building it replaced."

"It's so bad it makes my eyes hurt," Monica agreed, observing with a certain wryness that, after bickering the whole way here, she and her wife-to-be were able to find common ground over their mutual dislike of something. Was that a good or bad sign?

There was an information desk in the center of the lobby, and Monica approached it with as much confidence as she could manage. "Excuse me," she said to the elderly man behind the desk. "Where do we go for a marriage license?"

She held her breath, perhaps hoping the man would take one look at her and Ray, call them out as the frauds they were, and order them to leave at once. Instead, he glanced up with not even a flicker of interest and replied as if by rote, "Registry division, second floor. You'll need valid IDs and a fifty-dollar fee. Cash, debit, or credit."

"Sounds easy enough," Ray remarked, though there was a quality to her tone that made Monica think maybe she, too, had been hoping someone would stop them at the entrance and keep them from going through with their foolhardy errand.

No such luck.

The office they were looking for turned out to be every bit as drab as the rest of the building. In a way, Monica was grateful. If there'd been any attempt to add a romantic flair, she might not have been able to convince herself to walk through the door. As it was, the short trip from the entrance to the clerk's desk—where she would sign her life away to a woman she didn't even like—felt indistinguishable from booking an appointment for a routine cleaning at a dentist's office, and every bit as enjoyable.

Unlike the grumpy man in the lobby, the woman at the desk greeted them with a cheery smile. "How are you on this beautiful day? It's starting to feel like fall already, isn't it?"

Monica cut directly through all the chitchat. She had no time to discuss the weather. "We're here to get a marriage license."

If the woman was taken aback by Monica's abruptness, she recovered quickly. "Sure thing. You'll need to fill out these forms, show me your identification, and pay the fee. Then you can be on your way."

"Can we fill it out right here? Get the ball rolling on wedded bliss?" Monica reached for Ray's hand, squeezing the woman's fingers hard enough that she almost expected to hear them crack.

"Of course," the clerk responded, sounding like she wasn't sure whether to take Monica seriously or not. "Here's a pen."

"You'll have to do it," Ray said, shaking her hand vigorously as if to restore the blood flow once Monica let go. "I'm not sure I can hold a pen, and I know for certain I can't spell Panty-top—"

Monica gave Ray a glare that shut her up mid-joke. "I still don't understand why you have such a hard time with Panagiotopoulos. It's pronounced exactly the way it's spelled, except for the silent G, of course."

"What kind of a language has a silent G?" Ray demanded.

"I don't know, English? There's gnome, gnat, gnash"—Monica counted them off on her fingers as she went—"sign, resign, benign—"

"Sorry, babe," Ray said, cutting her off mid-recitation, "but you're always going to be Panty-topless to me."

The clerk gasped. "I knew I recognized your voice. Aren't you Monica, from *Monica Talks Matrimony?*"

Monica flinched. "I am."

"I love your podcast, and I read your blog religiously. You have become the absolute authority on all things wedding. I think I refer at least a dozen brides to your site every week." As she spoke, the woman's expression morphed like a cartoon lightbulb moment, and she snapped up straight. "Oh my God. You're getting married!"

"Y-yes." Monica struggled to get the words out. "I am..."

"Right here in Boston? This is the most exciting thing that's happened in ages," the clerk gushed. "You must have the most lavish wedding planned. I can hardly wait. You really have an eye!"

"Well, thank you," Monica said, recovering some of her composure. She looked at Ray, whose face hinted she'd been pushed into the deep end without a life jacket with all the wedding talk.

"When's the big day?" the clerk asked.

Monica's brow creased. "We were kind of hoping today."

"Today?" The woman's eyebrows shot up. "You can't get married today."

"Why not?" Ray snapped, a look of true desperation creeping into her eyes. "We're kind of in a hurry."

The clerk shrugged. "There's a three-day waiting period. We'll have the license ready for pick up on Friday."

"Friday?" Monica choked.

"That long?" Ray added.

The woman nodded sympathetically, as if this wasn't the first time she delivered the bombshell news. "Afraid so, except under a very specific list of exceptions. Neither one of you is pregnant, are you?"

"Uh..." Ray gave the woman her best *how the hell do you figure that would happen* look, which, Monica had to hand it to her, was pretty spectacular.

The clerk blushed and looked down at her desk, where she began sorting papers that Monica suspected did not really need to be sorted. "Right. I guess probably not."

"It's okay," Monica said as quietly as possible to Ray, who still seemed to be fuming. "Let's get the paperwork filed, and we can talk about this outside."

As soon as they'd stepped into City Hall plaza, Ray began counting. "One. Two. Three..."

"Is that some sort of meditation technique?" Monica arched an eyebrow, looking warily at Ray's glowing red chin dimple. "Are you trying to keep your cool?"

"No," Ray growled. "I'm giving you a ten-second head start before I race after you and kill you. You better get running."

"Knock it off." Monica slugged Ray's shoulder, meeting with a rock-solid resistance that reminded her how strong Ray's arms actually were. "In case you missed the memo, I'm not happy about this either."

"Coulda fooled me," Ray said. "What with all the fan-girling that woman was doing over your blog, you seemed to be having the time of your life."

"Yeah, I was really looking forward to spending

more time with you because of bureaucracy." Monica pulled out her phone from her purse. "You know what we should do? We should rent a car and drive to Atlantic City. It can't be more than four hours away, can it?"

"Atlantic City?" Ray made a face. "I think it's farther than that. Besides, what could we possibly want to do in Atlantic City?"

"It's like Vegas, right? Surely they have wedding chapels." Monica scanned the search results with growing dismay. "Damn. You're right. It's more like a five-and-a-half-hour drive from here. Plus, there's not a single 24-hour chapel or singing Elvis to be found."

By this point, Ray was also consulting her phone. "New Hampshire's wait for a license is also three days. Oh, we may be in luck. Vermont and Rhode Island don't have a waiting period. Connecticut either."

"How far are we to any of those?"

"Closer than Atlantic City. How bad is your geography?" Ray's sarcastic tone could have peeled off the top layer of Monica's skin. "It's getting late, though. By the time we got a car and drove to the closest place, they'd be closed. I think we're stuck for the night. Any bright ideas on what to do now?"

Monica narrowed her eyes, having had about enough of Ray's snarky attitude. "As a matter of fact, yes. I have an industry connection at a hotel nearby. I bet if I get in touch, she'd comp us a room."

"I'll believe it when I see it, oh great and powerful

wedding planner." Ray did an *I'm not worthy* bow a la *Wayne's World*.

"You doubt my abilities?"

"You didn't even know about the three-day thing," Ray shot back.

"Guess that's how you got your name. You're such a ray of sunshine." Monica snarled as she dashed off a text to the hotel manager she'd interviewed for a piece earlier in the year. "While we wait for an answer, we'd better do some shopping."

"Shopping?" The way Ray said it, Monica might as well have suggested an elective root canal.

"Given this latest mess," Monica said as patiently as she could, considering her companion was suddenly acting like a toddler, "we're going to need some clothes to tide us over for a couple of days."

"What's wrong with what I have on?"

"Nothing, except for the inevitable stench that will be baked in them by morning."

"Did you just tell me I smell?" Ray's voice went up a good half octave on the last word. "You did, didn't you?"

"I was applying it to myself, too," Monica assured her with a shake of the head. Unbelievable. What kind of grown woman put up this much fuss over something as simple as shopping? "Come along, wifey-poo. Let's go get you clean undies."

"I'm not your wife yet," Ray huffed, shuffling her

feet as she followed Monica, remaining several feet behind.

"Thank God for that."

'Til death do us part? At this point, Monica would welcome the sweet embrace of death with open arms if it meant getting some space from this sullen partner that fate, and her *yiayia*, had thrust upon her. A lifetime with Ray would feel more like a life sentence. It would take a miracle for them both to survive each other's company long enough to make it through the ceremony.

CHAPTER EIGHT

"Do you smell onions?" Ray breathed in deeply, her stomach growling at the scent of something cooking nearby. Her head swiveled in search of the source. "I think that's a food truck, or maybe a place with a grill. I'm starving. Are you starving?"

"No." Monica continued walking, eyes fixed forward as if Ray and her stomach didn't even exist.

Wow. Ray wasn't exactly surprised the princess never bothered to eat. Monica had an amazing figure, but she seemed the type who kept it that way by pounding a protein bar and a smoothie full of supplement powders once a day and calling it done. No zest for life, that one. If she had any manners, though, she could've at least offered to stop somewhere so Ray could grab a bite. She hadn't eaten since a breakfast sandwich at the airport, which was so small it barely counted as food. It was now nearly dinnertime, and if she didn't get fed soon, Ray might start to panic. She was a three square meals a day kinda gal, no exceptions.

Ray slapped a hand on Monica's shoulder and held her in place long enough to point to a sign across the road. "Quincy Market Food Colonnade, right over there."

Monica shook her head. "I told you we're trying to find Faneuil Hall Marketplace."

"And I told you I'm hungry." Ray pressed a hand to her sad belly. "I'm not sure what a food colonnade is, but little Ray-Ray likes the sound of it."

"You named your stomach?"

Ray shrugged. "Couldn't help it. The little fella has a personality of his own, which, I'll warn you right now, is usually somewhere between a grumpy old man and a toddler on a rampage when he hasn't been fed."

Monica shut her eyes and drew the type of deep breath that more often than not accompanied being on the brink of a full-blown nervous breakdown. "Great."

"Oh, hey, good news," Ray announced as she checked a roadside tourist map. "That Faneuil Hall place you're looking for and Quincy Market are right next to each other. You can go shop while I get food."

When they crossed the street, Monica headed directly toward a curved arcade with the types of clothing shops Ray normally avoided because they charged three times as much for the same thing you could get at a reasonably priced store that didn't have a trendy name. Ray, on the other hand, made a beeline for the food court, trusting her nose to sniff out the source of those mouthwatering aromas. When she found the long hall of food, she knew she'd hit the jackpot.

The onion smell had come from a stand selling Italian sausage. Ray bought one on a roll with extra onions and peppers, and she started woofing it down as she walked to the far end of the colonnade. She passed a bakery with delectable looking cream puffs but opted not to stop. Monica was waiting, and the little woman wasn't exactly the patient type. Of all the women out there, how had she gotten stuck with such an anti-foodie?

Ray paused at the entrance to the clothing store. Through the window, she could see Monica pawing at blouses on a rack. As a general rule, Ray stayed away from anything girly, but there was a white cotton button-up printed with blue flowers and birds that caught her eye. Too bad she'd never have a place to wear it, because it was actually kind of nice.

Swallowing the last bite of sausage, Ray walked into the store and headed directly for the men's department.

"Women's is over here," Monica corrected her.

"Which is why I'm going this way."

"They have some cute things," Monica tried again, as if Ray would react to the word *cute* like an eager puppy and come running.

Ray stood her ground, refusing to budge from the men's side. "They have some practical things over here."

"Let's make a wager." Monica's eyes twinkled with mischief. It was a look that, much to Ray's chagrin, instantly weakened her resolve. Damn it. Whatever Monica suggested, she was likely to get her way after only the briefest of struggles. "If I select an outfit from the women's side without you telling me your size and it fits, you have to get it and wear it tomorrow."

"Are you embarrassed by how I dress?" Ray guessed, and a flicker of something like guilt on Monica's face told her she was onto something. "That's it, isn't it? You don't like being seen with someone like me. I'm too butch for you."

"That's not it at all." Monica quickly crossed into the men's section, lowering her voice. "You're an attractive woman, Ray. I think you'd look even nicer if you took more care with how you dressed."

"By wearing blouses and pencil skirts?"

Monica let out an exasperated sigh. "If you want to dress in a more masculine style, that's fine. But buy something that fits. I'm not trying to be hurtful, but the men's stuff hangs like a sack on you."

Ray grasped her jeans, balling her fist as she tried to control her temper. There was nothing she hated more than being looked down on or judged. Unfortunately, the fact that she now held a massive bunch of fabric in her palm kind of supported Monica's argument that her clothes were too big. Infuriating.

Between her line of work and her somewhat boyish appearance, most people probably assumed Ray chose men's clothing to make a statement about her sexuality and gender identity. The truth was she found women's clothing confusing. Maybe it was because she'd been raised by her grandfather, but she'd never gotten the hang of girl stuff.

Like pants.

Pants should be easy, but in the women's department, some pants zipped in the front, others on the side, and some had all sorts of buttons and hooks she could never figure out. Then there were the ones that only came to the middle of the shin. Why? They weren't trousers, but they weren't shorts, either. What were they, and what purpose did they serve?

And don't get her started on how meaningless the sizes were. She could wear a size four, six, eight, *and* ten in the same store, depending what style it was. Was that sorcery or something? With men's pants, she could grab a pair without even trying them on and know, based solely on the measurements, they'd be fine. She'd have to buy them a few inches bigger than her natural waist measurement so that they fit her hips, but that was an easy fix. She just cinched them in with a belt until they…hung like a sack.

No, until they didn't fall down. That was what

she'd meant to think. Easy peasy and perfect every time.

Okay, even she wasn't buying her own defense.

"Whatever. All of this is on your dime, right? You did say you were covering my trip expenses."

"Er…" Monica's face contorted through a full range of unpleasant emotions before settling on a slightly pained smile. "Of course. I guess it's only fair since I told you not to pack anything. Thank God for credit cards, right?"

"If you can suffer the pain of the credit card bill, I can suffer uncomfortable clothes for a day, I guess." Ray crossed the aisle into the women's section, hoping her ploy with the bill would keep Monica from going too crazy with what she chose. "Okay, expert. What do you suggest?"

"How about some of these?" Monica took a pair of jeans from a rack. "They're the skinny style, but they have some spandex for stretch."

"You mean so they won't cut off circulation to my p—"

"Shhh!" Monica's head swiveled furiously as she scanned the store like she was on some kind of stakeout. Seeming satisfied no one had been close enough to overhear, she spoke in a stage whisper. "You can't say the word 'pussy' in a nice store like this."

"I wasn't going to," Ray assured her, wondering how angry it would make Monica for her to point out that she'd actually been the one to say that forbidden word out loud.

"Don't try to lie. I heard you. Unless..." Monica's eyes grew wider. "Oh, God. You didn't name that body part, too, did you? Is she called Petunia?"

"Really? Do I seem like the type to name anything on my body Petunia?" Ray gave an exaggerated shudder. "I'll have you know the phrase I was about to say, before you interrupted me with your vulgar language, was private parts. I'm not a complete Neanderthal."

Monica's face was pinched like a prune, and it was obvious she wanted to argue the point, but instead, she thrust the jeans into Ray's arms. "Here. Put these on."

"Right here?" Ray glanced around, shrugged, and put her hand on her belt buckle. "Okeydokey."

"In a fitting room," Monica shrieked. "Have you never tried on clothes in a store before?"

"Why bother?" Ray challenged, though of course she'd only been trying to get a rise out of Monica and had no intention of actually disrobing in the middle of a store. "I know my size and stick with the classics."

"Humor me?" Monica was so discombobulated by this point her face was flushed, and she was breathing heavily. Ray would need to remember this for the future, as it really displayed the woman's ample bosom. If they were going to have to spend a few more days together, not to mention get hitched, Ray had to find ways to make it fun.

"Fine."

Monica led the way to the dressing room, holding back the flimsy curtain like she was a maître d' presenting the finest table in the house. "Your dressing room, madam. I'll wait out here to see how you do."

"What, you aren't coming in to get a peek at Petunia?"

"In your dreams."

Inside the tiny room, Ray chuckled as she undid her boots then unzipped her jeans. The weird thing was, for as exasperated as she'd been all day, she couldn't remember the last time she'd laughed so much.

Ray held out the jeans and studied them with a shake of her head. No way were these going to work. "You never told me what I get if I win the bet."

"What bet?" Monica called out from the other side of the curtain.

"You know, if the outfit you chose doesn't fit. What do I get?"

"What do you want?"

Ray's body tensed as a current of electricity sparked through her. All of a sudden, thanks to Monica's sexy shopping voice, she wanted all sorts of things she shouldn't. "Uh...well..."

"Never mind. It'll fit." A saucy, evil little laugh accompanied her words, almost as if Monica knew exactly what ideas had begun racing through Ray's mind.

Ray grunted. "You sound pretty confident about that."

Certain there was no chance they would fit, Ray slipped one leg into the skinny jeans and then the other. They slid on like a perfectly made glove, the fabric stretching to embrace each curve with the soft touch of a cloud. These were like no jeans Ray had ever worn before. *Damn it.*

"How are you doing?" Monica prodded.

"If I admit the jeans fit, will you at least let me pick out the top myself?"

"Let me see."

Ray stepped out from behind the curtain, putting her arms out to each side. "Well?"

"Uh..." Instead of her usual snappy comeback, Monica seemed momentarily incapable of speech, her eyes glued to Ray's ass. "They, um..."

"They what?" Ray took a step closer because she knew it would make Monica squirm. She didn't have to like the woman to get a thrill of satisfaction in knowing Monica found her attractive.

Swallowing hard, Monica bent forward slightly, exposing several inches of bare chest and the hint of a lace bra as her shirt shifted. So unfair. Now Ray was the one who couldn't look away.

Monica reached out, gripping Ray's waistband in both hands. Shit, had Ray miscalculated? What were the odds Monica was planning to strip and have her way with her in the dressing room, like they were the main characters in some sort of erotic romance? An even better question, why wasn't Ray more alarmed at the prospect?

Their bodies were so close Ray could smell Monica's perfume. Alluring. Tempting. Dangerous. Petunia was throbbing.

Monica yanked Ray's jeans…up. "You're wearing them too low on your hips. Now they fit perfectly."

Well, fuck.

She was right, though. Ray wasn't accustomed to wearing them at her natural waist, but the jeans really did look and feel better that way.

Also, had she just mentally referred to her pussy as Petunia. Like, not as a joke?

Ray dashed back into the stall so as to make it easier to avoid thinking about anything she'd just experienced. "I'm about shopped out. If I agree to get the jeans, can we go?"

"We still need clean underwear," Monica protested. "They're having a sale, buy three get three free."

Ray groaned. "Time for a new deal. I'll let you pick out the underwear for me. Just don't make me shop anymore. Please?"

"I wish I could say yes, but you still need shirts. You should get three, in case we encounter any more delays." Monica paused a beat and then emphasized, "Women's shirts."

"I can handle shirts." Ray's mind flashed back to the blue bird print. She was going to get it, just to make Monica's head explode. As for the other two, she didn't even care at this point what they looked like. She only wanted to go to the hotel and go to bed.

"I know I've been giving you a hard time, but you're being such a brave little toaster." Monica put a hand on Ray's shoulder as they exited the dressing area. "I'm proud of you."

At the touch of Monica's hand, a zing of warmth flooded Ray's body, settling into the one spot that should have been an immovable fortress where this woman was concerned. Instead, it had definitely…moved.

Uh-oh.

While Ray had been exhausted a moment before, suddenly her imagination was flooded with all sorts of more invigorating uses for that aforementioned hotel bed than catching forty winks.

Oh, Petunia. We're in some serious trouble now.

"I UNDERSTAND THE NEW CLOTHES," Ray said, "and even the underwear, but explain to me again why you had to buy a suitcase?"

She was sitting on a park bench in the middle of a green space that overlooked the harbor, watching in bewilderment as Monica took the new items one by one from the perfectly good shopping bag they'd come in, refolded them, and placed them in the carry-on size rolling bag she'd insisted on purchasing from the corner drugstore.

"I told you the only people who arrive at a hotel without luggage are looking to rent a room by the hour."

"For someone who's living on plastic, you're spending money like it's water."

"I'll pay it off when we get access to the money from the savings bonds. Besides, I can't put a price on my good reputation."

"I still don't get it," Ray argued. "You said the woman at the hotel is a friend. They're even giving us the room for free."

"Yes, because I'm a respected expert in my field. If I show up looking like a disorganized bag lady, how long do you think people will take me seriously?"

Honestly? Here was a woman who thought writing little articles and blathering to herself about weddings was a real business. How seriously should anyone take her? But Ray pressed her lips together tightly, knowing better than to breathe a word of what she was thinking out loud.

Ray peeked over her sunglasses at a row of underwear folded with origami-like precision into colorful, silky squares. She pinched one with polka dots, plucking it from the suitcase. Instead of underwear, Ray discovered it was a bra. "No offense, but I don't think this is going to fit you."

"You've been sneaking peeks at my boobs?"

Ray snorted. "No need to sneak. They're not what I'd call subtle."

Monica pursed her lips. "As it happens, this isn't for me. It's for you."

"Yeah, I don't wear one."

"No need to inform people; trust me." Monica shot Ray's chest a reproachful glance. "Your nips do all the talking."

Ray crossed her arms over her chest, which, yes, was sporting two hard peaks at the moment, but it really wasn't her fault. The temperature had dropped significantly as soon as the sun started to go down. Plus, there was a cold breeze coming from the harbor. "Look. I went with the skinny jeans, but I'm drawing the line at bras. A girl has to have some respect."

"Seriously?" Monica mimicked Ray's arm position, but instead of resulting in a flattened chest, her action produced a deep valley of cleavage. The contrast couldn't have been starker. It might've bolstered her own anti-bra position, only Ray was too transfixed to formulate an argument. "Pretty sure wearing appropriate undergarments is part of the definition of being respectable."

"Pretty sure you're not going to make me change my mind on this one, so let's go to the hotel, okay?" Tearing her eyes away from Monica's overly prominent boobs, Ray took the rolling bag by its handle. "Let's roll—get it, roll? Because it's a rolling bag…"

Monica studied her in stone-faced silence.

"Come on. That was funny."

"Sure. If you have the sense of humor of a twelve-year-old boy, which clearly you do."

"Just for that, I'm not talking to you for the rest of the walk to the hotel." Time stretched on for an eternity with nothing to listen to but the clicking of luggage wheels against the cracks in the sidewalk. Finally, Ray broke down. "How far is it to this place, anyway?"

"Two-point-five," Monica responded.

"Miles? Hours left to walk?"

"Seconds. You lasted exactly two-point-five seconds from the point when you said you wouldn't talk to me. Would you like to try again? I bet you could double your time if you really focus."

"Sometimes I feel like you don't take me seriously."

"Only sometimes? I'm going to need to try harder."

Ray stopped walking and set the bag upright, removing her hand from the handle and giving it a good shake to restore circulation. "This thing weighs a ton. I think we should leave it behind. I'll never be able to drag it all the way to the hotel, however much farther it is."

"It's right there." Monica pointed a pink polished finger to a building directly across the street. She grabbed the suitcase and began to pull. "How is it possible you are struggling with this little thing with arms that look like yours?"

"You've been scoping out my arms?" Ray trotted to

catch up to Monica, who was definitely ignoring her and doing everything she could to pretend she hadn't basically admitted to lusting after Ray's arms. "Tell me more about my arms."

"Why don't you tell me about this old building?" Monica challenged, clearly changing the subject. "Since you're the expert and all."

Ray eyed the building. "Federal Style, constructed of Quincy granite. The classical column, flat facades, and three-part windows are the dead giveaways. My guess is it was constructed during Bullfinch's day. Hell, it might even be one of his."

Without saying a word, Monica eyed Ray with an expression Ray couldn't discern, but which might have been a blend of surprise and admiration. Before Ray could really dig in and try to weasel a compliment out of her, Monica shoved the suitcase handle at her so she could wave furiously to a woman who had appeared in the doorway of the boutique hotel.

"Monica?" the woman called out. "Oh my god, this is so exciting!"

Monica rushed across the cobblestone street and gave the woman one of those embraces women give one another when they aren't actually close friends but feel the need to show affection anyway. For some reason that had always escaped Ray's understanding. Meanwhile, Ray was left to wrestle an unruly rolling bag across one of the most unevenly paved roads on this side of the

Atlantic. Why had they required all this junk again? High maintenance didn't begin to describe that woman.

"I'm so glad to finally meet you in person, Mary," Monica gushed, confirming Ray's suspicion that this so-called friend of hers was basically a total stranger. "I have to say, though, I feel like I know you after the interview we did for my article."

"After you did your piece on us earlier this year, our bookings increased three-fold," Mary said, ushering Monica and Ray into a lobby area filled with sumptuous wood rubbed to a high shine. "It's done wonders for our economic recovery, but we can talk about that later. Right now, I want to talk about you and your big day."

"Big day?" Monica looked to Ray, her face clouded with confusion, but Ray was even more lost in the conversation than she was.

"Your wedding!" Mary put one hand on Monica's shoulder and the other on Ray's, encompassing them both with a million-watt smile. "I know it's technically not your honeymoon yet, but I took the liberty of booking you in our bridal suite for this evening. Shall we check it out?"

"Uh…" Monica gave Ray an *oh shit* look as Mary strode to the elevator.

"How does she know?" Ray whispered, genuinely perplexed. She'd figured Monica would want to keep their sham engagement on the down low as much as possible. Only one explanation remotely made sense. "Did you tell her to get upgraded to a better room?"

"What? Of course not," Monica denied. "If the only way to get a room was to admit publicly that I'm marrying you, I'd choose to sleep on a park bench in Boston Common."

"I, on the other hand, don't care what people I don't even know think," Ray explained. "I'd announce it to every bum out there right now if it meant I'd get to watch you try to get comfy for the night without a down pillow and satin sleep mask."

"How did you know I wear a sleep mask?" Monica demanded in a hoarse whisper. "Did you go through my things when you were painting my bedroom?"

"Relax, princess," Ray soothed, unable to hold back a slight chuckle. What was it about Monica that kept making that happen? Instead of being in complete agony at this forced proximity, at the rate she was going, she was going to have permanent laugh lines by the time this trip was done. There was no explanation for it. "The sleep mask was a guess, and not even a very lucky one. There was maybe a one percent chance you didn't sleep with one. I mean, have you seen yourself?"

Ray could've teased her for hours over this, but they'd reached the elevator, and Ray had enough desire to live until they made it to the room that she wisely stopped talking. She even managed to make it the entire ride up to the sixth floor without pointing out to Monica how quiet she was being. Honestly, it was killing her. What was the use of proving she could go this long without talking if she wasn't going to get any credit for it?

If it was a struggle to stay quiet on the way to the room, that difficulty ended as soon as Mary unlocked the door of the suite and allowed them to enter. In short, the room left Ray speechless. There were vases of fresh flowers on every flat surface, and red rose petals sprinkled on the crisp white sheets of the king-sized canopy bed. A bottle of champagne had been left to chill in the fanciest ice bucket Ray had ever seen, alongside a fruit basket that could feed a small nation.

Holy fuck, are those chocolate-covered strawberries? Ray was about to blurt this out when Monica broke the silence.

"You've really outdone yourself," Monica said.

Understatement of the century.

Mary waved a hand as if to say it was nothing. "I know you said you only wanted a room for the night, but after I saw the news on Twitter…"

"Twitter?" A hint of danger glinted in Monica's eyes. "You're going to need to tell me exactly what you've heard."

"It's not just Twitter. It's all over social media, under the hashtag, uh," Mary paused a beat, looking uncertain, "PantyWedding."

"*Panty* wedding?" It was hard to tell whether Monica was more likely to go on a rampage or hide in the bathroom and cry. "That's the worst hashtag I've ever heard."

"I think it's cute," Mary reassured her. "More importantly, it's memorable and trending big time. All of this is so exciting, and the fact that our hotel is playing a small part in the best day of your life—it's more than we could have asked for. Well, I'm going to leave you two lovebirds alone now."

With a suggestive wink, Mary left the room. Monica twirled to face Ray, her face beet red with rage. "Can you believe her nerve?"

"Mary?" Ray shrugged. "I mean, she thinks we're getting married. It's not that outrageous that she'd assume we were sleeping together, too. I'm pretty sure the Puritans left Boston a long time ago."

"Not Mary. That clerk at City Hall. It had to be her, sneaking photos and putting the news on Twitter. I'm going to sue." Monica snatched her phone and began to scroll. "Where's that lawyer's number?"

"Hold on, tiger. Don't you think it'll blow our cover if you start suing people for announcing our marriage? Not to mention destroy your business by outing yourself as a fraud?"

"This is even worse than I thought." Monica's shoulders slumped, her expression becoming sober.

"Cheer up. It's not that bad." Ray gave Monica's arm a playful punch. "Things will look much better tomorrow after we get hitched in Connecticut and head back home."

Monica shook her head. "Don't you see? This changes everything."

"What, you're thinking Vermont would be a better choice?" Ray shrugged. "I can go either way."

"No. I'm thinking there's no way I can elope now. You heard Mary. PantyWedding is trending." Monica threw her hands in the air and began pacing the room. "That terrible moniker is your fault, too. You had to make your stupid panty joke in front of that clerk."

"It's not my fault you have an impossible name. Maybe you should change it tomorrow when we get married."

Monica stopped pacing, spinning in her tracks. "Have you not heard a word I've said? We can't get married tomorrow."

"The deal's off?" Ray should've felt relieved, but instead she was agitated. Why did Monica get to call all the shots? Shouldn't she have a say in whether or not she got married, too?

"Are you kidding? Calling it off would be even worse." Monica sank to the edge of the bed. "We're going to have to make it look like we're having a real wedding, something I can feature on my website."

An actual wedding? Ray rubbed her chin, trying to concentrate and not give in to the urge to panic that bubbled up inside her the moment she started picturing bouquets and white dresses. "Okay, we can check around Boston tomorrow and see if we can find something that will work."

Inexplicably, Monica was shaking her head. "No can do."

Ray put her hands on her hips. "Why not?"

"Because people would see us. I have over a million followers. It's too risky."

"You make it sound like you're a long-lost Kardashian."

Monica glared. "I'll have you know I'm kind of a big deal, and the city of Boston is crawling with nosy wedding industry people. If anyone catches us bickering like this, they'll figure out we're fakes, and the jig will be up."

Ray couldn't believe this woman's overinflated ego. "Who could possibly care?"

Instead of lashing out, Monica took a deep breath and explained calmly, "Wedding planning is a multibillion dollar industry, and it's fallen on some hard times lately. I can think of plenty of people who wouldn't think twice about spreading malicious gossip to try to knock me down a few rungs."

"I hadn't thought of that." Ray sat down on a chair, the enormity of the issue sinking in. Suddenly, her spinning wheels hit upon a brilliant idea. "I know where we can go where no one will look for us."

"Where?"

"Our vineyard. I mean neither one of us knew it existed until today. It would be totally off the radar."

"We don't even know what it looks like," Monica argued, although Ray got the impression it was more out of habit and less because she had a specific objection to Ray's idea.

"Does it matter? We know there's a house on the property, and your grandmother's lawyer said we could get the keys to check it out. It's the perfect place to lay low for a few days and figure this out."

Doubt etched Monica's face, but she nodded slowly. "I guess you're right. We can rent a car in the morning and at least give it a look."

"Hey, vineyards are romantic. Maybe it will turn out to be something we can work with for the wedding."

She'd said it to cheer up Monica, but as Ray's eyes swept the room, taking in the champagne, the rose petals, and the rest of the trappings of the type of big day she'd never wanted, reality hit her with all the force of a two-by-four to the head.

She was getting married. To Monica.

And based on that woman's complete lack of understanding of the concept of moderation, it was sure to be the shindig of the century.

This was bad.

Really bad.

What the hell had she gotten herself into?

CHAPTER NINE

Monica gripped the steering wheel of the rental car, her fingers curling around the hard plastic like a python squeezing the life out of its prey. The road in front of her was more pothole than pavement, and the cracks in it had been patched in so many places the solar glare off the shiny squiggles of tar was nearly blinding. Several yards ahead was some sort of sign, which Monica couldn't read. If it was announcing another dead end, it would break her. She'd have to stop the engine, get out of the car, and scream.

"You okay?" Ray asked.

No, Monica was not okay. She'd spent the night alternating between guilt for taking the bed and terror that somehow Mary would figure out Ray had spent the night on the sofa, and their entire charade would be exposed to the world. When she'd finally drifted off to sleep, she'd had the most vividly realistic dream in which she'd stripped off all her clothing and invited Ray to join her, naked, on the king-size mattress. She'd woken up in pitch blackness with her heart pounding in her ears, convinced it had really happened, and it had taken the better part of half an hour to calm down and go back to sleep. Now her neck was stiff, her head was throbbing, and she might never be able to make eye contact with Ray again because every time she looked at her, she could feel the ghost of velvety skin against the length of her body.

"It's nothing," Monica replied, loosening her grip on the wheel ever so slightly and coaxing her shoulders downward from where they'd been hunched at her ears. It wasn't like Ray would understand any of what she was experiencing, even if she did try to explain. She'd laugh and call Monica high strung. "I hate driving when I don't know where I'm going."

"It's the next left. The GPS just said so."

The GPS had told them a lot of things that morning, none of which had prevented them from driving in endless circles as they encountered narrow city roads that lacked street signs and sometimes became one way with no warning. By the fifth time they'd passed the flag announcing the location of the original bar from the Cheers television show, the experience had lost its charm. Honestly, if they'd gone by a sixth time, Monica had been determined to pull over and go in for a drink. Who cared if at the time it had only been a quarter past seven in the morning? Considering she'd been right there in the passenger's seat to witness all of it, Ray's calm tone at the present moment made Monica immediately want to rip the steering wheel from the dashboard and crown her with it. In fact, picturing doing so made Monica relax a little.

"And by the next left, does that mean a dirt road or an actual road?" Monica asked, her tone saccharin sweet. "Or have you already forgotten being chased by that dog because what you thought was our turn was actually someone's driveway?"

"Considering what that sign says, I'm guessing we're close." Ray pointed at the cracked wooden sign staked into the ground. Now that they were closer, Monica could see her own last name was painted on it: *Panagiotopoulos Vineyards, 2 miles*. An arrow pointed left.

Monica sighed as she turned onto a road even less well paved than the one they'd been on. "You still can't pronounce my name, can you? You better start practicing for the wedding."

"Can't we go with first names only?" Ray asked hopefully. "Learning how to say it properly feels like a bigger commitment than actually getting married."

Monica stared ahead, ignoring her.

"'Two Mikes' Automotive,'" Ray read out loud as they passed a ramshackle mechanic's shop with a sign out front. "Now there's commitment. I mean, what if one of them dies?"

"What on earth are you talking about?" Monica had a feeling she would soon regret asking.

"I mean, I guess they could cross out the two, so then it would be Mike's Automotive, only the apostrophe would be in the wrong place."

"Frankly, it doesn't look like the type of place where they'd care about apostrophes."

Ray turned abruptly toward Monica, her tone sharp. "You know, you have a real chip on your shoulder."

Monica glanced at Ray, surprised to find her chin dimple glowing as brightly as Rudolph's nose. "About what?"

"Blue collar workers, that's what." Ray crossed her arms over her seat belt's shoulder strap. "Just because the Mikes work on cars doesn't mean they're stupid. They might have strong opinions on the Oxford comma for all you know. It's not like wedding bloggers have a corner on the grammar market."

The dismissive way Ray said wedding bloggers immediately raised Monica's hackles. "Sheesh, are you always like this in the morning?"

"What do you expect?" Ray pouted. "I've gone three hours without breakfast! I warned you about Ray-Ray."

"I gave you a granola bar at the hotel."

"That might constitute as breakfast in your world, but in mine, that's barely a snack. I pointed out a diner, but you refused to stop."

"Even if I could've found parking, which is a big if, that place was right near downtown and packed to the gills," Monica argued. "Anybody could've seen us in there. We're supposed to be laying low. What part of being on the lam are you not getting?"

"The part where I die of starvation."

"You're not dying! You ate a large pizza all by yourself last night." Monica hadn't planned to bring it up, but it was true. Ray had eaten the entire thing. "You can't possibly feel hungry after that."

Ray turned her head toward the window in a huff. "Don't tell me how I'm feeling. It's rude."

"So is eating a whole pizza while I'm in the shower." Did that really need to be explained?

"You told me a million times as I was ordering it that you don't eat gluten, and you don't eat cheese, and pepperoni's too fatty. I didn't realize that was Monica code for let's go halfsies. Besides, you got the last slice. You keep forgetting that part."

"Because I got out of the shower in the nick of time." Monica said, choosing not to address the rest of Ray's observations. "You had the slice in your hand."

Ray snorted, still seeming miffed. As seconds ticked away in uncharacteristic silence, Monica feared she may have upset the woman more than she'd realized. She'd thought finally getting Ray to stop talking would've made her happy, but instead, Monica shifted uneasily. It felt unnatural.

"I'm sorry." Monica glanced at Ray, looking for signs of softening. She thought maybe Ray's shoulders seemed a little less stiff and decided to take it as a win.

"We'll find you some food, okay? I'm sure the vineyard will have a restaurant."

Ray looked at Monica, head cocked to one side. "What do you think we're about to find?"

"I've been giving this some thought," Monica said, not mentioning the thinking had mostly been between the hours of three and four that morning when she'd been trying to distract herself from picturing Ray naked after dreaming they'd slept together. Some things were better left unsaid, after all.

"Uh-oh," Ray ribbed. "Why does that worry me?"

"Hey, I'll have you know I went to Napa Valley last fall with Bri on a week-long wine tasting excursion, so I've got some experience with vineyards."

"You're practically an expert, I'm sure."

"I know this is a smaller scale operation, but you may have been onto something with your wedding idea last night." Monica shrugged, not wanting to make too big a deal of letting Ray know she'd been right. "A vineyard wedding would be popular with my followers, and the media attention might mean a better selling price for the property."

"Is this where I say I told you so?"

"Not if you don't want to walk the rest of the way to the property." Out of the corner of her eye, she saw Ray stick her tongue out at her, which was so childish it was actually amusing. Monica chuckled, her spirits lifting considerably. "The vineyards I toured on the west coast were stunning. Rows and rows of grapevines rolling along the hills as far as you can see. When the sun hits the leaves in the late afternoon, they practically glow. And the place we stayed was like a Spanish villa. You pull up along this circular drive, and there's this fountain in the middle, and…"

Monica's voice trailed off as the road they were on came to an abrupt end in front of a monstrosity of an old house covered in weathered wooden shingles. Several of its shutters—that is, where they weren't missing entirely—hung at a tilt that gave her the distinct impression the house was suffering from a hangover. The yard surrounding it was so overgrown Monica was certain she was about to step onto the set of the next Stephen King movie.

"Where's Cujo?" Monica asked, hoping a joke would make her feel better about the sorry state of things. It didn't. Her companion, however, seemed to be experiencing the situation very differently.

"This looks amazing." Ray was releasing her seatbelt and had a hand on the door, looking as if she was going to open it before the car was completely stopped.

"Wait. You'll get hurt!" Despite every instinct telling her to hit the gas and hightail it back to Boston, Monica shifted the car into park and turned off the engine. "This can't be it, can it?"

Ray pointed to a sign on the rickety fence along the road, which was nearly identical to the one they'd seen a few miles back. Unfortunately, instead of directing them farther down the road, this one simply said, "Welcome."

"There's no way there are two Panty-topless vineyards in central Massachusetts. I doubt you'd get that many even in Greece."

"But—" Monica spun slowly in a circle, her heart sinking deeper the more she took in of the panoramic view. "Where are the vines?"

Ray pointed to a tangle of what looked like weeds weighing down a sagging arbor. "There."

"Just one row?" Monica threw her hands into the air, even as Ray opened the garden gate for a closer inspection of the property. "This isn't a vineyard. It's an old person's run-down garden. I doubt it yields a single grape."

Ray looked back from across the yard, regarding Monica with a curious expression. "I know at first glance this looks a little on the rough side—"

"What's your definition of a little or rough for that matter?" If she could've kicked something without fear of bringing the whole place down, she would have. Monica's dreams of selling this place for millions were fizzling before her eyes. "I guess we'd better get back on the road and head for Connecticut. The vineyard idea's a flop, but the land itself must still be worth something to an investor. The sooner we get it all ironed out, the sooner we can move on."

"What are you talking about?" Ray looked at her

aghast. "You can't possibly be thinking of selling to a developer. They'd tear the whole thing down."

"Not necessarily." Monica poked at the garden gate with distaste. "Setting fire to it might be more efficient. A good, controlled burn."

"But…" Ray's voice quivered, and much to Monica's amazement, she appeared to be on the verge of tears. "It's perfect."

"*This* is perfect?" Was she joking? She had to be, but Monica saw no trace of it on her companion's face. "What drugs are you taking, and can I have some?"

"I'm serious." Ray motioned for Monica to join her at the far end of the yard, where she stood beside a long line of neglected boxwood shrubs. "Let me show you something."

Monica approached timidly, scanning the ground for hazards like gopher holes or possibly landmines. She stopped a few feet from Ray and peered over the hedge barrier. There were the vines—for real this time —covering the rolling hills in what might once have been neat rows, but which now appeared every bit as wild as the rest of the property. Monica made a face. "I'm glad we skipped breakfast, because I think I might be sick."

Instead of answering, Ray moved closer to her. All at once, Monica was overcome with a faint scent of soap that mingled with something else, unidentifiable but oh, so enticing that it made her feel a little wobbly. There was body heat against her back, the kind that welcomes with the promise of a warm embrace or more. Monica bit her lip, forcing herself not to remember the dream she'd had the previous night of Ray's bare skin against hers. This was not the time or the place for that kind of thinking and *definitely* not the person.

"Now, I want you to stop looking." Instead of keeping a safe distance between them, Ray stood mere inches behind her and covered Monica's eyes with her palms. "Just listen to me. Can you do that?"

"Yes." Monica gulped as Ray's fingers shifted, feeling softer than even her best satin sleep mask. All the fight drained out of her, and Monica feared she might agree to anything if it meant standing where she was for a little longer.

"Okay, Miss Event Planner Extraordinaire, pretend this is Napa. Tell me what you need for a fantastic vineyard wedding."

Monica breathed in deeply and willed herself to focus. "A scenic spot for the ceremony is a must, flat enough to offer space for chairs, and with a focal point for the couple to stand for the ceremony itself."

"So, maybe a pergola or a gazebo overlooking a classic white New England church steeple, with vibrant fall foliage in the distance?"

"Uh, yeah." Try as she might, Monica couldn't fault Ray's suggestion. "That's pretty much spot-on."

"Good. Go on."

Monica crinkled her nose, trying to shift Ray's

fingers from her eyes, but they remained firmly in place. "Then you'd need a place for dinner. Covered is a must, and big enough to seat at least a few hundred people at long family-style tables."

"A tent?"

This time Monica shook her head. "I know they're popular, but it's not my style. At the end of the day, a tent is still a tent. Ladies get their heels caught in the grass, and the dance floors are never any good. It's a wedding, not a camping trip."

"Something permanent, then, with a real floor." While she thought, Ray made a low humming noise close enough to Monica's right ear that she could feel the vibrations in every inch of her body. "How about a carriage house?"

"Huh?" She'd kind of lost track of the conversation for a second. "Oh. It would depend, I guess. Ideally, I wouldn't want it to be so rustic it looked like a barn, or too closed in. I mean, if we're daydreaming right now, the perfect thing would be a building with big doors and windows that could be opened up to feel like you were outside."

"Sure. Something that would let in the fresh autumn smells and allow everyone to enjoy the colors of the season." Ray's voice was soft and gentle, trailing off in a dreamy way. Monica leaned back ever so slightly, her back resting against Ray's chest as it rose and fell in deep, steady breaths. Somewhere nearby, a bird chirped. "Monica?"

Monica jumped at the sound of Ray's voice saying her name, a rush of heat letting her know her face had definitely turned bright red. Good thing Ray couldn't see. "Yeah?"

"I'm going to remove my hands now, and I want you to open your eyes and take a closer look at this property."

Monica gave a slight nod, after which Ray's fingers fell away from her eyes, leaving her feeling strangely exposed. She scanned the property as Ray had asked, her pulse quickening as she spotted the white church steeple and recalled Ray's description.

She pointed at it, a slight frown tugging at her mouth. "But, there's no gazebo."

"Easily remedied," Ray said, exuding the confidence of someone who knew how to build things. "With a premade kit, I could do it in a weekend. Tell me what else you see."

Monica's eyes swept the property again, quickly recognizing a building she assumed must be a carriage house. It had large doors that could be opened wide as she'd described, but it was in at least as bad of repair as the farmhouse. "I don't know, Ray. That looks like it's about to fall down."

Ray stepped around her so she could look Monica in the eyes. "You know weddings, but I know architecture. One look tells me everything here was built to stand another hundred years, easily. All it needs is some elbow grease, and it will be exactly what you described."

"This seems like a lot more work than we bargained for." Even as she said it, the hope and excitement in Ray's eyes made Monica's resolve waver.

"How many days did that lady at City Hall say we had to get married once we get the license?"

Monica closed her eyes, trying to recall. "Sixty, I think."

"Right." Ray tapped her fingers as if doing mental calculations. "If we use some of the savings bond money, we can hire a crew to clear the weeds. Then I can tackle the gazebo and the carriage house with plenty of time to spare. I can draw up a renovation budget. You just have to handle the wedding details."

"There's no way we can get it all done in time." Monica's shoulders stiffened, ready for battle.

"Speak for yourself." Ray lifted her stubborn chin. "I can get my part of it done, but if you don't think you can pull yours together in 60 days, well…"

Monica put her hands on her hips. "I didn't say that."

"You seemed to imply—"

"It's tight, but I can pull it off," Monica countered. "Besides, it doesn't have to be a real wedding. It only has to look like one on Instagram."

"I don't think I'm following."

"What I mean is, we don't actually have to invite guests and all that, or even have a real ceremony and reception." Monica found herself warming to the idea as the possibilities unfolded in her imagination. "We need a good photographer and the proper staging, maybe a few fake guests brought in to make it look like a real event. I'll put together a budget, just like you."

"You want to make people think we had a wedding?"

"Of course. Venues do it all the time when they want to break into the business but haven't hosted an actual wedding yet."

Ray gave her a dumbfounded look. "Are you sure?"

"Trust me. I'm a professional."

"We both are, which means we can, and will, make this the best make-believe shindig anyone's ever seen."

Ray's smile radiated way more confidence than was probably warranted. But as her heart began to flutter, Monica had to admit the woman's excitement was more than a little contagious. Still, she wasn't quite ready to give in.

"I don't know. It's a huge risk. If I build this up on my blog and it doesn't work out, I'd be ruined."

"I know you don't really know me, Monica," Ray said, "but I need you to trust me. A restoration project like this could make my career, like the wedding itself could make yours. I can get my end of it done on time, if you'll give me a chance. If I don't, we can elope to Connecticut, or Vegas, or anywhere you'd like, and as soon as we're married, we can sell this place to a developer, and I'll sign over my entire portion of the proceeds to you."

"Every penny?" Monica looked at her like Ray had lost her mind. "What makes you think I won't sabotage the project simply to get the money?"

"Because you're a savvy business woman like I am." Ray motioned to the land around them. "This place could be more amazing than anything you saw in Napa. It just needs some polishing. I think you feel it, too."

"I do."

Monica swallowed as the enormous gravity of that particular phrase sank in, her head spinning even as she felt the strange urge to laugh. Sixty more days, and she'd be saying it again, right here, with all the internet as a witness in a faux wedding that could make both of their careers. When they'd first hatched this plan to get hitched, the idea of marrying a woman like Ray had seemed as distasteful to her as it was ridiculous. A mere twenty-four hours later, Monica felt nothing but a tingling sense of excitement at what was to come. Her only concern was could they really pull it off?

CHAPTER TEN

"Okay, let's get to work." Ray slapped her palms together, the sharp snap echoing in the open air. Giddiness overtook her as she surveyed the vineyard property. The moment that old farmhouse had come into view, she'd known this was a project she couldn't walk away from. The carriage house had sealed the deal. Original slate roofing and architectural details galore, with enough upkeep to suggest the buildings were in good condition, but not enough to signal major renovations that could have stripped away the charm. She was in heaven.

"Before we can do anything, we'll need to pick up those keys from the caretaker," Monica pointed out.

"That's right," Ray agreed. "Where did the attorney say we'd find Zorba again?"

By the way Monica sighed, Ray could tell she'd said something wrong. "Why do you hate Greeks?"

"I don't." Ray scratched her head. What had she done to give the woman that impression? "It's quite the opposite. I love Greeks. Well, more specifically, I love Greek food. But, I'll have you know *Zorba the Greek* is one of the best movies of all time. It was nominated for seven Oscars, taking home three."

"What does that have to do with anything?" Monica's tone suggested she was losing patience, but Ray barely noticed. As soon as she'd started to speak, the sun shone through a patch of clouds at just the right angle to turn Monica's hair into strands of fiery gold that held Ray almost as captivated as the copper valleys on the carriage house roof had done.

Monica had that look, like she was waiting for an answer, and Ray wracked her brain to recall what they'd been talking about. "The caretaker's name is Zorba."

"The caretaker's name is Christos."

Ray winced. "Oops. I knew it was something super Greek-y, and Zorba's the only name I could think of. Sorry."

With a roll of the eyes that said she considered Ray beyond hope, Monica pulled her phone from her bag. She pointed to the right. "The text said we'd find a brick path, over that way, that leads down to the lower portion of the property. Christos doesn't live here, but he's usually at the shop during business hours."

"That brick path?" Ray nodded in the direction Monica had pointed. "You're kidding me."

"What?" Monica cocked her head to the side, the way she did when confused. Or annoyed. It was a look Ray had seen a lot in the past twenty-four hours. Even so, she'd started to find it oddly adorable, like a look a puppy would give.

"It's yellow." Ray waited for a response and got none. "Follow the yellow brick road?"

"Let me guess." Monica started picking her way through the overgrown yard toward the path. "*The Wizard of Oz* is another all-time fave?"

"Nope." Ray trotted after her, quickly catching up since her boots made her much more surefooted than Monica's girly slip-ons. Not that Ray was complaining about Monica's choice of clothing. Ray might not be caught dead in leggings and a form-fitting cranberry sweater herself, but she couldn't deny their effect on Monica's shapely body. The woman looked like a million bucks. "I know *The Wizard of Oz* is a classic, but I've never been a fan. I do think the yellow bricks are a sign, though."

Monica gave her a quizzical look even as she struggled to keep pace. "What kind of a sign?"

"That we're fated to find our fortune." Ray stopped and held out her arm, pushing up her sleeve. "I'm getting all tingly. Feel the goose bumps on my arms."

Monica swallowed roughly, like something had suddenly become lodged in her throat. "I think I'll pass."

Monica's condescending look was like a bucket of

cold water over the head, reminding Ray that as far as this woman was concerned, she was nothing more than the hired help. Ray gathered the tattered remnants of her pride, kicking herself for opening up even for a moment. To think she'd actually started to find this snobby princess attractive.

Monica led the way, with Ray following reluctantly, shuffling her feet. It almost seemed like she wanted to say something, glancing over her shoulder at Ray on three separate occasions. Her lips—which Ray refused to note were particularly full and pink this morning, because honestly, she was really done noticing things like that where Monica was concerned—kept parting, but she never actually said anything.

As they followed the path through rows of vines, Ray soon noticed the vineyard was in better condition than it had at first appeared. Far from being barren, bunches of vibrant purple and green grapes peeked out from beneath wide green leaves, and the air was filled with a sweet, floral scent. Though she didn't know much about farming, Ray guessed the crop must be almost ready for harvesting.

Exiting the fields, a small building about the size and shape of a barn stood several yards ahead of them, and it was to its front door that the yellow brick road appeared to lead. An older gentleman in denim coveralls, his face grizzled and shoulders hunched, came out the front door and raised a hand in greeting.

"Good morning! You must be the young ladies Mr. Donahue's office called about."

Monica approached him, extending her hand. "I'm Monica."

"Of course, you are. You look just like your *yiayia*." Though he spoke with no discernible accent, he pronounced the Greek word as though it was his native tongue. As he took Monica's hand, his eyes seemed to grow misty. "I'm Christos."

"You knew my grandmother?" Monica asked.

"Your grandfather, too," the man confirmed. "We came from the same village back in the old country, though your grandparents were more my parents' age than my own."

"You knew them in Greece?" A look of curiosity passed over Monica's features, softening them. "I hardly know anything about when they lived there."

"No, I'm afraid they'd left when I was a young boy, but you know how villages are…" He frowned for a moment. "Well, perhaps you don't. Where I came from, everyone was like family, no matter if you were related or not. If someone got a letter from family in America, everyone turned out to hear the news. Of course, when I moved here myself, everyone told me I should look them up, and they were more than hospitable."

"I had no idea. I'm afraid my grandparents never mentioned you, or this vineyard, for that matter." Monica delivered the news with a measure of kindness and delicacy that surprised Ray, considering her own experiences with the woman's razor tongue.

"Ah, it was a lifetime ago." He waved a hand as if to say it didn't bother him. "I'm so sorry for your loss. Your grandmother was such a beautiful creature inside and out."

"I still can't believe she's gone." The words that came from Monica were heartfelt, her voice cracking with a raw emotion that tore at Ray's heart.

Without thinking about what she was doing, Ray put a hand on Monica's shoulder and felt her shudder. Certain the gesture was unwanted, Ray made to pull her hand away, but Monica reached up and grasped, pressing Ray's palm firmly against her.

"And who's this?" Christos asked, giving Ray a polite smile.

"This is my fiancée," Monica answered.

"Uh, Ray…er, Rachel…er, Ray," Ray stuttered as she put her free hand out for the man to shake. She'd been so thrown off by the matter-of-fact way in which Monica had introduced her as her fiancée that she'd momentarily forgotten her own name.

"So nice to meet you, Ray," Christos said, politely ignoring her fumbled introduction. "Would you two like a cup of coffee?"

"Please." Monica yawned. "I didn't sleep much last night."

Ray, who'd slept like a log despite her less than ideal accommodations on their hotel room couch, made a quick study of Monica's face. She looked beautiful—Monica always looked stunning, as it was basically part of her brand—but through a thin layer of foundation, Ray noted the shadow of dark circles beneath her eyes, along with faint wrinkles that no amount of moisturizer could smooth. Was it the stress of their bizarre situation that had robbed her of sleep, or something else?

Christos led them into the shop, which was a single large room in what had once been a barn, a very old barn, judging by the massive exposed beams. Bottles of wine were displayed on rustic wooden shelves, and there were a few tables that Ray suspected were used for tastings. Behind the counter was a jumble of oak barrels, plus huge plastic containers that looked like they could've come from the laboratory of a mad scientist giant. Through the white plastic, Ray could make out dark red liquid, giving her the impression that this was not only a shop, but the place where the wine was made and stored.

Christos ducked behind the counter, retrieving three white ceramic mugs and filling them with hot, dark coffee from a plain glass pot. "I put this on fresh, in case any tourists stop by today."

"Do you get many people coming all the way out here?" Ray asked, recalling the long drive from the city and how sparse the population had become once they'd made it west of the interstate.

"We've got some regular tour buses that come through every October. Outside of the leaf peepers, though, it's kinda few and far between the rest of the year," Christos admitted, but then his face brightened. "Wednesdays are the exception, which is why I always make coffee."

"Why Wednesdays?" Ray inquired, though she was only half listening. Mentally, she was replacing the current shelving with custom built wine racks and adding a lighted display area along the back wall, with maybe a bar and stools made from repurposed oak barrels for the tastings. If only that messy eyesore of a workspace could be moved elsewhere, it wouldn't take much to transform the barn into a top-notch shop, like one she'd worked on a few years back in the old section of Alexandria, Virginia.

"Wednesdays are when the local farmer's market takes place, up in the town common, across from the library. It's less than a half mile walk if you take the main driveway out to the road." He pointed in the direction directly opposite from how she and Monica had come.

"There's another entrance to this place?" Ray tapped her fingertips together, recalling the bumpy road and overgrown paths. "Is there a sign for it? All we saw were those wooden signs directing us to the old house at the top of the hill."

"Oh, that's right." Christos's shoulders sagged slightly. "I keep meaning to take those old ones down and replace them with something out on the big road. The county stopped paving the other one years ago. Seems like I never have the time or the energy, the older I get."

No signs to direct potential customers to the entrance? No wonder this place didn't get any business. Ray couldn't help noticing, too, that the bottles of wine in the shop had little more than white labels from a home printer to announce what variety they were. She was no branding expert, but even she knew there was plenty of room for improvement. Still, for a one-man operation, it wasn't too bad. Like a building for restoration, if the bones were good, the rest could be prettied up and put right with a little love and a lot of elbow grease.

"I think you're doing a nice job here, Christos."

He looked at Ray, as if deciding whether or not she was being sarcastic, but he seemed to pick up on the sincerity of her enthusiasm. "It's my happy place. I know many people who have to travel far and wide to experience land like this."

"It's good land, then?" Monica asked, breaking her long silence. By good, she meant valuable, of course. Ray could see it in her eyes, the way she was trying to assess the fair asking price without coming right out and saying it. It made Ray's skin itch, how detached the woman could be from what was clearly this man's life passion. Was there anything other than money that made her tick?

"Very good soil. Almost as good as back in the old country. I grew up on a vineyard there, which is part of the reason your grandparents put me in charge here when they moved." Christos leaned against the wall close to a window, looking out toward the vines. "I only wish there was more of me to turn it into a thriving place."

"The grapes were looking really nice out there," Ray offered. "I'm sure it'll be a good harvest."

"What I can get of it, anyway." Christos held up his hands, spotted with age. "I don't have the stamina I once did."

"By yourself?" Ray frowned. "Don't you have a crew of people who come in and help with the harvest?"

"Sadly, pickers are few and far between," Christos answered, "and in high demand. All the independent vineyards in the region struggle somewhat to compete with the bigger commercial operations for workers, but a little place like this doesn't stand a chance. It's too labor intensive to harvest those unruly vines, and I can't afford to pay what they'd make elsewhere."

"That's a shame. What about a landscaping crew? Not for picking, but is there anyone in the area who might be up to doing some cleanup work?" she asked, thinking of the tangled mess that made up the majority of the property. If they couldn't hire someone for that, there'd be no way they could pull off the wedding here in two months. That was one kind of manual labor even Ray balked at as being too back-breaking to tackle on her own.

"Oh, sure," Christos said. "There's a young guy across the way who runs a really nice operation."

"You think you could get in touch with him and see if he can clear the overgrowth?"

"You mean all of it?" Christos scratched at the fringe of hair along the edge of his mostly bald head when Ray nodded. "How soon?"

"The sooner the better." She might've said more, but at that moment, Ray's stomach grumbled loudly enough for everyone to hear. By everyone, Ray was pretty sure that included most of the surrounding counties.

Monica shot her a look of pure mortification. "Was that Ray-Ray?"

Ray pressed a hand to her empty belly. "Afraid the little fella's on the war path. It's almost noon. Is there a grocery store nearby?"

"There's one of them super centers about twenty minutes from here," Christos said, the distaste clear on his face, "but the produce is terrible. This time of year, the farmer's market is your best bet."

"I love a good farmer's market." Ray turned to Monica, clapping her hands together eagerly. "What do you say? Want to check it out with me?"

"The only thing I want to check out is the main house, specifically the bedroom." Monica lifted a hand to stifle a yawn. "I'm praying there's a bed."

"There's essentials, even if there's little else," Christos assured her, though having traveled with Monica twice now, Ray suspected his definition of what was necessary for comfort would be very different from Monica's, much like her own had been.

"There's a bed?" Monica looked at him sharply, almost as if she had been thinking along the same lines as Ray. "Sheets? Fresh towels?"

"Yes, all that," he answered.

"Thank goodness." Monica let out a long sigh, and once again, Ray was aware of how exhausted she looked. "You go ahead to the farmer's market without me. I'm all shopped out."

Ray reached into her back pocket and pulled out a notebook and pencil.

Monica frowned. "What's that for, a shopping list? If so, get me some granola bars."

"No," Ray replied. "I'm writing down this momentous date so I don't forget. September sixteenth. Monica Panty-topless is all shopped out."

Ray's walk from the vineyard to the town common was surprisingly short, only a few minutes along a winding, tree-lined road until she reached a spacious square of grass dotted with war monuments. There was a gazebo in the middle, festooned with a banner that announced a summer band concert series that had recently come to a close. All around the common were the quintessential buildings one associated with a small New England town: a church with a tall white steeple, a row of shops behind gracious turn-of-the-last century brick facades, a two-story wood frame building with a wide porch that had probably been a colonial era tavern, and a stone library clearly built in the days when libraries were taken very seriously even in the most out of the way little places.

The bells in the church steeple began to toll noon as Ray made her way to the jumble of tents that were the farmer's market. There were about two dozen stalls in all, each bustling with customers toting reusable shopping bags. Ray took her time, checking things out, her eyes wandering over the options. From fresh baked breads, to grass-fed meats, to fruits and vegetables bursting with end-of-season flavor, Ray knew she wouldn't go hungry.

Her first stop was a place called the Black Cat Farm, where apples, pears, cucumbers, peppers, and onions were artfully displayed in stacking baskets. Ray selected as many as her arms could hold, wishing she'd had the foresight to bring something to carry her purchases in. Instead of stocking up, she would have to settle for a few necessities and find out when the next market day was to get the rest. She began putting back a few of each item when an older woman approached her, silver hair pulled back in a bright red bandana.

"Would you like a bag?" the woman asked.

"I really would." Ray flashed her a sheepish grin. "I wasn't expecting to come out shopping today."

"Oh, what brings you into town?" she asked, pulling out a paper sack with handles from under the table. "Just passing through?"

"Actually, I'm going to be staying locally for a while, over at the vineyard." Ray prayed she wouldn't ask which one, because there was no way she would be able to say it without massacring the name.

"Do you have a car?"

"Back at the house, yes," Ray said, "but I walked down here. Total miscalculation on my part, considering I need a week's worth of groceries."

"Tell you what," the woman said, grabbing a basket filled with what looked like small fruits and vegetables made out of fabric. "If I can interest you in a reusable shopping bag, I'd be happy to drop your purchases off at the vineyard on my way home. Reusable is better for the planet, you know."

"Let me see." Ray picked up a strawberry about the size of her palm, and when she'd twisted the bag one way and another without figuring out how the thing could be expected to hold anything at all, the woman took it from her and popped it open into a full-size sack complete with long handles for carrying.

"That's fantastic." Ray grinned as she selected an apple, an eggplant, and an orange from the basket. "I'll get a few extra to be safe."

With enough produce to last several days safely stowed in one of the bags, Ray moved on to the next stall, which sold homemade baked goods. Ray's mouth started to water when her eyes roamed the scones, donuts, muffins, and cookies. Hell, even the pancake and donut mixes made Ray-Ray grumble loudly for all to hear. She selected two loaves of multigrain bread for home, and a huge blueberry muffin to placate her naughty belly.

With her hunger sated and enough groceries purchased to last a week, Ray stopped at a table selling socks, mittens, and cute knitted animals. One of them was an owl with huge, soulful blue eyes, which unaccountably made her think of Monica. The woman did have beautiful eyes, but why Ray would be thinking of them in the middle of a farmer's market was a mystery. Fortunately, the approach of a friendly looking woman in her mid-thirties, clearly the owner of the stand, meant Ray could ignore the question for another time.

"Morning. I'm Sally." The owner offered her hand.

"Hi, I'm Ray." She shook the woman's hand. "Did you make these?"

"I sure did. Knitting gives me something to do during the long winters."

Ray nodded, then picked up a dark brown bottle whose colorful label alone begged her to buy it. "Is the honey yours, too?"

"My husband's the beekeeper, but I designed the labels."

"No kidding?" Ray took a closer look and was even more impressed. "I have to be honest; the label is why I picked it up. I don't even need honey, but I'm going to buy this."

Sally laughed. "I'm going to let my husband know he owes me a commission."

"He really does," Ray agreed. "Are you an artist?"

"Graphic designer," Sally said. "My husband's in finance. We both work for companies in the city, but we can do it remotely, so we took a chance to get out of the rat race recently and bought an alpaca farm."

"Alpacas and bees? That's an interesting mix."

"Oh, you see a little bit of everything out here. You visiting the area?"

"Yes, well, no. I…er, we…will be staying at the house on the vineyard for the next few months." Ray pointed in the vague direction of the place over the hill and around the bend.

"Christos's place?"

"You know it?"

"Oh, sure. It's such a beautiful piece of land. It's too bad Christos doesn't do more with it. He'd make a killing if he did the farmer's market circuit. That man has a talent with wine."

"Is it really any good?" Ray frowned, remembering the generic bottles.

"One of the best I've tried, and I've done tastings at

dozens of wineries all around New England. If you mix his pink zinfandel with one of Brenda's wine slushy mixes, it's heaven in a glass."

"I've never heard of wine slushies."

Sally leaned forward, eyes wide. "You haven't lived. Have you been over to the Black Cat Farm tent yet?"

"I have. In fact, the lady over there with the bandana said she'd deliver all my bags to the house after the market closes."

"That's Brenda. She's really nice like that. Not to mention probably the best cook in central Mass. People come all the way from Boston for the farm to fork weekends at the Black Cat. That's probably half the reason Glen and I ended up out here." Sally turned toward the aforementioned tent and waved her hand in the air. "Hey, Brenda, you still have some of those wine slushy mixes? Put one in our friend Ray's bag, would ya? Charge it to my account."

"Aw, thanks," Ray said. "That's nice of you."

"Pink zin, don't forget, although honestly, every variety over there is amazing. I swear, I keep telling Christos he could sell twenty to thirty bottles every market day, but he says he can't keep up with that level of production. Crazy, considering how big that farm is."

"Yeah." Ray tapped her chin, recalling what Christos had said about the lack of pickers. If the wine was really that good, it was even more of a shame for the grapes to go to waste. "How many market days are there, exactly?"

"This one's twice a week, and there are others in surrounding towns. Between Glen and me, we try to do four per week from June through November, but some vendors do multiple stands every day, maybe ten or fifteen each week."

Ray did some quick calculations. Ten or fifteen per week, times thirty bottles at twenty bucks each equaled...well, a lot of money. "I'm not sure, though. Have you seen those labels? They don't exactly sell the product like yours do."

Sally's eyebrows arched. "Sounds like you have more than a passing interest in this vineyard."

Ray shrugged. "It's complicated, but yeah, my fiancée and I have sort of an ownership stake, I guess you'd say."

"Fiancée?" Sally's voice did that high-pitched thing women so often did when they smelled a wedding and were itching for the full scoop. "When's the big day?"

"That's complicated, too," Ray said with a chuckle. "Hey, I don't suppose that between your job and your alpacas, plus the bees and the knitting, you have any time to ever take on some design work on the side?"

"As a matter of fact, I do." Sally reached into her pocket and pulled out a business card, handing it to Ray. "I've been trying to get Christos to give me a shot at doing something with his labels for months. If you can send those my way, I'd sure rather spend this winter doing that than knitting owls."

"I'll see what I can do," Ray promised and grabbed up the owl with Monica's eyes. "I kinda like the owls, though. I'm gonna add this little guy to my purchases."

"Don't be silly," Sally said, taking the owl and adding it to the bag with the honey. "It's on the house."

CHAPTER ELEVEN

Considering the disastrous state of its exterior, the inside of the farmhouse had turned out to offer much less disappointment than Monica had been expecting. The cheerful floral wallpaper, so full of country charm that it would probably be considered on trend in certain crowds, was in surprisingly good condition. The wide plank floors, too, seemed free of any major defects besides a coating of thick gray dust. Brianna would be horrified by the place, but the truth was Monica kind of liked it. There was a hominess to it that had always felt lacking in Monica's place, or rather her former place, with Bri. If anything, it wasn't so much what was in the farmhouse that caused her dissatisfaction, but what was missing.

Basically, furniture. In that, there was none. Or not much, anyway. A single sofa sat in the living room, a small table and two chairs in the kitchen, and precious little else. The house had four bedrooms, but two of them were completely empty except for lace curtains on the windows, yellowed on the edges and in desperate need of a good washing. The other two rooms each had a twin bed with matching, rusty iron frames. No dressers, no nightstands, and nothing more than a thin cotton blanket and single pillow on each one to offer any sort of comfort. At that particular moment, Monica didn't really care. As long as the sheets were clean and the surface was flat, she wasn't going to complain.

Stripping off her clothes, she pulled her new nightgown from the suitcase and snapped off the tag. She hadn't been able to resist it in the store, but had been too embarrassed to wear it the night before with Ray in the room. It wasn't because it was sexy or revealing. Far from it, actually. The sleeveless gown fell nearly to the floor, a sheer cotton lawn in a blue floral print, trimmed in white lace at the neck and hem. Brianna had called them granny nighties, teasing so mercilessly when she came across a similar one in a drawer that Monica had gotten rid of it on the spot. But the truth was, she loved those shapeless gowns. They were cool against her skin and made her feel fresh and feminine, unlike all the Victoria's Secret nightmares Bri had loved her in so much but that made her feel like she was putting on a show that she didn't want to be in.

The funny thing was, Ray probably wouldn't have said a word about the nightgown, or even noticed. It was painfully obvious Ray wasn't into her. Not that Monica wanted her to be—of course not—but still, had there ever been a woman who'd shown *less* interest in her? Even straight women at least admired Monica for her fashion sense, even if they didn't want to sleep with her. But not the handy ma'am. Like it or not, Ray's total indifference, or disdain if Monica was totally honest, was a bit of an ego blow.

Meanwhile, Monica could barely keep from drooling.

She hated herself for how much Ray's presence threw her off. It's not like she even liked the woman. She was annoying, and argumentative, and such a know it all. But when Ray had held her arm out to her earlier and told her to touch it, Monica's panties had gotten wet. For real wet, like she was starring in a bad porno. Monica simply did not get turned on like that, ever. It had taken every ounce of strength for her to get out of the situation with her dignity intact. She felt hot all over just thinking about it, and the worst part was she couldn't decide if the heat she felt was good or bad.

Stop thinking about her, Monica begged herself, pulling the sheet over her head. At this rate, she would never get any sleep.

Eventually she dozed off, but it seemed like only moments later, Monica's phone blared with the dark drumbeat of "Enter Sandman" by Metallica. It was the song one of her cousins had ascribed to Brianna's number while they were sitting vigil at the hospital, and Monica had forgotten to change it.

"I'm sleeping," Monica snapped, having absolutely zero energy to put into politeness.

"Must be nice to be you." Damn Bri and that tone of hers that implied so perfectly that she thought Monica did nothing except sit around watching soap operas and eating bonbons all day. What the hell were bonbons, anyway? Monica was certain she'd never had one.

"It's always so charming to speak to you. Was that all you wanted, to call and get in a dig?" In the past, Monica had always let it slide, placating Bri to keep the peace, but in her sleep-deprived state, still raw from the loss of her grandmother and her house, she'd had about enough. She'd been so impressed with Bri's accomplishments when they'd first met, so wowed by the way her presence filled a room. How had she never realized before that Bri only had two modes, fake and mean?

"Like I have time for chitchat." Monica could almost hear Bri's eyes rolling through the phone. "We have to talk now that the house is sold."

"Yeah, I saw they changed the sign." Monica's words dripped with sarcasm. "Thanks for the heads-up."

"I can see you're going to make things difficult."

Right, because Monica was the unreasonable one in this scenario. "Cut to the chase, will you?"

"You weren't home, and I wasn't sure where you were or when you were coming back, so I've boxed up your things, and I need to know where I should send them."

Monica bolted upright in bed. "You've packed my things? I've only been gone two days."

"The buyers want a quick closing, and nearly everything in the house was mine, anyway, except your clothes and Mr. Fluffles."

"Mr. Fluffles also belongs—" Monica stopped mid-sentence as it struck her she didn't have the heart to abandon a cat, even one as high maintenance as Mr. Fluffles, to her ex's less than tender mercies. "You know what? Never mind. I'll take him. But can this wait until I get back?"

"Where are you, anyway, at your parents'?"

"I'm on my new vineyard." Monica may have been gloating a little when she said it. For once, she knew she had something that Bri would be envious of.

"Your what?" It was clear Bri wasn't taking her seriously.

"Vineyard. I own a vineyard." Monica relished delivering this bit of news. She only regretted not being able to see Bri's jaw hit the floor. "I inherited it from my grandmother."

"Seriously. I don't have time for your little daydreams and games. I need an address, or I'll drop

Mr. Fluffles off at a shelter and donate your stuff to Goodwill."

"You will do no such thing." Although honestly, Monica could picture her doing both, the heartless bitch. "How did I ever think I was in love with you? I don't even like you."

"I don't remember you complaining when you got to live in a nice house and drive that fancy car I got you, Moany. So, give me a break on the lectures. Where are you, really?"

"Boston. Or just outside, anyway."

"So it is true?" Bri's voice had a strange, strangled quality to it.

"What?" The conversation had Monica completely lost. Did Bri finally believe her about the vineyard?

"I saw the photos on Instagram, but I didn't think it was possible." Bri snorted. "I thought you had better taste."

"What the hell are you talking about?" Monica tossed the blankets off her, bolting out of the bedroom and descending the stairs toward the kitchen. She needed to pace away some of this nervous energy, since throttling her ex through the phone was impossible.

"The photos of you with that handy ma'am I hired. I had no idea at the time her list of services was quite this extensive. Of course, I also never knew you had a secret desire for a bull d—"

"She's no such thing!" Her vision going red,

Monica cut her off before Bri could complete her offensive description. Masculine of center, sure, or maybe soft butch would be a good descriptor, but Ray wasn't…the broader implications of what Bri had said finally sank in. "Wait. What do you mean by you saw the pictures?"

"It's all over social media." Brianna made a *tsk* sound, brimming with judgement. "I understand a rebound fling, Moany, but marriage? You really are taking this whole breakup worse than I imagined, hashtag PantyWedding."

"You're one of my social media followers?" Monica's body went cold. She stopped her pacing long enough to lean against the wall beside the refrigerator. It had never occurred to her that Brianna, or anyone she knew in real life for that matter, would follow her. It felt like a violation of privacy.

"Oh, get over yourself, Miss La-di-da Podcaster. You just want me to sound hurt that you're marrying that plaid-wearing lumberjack, or should I say Lumber Jane?"

"Stop. Insulting. Ray." Monica growled, channeling every ounce of irritation into the low, guttural sound. Bri could be horrible to her all she wanted. Monica was used to it. But somehow when she turned her vitriol on Ray, it crossed a line. "I'll have you know that woman is the most genuine person I've ever met. What's more, she's chivalrous, and she sure as hell is worth a million of you!"

Monica launched herself away from the wall and flipped around so she could resume her furious pacing in the wide-open stretch that was the almost empty living room. Her path was blocked by Ray, who was standing in the doorway between the kitchen and living room with an unreadable expression on her face.

Shit!

Ray crossed to the counter carrying a single bag, which she placed beside the sink. It was impossible for Monica to tell how much she'd overheard, or what she was thinking. Had Monica mentioned Ray's name, or anything else that would let her know she'd been the topic of conversation?

Her stomach in a knot, Monica turned her back on Ray and ducked into the living room, lowering her voice. "I've gotta go. I'll text you the address in Massachusetts, since it looks like I may be here for a few months getting things sorted out."

"Great," Bri said with all the cheeriness of someone wrapping up a business deal instead of a serious relationship. "I'll ship the clothing tomorrow."

"And Mr. Fluffles?" Monica felt a pang of sympathy for the poor cat. Brianna had never been perfect even on their best days, but she'd never dreamed the woman would be so heartless as to fluff off Mr. Fluffles. "Surely you can't be planning to send him through the mail, too."

"No, I'll arrange for a courier to bring him up this weekend. Enjoy your honeymoon."

As the line clicked silent, Monica sucked in a deep breath. Ray was puttering around in the other room, opening the fridge door and sliding out one of the plastic drawers inside. There was still no indication what Ray had overheard, or how it had affected her.

How should Monica handle this pickle?

She tiptoed back into the kitchen. "We're, er… getting the cat."

Ray blinked. "What?"

"Mr. Fluffles." Monica looked intently at the floor. "Bri's already packed up the house and is shipping my things here, along with the cat."

"She's shipping a cat?" Ray looked horrified.

"No, although I double checked because I wouldn't put it past her to try. He's coming this weekend by courier."

"Oh." Ray nodded, appearing to think this over. Monica held her breath, belatedly realizing that as fiancées, even fake ones, she probably should've run this past Ray before committing. Fortunately, Ray simply shrugged. "Okay, well, we might need a good mouser."

"Mr. Fluffles?" She couldn't help herself. Monica howled with laughter. "You've met him. Does he strike you as the mousing type?"

Ray cracked a smile. "Only if the mouse is served up on a silver platter, lightly sautéed in butter."

Still no hint Ray had heard what Monica said about her. In that case, Monica decided to take the easy way out and pretend it had never happened. She pointed to the bag and was about to ask if that was all Ray had bought, but as she looked closer, she realized the bag was red with white polka dots and a frill of green at the top, and was so taken aback that what actually came out was, "Where the hell did that come from?"

A flicker of annoyance creased Ray's brow. "I bought it at one of the farm stands. In fact, the owner, Brenda, will be coming by in a few minutes to bring the rest of the groceries."

"Brenda, huh?" An image formed in Monica's mind of a young, fresh-faced country girl with long, red braids, and Monica's jaw tensed. "You're making friends quickly, I see."

"She was very nice. Sally, too."

Sally, too? How many women were there in this one-horse town? "Looks like there's a pickup truck pulling into the driveway."

Ray opened the side door, waving to the woman who got out of the truck. Monica noted with some satisfaction the woman's silver hair and red bandana and hoped Sally would turn out to be her even older sister.

"In here," Ray called out, meeting Brenda halfway to relieve her of as many bags as she could carry. Apparently, Ray had bought out the entire farmer's market. Monica was certain she didn't buy half that much for an entire month.

"You'll want to add the pink zin and then put this

in the freezer right away so it doesn't melt." Brenda bustled into the kitchen and went straight to work like she owned the place, fitting a plastic bag of something red onto the top shelf of the freezer. When she was done, she gave the table and chairs a hard look. "I see Christos hasn't done much to spruce up the place before your arrival."

"It was very last minute," Ray explained, retrieving a bottle of wine and a corkscrew from the cabinet. "I haven't had a chance to look around yet."

"I'm afraid you're likely to find most of the rooms empty," Brenda told her. "If you're planning to stay a while, there's a used furniture store a few miles down the road with some real bargains."

Monica's lips curled in distaste at the word "used," while Ray's eyes lit up. "I'll have to check that out, although depending on what's needed, I have some things in a storage pod I might want to bring up. This could be just the place for them."

Things in storage? Great. Just what this run-down place needed, a mishmash of used crap. Monica wondered exactly when Ray had been planning to discuss this decorating decision with her, conveniently putting aside the fact she'd already committed them to a cat without any input from the better half. Based on Ray's enthusiasm for used furniture, not to mention plaid in all its many forms, Monica could only imagine what would be coming. Bookshelves made of cinderblock? Whatever. This was a temporary living arrangement, and it would be cheaper than buying furniture they'd have to sell when they put the vineyard on the market.

When it became apparent no one else was going to start introductions, Monica cleared her throat and said, "Hi. I'm Monica Panagiotopoulos."

Brenda gave her a sharp look, recognition dawning in her eyes. A smile warmed her face. "Of course, you are. I was so sorry to hear of your grandmother's passing. She and my mother were great friends. I still make your grandmother's baklava recipe every Easter."

Monica nodded, a bit dazed. It was weird to think her grandmother'd had this whole other life at one time, and she'd never been aware of it. Before she could come up with a reply, Brenda clapped her hands together in a sudden burst of excitement.

"Speaking of cooking, that reminds me. I wanted to invite you ladies to the farm and fork dinner Thursday night at the Black Cat."

"Sally told me about that," Ray said, and Monica was glad at least one of them knew what the woman was talking about. Farms? Forks? Cats? "Is there a website where I can sign up and buy tickets?"

"It's been sold out for weeks," Brenda replied, "but I want you two to come as my special guests, as a little engagement gift. I'll have a table for two set aside, six o'clock."

"How very generous," Ray said. "We'd love to."

Once again, all Monica could manage was a dumb nod. A muscle twitched in her neck. Was there anyone left in the world who didn't know all of her personal business? Not to mention this was now the second decision Ray had made without consulting her, which did not bode well for their fake future together.

When Brenda left, Monica let out a sound that was somewhere between a laugh and a sigh. "The list of people who know about this little arrangement of ours is growing by the minute."

"Oh?" Not exactly offering her undivided attention, Ray searched the cabinets, pulling out a cutting board. "Omelet?"

"Huh?" It took a moment for it to register that the woman was planning to cook something, like from scratch. Ray cooked? That was about the last thing Monica saw coming. "Oh, uh—sure."

"Spicy or garden delight."

Damn. All of a sudden, Ray was looking straight at her, and that woman's eyes were the very definition of spicy, reigniting the fever of those dreams that'd kept Monica up all of last night. *Just say no to spice.*

"Garden delight." Monica took in the growing pile of supplies on the counter. Did Ray really know what she was doing? "Can I help?"

"Can you cook?" Ray shot back.

"No."

"Then sit back, princess." Ray cracked an egg into a bowl. "Watch and learn."

Monica stiffened, mindful of her earlier conversation with Bri. "I'm not useless, you know. I can take care of myself."

"I didn't mean to imply otherwise," Ray assured her. She placed an assortment of veggies on the cutting board and began dicing with expert precision. "I meant that you still look exhausted. Did you manage to get a nap?"

"Not enough of one," Monica admitted, yawning. "Oh, guess what. Bri knows we're getting married. She was quite rude about it."

Ray put a skillet on the burner and poured in some oil. "I'm sure everyone knows by now. I'm surprised your mom hasn't called yet."

"My mom? Why would—" Monica's hand flew to her mouth. If Brianna had followed her on social media, what were the chances her mom did, too? And everyone else she knew, for that matter. "You don't actually think my family has seen the news, do you?"

Ray gave her a look that said *get real*.

Oh God.

Monica's heart started banging around her ribcage like a mouse trapped under a box.

"Have you checked your messages? I know it's not your thing." Ray winked, damn her, and Monica had to cross her legs to keep her body in check. At a time like this, with the prospect of explaining to her mother why she'd been the last to hear about her only daughter's impending nuptials, how was it possible that any part of her could be distracted by sex?

Hand shaking, Monica looked at her phone. Seventeen missed calls from her mother. Three from her cousin Nina. One each from Maddie and Trish. The corners of her vision blackened as she struggled to catch her breath.

"Hee…" was the only sound Monica could squeeze from her lungs. "He-he-he!"

Ray whipped around from the stove, alarm written all over her face. "Are you okay?"

"He-he-he!"

"Oh, God. You're hyperventilating. Bag. Paper bag." Ray's eyes swept the kitchen, seizing one with bananas in it, which she unceremoniously dumped onto the floor. "Here. Breathe into this. Slowly."

Monica did as she was told. She was in no shape to argue. Hands planted on the table in front of her, it was all she could do to keep from blacking out.

The reassuring comfort of a hand pressed into her back, rubbing in deliberate circular motions.

"It's going to be okay, sweetheart," Ray said, or at least that's what Monica heard. Had she really said it, or was it wishful thinking? Monica had no idea. "I'm here. I won't let anything happen to you. That's right. Keep taking in long, deep breaths. You're going to be okay."

As Monica rested her head on the cold Formica surface in front of her, all she could see was a stunning pair of dark blue eyes staring deeply into her soul. She'd be okay, Ray had said, and looking into those eyes, how could Monica not believe it?

CHAPTER TWELVE

Sometime later, after Monica had regained her breath, and enough composure to eat, Ray stood at the sink with a soapy sponge, finishing the last of the dishes.

"Are you sure you don't want help?" Monica asked, her voice still sounding a little shaky despite eating an extra-large omelet. "In my family, the rule was always the cook doesn't do the cleanup."

"Not a bad rule." Ray glanced over her shoulder, finding Monica looking as out of sorts as she'd sounded. "Given what happened earlier, it's probably better if you stay seated."

Fire flashed in Monica's eyes. "I'm not helpless."

Ray put up her soapy hands as if to ward off the woman's ire. "Not implying you are. Look, this might come as a surprise to you, but I'm the caregiving type."

"Really?" Monica's skepticism was plain on her face.

"I swear. Wish I could say it wasn't true, as it's gotten me into more trouble than you'd believe." Ray opened the freezer, poking at the pink bag inside. "I have some great news."

"This has all been a dream." Monica guzzled her water. "We're not really getting married, which means I have not ignored seventeen calls from my mother demanding to know why she wasn't informed of the wedding."

"Sadly, you're still engaged to me. But on the bright side, we have wine slushies."

Monica's face puckered. "I have no idea what that is, but it's a hard no."

"If you have no idea what it is, then why refuse before finding out?" Ray shook her head, bemused beyond all reason by this woman's snobbish streak. "For all you know, this is going to knock your socks off. Also, I think some booze might take the edge off your current mental state."

"Now I'm a mental case in addition to being weak?" Monica crossed her arms, showcasing her curves.

Damn. The woman could be infuriating and sexy as hell. Why, oh why, couldn't she just be annoying? Ray was used to dealing with straight-up bitches. They were easy to put in their place. But a sexy one with a vulnerable streak? That added layer upon layer of complications. Getting married was one thing, but having to tamp down parts of Ray that had been dormant, for good reason, was making everything so much worse.

"What time is it, anyway?" Monica swiveled her head as if in search of a clock. "It can't possibly be late enough for drinks."

"You know what they say. It's five o'clock somewhere. Come on. Let's move this party to the couch." Ray paused, feeling doubtful. "There is a couch, isn't there?"

"Yes, but not much else." Monica's expression clouded, her tone growing testy. "I guess it's a good thing you're bringing all that furniture."

"I'm sorry about that." Ray dried her hands on the single dish towel she'd found in a drawer. "I realized after I said it I probably should've run it past you first."

Monica gave a slight shrug. "It's okay. I should've talked to you about Mr. Fluffles. Good thing this is all only temporary, I guess."

Ray continued wiping her hands for several more seconds, even though they were good and dry. It gave her something to do other than say what was on her mind. The problem was, ever since they'd arrived at the vineyard that morning, Ray'd had the strongest feeling, like maybe this wasn't so temporary after all. She'd felt something she hadn't felt in years, or possibly ever: a sense of being home. But how could she explain that to Monica when their whole deal was based on cashing in and moving on?

Ray took the slushies from the freezer. She hadn't been sure how much pink zinfandel to add, so she'd gone ahead and used the whole bottle. She'd come across two big plastic cups and straws in the cupboard, the refillable type like the ones you could get from an amusement park or county fair. She divided the slushies fifty-fifty, then followed Monica into the living room, already anticipating the rant her companion would go on as soon as she saw she was being served a drink in a giant plastic cup.

"Here you go." The fact that Monica simply took the cup from her and sank into the corner of the couch told Ray more than words about the woman's mental state. "Still feeling those jitters?"

"You'd have the jitters too if you belonged to my family. I don't think you understand how them finding out is a game changer." Monica sipped so long from her straw Ray was sure she would get brain freeze. "That just-for-the-cameras fake wedding we had planned has gone right out the window."

"What do you mean?"

"My mother knows, Ray. She can't attend a fake wedding. We're going to have to do it for real."

Ray's throat closed a little, choking her as reality sank in. "Okay, but we can still keep it small, right? Not make it into too big a deal?"

Monica snorted. "I'm Greek. You've seen that movie, right?"

Now it was Ray's turn to be on the verge of hyperventilating. "I did not sign up for that. I am not converting to Greek Orthodox and roasting a full lamb on a spit in the front yard."

"No, I'm not asking for that. But we're both going to have to face the fact that the heat got turned up a notch on us. Leave my family to me. I'll do everything in my power to keep this from turning into a nightmare. I promise."

A real wedding with actual guests? What part of that wasn't already a nightmare?

Ray half sat, half tumbled into the sofa's opposite corner, leaving the middle cushion empty between them. Considering this most recent turn of events, she needed a drink. She took a sip of her own slushy, stifling a moan. It was every bit as good as Sally had promised. "What I don't understand is how you didn't think they'd find out? Didn't you ever plan on telling them?"

"Not a chance in hell!"

"But—it's all over your social media."

"How was I supposed to know my mom, aunt, and all my female cousins were following me on Instagram?" Monica took another long swig. "I feel like I've just found out I have stalkers."

"Isn't that the point of social media?" Ray felt like there was something she wasn't getting. Was she being slow? It was certainly possible. "I mean, isn't that what everyone wants, to have followers?"

"Yes, but not my family." After another sip of slushy, Monica's eyebrows shot to her hairline. "Oh, wow."

"Headache?" Ray leaned forward slightly. "You're not going to hyperventilate again, are you?"

"No," Monica assured her, shifting into a more comfortable position. "This is just super good."

Ray took a long, slow pull from her straw. "I know, right?"

"Better than good. Better than…" Monica pressed her lips together before finishing her thought, and Ray felt certain she'd been about to say sex but thought better of it. "You know, good."

"You need to trust me more, darlin'."

Ray gulped as she heard the term of endearment slip from her lips. It was the second time in as many hours, though she was pretty sure the first had gone undetected by Monica, who'd been preoccupied with trying to breathe. This time, though, Monica's chin snapped upward, and her eyes zeroed in on Ray's with laser-like focus. She'd heard it, all right. Now all Ray could do was suck on her straw like an idiot and do her best not to read too much into the warm sensation coursing through her, which wasn't due in even a small part to the frozen booze.

After several seconds, it occurred to Ray that Monica might let her little faux pas slide. She hurried to redirect the conversation to be sure. "Why didn't you think your family followed you on social media?"

"Because it's my job. I don't follow any of my cousins' professional accounts." Monica's head drooped, her focus shifting to the empty sofa cushion. "No need to remind myself how much more successful they are."

Damn it, there she went with the whole damsel in distress routine. It wasn't even like she was trying to milk the situation, at least Ray didn't think so. And she'd had enough experience with seemingly helpless vipers in her past to recognize when she ran the risk of being bitten by one. When Monica got that wounded look, it was all Ray could do not to swoop in and try to carry her to safety. No matter how many times she'd sworn she was done with all that.

Steeling her resolve, Ray turned to the generic pep talk approach to keep Monica at arm's length. "I'm sure your family's impressed by what you've accomplished."

"Let me see if I can explain." Monica took another sip. "My family has taken the American immigrant experience and super-sized it. My grandparents came here with very little. They worked hard. They put every one of their children through college. They became doctors and lawyers, and they put their kids through college, and now they're expected not to be doctors and lawyers but surgeons and judges. I majored in party planning."

"Is that an official degree?"

"No. See the problem? How does that compare to an uncle who was on the team that did the first heart transplant, or a cousin who's clerking for a Supreme Court justice?"

"Did you want to be a doctor or lawyer?"

"Not at all." More than three-quarters of Monica's slushy was gone, lubricating the free flow of her words as her body language became more animated. "It doesn't matter if I wanted to be a doctor or lawyer. I knew that's what they all wanted, so when I failed to live up to my end of the bargain, I let my family down."

"Are you sure they really felt that way?" Ray thought back to when she'd met Monica's family. She hadn't met the whole extended clan, but certainly Monica's *yiayia*, and even her parents, hadn't really given off the disappointed vibe Monica described. "Maybe you've read more into their expectations than were there."

To Ray's surprise, Monica let out a soft laugh. "No maybe about it. I have a knack for knowing what other people want, even when they might not know it themselves or be able to put it into words."

"Must be why you're so good at your job," Ray offered.

"And so bad at relationships," Monica countered. "The problem is, as soon as I meet a woman I like, I start picking up on what she wants me to be. I don't do it on purpose. I don't even know it's happening, until suddenly I realize I've changed everything about myself to make her happy, and she ends up hating me for it."

"You?" Ray couldn't hold in a snicker. "I can't imagine you giving in on anything."

"Well, that's because I'm not in a relationship with you." Monica giggled. "Aside from the tiny little detail of being engaged."

"You're the most stubborn woman I've ever met, next to me, anyway." Ray shook her head wistfully. "I don't give in on anything, even when maybe I should."

"You sure about that?" Monica gave her a funny look, one that said she wasn't quite buying what Ray was selling.

"Why?" Ray couldn't figure out what she was getting at, until she saw Monica staring pointedly at her floral print shirt. "Oh, this. You probably think I bought it to mess with you, and I did, but you wanna know a secret? Before I even walked into the store, I spotted this and really liked it."

"Oh, yeah?" Monica's eyes twinkled with mischief. "And how's that underwear I picked for you working out."

"Honest truth? My pussy has never been treated so well." As Ray made a show of wiggling her bottom against the couch, it occurred to her the wine slushy might be going to her head. "Too bad I have all these fancy undies and am cooped up here with a woman who recoils from my touch."

"I do not." Monica bolted upright. "When did I do that?"

"When we were walking down to meet Christos this morning, and I showed you the goose bumps on my arm, you looked at me like the thought of touching me was the worst thing in the world." Ray's insides twisted as she said it, and it was only then she realized how much Monica's reaction had hurt. She braced herself, expecting Monica to laugh at her revelation, but instead, the woman quietly scooted closer.

"You really thought that's what I was thinking?" Monica's face crumpled, stuck somewhere between concern and shame. "That wasn't it at all. I knew better than to touch you; that's all. Too dangerous."

Monica's whole demeanor was so earnest, her flushed pink cheeks and darkened pupils hinting at how hard the alcohol was hitting her system. Ray could put her on the spot, press for more details on exactly why a touch would've been so dangerous, but it would be wrong to take advantage to stroke her own ego.

"I've made it kind of a habit to fall hard for the super femme, helpless types," Ray said, as much to herself as to Monica. "Let's face it. The way I dress and present myself sometimes makes certain types of women think I'm a safe way to test out their own sexual curiosity. My problem is, I get attached too quickly without truly getting to know a person."

"They didn't feel the same?" Monica guessed.

Talk about an understatement. Ray shut her eyes, blocking out the bad memories. "Doesn't matter. I've learned my lesson, and that won't be happening."

"What won't, falling for the wrong woman?"

"Falling for anybody at all," Ray corrected. "Over the past few years, I've learned to shut that part down. My heart only does what it's meant to do now. It pumps blood to keep me alive."

"You're telling me you don't feel anything, no emotions at all?"

"I'm not a sociopath, Monica. I've figured out how to keep all the messy emotions at bay." Ray ran a hand down in front of her face, as if pulling down a window shade. "When I turned thirty, I had an epiphany. The only way for me to be happy is to be alone."

"You're not exactly alone right now," Monica pointed out, her face growing thoughtful.

Ray frowned. "What do you mean?"

"Well, we are getting married, not to mention we'll have to live in this house together while we plan the wedding. What if something happens between us?"

"Something, like what?" Ray wasn't dumb. She had more than an inkling where Monica's thinking was going, but the wine slushy had made the woman delightfully open to discussing things she never would normally and had lowered Ray's resistance enough that she could no longer stop herself from pushing buttons she knew she would be better off leaving alone.

"Earlier, you asked me why I wouldn't touch you. You want to know why?" Monica swallowed hard, touching her tongue to her lips in an unconscious gesture that made Ray realize too late she wasn't so much pushing buttons as playing with fire. "It's because last night in the hotel, I had a sex dream about you."

"You did?" The room seemed to grow warmer, and Ray could no longer ignore the tingling sensation coming from within the ridiculously soft underwear Monica had bought her. Damn that overly pampered pussy. Petunia would not be as easily reined in if Ray had on a scratchy pair of boy shorts. Why had she not shut this conversation down?

"It was hot. I mean, hotter than hot." Monica drew closer, her long lashes shading impossibly blue eyes. "And super realistic. Like, we were in the hotel room, right there where we really were, you know? You got up off the couch, and you stripped off all your clothes and climbed into bed with me. When I woke up, I could still feel your skin against mine, and it took forever to realize it had only been a dream."

"Oh." *Wow, Ray, good response there, buddy.*

Monica closed the gap between them, giving Ray a chance to notice how amazing Monica smelled. What was it, jasmine? Musk? They weren't touching, but their arms were so close Ray wasn't convinced even a spark of daylight would show through the gap. Not that there was much of that left. The sun had mostly set by now, casting the living room in deep shadow.

"If I'd known at three o'clock this morning you weren't into sex, I might've gotten more sleep." Monica poked her shoulder teasingly, then seemed to lose track of what she was doing, leaving her hand to rest on Ray's shoulder.

"I'm not opposed to sex," Ray heard herself say, though she knew it was exactly the wrong response. But the frozen wine had made her thinking fuzzy, and meanwhile, whatever was making Monica smell like that, Ray wanted to take a bath in it.

"How did we get into this?" Monica rested her head on Ray's shoulder, seeming to dwarf in size. "The wedding. My family…"

Sensing how overwhelmed Monica was, Ray instinctively wrapped an arm around her, pulling her close. That aforementioned heart—the one that she'd so carefully built into an impregnable fortress—lurched as it filled with the same sense of peace she'd felt when she first saw the vineyard, the unexplainable but achingly real sense of being exactly where she was supposed to be.

Monica let out a contented sigh.

Ray inhaled deeply, her sight blurring.

"Thanks for being so supportive." Monica's voice was low, brimming with sincerity.

"Hey, it's what fake fiancées do, right?" Ray tried to chuckle like it was no big deal, but she was holding Monica, and it felt so damn right, so perfect.

This was bad.

Disastrous, even.

Monica glanced up, batting those long lashes. "This feels good, doesn't it?"

Ray gulped but nodded because apparently, she'd fallen under Monica's spell, and it had become impossible for her to lie.

"You're really so sweet, and you have amazing lips." Monica ran a finger over Ray's bottom lip. "So full."

Petunia's zinging set off a red alarm, like a dam about to burst, but Ray was incapable of taking action, of moving to safety. Like an idiot, she kept sitting where she was, waiting to drown.

"I wonder what they feel like."

"Like lips." Ray struggled valiantly to keep her head above water, grasping at any life preserver she could find. "You're touching them right now."

"I didn't mean that way, silly." Monica inched so close Ray could feel the woman's breath against her neck. "Maybe I should try it and find out. Isn't that what you said earlier about the wine slushies? Maybe it would knock my socks off."

Before Ray could respond, their lips met in a moment of searing heat.

This shouldn't be happening.

But when Monica deepened the kiss, Ray not only let her, but she gave into the sensation, allowing her tongue to taste and explore and letting Monica do the same. Their lips crushed against the other, their bodies becoming entwined.

It was a good thing Ray was sitting down, because this wasn't a "socks getting knocked off" type of a kiss. It was the knee-buckling kind.

One she didn't want to end. Ever.

Every time she thought she'd need to break for air, Monica ramped things up, making Ray forget about everything, even the need to breathe. What was air when you had a woman like Monica kissing you?

Ray savored the taste of her on her lips, mixed with a hint of frozen pink zinfandel. That was what finally brought Ray back from the brink of sweet oblivion.

This is wrong.

Finally, Ray's senses started to come back to her, most importantly her senses of self-preservation and decency. Monica was drunk, and Ray was being a fool.

She knew where this would lead. The same place it had always led, every time Ray let herself fall too deeply and open herself up to the wrong woman. And was there any question Monica was the wrong kind of woman? They couldn't be in a room together for a minute without fighting like cats and dogs.

Meanwhile, Monica—who had not gotten the memo about Ray's sudden change of plans—slid her hand under Ray's shirt.

Ray pulled back. "We need to stop."

"But why?" Monica pouted and reached out to touch her again, but Ray held her ground and stood to put distance between them. "I thought you weren't opposed to sex."

"I'm not," which was probably more than Ray should admit, but she still found herself unable to lie outright to Monica, "but you've clearly had too much alcohol, and it doesn't seem right."

Monica's eyes flashed with anger. "Every time I think I'm starting to figure you out, you make a U-turn." Monica rose to her feet and wobbled.

Ray's arm shot out to steady her. "There's nothing to figure out." Much as it pained her, Ray slowly removed her hands from Monica's waist, making sure she could stand on her own. "You're drunk. I'm not. I'm doing the right thing. You'll thank me tomorrow."

"The hell I will," Monica spat, stumbling from the room.

The stairs squeaked under Monica's heavy footfall. Ray held her breath, expecting a terrible tumble, but after some impressive banging and thumping, she heard one of the upstairs doors slam. Even so, Ray found it impossible to relax or regain any sense of composure.

Ray could feel herself falling, and it had to stop.

As crazy as Monica drove her, that pampered princess was no different from any other woman who'd already wreaked havoc on her life. She'd breeze through, take what she wanted, and leave a trail of destruction in her wake. She might seem different, and Ray might be fooled into thinking she was worth it, but in the end, she wouldn't be. In the end, she would leave, and Ray would be alone.

It happened every time.

CHAPTER THIRTEEN

"What fresh hell is this?"

A chainsaw buzzed maddeningly, vibrating the very molecules of air in Monica's lungs as it chewed mercilessly through what certainly must have been the world's biggest tree. Given the terrible racket, she was half convinced she would open her eyes to find a crew of lumberjacks actually standing inside her bedroom.

Monica grasped her throbbing temples. Dear God, how much of that frozen wine had she drunk the night before? The chainsaw revved again, and Monica lurched out of bed and stumbled to the window. They weren't exactly lumberjacks, but half a dozen men in dirt-stained jeans and bright green T-shirts stood in the jumbled garden below, surrounded by landscaping equipment.

"Ray!"

There was a loud thud next door, as if Ray had rolled onto the floor. It was followed by an indeterminate grumble, which Monica could hear despite the thickness of the old plaster walls. From the sound of things, apparently her darling fiancée had over imbibed as well. Good. Considering the humiliating way she'd flat out rejected Monica's advances, that woman deserved the mother of all hangovers.

"Get in here!" Monica hollered, wincing as her voice echoed in the cavernous space between her ears where her brain usually was. Further proof she'd lost her mind, as her behavior the night before attested to. Had that kiss really happened? Maybe Monica would be super lucky, and it would turn out it was a dream, like the one she'd had the night before. A totally hot, really realistic dream.

"What's wrong?" The sheepish look on Ray's face and the way she studiously avoided Monica's eyes as she stood in the doorway, still wearing the now rumpled flower shirt she'd had on the night before, were all the clues Monica needed to know it had not been a dream.

Ignoring the flutter in her belly, Monica pointed a finger at the window and summoned as much rage as she could manage. The fact her head felt like it was about to pop from her neck helped raise her anger level to a solid seven, at least. "When did you hire a landscaper?"

Ray rubbed her eyes, tugging at the hem of her

shirt, which Monica only now realized ended to reveal a bare expanse of shapely thighs.

Shit.

"I haven't hired anyone."

"Yeah, right." Monica's anger meter shot to a nine, because how dare Ray wander around without pants? "You keep making decisions around here like you own the place."

Okay, fine, Ray would own half eventually, but she didn't yet. Neither of them did. Not until after the wedding. That wedding they were actually going to have to have now, with guests, and flowers, and a cake...

"Breathe, Monica," Ray urged, unable to hide her concern.

Monica sucked in a breath, realizing she'd been on the verge of hyperventilating again. On top of the killer headache, that was probably the last thing she needed.

Ray's expression grew more relaxed as Monica's breathing steadied. "I saw Christos pull up. Let me go outside and see what's going on."

Ray disappeared into her room, coming out a minute later wearing the skinny jeans Monica had chosen for her, along with a tight T-shirt that came from God only knew where. Had Ray bought it when they were in Boston, and if so, had she grabbed a child size by accident? Monica'd had no hand in picking it, that was for sure. As far as she was concerned, it needed to be disposed of immediately, because it was doing things to Monica's libido that were absolutely uncalled for at this hour of morning. She had to stop having these thoughts about Ray, or she was going to drive herself insane. The handy ma'am clearly wasn't attracted to her. Hell, she'd outright refused her the night before. Monica couldn't recall any other time in her life when that had happened.

The truth was, drunk as she'd been, it had still taken Monica half the night to get the rejection out of her head enough to fall asleep. That was two nights in a row she'd tossed and turned, all because her mind wouldn't stop thinking about some woman she didn't even like and who wanted nothing to do with her. What the hell was up with that?

And did she have to look so smoking hot in those jeans? Monica should've done herself a favor and let Ray stick with her shapeless men's trousers.

If Ray wasn't going to sleep with Monica and break this whole sexual tension nonsense they had going on between them, the only decent thing for Ray to do would be to look like shit. But no. Standing down in the yard, talking to Christos, Ray looked like a million bucks. Which, incidentally, was probably what they stood to lose if Monica chickened out and couldn't go through with this charade of a marriage, so it was time to buck up.

In the course of explaining something to Christos, Ray lifted her arm just right, scooting the T-shirt upward enough to give Monica a glimpse of a very toned and tanned stomach. Who still had a tan this time of year? Not to mention abs like that?

Monica saw red.

Not the type of red that meant *I'm really angry*, but actual red fabric, right along the edge of her denim waistband. Oh, hell no. The woman was wearing sexy, silky red panties. Monica knew exactly what they looked like because she'd picked those fuckers out from the buy three get three free bin herself. Monica fled from the window, taking a seat on the bed and crossing her legs for good measure, in case her traitorous pussy came springing into action again like it had the other day. She sat like that, not moving a muscle, until she heard the creak of footsteps on the stairs.

Ray tapped on the bedroom doorframe, even though the door was wide open. Nice of her to show manners now when ten minutes before she'd been prancing around without pants.

"Monica? It was Christos who brought the guys in. When I told him yesterday we were interested in clearing the weeds, he jumped right on it." Ray sounded so upbeat Monica kinda wanted to punch her in the face. "Talking to him now, Christos has some great ideas for this place. I think I'm going to go and get the full rundown on the wine-making operations after breakfast."

"Do you think it wise to get so cozy—"

Before Monica could remind her the plan was to sell the place, Ray barreled on, "I swear, he's been waiting for us to come along and help him bring this vineyard back to life. You wanna come, too? I think you'll really love it."

"No." The last thing Monica wanted to do was fall in love with a vineyard she didn't want to keep with a woman who didn't want to have sex with her. "What time is that forking dinner tonight?"

Ray's eyes narrowed. "Geez, Monica. If you don't want to go, you don't have to. There's no need to be rude."

"What?" Monica blinked in confusion. "I thought that's what it's called."

Ray put a hand on one hip and fixed her with a *yeah, sure* glare. "You thought they called it a fucking dinner?"

"A *forking* dinner," Monica said, emphasizing the problematic word. "I'm asking because I think I should go shopping this morning for something nice to wear."

"Oh." Ray nibbled her bottom lip bashfully as she seemed to realize her error. "It's not *forking*. It's farm to fork. And what's wrong with what you bought the other day? I was going to wear something I already had."

"Well, I'm not you."

What Monica had meant by that was Ray clearly could wear anything and look amazing in it, but it was only several seconds after Ray turned her back and left without a word that Monica realized that might not have been how it had come across.

Oh, fork.

Would Monica ever be able to communicate with this woman without making a total mess of things?

MONICA TOOK one final look at herself in the bathroom mirror, satisfied with the results of the day's shopping excursion. She'd chosen a deceptively simple cotton dress, not too fancy, that should be right for an evening on a farm. The secret weapon was the neckline, which was cut in a deep vee and which, when combined with the new bra she'd also picked up, *well...*

Monica's mouth curled into an evil smile. Frankly, this was a revenge dress. If Ray was going to torture Monica by looking so hot, it was only fair she should get to do the same.

"We should get going," Ray shouted from the kitchen. "I hate being late."

"Coming," Monica said, adding a dash of spice to her voice as she descended the stairs.

"Good, because—" Ray's eyes bulged from their sockets as they came to rest exactly where Monica had intended for them to.

"Because...?" Monica shifted one elbow slightly so as to showcase her assets even more prominently.

"What?" Ray visibly swallowed.

"Are you okay?" Finally, Monica was able to ask this of Ray, turning the tables on this whole game of sexual tension they had going on. It felt pretty fantastic.

Ray nodded. "Yep…uh…you look nice. Did you get that dress in Worcester?"

"Sure did." Monica hadn't. She'd started out there, but the mall's offerings had been kind of pathetic, and she'd ended up driving halfway to Boston, stopping at a mall in one of the chi-chi suburbs where perfectly polished women carried tiny dogs around in their designer handbags and dropped several grand in stores one rarely found outside Manhattan and Paris. Thank goodness she'd found something in her size on a clearance rack. Those extra three hours were definitely paying off now. "I thought you didn't want to be late."

"For?"

"Farm to fork. Surely you haven't forgotten about our plans this evening." Monica's voice dripped honey. "Or have you changed your mind about going?"

"Uh…" There was a look of absolute panic on Ray's face, and her eyes remained glued to Monica's chest. With visible effort, she dragged her gaze upward and squared her shoulders, tapping her chin as if to remind herself she was made of tougher stuff. "Nope. Let's go."

Ray bent her elbow for Monica to thread her arm through, but Monica wasn't going to give her the satisfaction. Not so early in the evening, anyway. Ray'd had her chance to have a piece of this the night before, and she'd turned it down. Where Monica came from, actions had consequences.

The drive to the farm was silent, but Monica noticed every single time Ray tried to sneak a peek. Noticed and absolutely reveled in it. Who knew such simple revenge could be so fun?

"I think this is it." Ray hunched down over the steering wheel. "Brenda wasn't kidding about tonight's event being sold out. Look at all these cars."

Nice cars, too, Monica noted. Expensive, some with plates from as far away as Connecticut and New York. As she saw the other couples and groups making their way up the hill, she was relieved to see she wasn't overdressed by any stretch of the imagination. There was some serious money here tonight. "I never would have thought fried chicken and checkered tablecloths on a farm would bring in this caliber of people."

"I doubt it would," Ray said, her eyes twinkling with knowledge she'd clearly not shared. "Brenda's a gourmet chef. Tonight's main course choices are either maple-cured salmon or chateaubriand."

Monica let out an appreciative whistle, willing to chalk a point in Ray's column for that little secret. "I guess it's a good thing I decided to come to this forking dinner."

Leaving the car, they followed the crowd to a big red barn. Almost immediately, Monica's social media influencer brain ticked into high gear. This was no ordinary barn. There was a string quartet in the corner, a full bar stocked with top-shelf selections, and several tables filled with tasty looking appetizers.

Brenda caught their eyes from across the room and bustled over. "So glad you two could make it. You really do make a stunning couple."

Almost as soon as Brenda had said it, Monica felt Ray's arm on her back, pulling her close to put on the required show. They were happily engaged, after all. "Thanks again for the invite."

"This place is incredible," Monica gushed. "I had no idea, and the turnout tonight is amazing."

"That's because dinner at the Black Cat is no ordinary affair," Brenda confided with a wink. "Since this is your first time, let me fill you in on the drill. You'll start with wine and appetizers here in the barn."

"Local wine?" Ray inquired, and Monica recognized her shrewd businesswoman persona peeking through.

"Chilean," Brenda said, taking two glasses from a nearby tray and handing them to Monica and Ray. Her disappointment in sharing the news of the wine's origin was evident. "I'm afraid I haven't found the right local option to pair with our food. If Christos could ever increase production, I'd buy every bottle."

"I'll keep that in mind," Ray said. "So, will we be eating at the little tables out here?"

"No, when dinner is ready in a few minutes, you'll hear me ring the metal triangle, and you'll all line up to be shown to your tables inside the farmhouse. I've assigned you to the fireplace room. A table for two. It's the most romantic spot." Brenda's eyes grew dreamy. "Ah, young love. The way you two look at each other, it's so clear it's meant to be."

Monica nearly choked on her wine, which actually didn't taste half bad but was nothing compared to the wine slushy she'd had the night before. What was it about seeing her and Ray together that made everyone think they were actually in love? The idea was preposterous.

"Make sure you leave room for dessert," Brenda cautioned, as if anyone would not do that. "And before you head home tonight, roam the property and take in the view by the pond."

"Interesting what Brenda told us about the wine," Ray said once the older woman had left.

Monica nodded. "I do wonder why Christos has never tried to ramp up production, at least to supply wine here. I mean, we're nearly next-door neighbors with the Black Cat, for heaven's sake. He really doesn't have a head for business."

"No, he doesn't," Ray agreed. "It's a shame, considering what I've been learning about the opportunities out this way. Take this dinner, for example. Do you know how much they were charging for tickets tonight?"

"Hmm..." Monica did a quick calculation of the

cost of a salmon dinner and glass of wine at one of the nicer restaurants in Baltimore. "Seventy-five?"

"Try double."

Monica's eyes doubled in size. "Are you serious? We're, like, in the middle of nowhere."

"We're plenty close to Boston, and even the Connecticut suburbs, to attract loaded foodies who will pay top dollar for organic meals and good wine."

Monica's brain whirled with the possibilities, but before she could ask Ray any more questions, the dinner bell rang. Ray guided Monica into the farmhouse, which was a complete delight. The setting was rustic with exposed wood tables, but elegant, too, with fresh cut flowers and candles. There was a fire going next to their table. A good thing since Monica's shawl didn't provide much warmth. As she settled in, Monica couldn't help but let the relaxed atmosphere of the farm seep into her, boosting her mood much higher than it had been, at least since the whole Ray turning her down for sex incident.

A waiter delivered their salads, and as Monica reached for her fork, her shawl drifted from one shoulder. When she looked up from her plate, Ray was frozen in place, a cherry tomato halfway to her mouth, eyes glued to…well, to exactly where Monica had intended them to be glued when she'd chosen this dress.

"I'm sorry about last night." Ray's voice was hushed, her tone sincere.

Apparently, the conversation was shifting away from business to something a bit more personal. *About time*, Monica thought, except it was odd because a part of her felt disappointed to leave the shop talk behind. There was a lot more to the vineyard that she was eager to explore.

"I think I understand," Monica replied, her heart clenching as she prepared to voice the painful truth. "We have an arrangement, and you aren't interested in anything else."

"You know I find you attractive, right?"

Oh, sure you do, Monica thought, but then she caught the way Ray was looking at her, licking her lips without seeming to realize she was doing it. "Then, last night, how come you walked away?"

"Not from lack of interest," Ray assured her. "If you were thinking that kiss didn't turn me on, well, you're wrong. But I think we have a good thing going here, and I don't want to jeopardize it."

"The inheritance." Monica uttered a knowing sigh. "You're afraid if we have a little fling now, it'll complicate dividing the assets down the road."

Ray leaned across the table, giving Monica a good eyeful of cleavage from inside her blouse—another print that Monica would've pegged as too feminine before, which she'd paired with jeans for a casual yet surprisingly sophisticated look Monica couldn't find a single fault with. Damn. Did she have to look so good?

"No. I think we could have a total game changer

here, and I don't want us to make decisions when our heads are clouded."

"What are you talking about?" She didn't say it in a condescending way. Monica really wanted to know what vision Ray had in her head.

"I was speaking with Christos about the harvesting today." The way Ray's eyes sparkled, it was clear she'd enjoyed the conversation. "He has the capacity to process way more than he does. The problem is getting the grapes off the vines before they rot. I think we could help."

A ghost of a frown passed across Monica's face. She wasn't dismissing the idea, but she didn't see how Ray thought it could work. "The two of us, helping an old man harvest over fifty acres of grapes?"

"Maybe not all of it, but with two more sets of hands, he'd have three times what he usually does."

Monica pressed her lips together, brain swirling as she considered what Ray had suggested. It didn't seem like enough. The waiter set down a bowl of soup in front of her with a gorgeous edible flower on top. A second later, there was a flash of light from across the room, and it was like a lightbulb had gone off in her own head.

"Look over your shoulder." Monica jerked her chin toward the source of the light, and Ray's eyes followed. "I'm willing to bet she's putting a picture of her soup on Instagram right now."

"And?" It was clear Ray was trying to follow along but wasn't sure where Monica was heading.

"People want experiences, and they'll pay a lot of money for them if they think it's worth it." Monica picked up her soup spoon and held it like she was using a pointer in a lecture. "When I was out driving today, I passed at least four pick your own farms, where people actually pay money to do the work of picking their own produce. You know why they do that? So they can put the photos of these idyllic farms on social media and make their friends envious."

"You think we should do a pick your own grapes thing at the vineyard?" Ray scratched her chin. "Wouldn't they want to take home the grapes?"

"Not if we make it more of an experience. Like this." Monica gestured at the room. "What if we advertised to the same people who spend big bucks to come out here for farm to fork dinners, offering them the chance to have a real harvest experience?"

"Pay us to pick the grapes?" Ray made a face. "What would they get out of it?"

"Well, what if we served them a sumptuous lunch in a beautiful garden, with the vineyard in the background? Photo ops galore."

"We do have a garden." A smile slowly spread across Ray's lips. "It's overgrown, but the guys will have it cleared out in a few days. I wonder if Brenda would be willing to help out with food preparation if we promised her enough wine by next year to serve at her dinners."

"Oh, good idea. But fried chicken and checkered tablecloths for this one, not a big, fancy dinner. We're not trying to compete." Monica pressed her hands together, having to physically stop herself from clapping. "I had no idea you were so savvy with business."

"I'm thinking the same about you." A hint of doubt crossed Ray's face as she looked around the dining room. "But how do we reach the kinds of people who would do this? We can't stand up right now and announce it during dinner."

"Social media, baby." Monica grinned. "I'm a macro influencer, you know. I only need some gorgeous photos of the harvest event—"

"Which we don't have."

Monica tilted her head to one side. "Don't you remember what I told you before? It's like the wedding. It doesn't have to be real, it just has to look real. How long until the grapes need picking?"

"A few weeks, according to Christos. Most of the varieties he grows ripen in October."

"Then I'll set up the photoshoot as soon as my boxes arrive this weekend." Monica smiled slyly. "And I'll put Mr. Fluffles to work, too. Who can resist a big, fluffy mascot?"

"At least you didn't say barn cat," Ray joked. "That would be a bit of a stretch for His Highness."

Soon their meals arrived, and they continued to

plan while savoring the delectable flavors of a New England fall, with perfectly cooked and seasoned meat, heaping portions of vegetables, and homemade rolls that were crusty on the outside and soft and steamy on the inside. The final temptation was a slice of apple pie the size of Monica's head. Brenda had been right, saving room for it was both a significant challenge and an absolute necessity. When the meal was finished, and their game plan for the harvest weekend thoroughly outlined, Monica sat back in her chair and sighed in satisfaction.

"We make a good team."

"We do." Ray shifted in her seat. "That's the other thing I wanted to bring up."

Monica's pulse ticked faster as she basked in the earnest intensity of Ray's gaze. Was this the part where Ray was going to confess she'd made a mistake the night before, that she wanted more? If she did, every inch of Monica's body sang out that she'd be a fool not to give it a try.

"Yes?" Monica's palms grew damp.

"The vineyard. I know we talked about fixing it up to either flip it or parcel the land, but I think we're sitting on a goldmine. Neither one of us has been doing great in our current employment." Ray threaded her fingers. "What if we combined our talents and tried to make a go of things here, not for a season or the wedding but long-term."

"You want us to be farmers?" That was not the

conversational turn Monica had been hoping for. She had a sudden vision of Ray and herself, standing side by side and holding a pitchfork, a la the couple in the painting *American Gothic*.

"Agricultural entrepreneurs. I've been doing some calculations. If we ramped up production, rebranded, and sold wine at all the farmer's markets, I'm thinking we can bring in nine a week."

"Nine hundred?"

"Nine thousand." Ray waggled her eyebrows. "Per week."

Monica's eyes widened. "Really?"

"That's only from farmer's markets. If we did tastings on the weekends and maybe supplied some of the local restaurants—"

"It'd make a fortune," Monica breathed.

They left the table, and remembering Brenda's advice, the two walked down to the pond, the moonlight glittering on the water.

"I really think this could work," Ray said, gazing out over the water, "but there's one problem."

Monica's shoulders slumped. Why did there always have to be a problem. "What is it?"

"Us."

Immediately, Monica felt the urge to contradict. "What about us?"

"We don't get along."

"We're getting along now, aren't we?" Even as she

said it, her tone was growing pitchy, hinting that they might not be getting along for much longer.

"Yes," Ray soothed, "but the other night…"

"I had too much wine slushy." Monica laughed airily. "I won't do that again."

"Was that the only reason you kissed me?" Ray's tone was unreadable, her face turned toward the pond and hidden in shadow.

It wasn't the only reason, but now with the business prospect on the line, Monica knew the last thing she needed was a messy relationship to interfere with her success. Well, her brain knew it. She would convince the rest of herself of this wisdom in due time.

"Yes, that was the only reason," Monica lied. "Come on, Ray. Do you really think I don't know how mismatched we are?"

When Ray chuckled in agreement, Monica blinked back an unexpected sting of tears.

Pull yourself together.

"So, what do you think?" Ray asked.

"Uh—" Monica was too busy not crying to remember what she was supposed to be thinking.

"Are we on the same page?"

"Remind me again."

Ray stared deeply into Monica's eyes, and for one crazy second, Monica imagined her saying she wanted to chuck the whole business nonsense and go all in on giving a relationship a chance. That's what she ached to hear, because right then and there, Monica wanted

Ray. Not just in bed, but all of her, everything she had to give.

"Are we going to roll up our sleeves and turn the vineyard into the most successful in the state or the country?" Ray beamed.

Of course. The vineyard was all Ray wanted, and there was nothing Monica could do about it but go along. "Count me in."

Ray stuck out her hand. "Business partners?"

It was exactly the right setting for a kiss, but instead, Monica took Ray's hand and gave it a collegial shake.

"Business partners," she agreed.

Before turning back to the barn, Monica took a deep breath, willing herself not to fall apart. The air had that delicious spicy autumn scent, crisp and cold with a hint of woodsmoke. In the darkness around them, the sound of crickets and toads croaking was like a symphony, punctuated once in a while by the hoot of an owl.

How unfair was it that, even with how it had turned out, this had been one of the most romantic nights of Monica's life?

CHAPTER FOURTEEN

"What do you think you're doing?" Ray made a dive to retrieve the escapee, but the snow-white feline darted to safety and gave his back an arch that would be the envy of any yoga instructor. "Monica is going to kill me if she finds you outside. She was clear about the rules before she left you in my care. You're an indoor cat. Always have been. Always will be."

The cat flexed his furry toes, his curved claws extending and digging into a pile of dirt that was rapidly turning his pristine fur into a dusty mess.

"Are you listening to me?" As she spoke, Ray tried to calculate how close she could get to the beast before he noticed she was moving. Considering this would make her fourth attempt, she already knew the answer was likely to be not nearly close enough.

Without deigning to acknowledge Ray in the slightest, the naughty kitty settled into a particularly filthy spot right alongside the garden fence and proceeded to lick his butt.

"Mr. Fluffles!" Ray put both hands on her hips and stared him down.

Apparently willing to respond to his full name, the behemoth of a cat momentarily stopped, his back leg still stretched in the air. He blinked as if to say that whatever she had on her mind, she'd better make it quick because he had important business to attend to.

"Get back inside this instant before your mother gets home." Ray pointed a scolding finger at the cat, not that he seemed to care. She switched tactics, folding her hands together and pleading. "Please, little buddy. For some reason she seems to like you, and she'll be heartbroken if you get hurt."

It had been nearly two hours since Monica had texted to say she was finally on her way back from Boston. Not that Ray had been counting the minutes or anything, but what was supposed to have been a quick and easy trip to sort out some paperwork regarding the vineyard's food and beverage licenses had turned into a three-day ordeal.

When they'd planned the harvesting event for the first weekend of October, Ray had known time would be tight, but she'd assumed she would be the one scrambling to complete the finishing touches that would make their vineyard photo-op ready. Instead, the last major item on her task list had been checked off the night before, and they were down to the wire waiting on Monica to be given a single piece of paper with the right stamp on it so they could legally uncork the wine and serve it to the over one hundred guests who would be arriving in a few short hours. Considering the whole draw of the event was wine, it was no minor detail.

The rumble of an engine caused Ray to snap her head up. Her heart was in her throat as she anticipated Monica's return. It had nothing to do with missing her during her absence, Ray assured herself. It was fear of getting in trouble over the cat.

"Plan B, buddy."

Ray dashed into the house and swiped a can of tuna from the cupboard, the real smelly stuff that, like the great outdoors, was supposed to be off-limits to Sir Fluffington. But it was easier, Ray reasoned, to hide the evidence of a tuna can than a huge white cat sunning himself at the edge of the driveway. As soon as she peeled the lid away, Mr. Fluffles came running. As Ray opened the kitchen door and let him in, he rubbed against her legs. He was decidedly dingy from his time outside, but if Monica had gone days without noticing when he'd been painted blue, there was at least a fair chance the beast would groom himself clean before his mom caught on.

As he trotted past to get to the tuna, Ray scratched his fuzzy back. "I never thought I'd be a cat lady, but you're winning me over."

Seconds later, Monica's truck pulled into the driveway. Once they'd made the decision to stay for the long term, they'd returned the rental car. Since the lease on Monica's Mercedes was up and Ray's car back in Baltimore was too unreliable to bother moving, they'd decided to spend some of their inheritance on an old farm truck. It still made Ray giggle a little to see prissy Monica behind the wheel.

Ray darted out to the driveway, putting herself between Monica and the evidence of the crime in progress in the kitchen. "How did it go in Boston?"

"Three days of my life I'll never get back. I'm sorry it took longer than I thought. Were you able to manage unloading your furniture without me?" Monica moved toward the kitchen door, making as if to look inside.

"You can take a look later." Ray slid in front of her, deftly blocking her passage. "Our first round of pickers are arriving in less than an hour."

"I want a quick peek." Monica continued toward the kitchen undeterred. "I can't wait to see all of it—"

"Brenda had some questions about how you wanted the centerpieces on the buffet table."

"Oh." As suspected, the prospect of an event emergency stopped Monica in her tracks. "I guess I'd better go talk to her."

"Yoo-hoo!"

The two of them turned to Sally riding her bike up the driveway, a laptop bag strung diagonally across her back. "I'm so excited to show you what brilliance struck in the middle of the night."

"We were on our way to check on Brenda," Monica said, not breaking her stride as she headed toward the yellow brick road. "Can you show us down there?"

"Sure thing."

Sally leaned her bike against the fence and sashayed toward Monica at such a clip that Ray was left bringing up the rear. It was less than perfect, leaving Ray to do her best not to watch the twist of Monica's hips as she walked. Her best wasn't nearly good enough, and by the time they were a third of the way down the path, Ray was pretty much ogling. Luckily, she couldn't be seen. To be fair, no one on the planet had hips that moved like Monica's did. She should be issued a patent. Or maybe Ray should be issued dark glasses and a cane, because telling herself not to look wasn't really cutting it.

Outside Christos's shop, two dozen long picnic tables had been set up, draped with the red and white checkered tablecloths Monica had envisioned. The smell of cornbread and baking rolls greeted them as they approached. As Monica went off to sort out the centerpiece issue with Brenda, which was a real question even if it hadn't been quite as pressing as Ray had made it sound, Sally took her laptop out of her bag.

"I know you weren't certain what you wanted, but

I did some mockups for an entire line of new labels, plus a logo for the website you're having me build." As she talked, Sally fired up her Mac, clicked the touchpad, and then swiveled the screen for Ray to see.

"Is that—?" Ray pointed to the fluffy white face on the logo.

"The one and only Mr. Fluffles." Sally clapped her hands together, unable to conceal her glee. "I remembered Monica calling him the vineyard mascot when he arrived. And let's face it, people love cute animals."

Ray spent a moment taking it all in, then pointed to the unfamiliar name written across the mock-up label. "White Cat Winery?"

"I wasn't sure what you would think," Sally said, "but it ties in so nicely with the Black Cat Farm, which is down the road and has a huge following. Plus, it's so hard to pronounce Panty-oh…Pan…"

"No need to convince me of that part," Ray assured her. "It's impossible to spell, too."

"It's spelled exactly the way it sounds," Monica said for probably the millionth time as she joined them at the table.

"I hate to break it to you, babe," Ray countered, "but it's really not."

Monica narrowed her eyes and stuck her tongue out at Ray.

Sally chuckled. "You two love birds crack me up."

"We're not—" Ray had been about to say they

weren't love birds, but as far as everyone was concerned, they were.

"Going to have time to see all the designs if we don't get a move on," Monica improvised, saving Ray from her close call.

"Right, well..." Sally pulled up a closer view of one of the labels. "I'm not sure of the names of the individual wines you're planning, but these images will show you the overall concept. Let's say you have a blueberry wine—and why wouldn't you, since they grow locally, right? So, here's Mr. Fluffles with a blueberry dangling from his mouth. This one has a grapevine. I'm thinking that will be the website logo, but for each variation of wine, there'll be something to signify the flavors. A bunch of cherries if it's a cherry dessert wine, or apples, or cranberries, or whatever."

Monica leaned closer to the laptop, and as she did, she accidentally brushed her leg against Ray. A jolt of electricity about stopped Ray's heart, and the effect on Monica must've been similar because both of them immediately retracted their legs while exchanging *I'm sorry* glances. One of the ways they'd worked out to keep them from unnecessary physical temptations was a strictly enforced personal space bubble. For the past two weeks, Monica and Ray had followed the rule with an almost religious fervor, to the point where an outsider would be forgiven for thinking they belonged to a strange cult in which members were never allowed to touch.

After a pregnant second, Monica refocused her attention on the computer. "I love it. He's such a handsome cat, and your color choices are bold, crisp, and stunning."

"Aw, thank you." Sally was beaming.

"This is so exciting, isn't it?" As Monica said it, she gave a little hop that started her breasts jiggling like a Jell-O mold. Ray stifled a groan, forcing herself to focus on a single red square on the tablecloth until the sudden turmoil the sight had unleashed in her body settled down to a low boil. Was Monica trying to kill her with her enthusiasm?

Ray plastered a smile on her face. "It's such a thrill when a plan comes together."

"Look at you two." Sally grinned as she closed the laptop. "You're like the new power couple of central Massachusetts, proving you can have everything. True love, a thriving business, maybe some little ones out there on the horizon someday."

"I'm afraid Mr. Fluffles is fixed," Monica stated.

Sally tilted her head to one side. "I meant babies."

"Babies?" Monica repeated the word like it was a foreign language.

"Human ones." Sally turned to Ray. "You two would make *great* parents, and there's no place better than a farm for raising a family."

"I...uh..." Fortunately for Ray's brain, there was a crunch of gravel outside, which stopped her head from imploding at the prospect of Monica and her raising babies, human or otherwise, together. "That'll be Christos getting ready. I should help him."

Ray ran toward the elderly gentleman like she was being chased. "Christos, is everything set?"

A smile split the man's face. "You bet. Can you believe every single slot has been filled for every picking session?"

"That photo shoot Monica did for Instagram paid off in spades." Ray stole a glance in Monica's direction, allowing herself a brief moment to admire her from a safe distance. Admire her business acumen, not her appearance. There was no rule against that. "I still can't believe she pulled it off."

"Looks like we'll get the entire harvest done this way." Christos followed Ray's example, which apparently had been a lot less subtle than she thought, and looked admiringly at Monica. "She's so much like her grandmother. Beautiful, loving, and smart. It's not often you get the whole package."

He nudged Ray's side with his elbow as if to say *you lucky dog*.

Ray cleared her throat, not exactly sure when that lump had formed there. "Uh…so…um…I'm going to let you lead the pickers, but if you need anything, let me know."

He looked at Ray oddly for a second, like he wanted to say something but wasn't sure how. Then his expression changed abruptly, and he snapped his fingers. "Oh, I almost forgot." Christos dashed into the shop, emerging with something inside a cardboard box.

Ray strained to make out what it was, but the loud crackle of Christos's voice made that unnecessary as it was now obvious to everyone in the county that the man was speaking into a megaphone.

"Got it from Amazon!" He said this directly into the contraption, so not only did Ray give his announcement two thumbs-up, but so did a couple of the pickers who were coming into view at the edge of the driveway.

Soon enough, more pickers arrived. Something about them as a whole screamed this was a group of people who spent most of their days working in office buildings, but they'd shown up dressed for the occasion. Or rather, they'd shown up dressed in the way people who work in office buildings think farmers dress for a day in the fields. Monica had been right. The type of folks who shelled out money for what they'd marketed as an authentic country experience planned to document the day in photos like they were a bunch of professional photojournalists.

Most of them had on pristine work boots that probably still had the tags on them that morning, or else were sporting knee-high equestrian boots that gave off a country manor house vibe. Men and women both wore snazzy fleece pullovers with flannel collars poking out at the neck. A few of the women had wool cable-knit sweaters tied at their waist, sweaters that—as Sally at one point whispered to Ray—retailed for several hundred dollars. Whatever magic Monica had used, she'd definitely roped in the right crowd.

Ray wanted to pat herself on the back—and Monica, too, except that would violate the personal space rule. Absolutely everything was coming together as they'd planned. In Ray's mind, that could mean only one thing. They'd made the right decision. Physical attraction was fleeting and fickle, whereas a good business partnership was worth its weight in gold. So what if it was sometimes a struggle to keep her eyes off Monica's hips, or if the house had felt so empty when she'd been away that Ray had thought she might die. It didn't mean anything. This success that she was witnessing today? That was what really mattered.

After everyone arrived, Christos directed them to the fields so that he could demonstrate proper picking techniques to his enthusiastic band of city slickers. "Okay. Does everyone have their clippers?" he asked.

Every single guest hoisted a clipper-bearing hand into the air.

"And your Band-Aids?"

Again, hands clutching bandages were raised in the air with more glee than Ray would have thought, considering that the need for them kind of implied management was more than a little convinced this whole endeavor was going to hurt. People who didn't have to make a living doing manual labor could really be strange in their enthusiasm for it sometimes.

"Two people should work together, one on each side. As you can see, there are yellow tubs under the vines, every twenty feet. You should be able to fill up each one as you go. The process is pretty simple." Christos took a pair of clippers, snipped a bunch of grapes. and tossed them into the bucket. "Don't worry about cutting the leaves in the process. They'll fall off in a few weeks anyway. Any questions?"

A man raised his hand. "How much do you expect each of us to pick?"

Christos raised the megaphone and answered. "Each one of you should easily be able to harvest three hundred pounds before lunch."

A chorus of nervous giggles, mostly female, rang out, while nearly all of the men puffed out their chests as if saying they'd do double.

"So, are you guys ready to earn your grub?" Christos grinned at Ray.

There was a cheer. With a satisfied nod, Christos led the group along the sprawling rows of vines. At each new section, pairs split off for their assignment with smiles on their faces. Ray, who'd had a chance to do some harvesting with Christos the week before, wondered how long those smiles would last when reality set in.

Hopefully long enough to bring in the harvest.

Christos and Ray took up the last row, stripping off their long sleeves right away. The air still had a slight morning chill, but they'd work up a sweat soon. The work could be exhausting but oddly calming and therapeutic. Ray hoped their guests would find it that way, too. If not, at least Brenda's upcoming feast should restore smiles to faces and guarantee them some good reviews on social media.

At times, Ray's attention strayed to Monica, who walked up and down the dirt paths, making sure everyone had water and also taking photos for the website. The guests were more than willing to stop and pose, and Monica had explained to Ray that she planned on live-tweeting the event. This meant posting every fifteen minutes which team was making the most progress. Ray almost burst out laughing at how the competition kicked some of the men, especially, into a higher gear.

"Josh, dude," one of the men in a nearby row called out loudly, "you better watch out, because I'm going to smoke your ass."

"Whatever, Scott." His tone reminded Ray of some of the guys she used to work with on the restoration projects. "You don't scare me."

The trash-talking continued for the first thirty minutes, but soon after that, things got real.

Ray knew this because by about the forty-minute mark her biceps, which were in great shape if she did say so herself, started to burn. By the end of the first hour, the talk among the men had subsided some. There were the occasional taunts, but it was clear they were putting on brave faces.

The women, on the other hand, chattered merrily. Two of them in the row behind Ray spent most of the time discussing the older woman's divorce. Ray couldn't help but overhear. After twenty years of marriage, the poor thing had been blindsided. Needless to say, it confirmed what Ray already knew. Love was a joke. If she'd needed any more proof that she'd chosen the right path, there it was.

The sky was a brilliant blue overhead, and the temperature was in the low sixties, but Ray still got hot and sweaty. Just when she thought she might expire, an angel appeared.

Not an angel. Monica.

"Here." Monica was standing beside her, smelling good. Ray swallowed, coughing. "Your throat's dry from all this work. Drink some water."

Ray reached for the bottle, her fingers accidentally brushing Monica's. She was pretty sure the work hadn't been the only reason her throat was suddenly so dry, but she laughed it off.

"Remember our bubble," Monica whispered, grinning. "No touching."

"Same with you," Ray teased. "Another brush of the finger and you won't be able to keep your hands off of me."

It was the same old silly banter, the same dumb jokes they'd been telling for two weeks. But when their eyes met, the laughter faded. Seconds ticked as they stared at each other, electricity crackling in the space between them.

Finally, Ray tore her eyes away and turned them toward her hands, which were trembling slightly as she twisted the cap off the water. "I better get back to work."

"Me too." Monica's tone was a little too cheerful, too forced, as she raised her phone. "A couple of guys at the front are acting like they're on the final mile of the Boston Marathon. Gotta get it all on Twitter."

"This really is working out, isn't it?" Ray said, feeling a little too needy for the reassurance of Monica's reply.

"Absolutely."

Except, once again there was that wordless stare before Monica wheeled about.

What did it mean?

Luckily, the time flew by with enough work that Ray didn't have much energy to think too deeply. Before Ray knew it, Brenda was beating the triangle to call everyone to lunch, which went off without a hitch.

The day had been perfect.

Many of the guests added their names to their mailing list, claiming they'd be back next fall and would tell all their friends. More importantly, there was no longer a doubt in Ray's mind that they'd harvest enough of the grapes to produce all the wine needed to put their plans into motion. As for other doubts that may have been lingering somewhere in the recesses of her skull, Ray had a plan. She planned to ignore them until they went away. She had a good thing going here, too good to screw it up.

As the cars pulled away, Ray stretched her arms overhead, inadvertently dragging her shirt several inches above her waist. She brought them down quickly when she noticed the hungry look in Monica's eyes as the woman stared at her bare stomach. Looks like that was more dangerous than a hundred accidental finger touches. They were like matches on dry tinder, threatening to set fire to everything in their path. Nobody needed that.

"I'm ready for bed," Monica said, a faint flush of pink on her cheeks.

Ray laughed. "It's only four in the afternoon."

"But I'm exhausted," Monica argued. "Besides, I haven't even seen inside the house yet, not since all your furniture arrived. Did you set up my room?"

"I did," Ray assured her. "I think you'll like it. Shall we go take a look?"

But before they could enter the house, a car turned into their driveway, slowing to a crawl.

Ray squinted. "Do you think one of the guests got lost and needs directions? Cell service can be spotty out here."

Instead of an answer, Monica groaned.

Ray turned to her, shocked to see her hands clasped to her head like they were the only things keeping it attached to her neck. "Monica, honey, what is it?"

"That's not a guest." Monica's eyes were wide, her expression vaguely shell-shocked. "That's my mother."

CHAPTER FIFTEEN

Monica stared in disbelief at the silver Lexus. She wasn't hallucinating. That was her mother's car for sure, right down to the Maryland license plate, which meant she'd driven all the way from Baltimore by herself. That couldn't bode well.

Beside her, Ray regarded the car with wide eyes. "You didn't think you needed to tell me your mom was coming?"

"I swear I had no idea." Monica shut her eyes and opened them again, but it was no use. The car was still there, her mother still inside, and what was more, she was definitely about to park. "Do you know how long the drive is from Baltimore? It has to be at least seven hours. She was on the road all that time, and she didn't call."

Ray gave her a disbelieving look. "Didn't you talk to her on the phone recently?"

"I…uh. I left a voice mail." Monica neglected to say she'd placed that call at three in the morning, knowing her mother kept her phone plugged into the charger in the kitchen overnight and would never hear it ring.

"I thought messages weren't your thing."

"It was the best alternative."

"To?"

"Actually talking to her." Monica shielded her eyes from the setting sun. Her mom was still sitting in the car, too preoccupied with something to open the door. Monica supposed it was too much to hope her mom had only stopped to check the map and actually had a different destination in mind.

"Let me get this straight." Uh-oh. Ray sounded on the verge of getting really mad. "Your mom found out via the internet two weeks ago that her only daughter was engaged to be married, and all she's had from you is a voice mail? I'm not a family person, but even I know that wouldn't work."

"I explained very clearly in my message. I told her we weren't planning a big wedding, I had everything under control, and I would call her when I had more to share." Yeah, even Monica wasn't convinced by her own excuses.

"Seriously, Monica, how did you not see this coming?"

Monica didn't answer because there was nothing to say. The truth was, she'd been a total coward, and she should've seen this disaster coming from a mile away.

Or rather 400 miles, the approximate distance her mother had driven to chew her out.

"What's taking her so long to get out of the car?" Either Monica was imagining things, or time had slowed to a crawl. Maybe it would start going backward, and she'd have a second chance to call her mother properly and convince her to stay home.

"Dunno." Ray squinted, studying the car. "Seems like she's trying to wrestle something from the back seat. I better go help."

"Good thinking." Monica followed closely behind Ray, who'd already set off in the direction of the car. "If she throws her back out, she'll be stuck here for weeks convalescing. That's the last thing we need."

"Seriously?" Ray tossed Monica a questioning look over her shoulder. "It never ceases to amaze me where your brain will go when allowed to roam free."

They were a few steps away from the car when the door opened. Monica rushed to offer her mom a hand in getting out. "Hi, Mom. What a surprise."

"Let me help you with your ba—" Ray choked. "Er, *bags.*"

Monica's eyes flew to the back seat, which was piled high with what must certainly be the overflow luggage that hadn't fit in the trunk.

Shit!

Far from a quick, overnight excursion, her mom had come prepared for an extended stay. "There's my baby girl!" Exiting the driver's seat, Monica's mom held her arms open wide. "I can't believe you're getting married, and you didn't tell me."

"It was unexpected," Monica said, stinging from her mother's extra heaping helping of guilt. She prayed she wouldn't be pressed for too many details since she had none to share. Fortunately, it seemed her mom had become preoccupied taking in the view of the property, which Monica had to admit looked pretty spectacular after all of Ray's hard work.

"Take a look at this!" Her mother stepped back and made a sweeping gesture with her arms, encompassing the whole of the vineyard. "I had no idea your *yiayia* had this hidden up her sleeve. Your cousins will be green with envy when they see it."

"See it?" Monica's heart clanged against her ribs. "Please tell me they aren't coming to visit, too. You're not meeting them here, are you?"

"No, of course not. I assumed you'd be hosting the wedding here." Her mother fixed her with that look she had that could induce guilt in a microsecond. "But what do I know. You don't confide in me anymore. I had to find out on the internet you were engaged."

"I'm sorry about that, Mom. The news wasn't supposed to get out so quickly." At least Monica wasn't adding lying to her list of bad behavior. If she'd had her way, her marriage would've been a secret forever.

"Well, never mind. We have so much to do before the big day. Your father said I should wait until you invited me, but what do men know, right?" She looked at Ray and arched an eyebrow, clearly expecting her soon-to-be daughter-in-law to share her opinion. As far as Monica could tell, Ray was trying to wish herself invisible.

"Dad was right, Mom," Monica chastised. "I plan weddings for a living, and I have everything under control. It's almost completely planned."

That was a lie. She and Ray had been so caught up in the harvest event and the logo redesign they'd both nearly forgotten about the wedding.

"Oh?" Her mother's face crumpled. "I guess you don't need me, then."

"Mom, that's not—"

"No, it's okay," her mom interrupted, waving her hand dismissively. "I can turn around and go home since I'm not wanted here."

Ray—who had wrestled the last of the bags out of the back seat and had loaded herself up with three straps crisscrossed over her chest, one small bag in her hands, and her other hand on the handle of a massive rolling bag—stood frozen in place and gave Monica a searching look, as if to demand *what the fuck am I supposed to do with the luggage?*

"Don't be silly, Mom." Monica detected a note of panic in her voice as she pleaded with her mom not to leave, even though the last thing she wanted was for her to stay. "Of course, we want you here. Don't we, Ray?"

"Of course, we do, mmm…mis…Mom."

If Ray had been standing closer, Monica would've given her a sharp jab in the side with her elbow. For God's sake, could she have been any more obvious that she'd forgotten Monica's mother's name. Monica was about to mouth *her name is Helen* when her mother broke into a grin.

"You called me Mom." Eyes sparkling with tears, she rushed to envelop Ray, along with most of her luggage, in a crushing embrace. "I'm so very happy you're already becoming part of the family."

By the time Monica's mom let her go, Ray looked completely stunned. As she made for the house, loaded up like a Sherpa, her grunting sounds were hard to discern. Was it from exertion? The fact that Monica's mom had packed for a year? Was she starting to exhibit signs of post-traumatic stress disorder at the prospect of being saddled with Monica's family?

Seemingly oblivious to Ray's shell-shocked appearance or Monica's worried looks, her mom looped an arm through hers and started toward the house. "This really is an amazing piece of land. The view is simply gorgeous."

Monica, seeing it through her mom's eyes, flushed with pride. There was so much left to do, but the truth was, what Ray had already made happen around the place in a few short weeks had utterly transformed it from the ramshackle property it had been when they'd arrived. "And, we're going to be able to get all the grapes harvested. That's what we've been so focused on."

Ray, who had slipped inside to deposit the bags, reemerged in time to catch the tail end of the conversation. "Would you like a tour of the grounds?"

"Definitely," Monica's mom assured her, "but tomorrow when my legs are fresher. Right now, I can't wait to hear all about the wedding. Have you set a date?"

No, they had not, and Monica could see Ray becoming agitated as she tried to answer. "November sixteenth."

She'd plucked the date from her memory, having made note of it as being the absolute latest they could tie the knot before their license expired. Monica watched as her mom pulled out her phone, her brow creasing.

"That's a Monday. Who gets married on a Monday?"

"Weekends are the busiest time for tourists," Ray explained smoothly as she opened the door to the kitchen. "Would you like to see what we've done with the old farmhouse?"

I sure would, Monica thought. She braced for whatever she might find, reminding herself that anything would be good enough for now.

"Oh, yes." Her mom placed a hand on Monica's shoulder. "Did you work on it together?"

"I let Ray handle it," Monica replied hastily. Not

that she wanted to totally throw her fiancée under the bus, but if it looked terrible inside, she didn't want her mom to become suspicious or anything. Better to make it clear the house was all Ray's doing.

"Well," her mom said in a confidential tone, low enough that only Monica could hear "I hope this place suits you more than your last one did. The only room that had even a spark of personality to it was the bedroom."

As her mom slipped into the house, Monica's eyes grew huge.

The bedroom?

Fuck.

She and Ray could keep up the charade that they were a loving couple while they were outside, but her mother wasn't dumb. As soon as she saw their separate bedrooms, she'd figure out in a heartbeat that something was up.

"The bedroom," Monica hissed the moment she caught Ray's attention. "She wants to see *our* bedroom."

"We need to distract her." Ray disappeared into the kitchen. A second later, she reemerged with a huge ball of white fur in her arms. She opened her arms, and Mr. Fluffles dropped to the ground and made a dash for the bushes.

Monica's mouth fell open. Had Ray sacrificed her cat as a distraction?

"Oh no! The cat's gotten out." Ray called out in an exaggerated tone.

"Mom, help!" Monica summoned the same level of fake drama as a vaudeville damsel being tied to the railroad tracks.

"Mr. Fluffles?" Monica's mom reappeared in the doorway. "Oh dear. I think I see him under the bushes along the fence."

Yeah, no shit he was under the bushes. As her mother scurried out to look for the cat, Monica was about to give that infuriating fiancée of hers a piece of her mind when Ray whispered, "Stall her. Five minutes and I'll have the bedroom fixed." Then she marched off without giving any indication of what her plan involved. Time travel? Magic?

It took fifteen minutes to round up the unruly feline, who showed zero interest in giving up his new life in the great outdoors. When he'd finally been cornered, Monica grasped the squirming, cobweb-covered beast tightly to her chest and followed her mom inside. When she had a chance to get Ray alone, she was going to throttle the woman.

About five steps into the kitchen, all thoughts of killing Ray had vanished. Monica looked around in awe, barely recognizing it.

Her mom gave an approving nod as she scanned the freshly whitewashed cabinets and the newly sanded and oiled butcher block countertop with a silver vase of fresh-cut flowers resting on top. "This fiancée of yours has amazing taste."

Yes, she does.

It wasn't only the kitchen that had been transformed during the seventy-two hours Monica had been away. There was a charming maple hutch in the dining room with a matching table surrounded by six ladder-back chairs. In the living room, the single old couch had been replaced with an overstuffed sofa and loveseat that looked softer than clouds. An antique tea cart served as one of the end tables, and a plump ottoman took the place of a coffee table, which Monica had no doubt would double as a cat bed of epic proportions for spoiled Mr. Fluffles. In fact, the way a blanket had been folded and left on top of it led Monica to suspect Ray had set it up that way precisely for that reason. Maybe she wasn't such a cat hater after all.

By now, Monica was dying to see upstairs, but remembering her mission to buy Ray time, she offered, "How about a nice cup of tea?"

"That sounds perfect." Returning to the kitchen, her mom groaned as she took a seat at the sturdy island that had taken the place of the old Formica-topped table. "Oh, these old bones."

An electric kettle was plugged in beside the refrigerator. Monica stared at the cabinets, wishing she had X-ray vision so she wouldn't have to guess where Ray had stored the mugs. And the tea. After a quick *eeny, meeny, miny, moe,* Monica selected the cupboard where she would've put the mugs, the one in between the kettle and the sink, and was surprised to find when she opened it that Ray had been similarly inclined.

"So," her mom said as Monica carried the mug over, "how many people are you inviting to the wedding?"

Monica had to clutch the mug with both hands to keep from dropping it. "We hadn't really thought that far ahead. Small, though."

It was at this point that Ray reentered the kitchen, giving Monica two thumbs up. Whatever she'd been doing upstairs, the space was now prepped for Monica's mom to see. "What's small?"

"The wedding guest list," Monica answered.

Monica's mom crossed her arms. "Define small."

"Ten?" Ray responded.

At the exact same moment, Monica said, "Fifty, tops."

"Fifty?" Ray looked like she might pass out.

"Fifty!" Her mother's shrill voice was eardrum-busting level. "There's no way we can cull that many family members from the guest list. You'll start a feud worse than the Hatfields and McCoys."

"Now, Mom. We want to keep this cozy." *Like, no guests at all,* Monica added silently.

Her mom swiveled in her seat in search of an ally. "What do you think, Ray?"

Though she tried to hide her face behind the mug

of tea she'd poured for herself, Ray couldn't disguise her "deer in headlights" expression. "I don't have much experience with family."

"Well, let me tell you," her mom said, "family and cozy go hand in hand. The more the merrier when it comes to Greeks. We're such a peaceful people."

Yes, because no one had ever heard of Helen and the Trojan War.

Her mother continued tutting. "There's no way we can have less than three-hundred and fifty."

Poor Ray. Not only was her chin dimple glowing, but her neck was getting little red blotches all over, and Monica was pretty sure if her eyes kept boggling like that, they were going to pop out of her head completely.

"Stop, Mom," Monica urged. "I think we've discussed the guest list enough for one day."

"You're right," her mom agreed, though something about her tone made Monica not trust her. "We have more important things to consider. Like bridesmaids. I can't see a way for you to have less than a dozen."

"A dozen?" It was Monica's turn to have her eyes nearly pop out of her skull. "But, Ray doesn't have any family, so I think we should skip bridesmaids."

Ray hopped up, moving in the direction of the kettle. She either planned to make more tea, or perhaps she intended to slip out the back door, never to return. Monica wouldn't blame her in the least.

"What about groomsmen?" Her mom demanded.

"I know Ray's female, but if she doesn't have her own bridesmaids picked out, there's always groomsmen."

"A dozen of them? I mean, I'm not a recluse, but I don't think I could come up with that many people, men and women combined, that I'd want to ask to be in my wedding." Ray offered an apologetic shrug. "Sorry."

Her mom tapped her fingers on the kitchen table. "I know what we can do. We'll reach out to the Chicago Panagiotopoulos's. They have a ton of boys in that family. You two wouldn't be opposed to them, right? It'll only add another hundred to the guest list." Not waiting for input, she barreled on. "This family hasn't had a proper reunion in over a decade. No time like the present, and isn't that what weddings are for? The joining of family to celebrate your love?"

Ray had her back to them, but Monica could see the tensing of her shoulders. Much to Ray's credit, she was able to hold it together enough to finish making her tea and retake her seat. It looked like plain black tea in her mug, but Monica wouldn't have judged her in the least if she'd put a shot of something stronger in it.

It was clear Monica's mom had her head in the clouds as she reveled in planning the family event of the century. "For the junior bridesmaids—"

"Are those understudies in case one falls ill?" Ray asked in all seriousness, leading Monica to wonder how many big weddings Ray had attended, if any at all.

"You act like you've never been to a wedding before," Monica chastised.

"Not royal weddings, I haven't. I've only been to normal people weddings, like at city hall or on a beach."

Her mom hooted. "I like you, Ray. This is going to be so much fun. For the ceremony, I'm picturing—"

"We already have a location, Mom," Monica interrupted.

"That's right," Ray added, looking relieved finally to have something to contribute to the conversation. "The kit just arrived, so I'll be putting up the gazebo next week."

"Oh, a gazebo." Monica's mom clapped her hands together. "I can picture it now, overlooking a pond, with a pair of swans."

"We don't have a pond," Monica said.

"Or swans," Ray added.

"That's easily solved, though, right?" Her mom directed the statement to Ray. "You're so handy. Look how much you've accomplished with the grapes."

"Uh..." Ray answered, which under the circumstances was not a terrible response.

By this point, her mom wasn't really looking for responses so much as a sounding board for what she clearly considered brilliant ideas. "Do you know who we can hire for hayrides?"

Monica shook her head, but Ray, perhaps hoping to

score a point or two for the pond disappointment, offered, "I could ask Sally."

Monica's mom's face lit up much brighter than a possible hayride seemed to merit. "I have the perfect idea. We should set up Slip N Slides for the kids so the adults don't have to watch over them."

Monica stared, aghast. "This is a wedding, not a carnival."

"The wedding's in November," Ray said gently. "It's pretty cold by then."

"Right. That's off the list." Monica's mom made an X in the air with a finger. "That doesn't mean we couldn't look into bouncy castles, cotton candy machines—"

"I think we have enough ideas for now." Monica rose, her chair scooting across the floor. "How about we continue with the house tour?"

There were four bedrooms upstairs, and when Ray opened the first door, Monica could see it had been set up as an office, with a large, heavy wooden desk and a leather swivel chair. Barrister bookcases lined one wall. If Monica hadn't known better, she would've thought she had wandered into the private study of some nineteenth century country gentleman. There was even a pair of hunting prints on the wall.

"Monica's office is across the hall," Ray explained. "I've put your bags in there for the time being, Mom. Once we know where you're staying, we can have them brought over."

"Where I'm staying?" The expression on her mom's face made it seem like she was trying to translate something from a foreign language. "In your guest room, of course. Is that this one?"

"No," Ray called out as Monica's mom reached for the doorknob of the room nearest to her. "That's, uh, our room."

"Look at that bed," her mom squealed, barging into the room before Monica had a chance to see. "It's fit for a queen."

When Monica finally caught a glimpse, her heart caught in her throat. The room was beyond anything she'd imagined. It was feminine without being too girly, and elegant without being too stuffy. If Monica could've designed her perfect bedroom, this would've been it.

"Is that an antique highboy?" Her mom plucked at Monica's sleeve. "And will you look at this painting?"

But Monica couldn't tear her eyes away from the centerpiece of the room, an intricately carved cherry four-post bed with what seemed to be a handmade lace canopy suspended above.

"What do you think?" Ray asked, her front tooth biting down on her bottom lip.

"I think," Monica's mom answered before her daughter had the chance, "that I need to excuse myself to find the ladies room after all that tea."

"Down the hall," Ray directed. Once she'd gone,

Ray picked up one of her T-shirts from the floor. "Oh, sorry."

"It's your room," Monica said with a shrug. "You can leave clothes on the floor if you want. My only question is how did you get all of my stuff in here so fast?"

Ray gave her an odd look, half shyness and half something Monica couldn't place. "This is your room. I must've dropped the shirt when I was moving my clothes in here."

"Mine?" Monica whispered, unable to comprehend that she'd be allowed to sleep in a space so beautiful.

It was perfect for her in every way, the stuff of dreams. After years of sharing a living space with women who insisted on their own style, Monica finally had a space that could've been plucked from her dreams.

But in reality, the contents had all come from Ray's storage pod. This was her stuff, not Monica's, yet Ray had clearly given her the very best. As she appraised the bed, the other furniture, and the artwork on the walls, all Monica could wonder was why.

CHAPTER SIXTEEN

As she listened to the chatting coming from the hallway, Ray realized she'd never known how truly exhausting family could be. There had been nonstop talking for at least six hours on everything from wedding plans to the state of each cousin's health in intricate detail, and even though Monica had said she needed to go to bed twenty minutes ago, she and her mother were still at it. What could they possibly have to talk about at ten o'clock at night that couldn't wait for morning?

"Good night, Mom." Finally, Monica slipped into the bedroom, closing the door. When it clicked shut, she leaned her back against it, sinking down several inches like she'd had the air let out of her. "Oh, thank God. I thought I would never escape."

Ray felt for her, even as she marveled at how much

stamina she'd shown. As soon as Helen had arrived, Monica's demeanor had shifted, as if she'd become a tightrope walker constantly balancing her own opinions with what her mom undeniably wanted to hear.

"Now what?" Ray whispered, eyeing the door and feeling more than a little grateful for Monica's body barricading it. "Do you figure if I wait an hour before I go downstairs, that'll be long enough?"

"Go downstairs for what?" Monica whispered back.

"To sleep." Ray pointed to the canopy bed. "Afraid we only have one of these."

"Are you kidding? One step on the staircase and she'll fly out the door wondering who's sick."

Ray scratched the side of her head, her eyelids battling to stay open. It felt like a week since the harvest event, but it had only been that morning that she'd woken up early to prepare the last-minute details. Between that and the future mother-in-law invasion, it was amazing she was still upright. "I don't know about you, but I could sleep through a nuclear explosion right now. I'm sure your mom must be even more tired after her long drive. She won't hear a thing."

"My mom has preternatural maternal hearing."

"Is that really a thing?"

"Yeah. It goes hand in hand with the extra set of eyes she has in the back of her head." Ray must've been looking at Monica like she had two heads because she responded with an expression of utter disbelief. "Didn't your mom skulk around at night, like a lioness protecting the boundary?"

"Uh, no." Either she hadn't been around, or she'd only stopped in long enough to steal money from Ray's piggy bank. But that wasn't a memory Ray felt ready to share, so she simply said, "The closest I came to having a mom was being raised by my mom's dad."

"Not exactly the same thing."

Yeah, not even close.

"When it came to kids, Grandpa Ray tried, but he really didn't have a clue."

"He didn't learn with your mom?"

As much as Ray didn't want to get into the details of her family, she probably needed to throw Monica a bone, or the woman's curiosity would keep her asking questions all night.

"My grandparents had what you might call a shotgun wedding, right before Grandpa Ray shipped out to Vietnam. He came back a year later to a daughter he'd never met and a wife who'd found someone else while he was gone. Even so, he provided for my mom however he could, and when her addiction issues made it impossible for her to care for me, he stepped up and gave me a home." Ray hitched a shoulder. "There may have been some gaps in my education when it comes to how normal families behave."

Monica's shoulders softened. "I'm sorry. That had to have been rough."

"It's okay. I mean, I've seen what your mom is like sometimes, and I'm not sure you had things any easier." Not wanting to continue with a topic she knew invited pity, Ray shifted to the problem at hand. "If we can't sneak downstairs, should I sleep on the floor? Unfortunately, I didn't put a spare bed in my office."

"I can't ask you to sleep on the floor."

"You didn't," Ray reasoned. "I'm offering."

"This floor is hard as a rock." Monica eyed the queen-size bed. "That bed is plenty big for two reasonable, rational adults to sleep in together for one night. Did you ever have sleepovers when you were a kid?"

Ray shook her head, and immediately Monica got that pitying expression, the one Ray had been trying to avoid. "My childhood is really hard to explain."

In truth, there was little to explain because Ray hadn't had much of a childhood. At least, not until she'd gone to live with Grandpa Ray. While other kids had parents who made them mouse-ear pancakes while they watched cartoons, Ray had often spent Saturday mornings scooping up the empty beer cans that had littered the apartment to take to redeem for deposits at the corner store so she could buy herself a box of Pop-Tarts while her mom lay passed out on the couch until noon. It hadn't been total misery, but a woman like Monica wouldn't be able to comprehend it. She simply lacked a frame of reference to a world that operated in that way.

"I guess it's never too late for your first sleepover," Monica said with a forced cheerfulness that suggested she had as many misgivings about this plan as Ray did.

"Will we be required to tell ghost stories?" Ray joked then watched with growing puzzlement as Monica started to climb under the covers, still clothed. "I didn't realize it was customary to sleep in your clothes."

"Oh, I..." Monica's face flushed.

"Your nightgowns are in the top drawer." Ray pointed to the highboy.

"Uh, that's okay."

"You've been wearing that outfit since early this morning." Ray eyed Monica's jeans with a hint of distaste. "In the fields. You're probably all covered in grape juice. Wouldn't you rather have on a nice, soft cotton nightie?"

Monica's arms folded protectively across her chest. "You looked at my nightgowns?"

"I put them away for you," Ray pointed out. "Kinda hard not to look."

"Well, go ahead." Monica tossed her head defiantly. "Laugh."

"Why would I do that?" She'd found them far from laughable. The gowns had looked so comfortable Ray had actually considered trying one on for half a second.

"Bri laughed her head off, calling me a grandmother."

Based on Monica's wounded expression, it occurred to Ray she might not be the only one struggling with baggage from her past. Slowly, Ray sat on the edge of the bed, not too close as she didn't want to give Monica any cause for alarm, and looked earnestly into her eyes.

"I won't do that. I know I might seem rough around the edges compared to a lot of other women, but I'm not mean." A flicker of doubt crossed Monica's face, and Ray reiterated, "I'm not perfect, but I'm never cruel."

Monica took a breath, letting it out slowly as if using the time to weigh Ray's words. "I guess I'll change in the closet."

"Don't be silly. I'll turn my back, and you do the same."

"I don't know…"

"Monica, I'm saying this for your own safety. I'm the one who unpacked all those boxes Bri sent, and I'm telling you now, if you try to get changed in there, you might be buried alive."

"Okay, fine. Turn around." Ray yanked one arm out of her shirt, then the other, undoing her bra and then removing it without showing an inch of skin.

From the other side of the bed, Monica giggled.

"You didn't peek, did you?" Ray accused,

wondering if she'd been caught in her bizarre undressing ritual.

"No. I was wondering what you wore for bed." Given the amusement the image had produced, Ray wondered if Monica was picturing her in one of those long cotton gowns.

"Nothing as fancy as yours. Can I turn around so you can see?" Monica said she could, so Ray spread out her arms, displaying a souvenir T-shirt she'd bought from Acadia National Park when she was a teenager, which she'd paired with cotton sleeping shorts.

When she'd turned all the way around, Monica had already dashed into bed and pulled the covers up to her chin. It was only when Monica eyed her chest that Ray realized how much more snuggly the T-shirt fit compared to when she'd first bought it. Were those really her tits? They seemed bigger than she remembered. Suddenly, hiding under the blankets didn't seem like such a bad idea.

Settled under the covers, Ray said, "So, these sleepovers. What were the rules?"

"No crossing the middle."

"Gotcha." Ray, laying on her side, gripped the edge of the mattress to prevent falling off the bed. As far as she was concerned, there might as well have been a crocodile-filled moat running down the middle. "Good night, Monica."

"Nightie, night."

Ray turned off the lamp on the side table and shut her eyes.

Her brain hummed with the awareness that Monica was inches away. All things considered, it might as well have been on the other side of the world. Hell, Ray wished that were the case. The last thing she needed was to be up all night, reminding herself of all the reasons they were wrong for each other, even as her body screamed for her to throw caution to the wind and give it a chance.

She tried to relax, but it was no use. It was impossible when all she could hear was Monica's gentle breathing as she drifted off almost immediately to sleep. This was going to be a long night.

At some point, Ray must have dozed off, because she awoke with a start, sweat slick across her face and chest. She'd dreamed she was a child again, her mother tiptoeing through the room, stopping to give her a kiss on the forehead. Even as she gave in to the warm rush of her mother's affection, young Ray knew that her piggy bank would be empty in the morning. Grown-up Ray tossed the blanket from her, twisting in bed while trying not to wake Monica.

Ray held perfectly still until she heard Monica snoring slightly. The woman had a delicate snore. Inside, the dream continued to cause turmoil. Ray fought back the need to sob. A hand pressed on her back, stillness descending on her at the touch.

Monica's hand ran up and down her spine, soothing. Was she awake?

But Monica was still snoring. Surely, she wasn't faking it, because what purpose would that serve? Had Monica sensed Ray's rigid body and desperate need to be comforted?

As if to say yes, Monica continued the light touch while Ray's eyes grew heavy and her mind finally began to still, until she was coaxed into a deep and peaceful sleep by Monica's soft caresses.

THE FIRST RAYS of dawn fell across Ray's cheeks, pulling her slowly out of the most restful sleep she'd ever had.

Monica's body pressed against her, still snoring softly.

Every morning for the past two weeks, ever since Helen had arrived, Ray had woken this way.

And, every morning, Ray carefully wiggled free and established a respectable space between them so Monica wouldn't realize she'd been doing it. Was that fair? Maybe not. But if Monica found out she was a secret late-night cuddler, that would certainly put a stop to it. As much as Ray hated to admit it, even to herself, it turned out she was the cuddling type. On more than one occasion, she'd woken in the predawn hours to simply feel Monica holding her. As far as Ray knew, Monica didn't have a clue that as soon as she drifted off to sleep, she sought out Ray with the accuracy of a heat-seeking missile. Perhaps some things were better remaining a mystery.

Monica stirred as if waking. Reassuring herself they were both completely on their own sides, Ray greeted her with a, "Morning sleepyhead."

"Hi," Monica replied in that gravelly, not fully awake morning voice. It was quite a turn on. As it turned out, so were a lot of things when you spent two weeks entwined in the arms of a woman you couldn't have and shouldn't want.

"The gazebo will be finished today." Ray opened her duffle from the closet floor, pulled out a pair of work jeans, and then took a flannel shirt off a hanger. The surest cure for unrequited lust was some good old-fashioned physical labor. Fortunately, with fifty-two acres of farm and a wedding coming up, there was no shortage of things in need of doing.

Unaware of Ray's internal struggle, Monica rubbed the sleep from her eyes. "Lucky you. I'm going dress shopping with my mom in Boston."

"That'll be fun." Ray would consider it torture, but Monica seemed to enjoy that kind of shit.

Monica sat up on her elbows, her crabby expression suggesting otherwise. "Clearly you've never been dress shopping with my mother."

"At least you'll get a nice lunch out of it," Ray said encouragingly. "She seems to love going out to lunch."

And dinner, too. They'd been to so many restaurants in the past two weeks, they were rapidly running out of new places for Helen to try. She'd been generous about it, insisting on picking up the tab each night, but Ray wondered if it was partially because her almost-mother-in-law didn't really believe she knew how to cook.

Monica yawned. "Oh, can you talk to Sally about the website?"

"Did you like that sample one I showed you?"

"Yeah, it was perfect," Monica said through another yawn. "It's nice to know I'm not the only one with style around here."

"I guess I know how to do a thing or two." Grinning in the still half-dark room, Ray flushed with pride. It felt good to be appreciated for her talent, and now that Monica had been convinced she knew her stuff, she'd pretty much been given free rein on everything to do with the vineyard grounds and rebranding efforts. "Now, why don't you close your eyes and get some more sleep. Stores won't be open for hours."

After a grunt from Monica in response, Ray left to change into her work clothes in the bathroom. Did she want to climb back in bed, too? Sure, and not just because Monica was still there. But another thing her grandfather had taught her was not to burn any daylight hours.

Downstairs, she turned on the coffee pot.

Christos pulled up in his truck as the last few drops

of coffee dripped from the machine into the pot. It had become their routine over the past two weeks as they'd worked on completing the first phase of landscape projects and launched into constructing the gazebo. He walked across the driveway, carrying his trusty steel thermos. That thing had probably been around since the invasion of Normandy—and had gone through it and survived, based on how banged up it was. It smelled strongly of dark roast black coffee even when it was empty.

Experience told Ray it would be in such a state now, which was why she'd started a pot of coffee even though Monica and Helen wouldn't be up for a few hours. Neither of those women could function without a cup of coffee the minute they got up. Actually, Ray was of the opinion Monica needed two cups before she was able to handle such complicated questions as, "How did you sleep?"

"Morning." Christos entered the kitchen door sipping the last of his coffee from the plastic lid. He unscrewed it without a word, and Ray filled it back up to the brim, setting the pot back on its burner before leaving. What remained should still be fresh when the other two women emerged, and it would give them a needed head start on their caffeine intake for the day.

Outside, the mid-October morning was on the right side of the line between crisp and raw. Ray sucked in a deep breath of fresh air as she surveyed the progress that had been made on the gazebo.

"This is looking good. It shouldn't take more than an hour or two." Ray inspected the remaining pile of parts, which had shrunken to almost nothing. If she'd had all the time in the world, she might have been able to design and build a structure that was nicer than the current one, but there was a lot left to do before the wedding.

Christos took a big swig of coffee. "What's next on our list?"

Ray pulled out a small spiral notebook from her back pocket to consult what Helen had referred to the other day as her honey-do list. The concept was entirely foreign to her, and yet the idea of having a list of requested projects from a significant other was oddly not as unappealing to her as it probably should've been. "The main thing is the carriage house. I've divided that into two phases, with the first being a thorough cleaning and basic repairs to make it good enough for hosting the reception, and the second being a full renovation, which I've put on my calendar for the spring.

"It'll be a beauty when it's finished," Christos said, and Ray could tell by his expression and tone that he meant it. "I don't think I've ever seen another one like it."

"Not outside a Gilded Age mansion," Ray agreed. She checked her list again and chuckled when she saw that someone—probably Helen—had added in pencil *Dig pond*.

"What's so funny?" Christos asked. He squinted when she showed him the notebook. "What pond is that?"

"Oh, it's something Helen requested for the wedding. She's got a bee in her bonnet about having a pond with swans out beyond the gazebo. Says it would be romantic."

Christos shielded his eyes with one hand against the brilliant morning sun. "We could do that. That spot, right there"—he extended his finger—"would be perfect for a small pond, and not just for looks. The wildlife would love it, too."

"Are you serious?" Ray looked at the tangle of brush and tried to picture turning it into a pond but had no idea where to begin. "The wedding's in less than a month."

"It wouldn't be that hard," Christos assured her. "The landscapers could do most of it, and it would be worth the investment for the tourist appeal."

"You really think it'd be a draw?" Ray put her hands in her back pockets, her thinking pose.

"You know it would because you keep talking about that night you had at Brenda's place and the pond there. You never shut up about it."

Ray studied his face and wondered if Christos knew the true reason for her talking about it. That was the moment Ray's life had changed, when she'd finally found her purpose in fixing up this vineyard and helping it to thrive. If only she hadn't spent every hour since then waiting for the other shoe to drop. Surely, when it came down to the wire, Monica wouldn't actually go through with any of this, right?

If there was one thing Ray's experience had taught her, it was that people were a constant disappointment. They abandoned you. They left in the dead of night with your hard-earned change clinking in their pockets. Sometimes, they died. It was only a matter of time, and even if Ray didn't want to see Monica walk out the door, she steeled herself daily for the inevitability of that moment.

"Now, I was never the marrying kind, but one thing I do know is if the little woman wants something, you do everything you can to give it to her." Christos raised his cup as a kind of salute. "If Monica wants a pond, she should have a pond."

"Pretty sure it's Helen who wants it," Ray said, but she couldn't find fault with the rest of his philosophy.

"Even better. It gives you a tick in the good daughter-in-law column."

Ray shook her head, knowing she was a fool for doing this, but that she would do it anyway. "Now, I need to figure out where to get swans."

She'd been joking, of course, but Christos replied, "That's easy enough. Ask Sally."

Ray chuckled. "Sally must be like the town magician. Whatever you need, she can get it."

"You know swans mate for life."

"They do?" Ray swallowed hard, sensing a meaning hidden in his words.

Christos nodded, tossing out the dregs of his coffee and twisting the lid back into place, ready to put hammer to nails.

Mating for life. Good for the swans, she supposed. She wondered what that would be like, to always have someone by your side. Too bad she hadn't been born a swan. As a human, Ray would never know.

CHAPTER SEVENTEEN

Monica sat at the desk in her office, holding her head as she stared at the email from the dress shop she and her mom had visited the day before. Monica had gone in with few illusions about the chances of getting her perfect dress at such a late date. She always told clients to allow at least seven months to order a dress, but she also knew there was some wiggle room in that rule.

A handful of designers could turn around an order in as little as two weeks—for an exorbitant rush fee, sure, but it could be done. Plus, most boutiques would sell sample dresses from the rack. Since Monica wore one of the most common sample dress sizes, she'd hoped to luck into something she could make work.

A few of the shops had laughed outright when Monica had told them her timeline, but the saleswoman at the last place had seemed so confident, not to mention she'd been a huge fan of Monica's blog, which was always a plus when it came to getting things done. She'd helped Monica compile a list of ten dresses she'd be willing to consider. Honestly, any one of them would've been fine. Which was why Monica had to read the email twice to absorb the news.

Discontinued.

Out of stock.

Backordered until spring.

Those were the replies for dresses one through nine, with a note on the final dress that a sample could be shipped in from another store as long as Monica thought she could squeeze into a size two. No shapewear in the world was strong enough to make that happen. Even if Monica stopped eating entirely until the wedding, there was no way she would fit into a size two. Her breasts alone made it impossible.

Right at the point where she clunked her head against the top of her desk, Ray walked by and paused in the doorway.

"What's wrong?"

Monica rolled her head on the desktop, cracking open one eye so she could see. "Do you know how hard it is to plan a wedding?"

"I thought this wedding shit was your wheelhouse."

"It is, but I usually have over a year to plan a wedding this size." Monica sat up, crossing her arms. "Plus, all my regular vendors are in Baltimore."

"What about the lady at the hotel?" Ray asked hopefully. "She seemed nice."

"She's very nice, but they only offer their services in-house, and they're booked solid. Even if we wanted to have the wedding there, we'd be out of luck."

"On a Monday?"

Monica nodded, chuckling slightly. Monday was a ridiculous day for a wedding, so she'd been shocked to find out the hotel was booked. "I have no idea why, but couples seem to be booking dates with the urgency of someone heading to war."

"Okay, well the good news is we already have the venue," Ray pointed out. "What else do we really need?"

"You sure you want to know?" Monica collapsed against the chair. "Florist. Baker. Caterer. Officiant. Music. Hair and makeup. Those are the biggies. And, that doesn't even include the rings or finding outfits for the wedding party." Monica displayed eight fingers, unsure if she'd ticked everything off and certain she was forgetting something.

"That's a lot." Ray looked a little pale, like she might topple over. "Why weren't you more concerned about this before?"

"Because before my mother got involved, everything was going to be staged. But my family thinks this is real, which means I now have four weeks to pull together a wedding that would usually take a year."

"Well, at least you can scratch off hair and makeup

for me. I don't need it." Ray gave her an annoyingly upbeat smile.

"Sorry to burst your bubble, but with a photographer, you have to wear makeup. Oh fuck." Monica held up a ninth finger as her breathing became ragged. "We need a photographer."

"Breathe." Ray dashed to Monica's side and squatted so they were eye to eye. "Do you know what you need?"

Monica shook her head as she gulped for air. "What?"

"Some time away from planning."

"Were you not listening? I can't possibly take time away with all I need to do."

"Are you kidding?" Ray challenged. "That's the best time to do it. I've found when I'm overwhelmed, what I really need is to give my brain a break. Some fresh air always makes it easier to find a solution."

"Fresh air?" It was like a foreign concept. Monica's usual approach was to put her head down and plow forward until the work was done. Or something broke. Maybe Ray had a point. "Fine. How do I do that?"

"Well, I was about to walk to the common for the Saturday farmer's market. Come with me."

Monica looked at her unanswered emails and sighed. "I really shouldn't."

"There'll be cake."

Monica perked up. "What kind of cake?"

"Any kind you want," Ray coaxed. "There's a baker,

Dorothy, who's supposed to be there. She runs a tea shop during the week, and everyone says she's dynamite. There's no problem in the world that cake can't solve."

This was literally Monica's life motto.

Still, she hesitated. "Something about this seems unfair. You're using my love of cake against me."

"I'm really not sure where the problem is." Ray winked.

"You win." Monica rubbed her hands together. "Let's roll."

Monica wasn't sure what to expect from the market, which generally meant that her expectations were low. She was pleasantly surprised when she heard music in the distance and could make out a jumble of dozens of colorful tents. There was an almost country fair quality to the experience that immediately lifted her spirits.

The only downside to the experience was that the morning air was colder than she'd expected, and her lightweight denim jacket did little to keep her warm. Monica stuffed her hands into her pockets, gritting her teeth as a particularly fierce blast of wind whipped across the town common.

"You okay?" Ray asked, seeming impervious to the weather.

"Yeah," Monica said, lacking conviction.

Ray stopped walking and frowned. "Let me see those hands."

Reluctantly, Monica removed her hands from her pockets and held them out. The skin was raw from rubbing them together, and her nail beds had a purple tinge.

"You poor thing."

To Monica's surprise, Ray took her hands and lifted them to her mouth, blowing hot breath across the fingertips. Immediately, parts of Monica's anatomy were on fire, though she doubted that had been Ray's intention. "Maybe I can buy some gloves."

"I know just the place," Ray said, keeping hold of Monica's frozen hands until they'd reached a table filled with knitted items.

Their friend Sally waved from behind the display. "You looking for anything special today?"

"Something warm." Ray took a periwinkle scarf off the table and wrapped it around Monica's neck. "Do you have gloves that match?"

"Sure do." Sally plopped a thick pair of gloves on the table then stood back and made an expression of approval. "You can sure tell Ray has a designer's eye. That color really brings out your eyes."

"Does it?" Secretly, Monica had suspected as much, even though there was no mirror.

"We'll take the whole set, my treat." Ray whipped out her wallet before Monica could argue.

"She's a keeper," Sally assured her. "Like most men in this state, my husband only picks out stuff with the

Red Sox logo, presenting items like he won the World Series for me when he barely gets off the couch."

Monica put on the gloves, blown away by how soft they were. "What's this made of?"

"Alpaca," Sally replied. "It's my favorite yarn. You can make just about anything with it."

"Oh, really?" Ray seemed to perk up, or maybe she was preparing to crack a joke. "How about a wedding dress?"

Yep, a joke. Monica was starting to learn the telltale signs.

"You never know," Sally said with a laugh. "Of course, it might take me all winter."

Ray snapped her fingers like tough luck. Monica shut her eyes, stifling a groan. Ray could be such a clown.

"If you really do need a wedding dress," Sally said, "you might stop by Michelle's consignment shop."

"Like a thrift shop?" Monica was pretty sure she'd sounded as horrified as she felt, and Sally must've caught on because she quickly started shaking her head.

"No, no," Sally assured her. "Higher end stuff. She caters to the wealthy suburban types. Designer labels, dresses for fundraising galas. She even brings some things in from Manhattan sometimes."

Monica's eyes scanned the stalls. "Where is she?"

"Over in the next row." Sally pointed vaguely behind her. "Right next to Dorothy's."

"Isn't that the cake lady?" Monica arched an eyebrow at Ray.

"Cake or dresses first?" Ray hooked her arm for Monica. "I'll let you decide. Lead the way."

"Have fun you two." Sally wiggled her fingers goodbye as she turned her attention to a man who was standing at the table, looking lost.

"I need a gift for my mom," Monica overheard him say. "Do you have anything Red Sox?"

Ray and Monica shared a chuckle as they headed to the end of the row. When it came to the design sense of men in Massachusetts—and probably a lot of women, too—Sally had totally nailed it. Perhaps because of how low the bar had been set, Monica was completely stunned by the natural beauty on display at a florist's stand in the next row.

"Oh, Ray. Look at those sunflowers. And, the pumpkins. Those would be fabulous as centerpieces. Maybe some of those deep purple mums, too."

"They would." Ray stopped and tilted her head to the side for a better look. "What about those fresh-cut bouquets for you and however many bridesmaids your mom talks you into?"

"Is that seriously the price?" Monica asked as she spotted a chalkboard with an amount marked on it that was half what she'd expect to pay. "What a bargain."

Ray stroked her chin. "I had a thought. All those services you listed off earlier, we could find someone to do just about every one of them right here. Flowers, cake, dress—there's a DJ playing music right now who sounds great, and see the sign on the gazebo?"

Monica turned her eyes to where Ray was pointing. "String quartet at 3:00 p.m.?"

"Exactly. It's the honors group from the local high school, so I bet they sound decent. Maybe they'd be allowed to take a few hours away from class on the wedding day if it were to raise money for the school."

"We could hire Brenda to do the catering," Monica suggested, quickly warming to the idea. "We know her food is spectacular, and she has plenty of waitstaff who work the farm to fork nights."

"The beauty is, if we skip the Boston vendors and go for local, it would probably cost less all around. Plus, it'd help us next season with the vineyard."

"How do you figure?" She didn't say this in an argumentative way. Monica was truly intrigued.

"You'd showcase them on your blog, right? Do a big write-up for each business, which means it'd up the visibility for this whole area, make it like a tourist destination. Your million followers would be dying to come here and try this all for themselves."

"You might be onto something," Monica confirmed. "In fact, my numbers are increasing by the hour now that I'm sharing the details of our wedding. It ups the stakes since I'm the bride. I'll be at two million followers soon."

"That's amazing." Ray's expression was so openly admiring that Monica quickly looked away.

"People like to get invested." Monica pointed to a tent filled with racks of clothing. "That must be the consignment place."

They approached the stall, and Monica quickly waved down the owner. "Excuse me; do you have any bridal gowns?"

"For you?" When she said yes, the owner, Michelle, looked Monica up and down. "Back at the shop, I have several that might work. I might have some photos on my phone."

"That would be fantastic." Privately, Monica worried what type of dress would end up in a consignment shop, but when she saw the pictures, she was pleasantly surprised with the options. "These are really beautiful. I have no idea which one to choose."

Monica showed the phone to Ray, who took it and flipped through the photos with a scrunched face. She pointed to a photo of the fluffiest white dress Monica had ever seen. "I kind of like this one."

"Oh?" Monica tried to keep her tone neutral, resisting the urge to gag. "That's an interesting choice."

"Fashion's not my area of expertise." Ray shrugged, clearly having picked up on Monica's unspoken opinion of her choice. "Is there anyone else you could show these to and ask?"

Monica had a lightbulb moment. "You know what?

I have almost two million people I could ask. I should post photos of all the choices and conduct a poll on my site."

Ray's face lit up. "Monica, that's brilliant. I subscribe to several interior design blogs, and there was something like that a while back, where you got to vote on your favorite stuff and they'd use it in the room. People loved it."

Monica turned to Michelle. "Would it be possible for me to come into the shop on Monday and take photos in all of the gowns for my blog? I'll give your shop full credit, of course."

"Did I hear you right that you've got almost two million followers?" The owner looked like she'd won the lottery when Monica told her yes, nodding vigorously. "Just link to my social media profile. I post new arrivals all the time, and I'll ship anywhere in the country."

As they left the stall, Monica made a motion like she was checking something off the list. "One more task down."

"Now for cake!" Ray smiled widely, the sparkle in her eyes doing things to Monica that had no business being done.

Planning your wedding doesn't mean you have to feel those gushy emotions, she reminded herself. *This isn't real. Think of it as another job, not some fairy tale with a happy ever after, because that ain't happening here.*

"What are you thinking?" Ray asked.

"Hair and makeup," Monica lied. "We haven't solved that problem."

They were standing in front of the bakery tent, eyeing a case of delectable cakes as they discussed this. When they mentioned makeup, the woman behind the case turned toward them.

"Did you say you need someone for hair and makeup?" she asked.

Monica nodded. "For a wedding. Mine, actually. Well, ours, that is."

"You need to talk to Tina. She does an amazing job."

"Tina," Monica repeated. "Is she here?"

"No. Saturday is generally a busy day for her, and I know for a fact Bill Crenshaw died last week."

"Oh no! Was he her husband?"

The baker laughed. "No. Tina's family runs the funeral home in town."

"She does makeup for dead people?" Monica slapped a hand over her mouth as she heard how close her words had come to a shriek.

"Oh, she does living people, too," the woman assured her. "Tons of 'em. She's done some work on films and that Stephen King TV show they were doing in this area a while back. I know the dead people thing is a little creepy sounding, but what can you do when your parents are in the mortuary business, right?"

Monica, who had some experience with the pressure families put on their offspring to join the family business, reluctantly agreed to check in with Tina at the funeral home, though she wasn't sure how to feel about it.

"What happens if someone dies on our wedding day?"

"What are the odds of that happening?" Ray asked. "It's not like this is a big city filled with people."

"I guess you're right," Monica conceded. "But I think after all this talk of funerals, I'm going to need some cake to cheer me up. What flavors do you have?"

"Is this for the wedding, too?" The baker gleefully handed them a printed menu. "Take your pick, or if there's something you don't see, just ask. My name's Dorothy, by the way. I own the tea place out by the main highway."

"Nice to meet you, Dorothy," Ray said, while Monica was too overwhelmed by the menu to respond.

She nudged Ray and showed her the sheet. "Look at all this. I can't decide."

Ray's expression was surprisingly grim, considering it was cake they were discussing. "We don't have to ask your followers about this decision, too, do we?"

"Hell, no," Monica declared. "This is much too important to trust them with. Dorothy, can we come in to your shop for a cake tasting?"

"Absolutely," Dorothy told them. "Any time."

"That settles it, then," Monica declared, relieved she and Ray had their priorities straight.

A FEW NIGHTS after the farmer's market, where almost as if by a miracle Monica suddenly found her vendor list nearly complete, she, Ray, and her mother decided to go out for dinner.

"I think I'll have the salmon." Monica's mom placed her menu down on the table. "You two are the experts, what wine goes best with it?"

While Monica's mind went blank, Ray moved to the edge of her seat, looking like that kid in class who was dying to get called on because they'd spent the whole year studying. "If it's seared, I'd recommend chilled Pinot Noir. For citrusy, Sauvignon Blanc. Or, Pinot Gris if it has a more Asian flavor."

"Sauvignon Blanc, then," her mother said triumphantly.

Monica looked sideways at Ray, perplexed. "Since when do you know so much about wine?"

Ray simply shrugged. "At first I had no idea aside from the different colors, but Christos has been imparting all of his wisdom."

"At least you won't have to worry about your wine order for the big day," her mom joked.

Monica wanted to palm-slap herself for not adding that to her list of things that needed doing. "Ray, does Christos have enough inventory for that? We'll need red, white, and champagne for a hundred guests."

"Better say a hundred and fifty," Monica's mom interjected.

Monica rolled her eyes. She'd thought she was being generous moving her estimate from fifty to a hundred guests, but her mother always had to push a bit more.

After a moment, which she'd probably needed to regain her composure after the shock of the head-count, Ray said, "The red and white, yes, but there's no champagne. White Cat doesn't make anything like that."

Monica's mom looked devastated. "What, nothing for a toast?"

To get her mind off it, Monica quickly shared with her mom the dress contest idea for her blog.

Her mother blinked. "You're letting strangers choose your dress?"

"Yep. So far, Ray's favorite is in the lead."

"It is?" Ray gave a goofy grin.

"No, are you kidding?" Monica gave an exaggerated shudder. "That thing was like the clown car of wedding dresses. You could fit a dozen brides in it, and no one would know."

"I thought it was pretty," Ray said with a huff.

Monica didn't know how to respond. Ray was talking about the dress like she actually cared. It threw Monica off her game and made her fear for a moment that she'd forgotten how to speak.

"What about the bridesmaid dresses?" her mom said after several seconds, filling the awkward silence.

"That's becoming an issue. It's way too late to order them from a dress shop, and while Michelle has plenty of options, they're all one of a kind. Looks like I won't be able to have a dozen bridesmaids after all."

Thank God.

Her mom seemed to mull this over while the waitress took their order. After the woman left, she said, "I have a solution. Nina can be your maid of honor. I was for her mother, and you were in Nina's wedding, so it's expected, but as long as you choose Nina, you don't have to have anyone else."

"Nina?" Monica groaned.

Her mother wagged a finger. "I don't know why you hate your cousin. She's just like you."

"Correction. She *looks* just like me." Monica turned to Ray, so eager to plead her case that she wondered if she'd missed her calling to be a lawyer after all. "Nina's a brain surgeon with two perfect kids and another on the way."

"An actual brain surgeon?" Ray's eyes had widened considerably.

"And they look so much alike they could be twins," Monica's mom added.

"Surely you don't look that much alike." Ray dipped a piece of bread into olive oil, wearing a pained expression that suggested she wished both other women would stop bickering so she could remove herself from being trapped in the middle.

"The last time we had dinner with all the family, Uncle Niko congratulated me on being named surgeon of the year."

"I didn't know there was such a thing," Ray commented.

"Me neither, so that was embarrassing. But the worst part?" Monica waited a beat to give the punchline. "Uncle Niko is Nina's dad."

"Her own father couldn't tell them apart," Monica's mom said, slapping her thigh.

As Ray and Monica laughed, their shoulders bumped together. Monica felt the heat rush to her face.

"Look at you two," her mother said fondly. "You make such a lovely couple."

Shit.

Monica had forgotten they needed to act like a real couple when her mom was around, but somehow, they were still managing to pull it off.

Just to be safe, Monica decided to lay it on a little thicker. She pulled her chair a little closer to Ray's and said, "We know each other so well by now I can tell you without a doubt what dessert Ray's going to get."

A look of surprise crossed Ray's face, but then she playfully tilted her head. "Oh, do tell. I'm dying to know what I think."

"Please." Monica gave Ray's arm a pretend slug, her heart skipping a beat when it met with solid muscle. Damn. She'd forgotten that was there. "You know you'll get tiramisu. It's your go-to every single time."

Ray's expression said *she caught me*. "Why mess with perfection?"

"See!" Monica flourished her wine glass before taking a big swig. Somehow that hadn't gone as smoothly as she'd planned.

Her mom turned to Ray. "Have you tried Monica's baklava?"

"Not yet," Ray said, waggling her eyebrows in a way that suddenly struck Monica as very naughty, as if baklava was code for something dirty.

Monica nearly choked on her wine. Ray hadn't meant it that way for real, had she? Impossible. Monica reminded herself, yet again, that they were playacting, and she chalked it up to Ray being a much better actor than Monica had realized.

Nothing to see here, folks. Move along.

Anything that appeared to be actual desire was pretend.

CHAPTER EIGHTEEN

After tossing the pruners back into the basket, Ray wiped her sticky hands on her jeans. She surveyed the rows of vines with pride, counting the yellow bins of freshly picked grapes even as she massaged her sore arms. She'd become so used to the daily tasks on the vineyard that she barely ached anymore, but picking half a dozen long rows with only Christos was pushing it. She glanced at the older man and wondered for about the nine hundredth time how he'd managed this all on his own.

"Is this really the last of them?" she asked. "If not, we should consider adding another harvesting event."

"I promise this is it," Christos assured her. "The Cabernet Franc and Riesling grapes are the last ones to ripen, and we don't grow enough of them to bother with one of those fancy events of yours."

"Fancy?" Ray laughed, comparing the simple

spread of fried chicken and checkered tablecloths with what she knew of Monica's plans for the wedding. "If you thought that was fancy, you haven't seen anything yet. But now that all the grapes are harvested, what do we do?"

"Squish them, mix them up, and *voila*!"

"Is it harder than my childhood chemistry set?" Ray made a face. "I still remember setting my carpet on fire."

Christos laughed, shaking his head. "Maybe you should simply watch this time. You'll learn it better that way."

"Excellent, I like to jump in headfirst, to soak up every single detail."

"I've noticed." He gave a chuckle that reminded her of the way Grandpa Ray used to sound. Ray's heart clenched with missing that man. "To answer your question, though, making wine isn't hard. Before anyone knew what they were doing, grapes naturally fermented."

"I'm sure it was a happy discovery. So, wine just kinda happens."

"Maybe not good wine, but, yes."

"We should make T-shirts that say *Wine Happens*."

He nodded. "I'd buy it."

"Me, too." Ray made a mental note to research sources for T-shirts they could sell at the shop. That reminded her she needed to speak with Christos about moving his wine making supplies, when the time was right. They could use all the space they could get for selling, and besides, she'd made a discovery while patching up the carriage house that she thought could be perfect.

They'd followed the yellow brick path all the way back to the farmhouse when Christos waved her over to where six gnarled old vines were growing on a red fence.

"This is where it all started," Christos said. "Monica's grandfather was gifted these vines by someone from his village who visited him from Greece. He planted them here, the start of his vineyard. He was like you. An eternal optimist."

"I'm an optimist?" Ray snorted. She was fairly sure no one had ever accused her of that before.

"We all are. You have to be to go into this business. Unlike other types of farming, the majority of the work you do on a vineyard isn't for immediate gain. You're always preparing, then waiting for the next stage, whether it be the following season, the wine maturing, or even the next generation."

Ray felt goose bumps. "So, why are these vines here, but the rest are behind the house?"

"Because Monica's grandfather learned something important. He wasn't fit for this life. He didn't love it enough, not like he loved learning and wanted an education for his children. But I did, and so he hired me. And by doing that, he saved me."

"What do you mean?"

Christos's eyes fell to the trampled and brown grass underfoot. "When I was your age, the world was a very different place. People like me and you and Monica weren't welcomed—"

"You're gay?" All at once, it felt like some missing pieces fell into place, completing the puzzle.

He nodded. "I had to leave Greece because my parents found out. They disowned me, and I thought all was lost. It's funny. Sometimes when you think you're at your lowest point, something good happens that changes your life."

Ray thought back to the moment she'd lost her job and all that had happened since. "I know what you mean."

Christos's eyes swept the horizon. "This place saved my life. The Panagiotopoulos family took me in. They needed someone to take care of this place, and I'd grown up around grapes back in the old country. They didn't care about who I loved or anything like that. That didn't matter. It was—what's the word…?"

"Fate."

"Yeah, fate, with a pinch of luck. Don't ever forget how luck plays a role. Good and bad. It's all part of the journey. You shouldn't take a day for granted. I haven't. How can I, when I work here every day?"

Tears stung Ray's eyes as she let all that she felt for this place wash over her. "I love it here."

"Me, too." Christos crooked a finger. "Let's go to my workshop, and I'll walk you through the basics."

Ray rubbed her hands together like she'd been given keys to a brand-new Porsche. "This is all so exciting."

"It really is. Every step of the process is a time-honored tradition that takes love and patience. It's like your relationship with Monica. If you treat it well, the love flourishes. If you don't, it shrivels to dust."

Ray started to speak, to refute what he'd said, but realized the thought of what she had with Monica slipping from her fingers would be devastating.

"This is where the magic happens." Christos opened the door to the shop. "Sorry it's such a mess."

They picked their way across the floor, which was even more strewn with vats than the first time Ray had seen it. "Oh, wow. You've utilized every square inch of this space."

"Yeah, it's small."

Ray gave a faint smile. If she suggested moving the workshop to the lower level of the carriage house, she was almost certain Christos would go for it. She'd draw up some plans to run past him as soon as she could. "Where do you stomp on the grapes?"

He laughed heartily with a hand on his belly. "I'm sorry to disappoint you, but that's not how it's done anymore."

"Really?" Ray's face fell. "I loved that episode of *I Love Lucy*."

"Everyone does." He held onto a metal lever. "Do you know what this does?"

Ray squinted at the unfamiliar device. "Raises a magic curtain? I assume the Wizard of Oz is around here somewhere, at the end of the yellow brick road."

"Always a comedian, you. Nope. It's how the corks are inserted."

"You do it by hand?"

"Yes. I've always had dreams of automating certain aspects, but I was never able to make them come true. Now that you and Monica are taking over—"

"We're not kicking you out!" Ray rushed to say, horrified he might think so.

"That's not what I meant. Remember what I said about thinking about the next generation? I've been worried for the last few years what would happen to this place. I don't have anyone to hand it off to. Or, I didn't. Now, I get to share what I've learned with such an eager pupil. Every person should be so blessed."

Ray felt her eyes get teary. "I never knew my father, and I wish I could say the same about my mom. You, though, remind me of my grandfather. I wish you two could have met."

"Was he good-looking?" Christos joked. "What can I say? I'm old, not dead."

"Now who's the comedian?" Ray laughed. "Of course, Grandpa Ray was handsome. Where do you think I got this chin from?"

Christos rolled his eyes. "Such humility."

Ray's stomach tightened. There was something she needed to ask Christos, and it was even more important than moving his wine workshop to a different space. "You know Monica and I are pulling this wedding together last minute…"

He nodded.

"The thing is, we don't have an officiant. Would you consider it?" Ray closed her eyes, bracing herself in case he said no. They weren't really family, after all, and who knew what his thoughts were on weddings?

Fortunately for Ray's nerves, Christos didn't hesitate. "It would be an honor."

"You mean it?"

"I do. What do I have to do? Do I have to become a priest or something?" Christos made a sour face. "I haven't always gotten along so well with the church, but if I have to…"

"There's a form you fill out, and the state gives you a certificate that says you can officiate as a one-time thing. That's it." Ray hugged Christos, then on impulse, she placed a quick kiss on his cheek. "You're the best."

Christos looked happy enough to burst. "I said I don't have family, but I did have a sister, though she's passed on now. She didn't turn her back like the others. After my mother died, she sent me a package and a letter. I know you probably have the rings taken care of…"

"Actually, we don't," Ray blurted out. It was one of the last things on the list and had been driving Monica crazy.

"My sister sent me the wedding bands that had belonged to our mother and grandmother. I think it was her way of saying she didn't agree with my parents' decision to make me leave. I don't have children to give them to, and it would be an honor to give them to you and Monica."

Ray pressed her hand to her heart, almost unable to respond. She wanted to take them to make him happy, but was it fair? After all, her relationship with Monica wasn't what he thought. On the other hand, how she felt about Christos was very real, and maybe accepting his offer would be the best way to show him that.

"Thank you," she whispered, wiping her eyes. For the first time since her grandfather had passed, Ray remembered what it felt like to have family of her own. "I should get back to Monica now."

"Here." Christos rummaged on one of the store shelves, grabbing a bottle, one of the new ones that was sporting a beautiful, redesigned label. "Take this up to your little lady and see what she thinks. It's one of my reserve wines. Very special."

"Thank you again, Christos," Ray said, this time at full volume.

She'd recovered from her emotional overload, and all she wanted was to race back to the house and share what she'd learned with Monica. Ray frowned to herself as she ran that sentence back through her brain. When had that desire started? It was becoming harder to ignore, the wanting to talk to Monica about everything. Was it a problem? Only time would tell.

Ray approached Monica's office, pulse racing. "Monica?"

When Monica saw Ray in the doorway, she popped off her seat with excitement, running to Ray. Her smile lit up the room, and Ray's heart ticked up even faster than before.

Monica clapped her hands together. "Guess what?"

"What?"

"I just hit my two millionth follower."

"That's fantastic!" Overcome with happiness, Ray picked up Monica and spun her around.

Monica let out an excited squeal, holding tightly onto Ray.

"We should celebrate," Ray said, setting Monica back down even though the last thing she wanted was to let go. She scurried to the doorway before the woman could figure out it wasn't simply pride in her achievement that made her want to hold Monica forever, but a stronger bond that was growing between them. "I've brought back a special bottle of wine, compliments of our officiant."

"Officiant? You mean Christos agreed to do it?"

"Yes, and I've got the rings sorted out, too."

Monica looked like she could float away on a cloud. "You're the best, Ray. Those were two of the last major things on my list."

"Does that mean you settled on a bridesmaid dress for your cousin?"

Monica gave what could only be described as a wicked cackle. "I sure did."

"Do I even want to ask?" But Ray couldn't help being amused at Monica's cousin rivalry, even if she knew for certain Nina couldn't compare to this woman in front of her. Not even close. "I'm starting to feel a little bit sorry for your cousin."

Monica gave an innocent shrug. "It's not my fault there aren't many bridesmaid dresses for pregnant ladies. Now, didn't you say something about wine?"

Ray ran downstairs, coming back up with two glasses of deep red wine. Monica went to drink hers, but Ray said, "Wait. We should make a toast."

"Like what?"

To our love was the first thought that flashed into Ray's mind. She swatted it away. Ridiculous idea, and the result of too many extreme emotions in one day.

"To our future on the vineyard," was her much safer choice.

"I like that." Monica clinked her glass to Ray's.

Monica's face transformed into sheer delight after tasting the wine. "Oh, wow. This is amazing. How is this the first time I'm trying this? Has Christos been hiding the best?"

"I'm thinking this will be the highlight of the next summer season, or maybe the year after." Ray recalled what Christos had said about the nature of vineyards.

"Winemakers. We're always investing in the future, you know. It makes us optimists, according to Christos."

"You're the most optimistic person I know," Monica agreed without hesitating one beat.

"Me?" Ray pointed a finger at her own chest. Surely Monica was joking, but she looked completely earnest. "First Christos, and now you. I guess I'll have to get used to the fact this is how other people see me."

"It's not a bad way to be seen."

Ray nodded. Maybe it wasn't.

"Please, Ray. May I have some more?" Monica held up her empty glass, giggling over her Oliver Twist impression.

"Anything for you."

Monica gave an odd slant to her head, studying Ray's face like there was something new there she needed to make sense of.

Whoops. Whatever weirdness was going on inside Ray right now, she'd pushed it a little too far. Time to switch gears to something safe.

"Hey, I almost forgot what I wanted to tell you. I spent the whole day going over the operation with Christos, and he has some ideas of how to expand. Some of them won't take much money. Just some elbow grease. What do you think?"

"You haven't told me the details." She laughed. "But, I trust you, and I think it's wise to focus on growing the business. It's why we're going through with the wedding, after all."

Ray swallowed the lump in her throat and, with it, her impulse to argue that wasn't the reason at all.

Of course, it was the reason.

"It is. So, I'll get some drawings onto paper for you."

"That'd be great." Monica left the room, taking the air from Ray's lungs.

Despite the rush of warmth brought on by the wine, Ray felt a chill come over her. What if someday Monica left for good? They were business partners entering a marriage of convenience. Nothing about that spelled forever. What if Monica decided she wanted to move on?

CHAPTER NINETEEN

The light in the bedroom was gray, the kind of early morning light that could fool you into thinking it was still night if it weren't for the incessant chirping of birds outside. Monica peeped one eye open, assessing the quality of Ray's breathing with the expertise one might expect of a seasoned nurse. Slow and steady. That meant Ray was still asleep. Monica held onto Ray a little tighter, trying not to dwell on how many more seconds until she would have to let go.

Several nights before, Monica had woken with a start in the darkness, horrified to find she'd wrapped her body around Ray as thoroughly as ivy around an old stump. The source of her dismay wasn't being close to Ray. Far from it. Canoodling with Ray was amazing, in all caps. The trouble was, Monica was pretty sure she would die if Ray ever found out about it.

Night after night, after her initial discovery, Monica had woken to find herself doing the exact same thing, Ray sleeping through it blissfully unaware. Instead of letting go immediately as she'd done the first time, Monica had dared to hold on a little longer each subsequent morning, first a few seconds, then minutes. It was a risk, she knew, and yet the closeness stilled her mind. That was the reason Monica held onto Ray. She absolutely needed this little bit of calm before the madness of the day kicked in.

Just one minute more.

Monica had always known that being an only child came with added burdens, but this was becoming especially clear the longer her mother stayed with them. Her mother was soaking up every detail of this wedding like she'd never experience anything like it again. Sometimes Monica wished she could tell her mom it was all for show, to get her to relax and take it down a notch. Or ten. Other times, these moments she and her mom—and even Ray—were spending together felt so special Monica wished it could be real.

It wasn't like Monica was falling for Ray, but she did like having her around. She enjoyed the company and the way Ray provided a much-needed buffer when her mom got riled up. It was Ray's soothing factor she was addicted to. That was all. It wasn't how hot she looked in her jeans, and it certainly wasn't love or anything crazy like that. It was that Ray was like a nice cup of herbal tea.

How many times would Monica have to chant that to start believing it?

Monica noticed the clock ticking ever closer to five in the morning, meaning her snuggle time was coming to a close. Ray never set an alarm, and she never overslept. It was an astounding feat, considering how deep a sleeper Ray could be. Not surprising considering how hard she'd been working to make everything on the vineyard perfect before the wedding, not to mention the time she'd put in on building their brand for the future. When the next season of farmer's markets arrived the following summer, White Cat Winery was poised to make a huge splash, thanks to Ray.

Pretending to be fast asleep, Monica edged back to her side of the bed. That way, if Ray happened to wake up, Monica could deny any knowledge of having trespassed on her side. Moments after Monica reached the edge of the bed, like clockwork, Ray rolled onto her back. It was Ray's habit every morning to lie there for a minute, awake but silent, as if steeling herself for the day.

"Morning," Monica said through a fake yawn.

"Back at you." Ray's smile was so infectious Monica couldn't help but mirror it. She must have looked like a grinning fool because Ray's eyes narrowed suspiciously. "What?"

"Nothing. It's just I don't think I've ever met someone who's as excited as you are to greet each new day."

"New days are an amazing gift." If anyone else had said something so corny, Monica would've teased them, but Ray's sincerity made it seem like a natural thing to say, like everyone would feel the same. "We're lucky to be able to have a clean slate every sunrise. To accomplish something new."

"You must be exhausted, though." In her mind, Monica could see all the projects Ray had completed, and she marveled at their number. "We've been running you ragged. I mean, you even dug a pond for my mother."

"The landscaping crew did most of the heavy work," Ray demurred. "And considering we're paying them out of the cash from those savings bonds your grandmother left us, we both should get half the credit."

"No, don't do that. I saw you out there doing your part." Okay, specifically, Monica had seen her out there on one of the unusually warm days, stripped down to a white tank top and cutoff shorts, her biceps rippling as she wielded a shovel the way Thor would wield a hammer. But it was probably better if Monica didn't elaborate on what exactly she'd seen or the physical effects it'd had on her. "I promise I'll make my mom lay off the insane requests from now on."

"Oh, let her have her fun." Ray rolled onto her side.

"I like your mom. At first, I was overwhelmed because I have zero reference point for a mother who is actually, well, nice. Now, though…it's kind of enjoyable being around her."

"I'm glad you think so," Monica tensed as she prepared to deliver this latest bit of news, "because she's going cake tasting with us."

"That's great." Ray sounded sincere and not the least bit flustered as Monica had been when her mom had announced her intention the night before. "I wouldn't have it any other way. I'm glad we're going with a local cake maker person."

"You mean baker?" Secretly, Monica loved it when Ray was exhausted and her brain sputtered like that, leaving her unable to think of a simple word. "You'd better like it since it was your idea."

"Well, it made sense to me to use all local businesses." Ray frowned. "But if you'd rather go with a bigger name in Boston, we can do that."

"Not at all. When it comes to going local, we're in complete agreement," Monica reassured her. Strangely, when it came to almost any part of this fake wedding of theirs, it had been the same. She and Ray were pretty much in full agreement over everything, or at least the decisions where it really counted.

"Good. The more we help get exposure for our fellow farmer's market businesses, the more of your blog followers who'll want to come to the area."

"You can't underestimate the importance of that

type of exposure," Monica said. "Did you know that when Prince Harry and Meghan selected a small shop for their cake, the woman who owned it was swamped with business even a year later."

"Just so I make sure I understand, are you picturing yourself as Prince Harry or Meghan in this scenario?" Ray flashed her killer teasing smile, the one that spurred heat to flood Monica's systems. "Because I kinda have you pegged more as the royalty type, but I can't picture Harry pulling off one of your little pencil skirts like Meghan could."

Monica stuck her tongue out at Ray, relishing the delight in the woman's eyes. The funny thing was, since they'd arrived on the vineyard and embarked on country life, those pencil skirts—along with the blouses and heels that went with them—hadn't seen the light of day. Monica had pretty much been living in leggings, cozy sweaters, and equestrian boots, and loving every minute.

"Are you sure it's okay if my mom joins us? I can tell her no."

"Can you really, though? I have yet to meet someone who can tell your mother no. Hell, I'm still on the lookout for a pair of swans." Ray patted Monica's hand, a throwaway gesture she probably hadn't even realized she'd done and certainly wouldn't expect that it had turned Monica's brain to such mush she could barely concentrate on the rest of Ray's words. "Seriously, it's perfectly fine with me—no, not fine. It's what I want. You're lucky to have such a mother like her. I'd never do anything to upset her, and I'm sure she's dying to try the cake as much as you are."

"What do you mean, as much as I am?"

"Oh, please. You printed out pictures of the cakes from Dorothy's website and keep them on your nightstand."

"I do like cake," Monica admitted.

"No, I like cake," Ray corrected. "What you feel for cake borders on unnatural. I'm surprised you didn't put those pictures in a silver frame."

"So," Monica said, doing her best to redirect the conversation away from her obsession with cake, "tell Mom it's okay?"

"Of course. She drives you batty, and it's fun to watch. Don't deny me simple joys."

Remembering what little Monica knew about Ray's mom, she understood what Ray meant. Monica had always taken her mom for granted, but she'd begun to learn, through Ray's eyes, how special the bond between mother and daughter could be. This was one other time when Monica truly wished her relationship with Ray was real. Monica couldn't heal the breach between Ray and her mother, but if they were honestly getting married, she would've been able to let Ray become a part of her family. It hurt that she couldn't make that happen when it was so obvious how much Ray needed it.

THE BELL on the cake shop tinkled as Ray opened the door, holding it wide so Monica and her mother could pass through first. In the months they'd known each other, Monica couldn't remember a single time Ray hadn't opened the door for her. It was a strange sensation, the way Ray treated her with respect. She was so unlike Monica's ex-girlfriends, who, she was realizing more and more, had been quite an impressive collection of self-centered divas. It wasn't like Monica demanded special treatment. As much as Ray joked, Monica didn't need to be treated like a princess to be happy. That didn't mean she couldn't enjoy the way it made her feel, like someone was watching out for her and taking care of her.

"Look at this place," Ray said in a hushed tone when she stepped inside the shop, which had a stone fireplace along one wall, flanked with shelves filled with teapots, lace doilies, and other adorably vintage decor. Two massive cases at the front were filled with cakes and pastries, and the shop had several cozy groupings of tables and chairs to provide plenty of seating for guests in front of wide windows that overlooked a gorgeous fall garden. "It's an Instagram dream."

Monica had been thinking the same thing. In fact, she was already reaching for her phone to snap some pics. It was funny to hear Ray say it, though, considering the woman had probably never heard of social media before they'd met. Now Ray was becoming a real pro, studying the photos that got the best results so she could help Monica with staging all around the vineyard. When Monica had hit two million followers, Ray had brought home a bottle of Christos's best reserve Cabernet Sauvignon to celebrate the milestone. Brianna never would've done that. She'd thought Monica's blog was a waste of time and had been consumed with jealousy over what she'd considered an easy and glamorous job. But not Ray, who praised Monica daily for her shrewd business acumen and recognized the hard work that went into what she did.

"Oh, look at all those lovely cakes." Monica's mom bent over to peer at all the delicacies. "How many do we get to try?"

"Easy there," Monica teased. "With the wedding a week away, I don't think any of us wants to have our outfits let out."

"I'm not afraid to buy a new dress if I can eat more," her mom replied, and Monica thought she might be serious.

Ray chuckled. "The beauty of wearing a suit is I can always hide an extra pound or two under the jacket."

Actually, Ray's wedding outfit had been a compromise and wasn't nearly as roomy as she liked to joke, thanks to Monica's eye for clothing. A dress had been out of the question, of course, but so, too, had a man's suit like the one Ray had gravitated to at first. Not that there was anything wrong with the concept, but it had hung on her like a sack. After some cajoling, and an appeal to the importance of looking good in wedding photos that two million people would see on the internet, they'd found an amazing tailor near Worcester who had custom designed a suit with the perfect blend of masculine style with feminine shaping. Of course, with Ray's metabolism and the amount of work she'd been doing, no number of cake samples would threaten her figure before the wedding.

"Hey there," the shop's owner, Dorothy, said as she came out from the back.

"Hi, Dorothy," Monica said. "Thank you so much for being willing to take this on with such short notice."

"Are you kidding?" Dorothy's eyes twinkled. "This is one of the most exciting projects I've had all year. It's no trouble at all. Have a seat at the table, and I'll bring out tea and cakes for you to try so we can finalize your order today."

When they'd chosen a table, Ray pulled out Monica's mom's seat and then Monica's before taking her own. She'd done so each time they'd gone to restaurants, too. Even so, Monica was pretty sure she'd never tire of Ray's good manners.

Dorothy appeared with a tray holding a white teapot with delicate blue flowers on it, and matching cups and saucers. After setting these on the table, she disappeared again, returning with another tray, containing small cakes and three forks. "I'm so excited for you to try these."

Monica and her mom made approving sounds while Ray eyed the tray apprehensively. "They look a little too pretty to eat."

"You won't say that when you hear the flavors," Dorothy said. "This one is a tiramisu. Then we've got a chocolate salted caramel, because sweet and salty are pretty much the perfect combination. There's a classic vanilla jam cake if you want to play it safe, or for a daring option, this one here is a coconut pudding cake. All three layers are made of vanilla sponge cake and have coconut pudding filling, drizzled with white rum-coconut milk syrup."

"That's..." Ray touched her tongue to her lips. "Oh my God."

Dorothy grinned. "Finally, here's the one I'm particularly proud of. It's a chocolate violet cream cake."

Monica's eyes glistened as she admired the cake, which was covered in a delicately hued violet buttercream frosting that had been piped to look like the most amazing flowers. "It's beautiful."

"It's three layers of dark chocolate devil's cake, drizzled with vanilla bean syrup. Inside there's buttercream, with the sides a slight shade of violet." Dorothy paused for a second before adding, "Of course, since this is for a wedding, we can always go with traditional white if you prefer."

"Not at all," Monica commented. "The color is spectacular, and I'm all for shaking things up."

"I don't care how they look, as long as they taste good." Monica's mom gripped her fork. "I'm going for the chocolate salted caramel first."

Dorothy nodded her approval. "I'll leave you three to it. Enjoy."

Monica made an "oh my god, that's delicious" sound after sampling the chocolate violet cream, and Ray did the same with the tiramisu. By the time they'd made it through all of the options, Monica felt like she'd been transported to another realm.

"I'm going to need to try these all again." Monica shut her eyes, reveling in the ecstasy that was her taste buds at that moment.

"I agree," Ray said. "This might be the most important decision I will ever make in my life." She reached for the teapot and refilled all three teacups.

"Thank you, dear," Monica's mom said.

"Anything for you, Mom." The ease with which the name Mom rolled off Ray's tongue hurt Monica's heart. When all of this was over and they'd settled the inheritance and ended their marriage, what was her mother going to think?

"Do you really mean that, Ray?" Monica's mom spoke in that tone she used when she was about to ask for something big. "In that case, is it possible to add a few more tables for the reception?"

Monica's fork clattered onto the table. "Mom." She took a cleansing breath. "We settled on the guest list weeks ago. The invitations have gone out, the RSVPs are all in, and I gave our preliminary headcount to the caterer this morning."

"I know, but we can still add to that until Friday, right? If I didn't have to, I wouldn't ask."

Monica's eyes narrowed. "Why do you have to ask?"

Her mom looked studiously at a spot of tea on the tablecloth. "It seems your father and I had a communication issue."

Uh-huh. Monica wasn't buying this. "You're saying Dad wants to bring random people to my wedding?"

"Not random. He knows them all. In fact, so do you."

Monica's stomach tightened, which was most unpleasant considering how full it was. "Who?"

"The people at the office." Her mom held up a finger to ward off the complaint Monica was preparing to raise. "Most of them have been with us since we opened the firm. They're like family. They've known you since you were little."

Monica blinked. "But I'm sure they don't expect to be invited."

"They sort of already have been."

"Mom!" As Monica's temperature skyrocketed, Ray

sipped her tea as quietly as a mouse, as if hoping to stay out of the fray.

"It was an accident," her mom insisted.

"How do you accidentally invite an entire office?"

"Well, you know your poor dad and technology." Monica's mom chuckled, irritating Monica to the core. Now was not the time to try to make her feel sympathy for her dad's total inability to operate a computer. "He was trying to respond to a photo I'd shared with him of how nice the vineyard is looking, and he accidentally emailed it out to the full company email list."

"Okay, and?" Monica's body tensed, waiting for the conclusion of the story, the part where disaster struck.

"I guess the way he'd worded his response to me kind of made it sound like he was inviting everyone, and then they all got so excited and started emailing him that yes, they'd love to come to the wedding. It's turned into the most exciting thing to happen since the time in 2001 when we were preparing that case for the Supreme Court. I mean, honestly, Monica, how can you expect him to disappoint them all after that?"

Monica's nostrils flared as she tried not to lose it completely. "How did my father, a lawyer, manage so poorly to word an email that he invited an extra dozen people to my wedding?"

"Two dozen."

"Since when do you have that many people working in the office?"

"They have to be allowed to bring dates. As for how it happened, your dad's never been good at wording things," her mom answered as if that somehow explained it. "That's why I usually take care of company correspondence."

"I hope the next correspondence you plan to write for him is his retirement letter. I think you two moving full-time to Florida would do everybody a lot of good." Monica was about to lay into her for real when her mom's phone vibrated.

"Oh, that's your father now. I'm going to step outside." Her mom grabbed the phone and scurried to the door as if barely able to believe the good fortune of her timing.

"I can't believe her." Monica's whole body shook as she tried not to scream. "If she thinks I'm falling for the accidental email or whatever, she has another thing coming. We can't add two dozen more guests. That's three more tables."

"If we take a little space from the dance floor, it could work." Ray rested her hand gently on top of Monica's, soothing her somewhat, though not enough for her to let it go.

"No." Monica used her free hand to slap the table. "I'm putting my foot down."

"It's not like we can uninvite all of their employees. Not when they're taking time off and coming all this way. That's mean."

"But *we* didn't invite them." Tears stung Monica's

eyes as she folded her arms over her chest. It wasn't nearly as effective as a hug from Ray would've been. Oh, why couldn't she fall into Ray's arms and sob like she wanted to? "I knew something like this would happen. This is a disaster."

"It's not a disaster." Ray's tone was calm and quiet.

"It is!" Monica cringed. A tear slid down her cheek, and she didn't even try to stop the rest from falling. It was no use. "I'm a professional wedding planner. I'm supposed to see this kind of shit coming from a mile away. What's wrong with me?"

"Nothing is wrong with you." Ray scooted close enough that she could rest one hand on each of Monica's shoulders. It felt like they were the only things keeping her from bursting apart. "There's a reason surgeons don't operate on themselves or why lawyers don't defend themselves in court. It's a whole different ballgame when it's your own wedding."

"It's not supposed to be." Monica wished she could yell but instead spoke barely above a whisper. "It's not like it's a real wedding."

Hurt flashed in Ray's eyes, but when she spoke, there was no trace of it in her voice. "The wedding itself is very real. It's not like it becomes easier to throw a party for hundreds of people just because the relationship itself is f—untraditional."

Monica swallowed, willing herself to stop crying, all the while wondering if there had really been a slight slip in Ray's words. Had she meant to say fake and changed her mind, or was Monica imagining it?

"This whole thing is getting out of control." At that moment Monica wasn't sure if she meant the wedding or all of it.

"Listen," Ray soothed. "We'll do some rejiggering of the tables. Amend the food order slightly to keep costs down if we need to. Look at the bright side. We haven't picked out the cake yet, so we can place a large enough order now and not need to worry."

Monica shot a seething look at her mother, who was still outside, although whether she was actually on the phone or pretending to be to avoid her daughter's wrath was anyone's guess.

"She shouldn't get to win." For some reason, Monica didn't want to give an inch on this.

"You need to give up now. I know you're stubborn, but"—Ray pointed to the dimple on her chin—"I've got you beat. This isn't worth a war or your mental health."

"But, Ray—"

"No buts. We're going to tell your mom fine on the extra guests, place our order for the cake, and then I have an idea. What's on your calendar the next few days?"

"A ton." Monica gave her a look she hoped implied how stupid a question that was when they were planning a wedding.

"For real?" Ray pressed. "Because I know I have a

ton on my plate for the weekend, but right now, I'm kind of in a lull. I thought it might be the same for you, too."

Monica pressed her lips together, tightening her jaw. Ray was right, damn it. Once the cake was sorted, the next couple of days were wide open, the calm before the storm.

"That's what I thought." Ray held her eyes, and it was impossible not to see her look of triumph. "You know what you need? A break. What about along the coast? We'll get in the car and find a charming seaside village somewhere in Maine to rest our minds and bodies."

"How are we supposed to rest? We're getting married next week."

"Didn't you say everything is taken care of for now?"

"Yes, but—"

"But nothing. After how hard we've worked, we deserve a break, and if we don't take the opportunity, one of us might end up murdering someone before it's all through."

Monica sighed, knowing she was beat. "Murder does put a damper on things."

"What puts a damper on things?" Monica's mom returned to the table, looking somewhat repentant. It didn't make up for what she'd done, but it was a start. "Not our little mistake, I hope. Your dad and I are so sorry."

"No worries. We've worked it out," Ray told her. "I'm hoping you'll hold down the fort for a couple days, make sure Mr. Fluffles gets his fancy food every day the way he likes it."

Monica's mom covered her mouth with one hand. "You're not eloping, are you?"

Ray chuckled. "No. Monica and I are heading to Maine. We need a mental health break."

"Having the honeymoon before the wedding? I don't get your generation. The way you do everything backward." Monica's mom winked. "I'm joking. That's so romantic. Don't you worry. Mr. Fluffles and I will do fine at the house."

Dorothy returned to the table, wearing a hopeful look. "Do we have a winner?"

Monica tensed. With the guest debacle, they'd forgotten about the task at hand. She knew which one was her favorite, but... "Ray loves tiramisu. We should go with that."

"I do," Ray countered, "but the violet one is so pretty. Totally Instagrammable and you know it."

"Yeah," Monica conceded, "but how do you know it?"

"I've picked up a few things in our time together. Besides, purple is your favorite color."

There was another detail she'd picked up on. Monica's favorite color was, indeed, purple, but she was certain she'd never mentioned it to Ray.

"The violet one?" Dorothy repeated, looking to confirm the order.

Monica met Ray's gaze and nodded. "The violet one."

"Look at you two, how well you work together." Monica's mom placed a hand on each of the brides. "I know in my heart you two are going to make each other so very happy for the rest of your lives."

For the second time that morning, Monica wished she could curl up in a ball and sob.

CHAPTER TWENTY

The sign for Brunswick, Maine was ahead, their exit another mile down the road. Ray gripped the steering wheel, her heart thudding in her throat, nearly strangling her. What had she been thinking, inviting Monica for a trip away like this, alone? They were getting fake married in less than a week, but somehow, that raised the stakes for their pre-honeymoon significantly. Ray couldn't shake the feeling that this was it. If she wanted Monica to know how she really felt about her, it was kind of a now-or-never scenario.

"I can't believe how excited I am to get away for a couple of days. I love my mother, but she can be intense about some things. My clients thought I was a perfectionist, but..." Monica shimmied in the passenger seat, giving the impression she was shaking a monkey off her back.

"You're sure you're not freaking out about the time away?"

"No. I've accepted you might be right about me needing it. Besides, I get to see how good my future wife is at picking *romantic* getaways." Monica made playful quote marks in the air, clearly expecting romance to be totally off the menu.

How to play it? Ray wondered.

Cool, calm, and collected?

Go hard or go home?

"Do you trust me?" Ray asked, not entirely sure where she was going with it but praying it would be brilliant.

"Considering we're business partners in a potential million-dollar venture, I'd sure hope so."

"Good to know." Ray hated being reminded that business was the only real link between them. Yes, it had started out that way, but the past fifty-plus days had shown Ray one thing. If there had ever been the right woman for her, Monica was it. The only problem was she clearly didn't think the same about Ray.

"So where are we going?" Monica asked.

"I told you it's a surprise. I thought you said you trusted me."

"I do, but—"

"No take backs. Let's make the surprise more fun." *And give myself time to throw the car into reverse*, Ray thought, *if it turns out this Airbnb is a total sham.* "Wrap your scarf around your eyes."

"A blindfold?" Monica turned in her seat, training those lovely eyes onto Ray, practically searing holes into her. There was laughter in them and maybe a hint of something else that Ray couldn't read. "I didn't know you were into kink. Any other secrets I should know before we walk down the aisle?"

"I'm serious. Do you trust me?"

"Yes, but..."

"Either you do or you don't." Ray stuck to her nerve, mostly because she was curious if Monica would give in.

"Fine, but I don't see the point—"

"You not seeing *is* the point. We're a mile away." Ray jabbed a finger at her phone, which was clipped into the air vent and had the GPS on display. "It won't be for long."

With a deep sigh of resignation, Monica took the purple scarf Ray had bought her at the farmer's market and wrapped it around her eyes. "This is really soft, by the way. Thank you again."

"Sally was right. There's nothing softer than alpaca. It'll be about ten degrees cooler up here in Maine." Ray glanced at the cloud-filled sky, recalling the updated forecast that called for thunder and lightning, but decided not to mention it. "I can't have you freezing."

"You really do take care of all the details."

"Hey now, when I say I'm taking you away for a weekend to relax, I mean it."

"I've never had someone pack my bag for me before, unless you count Bri boxing up my stuff so she could move me out." As she said it, Monica wriggled her head up as if trying to steal a peek.

"No cheating!"

Burying her head back into the scarf, Monica crossed her arms tightly over her chest. "How much longer?"

Ray pulled onto a gravel drive. "Soon, princess."

"I don't think it's fair you call me princess when I've never demanded special treatment. You're the one who insists on opening doors and pulling out chairs and all that."

"Oh, should I treat you monstrously?" Ray joked.

"No, please don't." Monica's voice grew softer, giving Ray a tickling sensation that ran from her neck to her toes. "I like the things you do."

Ray fumbled for a comeback, but then the house she'd rented came into view, and the best she could manage was, "Oh, wow."

"What?" Monica started to nudge her scarf upward. "Is it good? Is it bad? I want to see."

"Not yet." Ray took in the massive deck jutting out from the side of the house with an unobstructed view of the lake. That was the spot Monica should see first. She'd get her reaction on video. It would be internet gold. "Keep the scarf over your eyes while I get you out of the car."

Ray slammed the car into park and hopped out,

dashing to Monica's door before the woman lost control and ruined the effect. "Okay, put your feet on the ground. I'll guide you."

"You're taking this a little far, don't you think?"

"What can I say?" Ray gave what she knew was a thoroughly evil chuckle. "It's fun having you at my mercy."

Monica let out a throaty growl that made her sound like Mr. Fluffles when he saw a bird in the garden, but Ray knew the woman well enough now to be confident Monica was enjoying the game.

Ray put her hands firmly on Monica's shoulders. "Walk straight ahead, slowly. In about ten steps, we'll reach a small staircase. That's right. One foot after the other. It's like you've been walking all your life or something."

"You think you're so funny!"

"I'll be here for the next two nights, ladies and gentlemen," Ray teased in her best imitation of a standup comic. "Okay. There are seven steps, and then we're going to the left."

Carefully, they climbed the steps.

When they reached the deck, Ray positioned her in the best spot to maximize the view. "Give me your phone."

"Why? Are you planning to kill me, and you don't want me to be able to call for help?" Monica put her hands on her hips. "You know, you only inherit my half of the vineyard *after* the wedding, poopsie."

At the mention of their arrangement, Ray had immediately bristled and was fighting to remain upbeat. Why did she have to keep hinting at how fake this all was? "Come on, Monica. I want to take a video for your blog."

"What? It's not that kind of blog."

"It's not that kind of video," Ray countered. "On yesterday's podcast, you mentioned I'm whisking you away for a romantic getaway—like a reverse honeymoon. Let's get a video of your reaction to wow your followers."

"Oh, good idea." Sounding somewhat surprised, Monica handed off her phone. "Let me know when you're ready. I'll really play it up."

"Yes. Do your best." Ray's gaze swept the view, which was magnificent. There would be no need to pretend. "What's the passcode for the phone?"

"One-one-one-six. I use it for everything."

"Eleven sixteen," Ray said as she pressed the numbers. "Our wedding day?"

"What? No." Monica let out a high-pitched, manic sound that was probably supposed to have been a laugh. "That's a total coincidence. That happened to be my high school locker combination."

The hell it was.

Ray swallowed a lump in her throat but managed to ready the phone. "All set."

Monica pushed the blindfold off, blinked several times, and then turned tear-filled eyes to Ray. "Oh my

God. This is amazing. It's so beautiful. I can't believe you pulled this off in such a short amount of time. You're the most amazing woman I've ever met."

If any of that had been an act, Monica deserved an Oscar.

"Oh, Ray, take a look at this." She pointed to where the caretaker had prepped the outdoor fire pit. All it needed was a spark. "Would it be terrible if we had s'mores and hot chocolate for dinner?"

"Absolutely not." Ray kept the video rolling a moment longer before shutting it off, capturing an expression of hopeful innocence and excitement playing across Monica's features that she would cherish for the rest of her life. "In fact, I think it's a must. I was told there would be supplies for both in the kitchen inside."

Monica rubbed her hands together in absolute glee. "I was hoping you'd say that. Can you get the fire going while I take care of the hot chocolate?"

The sun was setting over the lake, the remaining rays licking the surface of the water, turning it a brilliant orange red. As Monica rummaged in the kitchen, Ray snapped several more photos, knowing they would be perfect for the blog. She managed to catch a few candids of Monica, too. Ray wondered if she could convince Monica to caption the one of her pouring an envelope of Swiss Miss into a mug *Domestic Goddess at Work*. After all, thanks to the dinners Ray had cooked, Monica's readers were well aware by now which of them had the culinary skills. They would eat this whole thing up, for sure.

The truth was, as they settled into side by side Adirondack chairs in front of the roaring fire, they made an excellent team. Never had Ray worked so well with someone else, other than the guys on her restoration crews—and she was damn sure none of them had ever given her the types of thoughts she got every time she looked at Monica. It wasn't just when she was all dressed up, like she'd been the first day they met. In fact, if anything, that had been Monica trying too hard. Ray liked her better now, the softer, more casual Monica who could throw on a sweatshirt against the morning chill, who pulled her hair back into a messy ponytail and toasted marshmallows on the end of a stick with an almost childlike appreciation.

"You're catching it on fire," Ray cautioned, pointing to said marshmallow on a stick.

"Of course, I am," Monica replied. "I like to get them all gooey first and then torch 'em to get a perfect charred crust."

"That's sacrilege." And even this terrible revelation did nothing to sway Ray's belief they were perfect together. That had to be a sign.

"Would you like a glass of wine?" Ray offered when their hot chocolate mugs were thoroughly drained. "I brought that one from the New Hampshire winery Christos has been talking up. I'm thinking if we place an order with the juice supplier in Italy right after the wedding, we can get a batch going and give them a run for their money."

"I think it's sweet how much time you spend with Christos."

"I've learned a lot from him," Ray said. "The man knows his wines."

"He's also old and lonely, and having you as his student has given him a new lease on life. Another person you're taking care of," Monica ribbed her gently.

"I guess so," Ray admitted.

"Is it because of your childhood, your mother? I've been reading how sometimes kids whose parents are addicts kind of reverse roles." Monica's voice was low, and she looked into the fire as she said it. Even so, Ray found it jarring. Monica had never asked about Ray's history so directly before. And when she said she'd been reading about it, was that because of Ray?

"Yeah. I guess that's how it was. My mother wasn't able to take care of anything, including herself. I took on a lot, at a really young age."

Ray shifted in her seat, not wanting to talk about it but knowing she needed to. If this thing between them was ever going to be real, she had to be an open book. She told Monica about the times there was no food in the house because her mom had been too high to go shopping, and the random strangers who would be invited to stay for days in their spare room because her mom was a generous drunk. The birthday money that inevitably went missing. The presents from Grandpa Ray that ended up at the pawn shop. Making her own lunch and getting herself to the bus stop when she was only in first grade.

"I'm sorry, Ray," Monica said when Ray was done. "No one should have to give up their childhood like that."

"I didn't realize it at the time." As hard as it was to believe sometimes as an adult, Ray knew this was true. She'd thought it was normal. "I mean, I knew my situation was different from my classmates, but I didn't really understand how much I was taking on. And then it became a habit. A really hard one to break."

"What do you mean?"

"Every relationship I've had has starred me as the caretaker. Broken women seem to flock to me like a moth to a flame. They love the attention and feeling special, but it becomes a one-way street." Ray hadn't been one for therapy, quit after a few sessions, but she'd read every book she could find and diagnosed herself over time. "Here's a little-known fact about caretakers. Sometimes we need help, too."

"Of course, you do." Monica leaned forward, the fire making her eyes sparkle, or perhaps it was a misty sheen of unshed tears.

"The problem is, if you ask for it, my experience is that most don't like it."

"Girlfriends?"

Ray nodded, ticking them off in her mind. "Every

time. Like I'm breaking some covenant of always being the bedrock, never crumbling no matter how hard things get. It's exhausting to keep that up."

"I can imagine."

"After the last time, which ended with me losing my condo because of her bad debt and moving back in with Grandpa Ray, I decided I was done with relationships. I couldn't put myself through that again."

"How long ago was that?"

"Five years. I mean, there's been physical stuff," Ray added quickly, not wanting Monica to think she was too bizarre. "I haven't been celibate all that time. But a real relationship? No."

"Do you want one?"

"I want to be on equal footing. That's hard to find. I can't be a caretaker anymore."

"I hope I don't fall into that category."

"Monica, you're probably one of the most capable people I've ever known." *You have to say it,* Ray urged herself. *You have to tell her.*

But as the seconds ticked past, she couldn't make the right words come out.

"I think my mom is seeing I'm actually good at my job, even if I didn't become a lawyer, and it's kind of a threat to her."

Damn it. The opportunity was gone. "What do you mean a threat?"

"I don't know, but I think that's why she's gone so nuts with all this wedding shit. Me being good at it is causing her to kick it into a higher gear so I'm still her little girl on some level."

Ray chuckled. "It's amazing how quickly she can get under your skin."

"Mock all you want."

"I'm sorry." Ray met Monica's eyes. "I wasn't mocking. Honestly, when it comes to your mom, I'm extremely jealous."

"Would you like to have a closer family?"

Ray took a deep breath, wincing at how much the question stung. "I know it will never happen, given the way my mother is. I mean, I haven't seen her in years, and I'm better off for it. But do I wish it could've been different? Yeah. I think having a close family is what every kid from a messed-up home dreams of."

There was no doubt the fire had nothing to do with it this time. Monica's eyes brimmed with tears. But whatever she was about to say was lost as a flash of lightning briefly turned the lake an electric white. It was followed seconds later by a crack of thunder. Ray jumped.

"You okay?" Monica asked.

"I'm not a big fan of electrical storms," Ray confessed. She wasn't sure if she'd shared that with anyone else before. "I know it's stupid."

"No, it isn't. Maybe we should get inside."

"Yes, it's getting late anyway." Ray rose and headed to the door. "Oh, here's some good news for you. This place has two bedrooms. You get the fancier one, naturally."

"Why do I get the fancy one?"

"Because that's the type of person I am."

"Yeah, I know, but it's not how I am." Monica rose to her feet, resting a hand on one hip and giving Ray a level stare. "I don't want you to confuse me with those exes of yours, those takers. Not ever. We should be fair about everything."

"Seriously, Monica." Ray sighed. She should've seen that coming. "I didn't share those details to guilt you into things."

"I don't feel guilty." Monica reached into her pocket. "Let's flip a coin."

There was another brilliant flash of lightning followed by a thunderous clap.

"Okay, but inside."

Monica swept up the hot chocolate mugs and ducked through the door, while Ray tailed her with a pile of blankets they'd wrapped over their legs. They got inside not a moment too soon. As Ray was sliding the door shut, rain began to pelt the glass like someone had turned a fire hose on the side of the house.

Monica, undeterred by the spectacular deluge, held a quarter in her hand. "Do you want heads or tails?"

Ray groaned. She hated to admit it, but this woman was every bit as stubborn as she was. "Tails."

Monica flipped the coin and caught it in her hand. "Tails it is. You win."

Ray grinned. "Excellent, in that case, I choose the small room."

"Nope. That's not how it works." Monica wagged a finger in the air. "The winner gets the large room."

"That's...cheating." Ray couldn't really explain why, but it had to be.

"No." Monica planted her hands on her hips. "It's heads or tails. It's not complicated."

"Doesn't the winner usually get to pick which thing they want?"

"Not this time." Monica waved off Ray's suggestion, yawning. "Little bedroom's over here?"

"Yes." She said it calmly, but inside, Ray was screaming at her earlier self for being so stupid as to book a place with two rooms. After so many weeks of sharing a bed with Monica, she didn't want to be alone.

"I guess this is good night, then." Monica's smile faltered. Was it possible she'd gotten used to their arrangement, too?

Ray didn't want it to be. Why wouldn't the words come out? How hard was it to say I love you and I don't want to be alone anymore?

Pretty fucking hard, as it turned out.

Ray gulped. "I guess it is."

Monica held Ray's gaze for several seconds, before saying, "Nighty, night."

For the first time in ages, Ray had a king-size bed all to herself. Instead of spreading out and luxuriating in all that space like royalty, Ray tossed and turned, unable to close her eyes for longer than five seconds. If the clock on the nightstand could be believed, it was past midnight, but the storm seemed to be picking up again. It wasn't just the thunder keeping her awake. It was the emptiness in the bed.

She hadn't slept alone for weeks now, and she needed Monica's calming presence, craved it with such an intensity that Ray finally realized a little of what her mother must've gone through, wanting to feel better and thinking only drugs could help.

Ray didn't want drugs. She wanted Monica.

But she couldn't have Monica.

Maybe there was chamomile tea in the kitchen.

Even as she told herself she was an idiot for thinking a cup of flower petals soaked in boiling water could substitute for a living, breathing woman, Ray tossed the covers back and scrambled out of bed, putting bare feet onto the frigid wood floor.

In the kitchen, she spied a glass jar with tea bags, and after sniffing them, she decided they were definitely not chamomile. They weren't really anything recognizable, but based on the fact they looked like dried lawn clippings, they were probably an herbal variety, so at least there would be no caffeine. Not that it mattered. Ray was certain she wasn't going to get any sleep. She was going through the motions to give herself something to do.

She filled the electric kettle, flipped it on, and then turned around to look in the cabinets for a mug. Finding one, she reached for it, right when there was a deafening clap of thunder. Ray let out a yelp, and the mug fell from her hand, shattering on the floor.

"Ray! Are you okay?" Monica flew out of her room.

"Careful where you step." Ray pointed to the shards on the floor.

Monica's eyes flickered downward for a fraction of a second, but then she was staring at Ray's face, assessing her as if the broken bits didn't matter at all. As if there was something much more important to her in need of tending. "Did you hurt yourself? Are you cut?"

"I don't think so." Ray looked at her feet and shin, not spotting any blood. She felt out of sorts but not injured. Why was Monica there, looking at her like that? "The thunder startled me; that's all."

"Come here." Monica skirted the broken pieces and pulled Ray into her arms. "You're shaking like a leaf."

Ray stiffened, even though the only thing keeping her from melting into a puddle was her firm resolve. "I'm acting like a child."

Monica held on tighter. "Shh, everything's going to be okay."

Ray leaned into the embrace, feeling Monica's

nipples pressing into Ray's thin T-shirt. Her resolve was growing less firm by the second, in direct proportion, as it happened, to how rapidly her own nipples were growing hard. Had she discovered a mystical balance to the universe?

Had she actually opened that bottle of wine she'd offered Monica, even though she didn't remember doing so, and was now impossibly drunk?

Another lightning strike was quickly followed by thunder. Her heart jumped like a panicked rabbit.

"I think that was right overhead." Monica protected Ray's head as if there was actual danger. "I've never been in a storm like this. Have you?"

"Not that I can remember, but as you've probably guessed, I've never liked them."

The kettle clicked off as the water reached a boil.

"Do you still want tea?" Monica asked, loosening her grip a fraction.

"No." The only thing Ray wanted was for Monica to never let go.

"Shall we get you back to bed?" Monica's voice was filled with an emotion Ray couldn't put her finger on.

"Maybe I'll sleep on the couch. Having the back of it might make me feel safer."

"No way am I letting you sleep on the couch, not when you have a king-size bed."

It's lonely without you, Ray's brain whimpered.

"Do you want me to come in with you until you fall asleep?" Monica offered. Had she read Ray's thoughts? Or, more likely, were they written all over her face?

She should definitely say no. It was the only proper thing to do.

"Yes," she answered instead, because screw being proper. Ray couldn't force her head away from the safety of the crook of Monica's neck.

Monica ran her hand up and down Ray's back, like she'd been doing most nights when they shared a bed.

Ray's muscles started to unclench in response.

"There you go," she soothed. "You're starting to relax. Look at me."

Ray burrowed her face further into Monica's shoulder.

"Please, Ray. Look at me."

Slowly, Ray lifted her head and was startled by the unmistakable longing in those clear blue eyes. Monica cupped Ray's cheek. "I won't let anything happen to you."

Ray's mind was going a million miles a second thinking of all the things she wanted to happen to her. As Monica's pupils grew impossibly large and dark, it was possible she was of the same mind.

Ray moved her head closer, Monica mirroring the action.

Their eyes met, as if each was asking of the other if this was okay.

Yes. Yes, it was.

Neither spoke, but the force pulling them closer

became increasingly impossible to resist, until, at last, their lips collided with need. As soon as the initial hunger was sated, a tenderness took over, allowing Ray to savor the moment. If this might be the last kiss they ever shared, she wanted to make it memorable.

Monica's velvet lips smothered Ray's, each caress healing a part of the scarred woman Ray kept under wraps. It was magical.

Then it happened. Monica opened her mouth, allowing Ray's tongue to explore and taste to her heart's desire. It wasn't solely Ray whose need was rapidly reaching a crescendo. As Monica hungrily explored Ray's mouth with her tongue, her fingers dug into the back of Ray's head with such force Ray might've screamed had she not been too distracted to notice.

Monica pulled back, breathing heavily. "Where?"

"What?" Ray gulped. Why was Monica asking her difficult questions when her brain was about to explode?

"My bed or yours?"

The meaning of Monica's question dawned, but was this really going to happen? There was no doubt in Monica's tone or intense stare. All Ray had to do was make a choice. Heads or tails.

"Mine."

Monica took Ray by the hand and marched them into the bedroom with a pace that clearly meant no take backs. Ray had been daydreaming about this moment night after night—right down to Monica's total bossiness—thinking it would never happen.

Now it was about to.

At the foot of the bed, Monica reached under Ray's shirt, their lips meeting again, while her fingers walked over Ray's bare skin. Yearning for more, Ray reached for Monica's nightie, only to be met with yards of fabric. What had looked so pretty folded up in a drawer, inspiring several nights of strange *Little House on the Prairie* inspired fantasies, turned out to be a pain in the ass when actually trying to remove it from a real woman.

"How do I get in?" Ray demanded. She was pretty sure that even in the heat of the moment, Monica would never forgive her for ripping it.

"Ask nicely."

Ray's pulse pounded in her throat. "Monica, dear, can I touch you?"

Monica didn't move or answer, her eyes digging into Ray.

"I know you've been teased before about that"—Ray pointed to the cotton nightgown—"but if you want to know a secret, I think it's kinda hot. Except now, I want to see what's underneath."

"Do you mean all of these times we've undressed for bed, you haven't peeked once?"

Ray shook her head. "Have you?"

"Not then."

"When, then?" Ray asked with a smirk.

"It's possible, when you're working in the field with Christos, your shirt slips up, and I can't help but see…things."

Ray cupped Monica's cheek. "Things?"

"Very nice, soft things."

"You're fully admitting you've been ogling me."

"Very much so."

"Before this moment, I never liked thunder, but I'm starting to change my mind."

The air crackled with electricity that had nothing to do with the storm.

Ray's eyes zeroed in on a long row of buttons on the front of Monica's nightgown. "Ah, the keys to the castle." She undid one, quirking an eyebrow as if asking if she should pop the next one open. Monica's facial expression didn't change, so Ray did, revealing tantalizing cleavage. Another button offered enough room for Ray to reach a hand in, her fingers teasing a nipple, which sprang to life with the first gentle tweak. Once again and it hardened even more, eliciting a low groan from deep in Ray's chest.

Monica sank her teeth into her bottom lip, her head tilting back as her eyes fluttered closed.

Ray was able to undo a few more buttons, allowing her mouth to take a nipple, causing Monica's breath to hitch. Without words, they fell onto the bed, Ray on top and Monica beneath. She maneuvered them both carefully so their heads were closer to the top of the bed, constantly mindful not to put too much weight on

Monica, or to do anything else that might spook her and send her running.

Ray continued undoing the buttons, which beyond all reason, appeared to stretch from the neckline all the way to the hem. At best, she was only halfway to the goal. "Do you do this every morning?"

"I usually just rip it over my head," Monica confessed. "This might be the first time the buttons have ever been undone."

"I like the thought of that, being the first to undress you like this. I think I prefer the slow way. It's —" Ray swallowed.

Monica sucked in a deep breath, while Ray's fingers roamed over the newly freed skin, each caress lighting up Monica's nerve endings like never before. She closed her eyes, giving in to the sensation.

"You have an amazing body." Ray's eyes roamed the exposed skin, the endless curves, and continued undoing the buttons. Not in haste, enjoying the slow unveiling of Monica in all her glory. It gave Ray time to notice every detail. The scent of rain that hung in the air, along with the wood from the cabin. The flashes of light from the storm that had become less frequent and intense. The ripples in the quilt beneath them. The sound of rain. She would remember it all, forever.

Monica, seeming to lose patience, pulled Ray's mouth to hers, while Ray continued to stroke her fingers up and down Monica's sublime body. Monica deepened the kiss, raking her nails up and down Ray's sides.

Ray moaned in delight.

"I see you like that." Monica nibbled on Ray's earlobe, pulling out another moan before slipping her tongue deeper into the ear.

Ray's insides lit up, but her hands never stopped their exploration. After all those sleepless hours wondering what it would be like to do what she was doing now, Ray didn't want to waste a second.

"I love touching you," Ray confessed.

"I'm enjoying it immensely myself."

"I can tell," Ray teased, even as her fingertips tiptoed lower, broaching an expanse of the softest skin she'd felt.

Their bodies started to move together, Ray's hip thrusting into Monica, who snapped her eyes shut, the back of her head pressing into the pillow.

"I need you, Monica. You have no idea how much."

Their lips collided again, their tongues seeking the other, as if expecting to find the way to the other's heart.

Ray cradled Monica's cheeks. "I love the color of your eyes. Such a soft and endless blue. Like the sky stretching over the horizon, never giving up. I could stare into them forever."

Monica leaned her cheek into Ray's right hand. "I love your deep blues. I feel like there's a mystery there, but the more I stare, the closer I get to the answer."

I'm falling madly in love with you, was what Ray's heart cried out, but her lips stayed silent.

For what seemed like an eternity but was only a few heartbeats, they continued to stare, causing Ray to wonder what it meant for Monica. Was she also falling for Ray, or was it simply carnal desire?

"You really are an amazing woman," Monica said in the sweetest voice.

"I never knew there was someone like you out there, or I wouldn't have stopped looking." Ray ran a finger over Monica's full lips. "Every woman who's treated you poorly is a fool."

"I feel the same about you."

Their mouths collided again, the warmth of their tongues and caresses revved to raking the other's skin. Ray fisted Monica's hair, her tongue going in deep. Monica's body trembled underneath Ray, proving she wasn't alone in this desire.

Ray lurched up, yanking her shirt off and casting it to the floor.

Monica let out a soft whistle. "My glimpses were never enough to get the full picture."

"And now?"

"Fucking amazing."

Even as she burst out laughing at Monica's bluntness, Ray enjoyed watching as the woman's light blue eyes explored her, clearly savoring the moment.

Monica bucked up, wrapping her arms around Ray, nipping and kissing her neck. Ray, not wanting to lose the upper hand, eased Monica onto her back, the sensation of skin on skin causing Ray to give her most devilish *fuck me* grin. Except it was Ray who had every intention of making love to Monica.

Ray made her way to the left nipple. Monica's chest hitched, making Ray's clit come alive.

Jesus. Just the act of licking Monica's nipple was doing things to Ray's libido—sensations she never thought capable of experiencing.

Ray moved to the other nipple, giving it even more attention, taking it between her teeth.

Monica released a moan that was music to Ray's ears. The woman tried to roll Ray onto her side, but Ray resisted.

"Patience."

Monica growled, but her eyes didn't show anger.

Ray's hip separated Monica's legs, their lower bodies moving in time together. Ray continued to give a nipple attention, yanking more delighted moans from Monica. Ray's right hand traveled up and down Monica's torso and cupped the available breast.

The desire in Monica's stare thrust Ray into a frenzy of wanting. Her tongue started the trek down Monica's stomach, leaving a trail of soft kisses. Ray's pussy leaped with desire as she traveled.

Farther and farther down.

Closer and closer to the prize.

Monica whimpered in her need for release.

Ray's hand was between Monica's legs, and a finger ran up and down swollen, wet lips. "Is this…?"

Monica smiled, "Don't stop what you're doing."

Ray entered with one finger, slowly moving in, the warmth welcoming her. Soon, she added another.

"That feels wonderful." Monica held onto the pillow under her head.

Ray needed another kiss, loving the way their mouths fit together. Monica welcomed it with ardor, while Ray continued to ease her fingers in and out of Monica.

"I love—" Ray froze and quickly added, "Kissing you."

Why won't the words come out?

"Me too," Monica said, and again, Ray suspected they were on the same page.

This time, Ray worked her way all the way down to Monica's pussy, making her back arch off the bed.

The first flick of Ray's tongue made Monica bend even more. Ray moved her body to allow her mouth and fingers to hit all the right spots, enjoying the feeling of being between Monica's legs.

The time for teasing had ended, and Ray moved deep inside, focusing her tongue on the right location. Monica's body writhed, getting closer and closer to tipping over into ecstasy. Her noises and frantic movements under Ray could only mean she was on the edge. Ray sensually lapped the magic spot and curled her fingers upward. Monica grasped the sides of Ray's head, holding it in place.

"Ray..." Monica wasn't able to complete whatever she wanted to say as her juices spurted over Ray's fingers.

Ray had no intention of stopping, wanting to give Monica the release she so needed, and then some.

Monica's ragged breathing didn't deter Ray, and Monica's groans urged Ray on.

She moved her fingers in and out.

Monica lurched upward, but Ray still didn't stop.

The words "Oh fucking hell" seemed to tear through Monica's core, bouncing off the walls.

If Ray could've grinned in triumph at that moment, she would've, but as her mouth was otherwise occupied, she settled for a throaty chuckle. Ray had known from the start she would remember every detail of this night. Now she could rest assured Monica would never forget it, either.

CHAPTER TWENTY-ONE

That had not gone as Monica had planned.

It had, however, gone exactly the way she'd imagined it would, right down to the earth-rocking orgasm at the end.

But how had she gotten here? She honestly wasn't sure. There'd been a deafening sound, like a bomb overhead. A shout. She'd rushed to check on Ray, and then?

And then, her body had taken over, perhaps sensing that when it came to transforming her relationship with Ray it was now or never.

She'd chosen now, but the exact nature of the changes she'd set into motion remained unclear. Did it matter? Maybe not. They were still in the moment, and Monica intended to make the most of it before reality intruded and the hard-to-answer questions could no longer be ignored.

Monica stretched her arms above her head, pointing her toes and allowing her body to flatten along Ray's downy-soft mattress. Beside her, Ray lay on her back, close but not quite touching. That wouldn't do at all.

Monica rolled onto her side, propping herself up on one elbow and studying Ray's peaceful face, eyes closed though she was certain the woman wasn't asleep. To be sure, she hoisted one leg and flung it across Ray's prone form. Immediately, Ray's eyes flew open, shocked but not in a bad way.

"You know"—Monica shifted her bottom so she was astride Ray, then stared down into those stunning blue eyes—"given our conversation earlier, I think it's important that we're on equal footing."

"Meaning?"

"Tit for tat." Monica traced a circle around Ray's left nipple. "The tit part, specifically. I'm not really sure what a tat is."

Ray snorted gently, obviously amused. "Oh. By all means, I wouldn't wish to deprive you of your equal tits. Although, mine aren't nearly as big. I think you're getting the short end of the bargain."

"Do you hear me complaining?"

"For once, no."

Monica gave Ray's shoulder a teasing swat, then walked her fingers up and down Ray's muscular arms, all the while using her unique vantage point to marvel over Ray's perky breasts, so prominently on display.

"What are you doing?" Ray asked.

"Admiring." Even in the semi-darkness, Monica could tell Ray was blushing. "You hate it, don't you?"

Confusion clouded Ray's eyes. "Hate what, sex?"

"No, not sex." Monica dipped her head and placed a light kiss on Ray's bicep. "You've done a fairly good job of convincing me you like sex. I was talking about being the center of attention."

"Oh, that. I really don't like that." Ray's brow creased. "Wait, I only did a fairly good job of convincing you?"

Monica giggled wickedly. "How are you going to handle the wedding, then, if you don't like attention?"

"I'm figuring all eyes will be on you. You'll be the one in the elaborate white dress, after all. Are you wearing a veil?"

"Of course. Personally, I think they're awful, but they're totally on trend this year, and that was one of the details I let my followers vote on."

"You didn't decide to wear one so you can play a nasty trick on me?"

Monica searched Ray's face, sensing that even though her tone was lighthearted, there was a shadow of real fear lurking behind the question. "What kind of trick?"

"I don't know, like sending an entirely different woman down the aisle, and I won't know until I lift the veil."

"Why in the world would I do that?"

"I don't know. People can be cruel." Ray was serious. Maybe not about the specific trick but about the cruelty.

The sadness in Ray's eyes pulled Monica further into her orbit. "Listen to me. I would never do anything like that. I'm not cruel."

Doubt flickered across Ray's face, just a hint but enough to wound Monica to the core and make her absolutely determined to chase it away.

"Does this help you believe me?" She leaned down and placed a delicate kiss on the hollow of Ray's throat.

"It doesn't hurt your case."

"And this?" Monica trailed her tongue to Ray's right breast. She teased the pink nub until it slowly hardened in her mouth.

Ray sucked in a breath.

Encouraged, Monica took it entirely into her mouth.

Ray let out an adorable squeak.

Monica continued lavishing attention on the nipple, not wanting to leave it, but there was still so much more of Ray to explore. Monica delighted in the way Ray's hips moved against her, as if making sure she didn't forget there was much more for her to do down there.

Monica glided her hip into Ray, allowing the two of

them to move together. Ray's hands pressed into Monica's back, and Monica wished she would keep them there forever.

How was this happening?

How could something that was supposed to have been a business arrangement and nothing more have turned out like this?

Nothing about this night was fake. At least not for Monica. And their shared business interests were the furthest thing from her mind.

Monica's mouth started journeying down, not taking the shortest route but stopping in random spots—a lick of the soft skin inside Ray's elbow, a nip of a fingertip—each destination offering something new to experience. It was like being on a road trip during leaf peeping season, stumbling upon a farm stand with particularly delectable late season fruit or a freshly baked pie. Monica's body still thrummed from Ray's earlier attention, but with each stop on this map, it was coming even more alive.

Making love to Ray was turning out to be even more arousing than having her own orgasm.

Which made no sense.

Then again, nothing about Ray and Monica as a couple made sense, aside from how incredible it felt when they were together.

Monica continued moving southward. From the sound her hip made as it pressed between Ray's legs,

ACCIDENTAL HONEYMOON

she was more than wet, practically bursting with readiness.

Monica peered upward to catch Ray watching her, pleading with those dark blues.

She raked her teeth on Ray's pubic hairs, and the moan it elicited sent shivers along her spine. She ran a finger up Ray's pulsing pussy lips, tracing along the enticingly wet surface. "I could do this all night."

Ray's chest hitched. Monica wasn't sure if that meant she wanted Monica to do that all night or if she was in agony at the prospect of not getting more. Probably the latter. Monica giggled softly, and Ray's thighs quivered in response.

"Okay, maybe I'll do this, too." Monica's mouth met Ray's clit, giving it a single lick before exploring the rest of the area. No sense rushing to the final destination when there were so many scenic byways to check out.

Ray reached over her head, gripping the corner of the pillow, her knuckles whitening. She widened her legs, allowing Monica complete control of what was going to happen.

What if Ray could do that with everything, not just her body but with their future? If Monica had complete control, what would she do? She shut her eyes, not willing to think about something that would never happen. What she had was this moment, and she was going to make the best of it.

As if spurred on by this thought, her tongue went

inside Ray, savoring the taste. She needed to go deeper. Monica withdrew her tongue, replacing it with two fingers. Ray was more than wet enough. The woman felt so fucking fantastic it made Monica see stars.

Monica dove in deeper, as if wanting to connect all the way to Ray's heart, praying Ray wouldn't shut her down. She couldn't take that rejection. The thought of it made Monica pull back for a moment, terrified. What would she do if Ray rejected her after all of this?

"Please…?" Ray pleaded. "I need you."

She'd said it before. Monica was not cruel. As Ray's pleas hit her ears, she resumed her intense, rhythmic lapping, bending her wrist at the same time to give her even more access inside. Each thrust went in deeper and deeper, while Ray's breathing became more ragged and huskier.

Finally, Ray's body grew taut, and she called out, "Yes!"

Monica's eyesight started to blur, much to her amazement, but it wasn't the moment to focus on herself. She wanted to give all she had to Ray.

Everything.

All night.

Every night.

How could she ever face a night without her? Monica loved this woman more than she thought possible.

Ray reached for Monica's free hand, threading their fingers like an unbreakable bond between them. All it took was for Monica to go in deep, one last time, and Ray's whole body shook—and continued shaking for so long it was like time had lost all meaning—until Ray collapsed back onto the mattress.

Monica sucked in air, moving her head even as she left her fingers inside, still as can be. Could they stay this way forever? Then Monica wouldn't have to explain that what she felt for Ray was real and risk the rejection of Ray telling her she didn't want more. That their business agreement was enough. That being with Monica wasn't worth it to her.

But maybe Ray wouldn't say that. Maybe she would say she felt it, too.

I should tell her.

"Ray?"

"Shh." Ray yawned as she motioned for Monica to move up. "Too tired. Hold me?"

Monica crawled back to the top of the bed, resting her head against the pillow and twining her naked body around Ray's. She knew the position well, having snuggled like this countless nights before, but the absence of clothing between them turned it into something new, something powerful and beautiful.

Could she start with that? Confess to all the nights she'd held Ray in exactly this way?

Already, the woman's rhythmic breathing told her Ray was sound asleep.

Maybe this wasn't the moment to talk after all.

"Leave."

Monica woke with a start, heart racing. She'd heard something, something terrible that had pulled her from her dreams, but she couldn't remember what it was. Had the storm returned? No, it was quiet outside, not even a hint of wind rustling what was left of the fall leaves.

Beside her, Ray kicked, sending the quilt sliding to the floor.

Had Ray cried out in her sleep? That was something new.

Leaning in, Monica could hear Ray muttering something unintelligible as she struggled with the bedsheets. Monica drew closer, sliding her arm around Ray's rapidly cooling body and attempting to spoon her the way that always had brought Ray comfort in the past.

"Monica." Ray pushed her away.

"I'm right here." In the dark, she couldn't tell if Ray's eyes were open or closed.

"Leave."

Monica's insides froze. Had she heard correctly? "Ray?"

"Monica. Leave."

Oh fuck.

Springing from the bed, Monica scooped up the discarded quilt and wrapped it around her shivering body before fleeing the bedroom. She scrambled onto the couch, burying her head inside the quilt. Her breath came in ragged bursts, and she knew from past experience she was on the verge of hyperventilating. She needed Ray to help stop it, to bring her a bag to breathe into and soothe her until she was calm.

Then reality struck.

Of course, Ray wanted her to leave.

Since the day they'd met, Monica had been nothing but another helpless woman in need of a caretaker. Other than inherit the vineyard, what had Monica actually done? Ray had cleaned up the fields, replanted the garden. It was Ray who had forged the relationships with the other farmer's market sellers to convince them to provide all the necessary services for their wedding. It was Ray who had furnished their house. And it was Ray who was rapidly becoming an expert in wine making.

And Monica? She'd taken a bunch of pretty pictures of all the hard work Ray had done and posted them on the internet.

Big. Fucking. Deal.

They'd been clear from the beginning that their relationship was an equal business partnership, yet Monica could see now how she'd failed spectacularly at it. She hadn't done an equal share of the work, and then she'd gone and wrecked it completely by taking advantage of a very rare weak moment in order to seduce Ray and turn everything on its head.

Now that they'd crossed the Rubicon, what would happen?

The truth was, Monica would trade everything—the vineyard, her wedding planning business, her two million followers—for a shot with Ray. Not a business arrangement and a sham wedding, but an actual relationship and equal partnership in all things.

But that wasn't what Ray wanted, not at all. She'd said it herself. She wanted Monica to leave.

And if that was what Ray wanted, that was what Monica had to do.

Right now.

If she waited for the sunrise, she'd probably lose her nerve, and Ray was too honorable to actually push Monica out. She'd go through with a wedding she didn't want. Hell, now that they'd slept together, Ray would probably feel honor bound to do it and stick with the charade forever unless Monica decided it was time to walk away. And how would she be able to do that later, when her love for Ray would surely be even deeper, if she could barely do it now?

No, she *had* to do it now.

Silently, she slipped into the small bedroom where she retrieved her clothes, dressed quickly, and made her way to the kitchen to find her boots. As she stumbled in the darkness, a sharp stab tore through her foot.

"Fuck!"

She smothered her mouth with one hand to keep

ACCIDENTAL HONEYMOON

herself from screaming, then flipped on the overhead light and leaned against the counter to retrieve the shard of broken mug from the bottom of her foot. A trickle of red oozed to the surface, and Monica winced. She wanted to cry. She wanted Ray to come baby her, put a bandage on the wound, and tell her it would be okay.

Was it any wonder Ray was done with her? Frankly, Monica was pretty much done with herself. She slipped her injured foot into her sock, gritting her teeth as she then shoved it into her boot.

Suck it up, buttercup.

At least she wouldn't have to dance on it at the wedding, because there wasn't going to be a wedding. Monica was in love with Ray. Ray didn't reciprocate. The best course of action was to leave, like Ray had told her to. Do it now. It wasn't like Ray had come running out of the bedroom to stop her from going. In the morning, Ray would probably appreciate that Monica had left without an awkward goodbye.

Ray would also certainly appreciate it if Monica called an Uber instead of taking the truck and stranding her in the Maine woods. It wasn't Ray's fault Monica had fallen in love and shattered their pact. Sure, the woman made it impossible not to fall head over heels, but still, Monica hadn't lost her sense of right and wrong. Ray shouldn't have to suffer. Monica would do what she should have done all along, take care of herself. She would call for her own ride and simply go.

As for the vineyard, the inheritance, and the rest of their arrangement, Monica would call Larry Donahue in the morning and tell him to let it go to the trust. Christos would be a good caretaker, and there was no doubt he would keep Ray on to work with him and probably name her as his heir. Eventually, Monica was sure Ray would be able to purchase her share. Ray didn't need to marry Monica to make her dreams come true. She needed Monica to get out of the way.

That was exactly what Monica intended to do.

Activating the Uber app on her phone, Monica's mind went blank. The only address she could think of was her home with Ray on the vineyard. Going there was out of the question. It was a little after four in the morning, and she didn't want to sit at Logan International Airport or one of the train stations. Finally, she punched in the only other address she could think of that wouldn't max her credit card, and then she prepared for a long wait.

Surprisingly, a driver was only minutes away. Considering it was still dark out and she was basically in the middle of nowhere, all the signs were pointing to this being the right decision. She'd started to gather the last of her things when the bedroom door creaked open.

Ray, wearing only a shirt, staggered into the living room. She stared at Monica with that sleepy, confused look that was utterly adorable, and under the current conditions, heartbreaking.

"Why are you dressed?" Ray asked through a yawn.

So much for a clean getaway.

"I have to go." Monica looked at her phone. The driver was one minute away.

"Go? Where are you going?" Ray glanced around the room as if trying to find clues.

Outside in the driveway, a dark sedan pulled up and stopped.

"I have to go." Monica grabbed her purse and dashed to the door. Whatever else she'd brought with her would have to be left behind. Maybe Ray would box it up for her, like Brianna had done.

"Wait!" Ray scurried after her.

"My car's outside." Monica yanked the doorknob. The minute she did, the skies seemed to open up, and the rain began to pour.

Monica scowled upward as she raced to the safety of the car. "Don't you think you're overdoing things?"

Needless to say, God didn't respond.

Monica had thought being barefoot and without pants would slow her down, but Ray gave chase.

"Monica! Tell me what's wrong."

"It's all wrong." Monica scrambled into the car.

"Please, I can't fix it if I don't know what I did wrong."

"You didn't do anything wrong." Tears welled in

Monica's eyes. "You've done everything right. That's why I have to go."

The driver looked back from the front seat with an exasperated expression on his face. "Lady, it's raining. Close the door."

Monica gave him a *hold your horses* wave.

"But when are you coming back?" Ray's pupils were dark, her expression more terrified than she'd been at the height of the thunderstorm. "The wedding's in two days."

"Oh, Ray." Monica's stomach twisted. "I can't marry you."

Ray staggered back a step, mud splashing on her bare shins. "What? Why?"

"Come on, lady," the driver growled. "You're gonna soak the back seat."

Her head spinning, Monica put her hand on the door handle, preparing to pull it closed. "Don't you see? I can't marry you because I'm in love with you."

Ray was reaching for the car door, but at Monica's declaration, she froze for a fraction of a second. Monica seized the opportunity to slam the door shut.

"Can we go now?" the driver demanded.

Ray pounded on the window.

Tears rolled down Monica's cheeks.

You have to be strong, Monica reminded herself. This was for Ray's own good.

She nodded to the driver. "Yes, we can go."

Ray pounded on the window again, shouting Monica's name.

As the car pulled away, Monica could've sworn Ray called after her, "I love you, too."

But it was only wishful thinking, surely. And when Monica turned around for a last look, the back window of the car was so covered in rain that she couldn't see a thing.

CHAPTER TWENTY-TWO

Rain pelted Ray's head, streaming in rivulets down her face and body as she watched glowing red taillights disappear into the night. She was soaked, half naked, and completely alone, like she had been in the dreams that had plagued her sleep. Only this was very real, which made it even more baffling.

What in holy hell happened?

Monica had declared her love for Ray and called off their wedding, pretty much in the same breath. This proved the only thing Ray would ever truly understand about women was that they were impossible to understand.

The car was out of sight, but Ray struggled to go back inside, fearing once she turned her back, it would blow out the flame permanently on the relationship, even as it had only recently been lit.

On the other hand, she couldn't stand in the rain for the rest of her life.

No, Ray needed to dry off. Then, even though they technically had the house another night, she was going to pack up their belongings and head back to the vineyard. Monica had left with only the clothes on her back. Was she heading home? Even if she wasn't, it was the only place Ray could think of, so that was where she would start.

Ray spun through the Airbnb like a whirling dervish, tossing on clothing and throwing things into a bag. It felt like only minutes later that Ray was inserting the key into the truck as her heart clenched at the memory of going with Monica to pick out the beat-up old Ford. Though Ray loved to tease her for being a pampered princess, what other woman could've gone from a Mercedes to this old thing without so much as batting an eye? The perfect farm truck, Monica had said. She could be so practical when it came to business decisions.

And batshit crazy when it came to emotional ones.

But now wasn't the time to analyze why Monica had run out on her before dawn, hours after the most amazing sex Ray had ever experienced. No, thinking about that for any length of time would cause her to curl into a fetal position and start sobbing. Now was the time for action. Thinking could come later.

The sun had only started to turn the sky a light pink as Ray tore down the road, praying the early hour meant the cops were still in bed and not setting up speed traps. The truth was, unless someone physically tried to stop her, Ray was going to push the truck to the point where its parts started to fall off.

She had to get home. She needed...

She needed her mom. Not her actual mom but a real mom. This was one of those times Ray wished she had a mother to go to. Someone to offer her wise words and a comforting shoulder. Someone like Monica's mom.

Oh fuck.

What was she going to tell Helen?

Maybe she wouldn't have to worry about that. Maybe when she arrived back at the house, Monica would be there, and she would've already taken care of telling her everything she needed to know. Ray was pretty certain the prospect of telling her future-mother-in-law the wedding was off because she somehow had broken Monica's heart while sleeping with her didn't really appeal to her all that much.

When she reached the house, there was no sign of Monica, but then again, why would there be? As much as Ray might have wanted it, it wasn't like Monica would have gone to all the trouble of running away just to head right back home to sit on the front doorstep, waiting for Ray to get home so she could throw herself into Ray's arms. Then again, maybe she'd gone inside and was waiting there.

Please let her be here.

"Monica?" Ray slammed the front door open. "Monica!"

Monica was nowhere in sight, but Helen sat at the kitchen table with a mug of coffee by her side, holding a utensil in her hand.

What the...? Ray blinked, momentarily taken aback. It appeared Helen was feeding Mr. Fluffles tuna with a fork.

"What's wrong, Ray?" Worry etching her face, Helen put down the fork. The cat shot daggers from his eyes, clearly not thrilled over the interruption of his breakfast.

"Is Monica here?"

"Did you two fight?" Helen asked, not accusingly but with concern.

"Yes. No." Ray wanted to dash up the stairs and check every room. Instead, she collapsed onto one of the kitchen chairs. "The truth is I have no idea what happened."

Helen gave a knowing nod. "My daughter can be a challenge to understand sometimes. Why don't you tell me what happened from the beginning, and I'll see if I can help?"

The beginning?

Ray swallowed hard as she contemplated all that starting from the beginning would entail. "I may need some caffeine first."

She poured herself a cup of coffee and settled back into her chair, allowing herself several sips before tackling this most unpleasant task. What would Helen think of her when she knew the whole truth? And would she be angry at Monica for lying to her?

Ray's belly flip-flopped. "I don't want you to hate me or think poorly of Monica. You two are so close. I'd hate to do anything to pull you two apart."

Helen leaned forward, covering Ray's hand with hers and giving it a gentle press. "Nothing will ever do that. I need you to trust me because once I have the full picture, I can help make everything better."

Ray bit down on her bottom lip to keep herself from bursting into tears. "It's over. I don't know what I did, but I ruined it."

Helen bounced out of her chair, pulling Ray into a hug. "Now, now. It's going to be okay. I know it in my bones. Start telling me the whole story."

"She's called off the wedding."

"Who has?"

"Your daughter."

Helen looked to Mr. Fluffles, who offered little help as he had his eyes firmly fixed on the tuna can. "Do you love her?"

"One hundred percent." At least that was a question Ray could answer easily.

"I'm sure it's only cold feet."

"No, it's not that." Ray ran both hands through her hair. "I need to tell you the whole story, but I don't know how to."

"One word at a time."

"Okay." Ray took a breath, letting it out shakily. "To begin with, Monica and I haven't known each other nearly as long as you think. When you came to the townhouse in Baltimore, we'd only met that week."

Helen nodded slowly. "I see. I wondered about that."

"You did?" Ray studied the woman's face like she was a mysterious, and possibly dangerous, artifact. Preternatural hearing, eyes in the back of her head, and now this?

Helen chuckled as if she could read Ray's mind. "Not at first, although I will say I'm not as bad with names as my husband, George, so I was very confused when Monica introduced you because I could've sworn her girlfriend's name was Brianna."

"It was, but they'd broken up a few months before."

"So Brianna was the one who decorated that house?"

"She was," Ray confirmed.

"That's what really threw me off," Helen confessed. "When I first arrived here and saw this house, I knew there was no way it had been the work of the same person who did that tacky townhouse."

Ray snickered. She couldn't help it. "No, Brianna was actually the one who hired me to fix up the place so she could put it on the market."

"Yes, I saw it had sold when I drove by trying to

check on Monica," Helen said. "My daughter didn't even bother to tell me. I take it that wasn't the only detail she failed to mention."

If only, Ray thought. Out loud she said, "Did she mention we weren't actually a couple?"

Helen blinked slowly. "I'm not following. When weren't you a couple?"

Uh, like, ever? Ray wanted to say but instead went with, "When you came to the house that first night with the news Monica's *yiayia* was sick, I was there finishing up some work."

"You came with us to New York and didn't say a word!" Helen looked stunned, but then her eyes twinkled. "You loved her even then?"

Ray couldn't keep in a loud snort. "Quite the opposite." Ray leaned forward, lowering her voice conspiratorially. "In fact, if I'm completely honest, I thought she was the most annoying woman on the planet."

Instead of being offended as Ray had feared she might be, Helen smiled fondly. "Monica is so much like her father. You know, George had to ask me out twenty times before I finally said yes. Mainly I did it to get him to stop asking me. He was so smug and sure of himself; sometimes, I wanted to punch him in the nose."

"I know the feeling."

"But you went with her to New York and let the family think you were her girlfriend." Helen arched an eyebrow. "Why?"

"She was so afraid of disappointing her grandmother," Ray explained, her chest contracting as she recalled how vulnerable Monica had been. "With as accomplished as everyone is in your family, her biggest fear is being seen as a failure."

"It's nice how you tried to help my daughter, but her *yiayia* would've been proud of her no matter what."

"I agree." Ray stroked her chin, eyes focused on the table. "The thing is I think Monica and I did a little too good of an impression on her grandmother."

Ray proceeded to explain the meeting they'd had with Larry Donahue and the terms of Monica's grandmother's will.

"You two wanted the vineyard, and that was why you decided to get married?"

"It was supposed to be on paper," Ray admitted. "A formality. It's why she didn't tell any of her family she was engaged."

"But at some point, it changed." Helen didn't say this as a question but as a fact. "When did you figure that out?"

"Honestly?" Ray let out a somewhat bitter laugh. "A few hours ago. She told me she loved me, right before getting into an Uber and riding out of my life for good."

"Ray, I need you to look me in the eyes and tell me if you want to be with my daughter."

Ray stared right into those soft blue eyes, so

similar to Monica's that she was on the verge of tears. "I do."

"Then we need to find Monica."

"I thought she'd be here, if only to come back for her computer. It has all her work on it." Ray clasped a hand to her mouth, her eyes growing wide as the consequences of Monica's departure sank in. "She was supposed to do a huge blog post tomorrow, a final one before the wedding. Two million people will be waiting for it."

"I'm sure she'll come back." Helen's reassuring smile faltered as her phone buzzed with an incoming text.

"Is it her?"

Helen's frown deepened as she scanned the message on her screen. "She says she's safe, and she needs some time."

"Ask her where she is."

Helen typed in the message, and they both waited, attention riveted on the phone. Nothing happened. Finally, Helen tapped the screen. "I'm going to call her."

Ray clenched her hands together, squeezing tightly as she waited. Surely Monica would answer when she saw it was her mother, right?

Helen shook her head, whispering, "Voice mail."

Ray's shoulders sagged as Monica's mom left a message to call back. What was the point? Monica never listened to voice mail, and since she'd just texted, she'd clearly chosen not to answer. Without knowing where she was, there was little left to do.

Ray rested her head in her hands. "She's not coming back."

"She will eventually," Helen soothed. "You'll get it sorted out. Maybe not in time for the wedding, but so what? You can always plan another wedding, a real one this time."

Yes, they could, but...

Ray's head snapped up. Two million people had been following this wedding for weeks. They'd voted on flowers and veils. They were expecting a grand finale on Monday. "If this wedding doesn't happen on Monday, she's going to lose all her followers. It'll destroy her business. She doesn't think anyone values her work, but I've seen firsthand how much passion she puts into it. She's amazing at it, and she doesn't deserve to lose it all because I screwed up."

"What about the vineyard?" Helen asked gently. "I see how much you love it, and now you might lose it. This is hurting you, too."

"I don't care about that." Ray collapsed into the back of her chair. "All I care about is Monica."

"That's music to my ears, Ray. That's what every mother wants to hear from a daughter-in-law." Helen gazed thoughtfully at the table, lips twitching as if silently running through ideas. Finally, her face lit up. "This was supposed to be a fake wedding all along, right?"

Ray nodded. "Yes, but I don't think she sees it that way now. Neither do I."

"I understand that, but before the family found out and three hundred people decided to come, what was the plan?"

"Definitely not that," Ray muttered, even as she noted the number of guests had grown again since the most recent head count. "We were going to stage a photoshoot. No guests, no ceremony, just a lot of great detail shots for the blog and maybe a few models standing around to make it look like the real deal."

"Well, we have no shortage of guests coming, and all the details are in place." Helen grinned. "We'd better get to work, Ray. We have a fake wedding to save."

Ray opened her mouth to argue, but then it finally hit her what Helen was proposing. "You mean we stage the wedding as a photoshoot and post it to her blog, and her followers will never know? That's brilliant!"

"We have everything we need," Helen agreed.

Ray's face clouded. "Except Monica."

"We have the next best thing." Helen gave a wicked grin. "Her cousin Nina looks so much like her, even her mom and I can't always tell them apart, and heaven knows after all the hair and makeup, no woman really looks very recognizable on her wedding day."

"There's just one problem. Isn't Nina pregnant? Like, really pregnant?"

"Oh. Right." Helen tapped a finger against her lips. "I think I know what to do. Remember that dress you said you liked so much?"

"The one Monica said you could hide a dozen brides in?"

"We don't need to hide a dozen brides." Helen grinned. "Just one baby."

"I don't know," Ray said. "Monica wouldn't be caught dead in that dress. She'll be so mad when she sees the pictures."

"Then she should show up for her wedding, so she can choose what dress to wear." Helen's frustration with her daughter was clear. "We'll call the shop and see if they can send over the dress. It's worth a try."

Ray's stomach fluttered. This insane plan might work. "When does Nina arrive?"

"Today. Her plane lands later this afternoon."

"We'll have to explain it to her, though. Actually, we'll have to explain it to everyone." Ray groaned. How were they going to break this news to so many people?

"I'll take care of that part," Helen assured her, already reaching for her phone. "I'm calling Christos to see if he can get in touch with all the vendors. After that, I'll send out an SOS to the family. Don't you worry, Ray. Monica gets her stubbornness from every branch of this family tree. Once we put our heads together, we'll pull off this wedding without a hitch."

"Literally." Despite the fact she was so nervous she thought she might puke, Ray couldn't help laughing at Helen's word choice. "It's the first wedding in history where no one is getting hitched."

"Clever one, my dear. You're going to fit right in with this kooky family of ours; mark my words." Helen let out a quick breath, like an athlete gearing up for the big competition. "Right. We'd better get to work. There's so much to do. Luckily, we had the best wedding planner in the world put the playbook together for us, but it still won't get done on its own."

"Speaking of playbook," Ray said, "do you have a copy of Monica's planning notes?"

Helen pressed her mouth together in a thin line. "They're on her computer. Do you have the passcode?"

"I might."

Ray's mind flashed back to the code for Monica's phone, and she smiled. Hadn't Monica said she used the code for everything? Retrieving Monica's computer from her office, Ray quickly typed in the date of their wedding and was rewarded with an open desktop.

"Success!" Ray cried, but then her spirits fell.

Monica's final blog post was open on the screen. It was set to go out Sunday night, the last update before the big day. Monica had said it would be an extravaganza of a wrap-up, and Ray had no doubt it would've been…if only the file wasn't blank. Ray recalled Monica had planned to write it when they got back from their trip. Clearly that wouldn't be happening now, with the bride-to-be MIA.

Which meant only one thing.

Ray would be writing the blog post to Monica's two million avid fans herself.

CHAPTER TWENTY-THREE

Monica sat on the daybed in Sally's guest room, her body pressed into the corner with her back against the wall and her knees tucked up against her chest. She'd been like that for hours. Prior to her current position, she'd been curled in a ball with her head under the blankets, and before that, she'd been facedown in the pillows, until her sinuses had become so stuffy from crying that she'd needed to come up for air. Somewhere in there, she may have slept. She wasn't sure. It was all a little blurry.

She'd arrived at Sally's place sometime on Saturday, red-nosed and weeping, after paying over three hundred bucks to a very cranky driver who, even with a generous tip for the three-and-half-hour trip, was clearly glad to see the last of her. Apparently, Uber drivers were not like bartenders. You couldn't pour out your heart to them and expect an answer to your problems. Or even a stiff drink. She made a mental note that next time her life crumbled to bits, she would skip the two-hundred-mile car ride with a total stranger and head to the nearest bar.

After rescuing her from her doorstep like a feral cat, Sally had offered a sympathetic ear, but by then, Monica had been all done with talking. Exhaustion had turned her bones to dust, and when she'd dragged herself to the guest room with her last ounce of energy, that was where she had stayed. She'd emerged once, maybe twice, to use the bathroom. Other than that, she'd remained holed up, wishing the world would do her a favor and simply come to an end. It hadn't. It was now early Monday morning.

Her wedding day.

Fresh tears started to fall. Maybe that was why she hadn't needed to pee more often. Every bit of moisture in her body was too busy making its escape through her eyes. As she pulled the last tissue from the box beside the bed, a tap on the door vaguely pierced the fog in Monica's brain.

"Yes?" she managed to say in a voice that was half croak, half squeak.

"I take it you haven't slept." Sally stood in the doorway, peering through a crack as she eyed Monica as if she were a science experiment gone wrong.

Unable to form the simple word no, Monica shook her head, sending all the congestion from one side to the other like she was wearing an overfilled water balloon on top of her neck. She pressed her lips together, focusing completely on getting out a single, vital word. "Coffee?"

Because, oh dear God, did she need coffee. And maybe a new heart to replace the sad, shattered thing in her chest that had been smashed to smithereens. But coffee would be an acceptable start.

"I'll make you a deal," Sally coaxed. "Follow me to the living room, and take a seat on the couch. Then I'll bring you a cup."

The woman drove a hard bargain. On the other hand, now that the door was open, Monica could smell a freshly brewing pot, even through her stuffy nostrils. With a sigh, she rolled herself off the bed and shuffled to the living room. She sat down in the corner of the sofa, pulling her legs up and assuming the exact same position she'd had on the day bed.

Sally came in with two steaming mugs. Monica took hers and sipped in silence, staring out the window. She could tell from the slight leak in the seal around the window that there was a chill in the air outside, but the sky was a brilliant blue that promised enough warmth in the afternoon. The leaves on the trees were a bit past peak color, offering shades of rust and faded gold that would've photographed to perfection against the stark white of the gazebo. In short, everything for her wedding day was going perfectly to plan, aside from the fact she'd called the whole thing off.

"Have you talked to her yet?" Sally asked, fortunately only after Monica had finished enough coffee that the chances of her breaking down into wild sobbing had diminished somewhat.

Monica shook her head and was relieved to discover the change of position and ingestion of hot liquid had cleared her sinuses enough that she no longer felt like she was about to drown.

"Are you sure you don't want to talk to her at all?"

"I can't. It'll hurt too much."

Monica's cell phone was on the coffee table, the screen black. It had been nearly out of battery the day before, though a cord coming from the bottom told her it had been plugged in to charge.

Sally nudged the device closer to her with an encouraging look. "You might at least check your messages."

"I don't do voice mail," she replied automatically.

"Okay, then start with texts." A look of defeat shadowed Sally's features when Monica shook her head, but she rallied and tried again. "Email? Come on. You can't hide forever."

"Pretty sure I can."

Sally's expression told Monica it was no use. In her weakened state, this was an argument she would eventually lose. Shoulders slouching, Monica took the phone from the table with all the enthusiasm she might've shown for a plate of week-old sushi.

She opened her email and frowned. Her inbox was

filled with responses from fans about her Sunday blog post. The one she'd never written.

"I'm confused."

Sally tilted her head to one side. "What is it?"

"I don't suppose you happen to follow my blog," Monica began.

"Of course, I do."

Monica swallowed. "This might seem like a strange question, but did I post anything last night?"

"You sure did," Sally answered, causing Monica's stomach to clench.

When she and Ray had left on their getaway, the file had been open on her desktop, completely blank. Whatever had gone out to her readers, Monica'd had nothing to do with it. It had to have been Ray. And considering what Monica had done, whatever Ray had posted was probably bad. Really bad. No doubt she'd announced to all two million followers that the wedding was off because Monica was a cold-hearted bitch.

She probably deserved it for seducing Ray and ruining their perfect business partnership. No, she did deserve it, no probably about it. She'd been selfish and hadn't given any thought to what Ray wanted at all. But it didn't make the consequences any easier to face.

Monica winced as she scrolled through the unopened messages. There had to be over a hundred of them, each one telling her in no uncertain terms that she was the worst person on the planet. She was a liar. An opportunist. A fraud.

"I have to hand it to you, Monica," Sally said. "You're an excellent writer. I don't know what happened between you and Ray on your trip to have brought this mess on, but that post you wrote before you left was a work of art."

Monica's breath caught in her throat. Sally's words simply didn't make sense. "What?"

"It was so romantic and beautiful it made me cry." As if to prove it, Sally gave a sentimental sniff. "I know it's not my business, but all I can say is, if you really meant what you wrote, the two of you need to patch up this misunderstanding right away."

Realizing she couldn't exactly ask Sally to tell her what she had supposedly written on her own blog without having a lot of explaining to do, Monica pulled up the most recent entry on her phone. The page was filled with photos she'd never published, including a clip of the video Ray had taken in Maine. Monica scrolled farther and began to read.

A relationship is like tending a vineyard. It's hard work, and sometimes the rewards seem few and far between. Sometimes, it seems like everything you've done might be for nothing. The grapes threaten to shrivel on the vine, unharvested. The wine will go sour and never ferment. But a wise man once told me that tending a vineyard is a sure sign you have hope for the future. The vines you plant today will take years to grow to maturity. The fruit they bear may be for future generations to enjoy. But you do the work today, believing in the hope of tomorrow. Love is the same. When you find the perfect partner, like the perfect blend of grapes, you know that whatever happens, it's only a matter of time before it ages and matures into something better than you could've hoped it would be.

There was more, but Monica could no longer decipher the letters through her tears. It didn't matter. What she'd read had told her the one thing she needed to know. Ray loved her. And if the words on the page hadn't said it clearly enough, Ray's actions did. Even after Monica had left her in Maine, Ray had come back home and completed her blog post for her. Instead of using it for revenge, she'd written the most touching love letter Monica had ever received and saved Monica's livelihood in the process.

"Have you checked the live feed?" Sally asked.

"What are you talking about?" Monica looked up in confusion. "What live feed?"

"Brenda called earlier to tell me, but I wasn't sure if you'd want to know. Ray's staging a mock wedding without you, to save your business."

"What do you mean she's putting on the wedding?"

"Ray's been live tweeting all morning from your account, like you planned. From what I hear, everyone in your family is pulling together so your followers won't find out. They're doing a damn good job. No one around here will say a peep. Actually, aside from Christos and me, I don't think anyone suspects."

"But...but, I'm not there. I'm here."

Monica's head was spinning. She clicked on the link to the live feed and saw a photo of her cousin Nina having her hair done. Of course. Everyone had always said it was impossible to tell them apart. The wedding was on, and Nina was going to walk down the aisle in her place.

"It might not be any of my business," Sally said, "but maybe, rather than being here, it would be a better idea for you to be there, instead."

Truer words had never been spoken.

Monica lifted her chin, straightened her back, and forced herself to her feet. She wobbled a bit, and it occurred to her that she hadn't put anything but coffee in her stomach for a couple days. No matter. There would be food at the house. Her mother was Greek. Even if it was a fake wedding, food would be a given.

"Sally, I know I've already imposed on your hospitality enough for a lifetime, but I have one more favor to ask."

"I'm happy to help," Sally assured her.

"In that case, I need a ride to the vineyard. I have a wedding to attend."

MONICA'S HAND hovered over the door handle, not quite waiting for Sally's car to shift into park before yanking it open and making a dash for the farmhouse.

"Ray?" Her voice echoed in the empty kitchen.

"We're upstairs," someone called out. Monica was pretty sure it was her mother and was certain it wasn't Ray.

She raced up the stairs to the bedroom. A massive white gown had been artfully arranged on the bed, a fresh farmer's market bouquet beside it. Her cousin Nina stood in one of Monica's frilly robes that matched her granny nightgowns. She held onto the bedpost, her now perfectly coifed blonde hair shining in the light that streamed in from the window. Monica's mother stood to one side with her phone held up as if to take a picture.

"Move your head a little to the left," her mom said. "I can tell you aren't her from this angle."

"How's this, Aunt Helen? The baby bump isn't showing, is it?" Nina asked as she turned. Her eyes caught Monica's reflection in the mirror, registering surprise. "Oh, hi."

"Oh, hi, yourself," Monica snapped. The sight of her rival cousin taking Monica's place on her own wedding day was too over-the-top for her to bear, even if the woman was trying to do her a favor.

"Look who decided to show up after all." Her mom's eyebrow arched, and Monica couldn't tell if she was happy to see her or mad.

"Of course, I showed up," Monica answered, jutting out her chin. "It's my wedding day, isn't it?"

"That's a good question," her mom replied and

turned to Nina. "I think we have enough pictures for now. Maybe you can give me a few minutes alone with your cousin before we decide what to do next."

Nina nodded, wrapped her robe a little tighter around her chest, and scurried from the room.

"I need to talk to Ray," Monica told her mom, her eyes pleading for cooperation. Why did the woman suddenly look so stern? "Where is she?"

"I'm fairly certain, according to your own schedule"—Monica's mom consulted a piece of paper she'd pulled from her pocket—"she should be getting a last-minute pep talk from Christos in the old barn. With video, of course."

"They're still doing that?"

Her cousin had been ready to don a wedding dress to pretend to be her, and her fiancée was having a fake heart-to-heart talk on video for the benefit of two million strangers. Monica chewed her bottom lip, certain the situation couldn't get any more surreal.

"It was a very picturesque location, and Christos had prepared such a lovely speech for the occasion that it seemed a shame to let it go to waste."

Monica frowned. "Seems like you have everything under control without me."

"Well, we weren't certain if you were planning to show." Monica's mom gave her a thorough up and down assessment, the kind that she used to do when Monica had been naughty as a child, and she was deciding what to do about it. "Which does bring up the question, why are you here?"

"I, um…" Monica squirmed under her mother's gaze. "I guess I should explain."

"Ray's already told me everything."

"Everything?" Monica gulped, nearly choking. That explained the stern expression and the less than warm reception she'd received. "Mom, I can—"

Her mother put her hand in the air, stopping Monica's words as effectively as a mute button on a remote control. "Why are you here, Monica?"

Monica's insides trembled, her heart beating in her ears.

Answer the question.

"Because I love her."

Her mother pointed to the bed. "Then put on the dress, go downstairs, and get married."

"But…" Monica's eyes fell to the floor, a wave of doubt overcoming her. "I don't know if I can," Monica said in a whisper. "What if she doesn't even want to see me?"

"Listen to me." Her mom dug her fingers into each of Monica's shoulders, but her expression had softened, sending tendrils of warmth to calm Monica's nerves. "Your father and I have been married for almost forty years, and do you want to know the secret?"

Monica gave a vigorous nod. Whatever the secret was, she needed it, like *now*.

"The secret is, there is no secret." Her mom chuckled, clearly sensing Monica's dismay. "But there is a prerequisite, and that's showing up. I've gotten to know that fiancée of yours pretty well over the past few days, and if there's one thing I'd be willing to bet on, it's that she wants to marry you. And you want to marry her. But for that to happen, you're going to have to take the first step. Put on the dress."

"What if she says no?"

"Then at least you know. I read somewhere recently that sometimes you have to do the work today and believe in the hope of tomorrow."

"Funny," Monica said, "I read that somewhere recently, too. On my own blog. Only I didn't write it."

"Well, it's about the best definition of getting married that I can think of." Her mother's eyes sparkled with humor. "I'm guessing the person who *did* write it is the kind of person who wouldn't say no when her perfect partner comes along. But just in case, you might want to lead with an apology."

Monica nodded.

Best. Advice. Ever.

Monica reached for the pile of white on the bed and frowned. "What is this?"

"A wedding dress," her mom replied, the tone of impatience still quite evident.

"Not the one I chose, though." She poked at it, recognition dawning. "Oh God. Is this that giant fluffy one?"

"It was the only one that would hide Nina's baby bump." Her mom put her hands on her hips and fixed Monica with a stern stare. "It's white. It's a dress. Are you going to quibble, or are you going to put it on and fix this mess?"

Monica lifted the dress by its shoulders, biting down on her lip as she tried to quell her disappointment. Then again, Ray *had* said it was her favorite. Maybe that would make it good enough. "I'll put on the dress."

When her mom had gone to break the news to Nina that she would be swapping the world's fluffiest wedding gown for the world's ugliest bridesmaid's dress, Monica stripped off her clothing and donned the enormous white monstrosity. She stood back and looked at herself in the mirror. She blinked back tears.

Damn it. Ray had been right. Again.

To hell with sleek and sophisticated. This was the perfect dress for her after all. Today, she felt like a princess. But if Ray agreed to marry her—for real, with all that it implied—Monica vowed to do everything she could to never act like a spoiled princess again. Ray deserved better than that. Given the chance, Monica planned to spoil Ray every bit as much as Ray had spoiled her, each day for the rest of their lives.

Tina, the makeup artist who had done Nina's hair and makeup, was long since gone. Monica wasn't surprised. She'd seen the orange cones and hearse outside St. Mark's church on the drive over and figured it was a pretty busy day for the local funeral home. Monica applied simple makeup herself, swept her hair into a plain chignon, and topped the whole thing with the massive white veil her fans had voted on for her, which she'd secretly nicknamed Bertha.

Once again, it wasn't the style she would've chosen, but it was exactly right. The moment the veil touched her head, it was like a fairy godmother's wand, turning her into a real bride.

Now if only Ray would say yes and turn her into a real wife, too.

Downstairs, Monica's dad waited, nervously shifting from one foot to the other.

"Oh, there you are, Nina." He crooked his arm without giving Monica's veiled form a second glance as he proceeded to lead her to the door.

"Hi, Dad."

He froze mid step, whipping his face toward hers and squinting to see through the layers of tulle. "Monica, is that you?"

"It's me."

"Are you sure about this, honey?"

"I think so." Her voice wavered.

"An honest answer." He smiled, giving her a reassuring pat on the hand. "I felt the same way when I married your mom."

"Do you ever have regrets?"

Her dad shrugged. "Only every other day or so."

"I heard that!" Monica's mom called from outside.

Her dad winked. "She's an easy target."

Monica laughed. "And to think Ray didn't believe me when I told her Mom has preternatural hearing."

Outside at the gazebo, row after row of chairs had been set up. She'd been expecting a photoshoot with a few people milling around to serve as extras. When Monica realized there were close to three hundred guests filling the seats, her knees wobbled.

"Dad, what are they all doing here?"

"It's a wedding, pumpkin. They're here for the same reason people always come to weddings. The food."

Despite her father's joke, Monica's heart raced. "How am I going to talk to Ray?"

"Well, she's waiting right up there." Her dad motioned toward the gazebo.

Sure enough, Ray had stepped into view with Christos beside her. Her short, dark curls had been tamed into beautiful, glossy waves. Her cream suit fit every curve and made her look like a million bucks. As she gave last minute instructions to the photographer, Ray looked calm and in charge. There was no way she would want to be stuck with a hot mess like Monica had proven herself to be.

Monica clutched her father's arm. She was about to tell him to turn around and take her back to the house when a string quartet struck up the first chords of the wedding march. She didn't even know where the string quartet *was*. Had she hired one? Oh, right. It was the honors quartet from the local high school, seated discreetly behind a screen beside the gazebo. It had all been in her notes, but one question remained unanswered.

"Why is there music?" Monica whispered. "It's supposed to be a fake wedding."

"Video," her dad said. "For your blog."

"Please tell me the video isn't being streamed right now." Monica's breathing quickened at the possibility. "I can't talk honestly with Ray while two million people are watching."

"Nope. We decided there was a greater than zero risk that Maddie and Trish would streak naked down the aisle as a prank and thought it would be best to reserve the ability to edit that out."

"Good call."

"Okay, are you ready?"

No, Monica wasn't ready. She hadn't even spoken to Ray. She needed time to apologize, to convince Ray to give her a chance. She needed there not to be hundreds of sets of eyes staring at her as she prepared to grovel for forgiveness from the woman she loved.

Too bad, princess, Monica told herself as her father took a step, pulling her along beside him. She was going to have to work with what she had.

About halfway to the gazebo, it struck Monica that she was doing exactly what Ray had feared she would do. She was sending a different woman up the aisle, to surprise Ray when she lifted the veil.

What if Ray thought she was doing it to be cruel? What if she caught one glimpse of Monica's face after lifting the veil and took off running?

With each step, Monica couldn't shake the feeling that she'd made a terrible mistake.

Ray couldn't possibly love her, could she? She had good manners and wanted to do the standup thing in saving Monica's business. That didn't mean she wanted to agree to a lifetime of waking up with Monica by her side.

Monica's feet ground to a halt. Her dad patted her hand.

Then he pulled her along like she was a timid puppy getting used to a leash.

Why was this happening so fast?

All too soon, Monica was standing at the steps of the gazebo with Ray in front of her. Christos stood a step above them, looking very much like a real officiant in his dark suit. Her father gave her hand a squeeze then went to find his seat beside Monica's mom in the front row, leaving Monica to face the hardest part alone.

Hands shaking, eyes glued on Ray, Monica raised the veil from her face.

Ray's eyes grew impossibly large as recognition hit. She sucked in a breath, nearly a gasp. "It's you."

CHAPTER TWENTY-FOUR

Ray stared at the face of the woman in front of her. It wasn't the person she'd expected, but it was very much the person she'd wished so hard it would be. Could this actually be happening?

"Monica?"

"I..." Monica hesitated, and Ray was certain she was going to finish the sentence *I can explain,* and Ray was already gearing up to refute whatever excuses she'd concocted. Instead, the words that came out were, "I'm sorry."

It was a surprise and exactly what she needed to hear. Ray's chin dipped as she gave a single nod, letting all the hurt and fear of the past few days go in an instant. "It's okay."

"No, it isn't." Monica appeared to be quaking beneath her massive dress and veil, so much so that Ray was afraid she was going to fall over, or start hyperventilating again. However, she squared her shoulders and continued with perhaps more stubbornness than even Ray could have mustered. "I'm madly in love with you, Rachel Walsh, and the way I acted was unforgivable. I want you to know that you don't have to marry me. I'll call Larry right now and tell him to let the vineyard go back to the trust. I'll walk away. You can run this place with Christos, you'll be his heir. You could easily earn what you need in order to buy it outright when the time comes. You belong here, Ray. You don't have to marry me to get what you've always wanted."

"Actually, I do."

"No, you don't," Monica argued, clearly for the sake of arguing. Ray tried not to laugh. Monica wouldn't be Monica if she didn't make everything harder than it had to be sometimes. "I need you to understand. I'm standing here right now because I love you. I didn't mean to fall in love with you. It just happened. But, I don't want you to feel like you have to go through with this for the sake of the inheritance, or to save my business, or to rescue me. I know in my heart of hearts that I want to marry you. To wake up every day with you. To face all the ups and downs with you by my side, but I can't go through with a fake wedding. I know that was the plan, but I can't do that. You deserve so much more, Ray. You're the sweetest, most amazing woman I've ever met."

Ray started to speak, but Monica barreled on, "No,

I'm getting there. You've gone to a lot of trouble to save my bacon over the past several days, but if this isn't real for you, then I need you to tell me and walk away."

"I have no intention of walking away, ever." Ray took Monica's left hand, running a finger over where a ring would soon be going if they went through with this. She could almost feel herself sliding it into place. It felt so right. "How can I say this so you'll understand and not try to twist my words to fit that script in your head to prove you're right? No matter what."

There was knowing laughter in the audience.

"The night at the lake house wasn't a lie to me. It was the best night of my life, until you ran away." Ray held Monica's hand tighter, savoring the way Monica clung to it as if it was the only thing in the whole world. "I don't know the moment I fell in love with you. I feel like I should be able to pinpoint it, but I can't. I just know every day I felt more and more. Even during the past forty-eight hours when I didn't see you, my heart expanded, aching for you. Honestly, I didn't know how I was going to get through this without you. That's the thing. I can't be without you. I don't want to be. You're stubborn, opinionated, beautiful, annoying, funny. You never check your messages. You're determined. Loving. Did I mention opinionated?"

"Twice."

Ray slanted her head, shoulders shaking from the

laughter she was trying to keep in check. "You like to keep score, darling."

"Clearly, so do you. You make me sound like a nightmare."

"No, the nightmare is you not being in my life. With you gone these past few days, I've never felt so terrified and alone. I never want you to leave. I know marriage isn't a cakewalk. I know I'm not perfect and neither are you, but together, we are. That's why I'm still standing here, and why I'll keep showing up every single day until death does us part."

Tears flowed freely down Monica's cheeks. "Ray, do you want to marry me, for real?"

"I do." She'd never meant anything as much as she did those two words, and all they stood for.

"Me too." From the emotions shining from Monica's deep blue eyes, there was no question she meant it completely.

Christos cleared his throat, and both Monica and Ray turned to look at him. His eyes brimmed with tears as he grinned at the crowd of guests, many of whom held tissues to their eyes. He held out his hand, dropping two gold bands into Ray's palm. As if in a trance, Ray slid the ring onto Monica's finger and felt a band coming to rest on her own hand, still warm from Christos's pocket.

"Okay," Christos announced loudly when the exchange was done. "You heard 'em folks. With no further ado, by the powers vested in me by my very official one-day designation certificate granted by the great Commonwealth of Massachusetts, I declare these women married."

Wait. That was it? Were they actually married?

Ray's head swiveled back to look at Monica, whose eyebrows had shot all the way to her hairline.

"Go on," Christos urged Ray with a chuckle. "Kiss your bride."

Ray reached for Monica, dipping into the poof of veil that framed her face until their lips met in a brush of velvet softness. Ray wanted more—so much more—but they had a lifetime ahead of them for that. She lingered a moment longer and let go.

"I love you," Monica whispered, sending a thrill through Ray's heart.

"I love you, too," Ray said softly, her words nearly drowned out by the cheer that erupted from the watching crowd.

The DJ from the farmer's market had already pumped the music by the time they made it down the aisle and into the carriage house for the reception. Tables and chairs for two hundred and forty-nine guests filled the space, draped in crisp white linens and topped with arrangements of apples, sunflowers, and pumpkins that hinted at the amazing fall feast Brenda would soon be serving. As they crossed the room, Monica gripped Ray's arm with increasing pressure.

"Ray, this looks amazing. I can't believe what you did with this space."

As she took it all in, Ray had to agree. There was so much left to do—beams that needed stripping and a massive fireplace that would only be useable after a thorough repointing of the bricks but might someday offer warmth to future newlyweds—but what had been accomplished in less than two months was worth Ray allowing herself a pat on the back.

"I'm glad we decided to go ahead and buy the tables and chairs outright instead of renting," Ray said.

"It's a good investment," Monica agreed. "I have a feeling White Cat Winery is about to become the hottest wedding venue in all of New England."

"And you the most sought-after wedding planner," Ray added.

"For a minute there, I was sure my career was toast," Monica admitted. "I know I joked about being a wedding Grim Reaper before but my near sabotage of my own wedding brought it to a whole new level."

"I think it's safe to say your Grim Reaper days are done. In fact, when you get a chance, why don't you order another few sets of tables and chairs? I didn't want to let on when your mother was around to hear, but we could've easily seated another fifty people."

"Speaking of guests, should we start around the room and greet everyone?" Monica's expression suggested she had as little enthusiasm for the task as Ray did.

"Why don't you come down to the lower floor with me first, and I'll show you the new workshop Christos and I put together?"

Holding hands, they slipped to the stairs and descended to the space that had originally been built to house the horses. Now, the stalls were filled with a vast assortment of new plastic tubs, plus dozens of barrels made of either oak or steel, which Ray had purchased to expand the vineyard's capacity. Already, more than half of them were filled with the juice from this year's harvest, and the rest would soon be used for the juice orders she and Christos had placed from the suppliers in Italy.

This was their future, all around them. Unless, somehow, Ray was dreaming.

Ray held up her ring finger to be sure. The plain gold band that had once belonged to Christos's grandmother sparkled reassuringly. She turned to Monica, who was watching her quizzically. "Are you positive about this?"

"No take backs." Monica held up her own hand, where Christos's mother's band sat as if it had been made for her.

Somehow, bless his heart, Christos had known. Even though the wedding had been called off, and Ray had told him they wouldn't be using his family rings after all—partially on account of Nina's fingers being too swollen from pregnancy for any type of ring—he'd put them in his pocket just in case. In the absence of families of their own, Christos and Ray had become like family to each other, and it meant more than she could express to honor him in this way on their special day.

Ray pressed her forehead to Monica's, emotion forming a lump in her throat. "Don't ever leave me again."

"I only left because you told me to."

Ray pulled back slightly, searching Monica's face, which was dead serious. "What are you talking about?"

"The night at the lake, after we made love, you told me to leave."

"I was fast asleep," Ray argued.

"You were talking very clearly," Monica countered. "You said *leave, Monica*. You said it twice."

Ray shook her head. "I was having a bad dream. I remember it now. You disappeared, and I called out, 'Don't leave, Monica. Don't leave.'"

"Really?" After a brief pause, Monica started to laugh. "Now you tell me."

"You could have asked first, instead of going full runaway bride on me."

"You're probably right." Monica sighed. "I can't believe you all managed to pull this together without me. It was the perfect day."

"I have an excellent wedding planner."

"Oh yeah?" Monica quirked one eyebrow. "What's her name?"

"Monica Panagiotopoulos."

Monica pressed a hand to her mouth. "You finally learned how to say my name."

"I can spell it, too," Ray added with a shrug, as if it were no big deal and hadn't taken her the better part of two months to accomplish. "If that doesn't prove how much I love you, I don't know what will."

They drew closer, their lips about to touch, when there was a loud pop from the direction of the wine storage racks, followed by a hissing sound.

"What the fuck is that?" Monica pressed up against Ray as if she expected to come under heavy artillery fire at any moment.

Ray held her close, sniffing the air. "Based on the smell, I think Christos and I need to reformulate the blueberry wine again."

Another cork popped, and then another.

"This has to be a sign," Monica said with doom in her voice.

"It sure is." Ray grinned, unwilling to let anything cast a shadow on their day. "It looks like we have plenty of bubbly for that toast after all. Let's go get Brenda to break out the champagne glasses and pass them around. It's time to celebrate."

MUCH LATER THAT EVENING, when the last of the guests had left and they had the house all to themselves, Ray collapsed onto the bed, staring up at the lace canopy. "What a day!"

"For someone who just had the best thing happen to her," Monica said, sitting on the edge of the mattress, her huge white dress billowing all around her, "you need to work on your enthusiasm. You seem a little too downcast."

"Best thing, huh?" Ray popped up her chin. "I see your self-confidence is back."

Monica shrugged as if to say *damn straight*. "Think you can handle it?"

Ray pulled Monica on top of her, white lace flying. "I think you'll find, out of the two of us, I'm much more stubborn. I got the chin to prove it."

Monica kissed the dimple. "I love your chin."

"Is that right?"

"What can I say? I'm a sucker for punishment." Monica laid her head on Ray's chest. "The house is so quiet. Not a creature was stirring—"

"Meow." Mr. Fluffles jumped onto the foot of the bed.

"Really, cat?" Ray gave a resigned laugh that would've been immediately recognizable to cat owners everywhere. "After chasing you down for weeks, this is the moment you want to stay inside and not escape, right when I was about to strip this dress off and get the honeymoon started?"

"Oh, you were, were you?" Monica's eyes darted to the white blob of fur, which was nearly obscured by a

ACCIDENTAL HONEYMOON

layer of petticoat. "If we open the window, do you think he might decide to hop out?"

"We're on the second floor." Ray's eyes narrowed. "Was that a test to see if I'd go along with it?"

"Sure, we'll call it that." It was obvious from her suddenly pink cheeks that in her enthusiasm for starting the honeymoon, Monica had momentarily forgotten how high up they were.

Gently rolling Monica off her chest, Ray sat up and coaxed Mr. Fluffles to the bedroom door, shutting it behind him. "There we go. Alone at last."

"Truly alone, since my parents decided to spend the night at a hotel," Monica said, once again sitting upright, although her dress had shifted, leaving her breasts tantalizingly on display, covered only by the barest wisp of lace neckline. I guess they thought we could use some privacy."

Ray sat down beside Monica—her wife—and stroked the exposed mounds with her fingertips. Suddenly, it struck her that a farmhouse bedroom was no place for doing what she was longing to do. Not on their wedding night. "I'm sorry, my love. If I had realized how all of this was going to work out, I would've booked us a room at the best hotel in the area."

Monica stared into Ray's eyes, her pupils dark with the desire that seemed to have begun building the moment Ray's hand had touched her chest. "Don't apologize. I have everything I need."

"But after planning such a perfect wedding, you're

being deprived of an equally spectacular honeymoon. That's my fault."

"Don't be silly." Monica rose and walked to the window, motioning for Ray to join her. "Look around us. I'm with my hot new wife, in a room with an antique canopy bed, in a farmhouse that looks like it came out of *Architectural Digest*, with a stunning view of a vineyard with majestic fall colors. I can think of two million followers who will absolutely eat that up."

"When you put it that way," Ray conceded, "it doesn't sound half bad."

"Not half bad? Darling, ever since we got here, we've been enjoying the perfect honeymoon."

Ray swept a strand of golden hair from Monica's face. "We have, haven't we?"

"If only someone had let us in on the secret that we were both madly in love with one another."

"I'm not sure that was as hidden as we think. I mean, everyone kept saying it was obvious we were made for each other. You're the professional romantic," Ray added with a wink. "Why didn't you get the message?"

"I've told you a million times," Monica replied without missing a beat. "I don't do messages."

"Do you do this?" Ray kissed her softly on the lips.

"Oh, yes. I definitely do that. And this."

Monica deepened the kiss, causing Ray to see stars as the world around her spun like she'd had too much wine. But that wasn't the reason. It was what happened when she and Monica were together. As they continued to kiss, Ray's hand sought the hidden zipper she knew was somewhere on Monica's back. After a bit of desperate searching, her fingers brushed against the magical key that would allow her to unlock all the treasures the night ahead of them promised.

As Ray slid the zipper open, Monica moaned against her, the sound causing a spark inside her that would soon burn out of control.

And why shouldn't it?

This was their wedding night, after all. They had their whole lives ahead of them, to spend together, achieving their dreams. What had started as an accident had become the perfect honeymoon indeed.

Printed in Great Britain
by Amazon